£1-50

13-5

Jacqui Reid's
Book?!

D1387857

FAR and AWAY

FAR AND AWAY

A novel by Sonja Massie
Based on a screenplay by Bob Dolman
Story by Bob Dolman & Ron Howard

BCA

LONDON NEW YORK SYDNEY TORONTO

This edition published 1992
by BCA
by arrangement with Boxtree Ltd

Third Reprint 1993

This edition first published in the USA 1992 as A BERKLEY BOOK,
published by THE BERKLEY PUBLISHING GROUP, 200 Madison
Avenue, New York, New York 10016

Copyright © 1992 by MCA Publishing Rights,
a Division of MCA, Inc.

CN 9116

Except in the United States of America, this book is sold subject to
the condition that it shall not, by way of trade or otherwise, be lent,
resold, hired out or otherwise circulated without the pubisher's
prior consent in any form of binding or cover other than that in
which it is published and without a similar condition including this
condition being imposed on a subsequent purchaser

Printed and bound in Great Britain by
Mackays of Chatham PLC, Chatham, Kent

One

═══

"MAY the devil cut the heads off all landlords—the bloody lot of them—and may he make a day's work of their necks." Patrick, the village cooper, drew a long draft of his ale, a smile on his round face. He glanced around the pub, his eyes sparkling with satisfaction. His curse had been the most colorful thus far in a circle of men who held the deadly serious art of cursing in the highest regard. His unspoken challenge: Top that one.

"The curse of the crows on them, a fox on their fishhooks, and may they be afflicted with an itch and have no nails to scratch with." Patrick's brother, Ryan, leaned back on his stool, his pipe puffing into the air, which was already pungent with the smell of the turf fire blazing on the hearth and the stench of damp woolen clothing. "And may the devil swallow them sideways and choke on their peckers."

"May they all be condemned to hell without a drop o' ale to quench their eternal thirsts," added Denis, a red-haired, freckle-faced farmer as he slid his empty mug down the bar to the tavern keeper, who immediately refilled it to the brim.

Half a dozen others followed Denis's lead, uneasy at the very thought of eternal damnation without the healing comfort of a cool ale.

"Ye'd better keep hold of yer tongues, lads," said Danty Duff, a grizzled kelp harvester at the far end of the bar. He and his best friend, Joe Donelly, had arrived earlier and had drunk harder than any of their companions, and they were feeling no pain at all. "Ye never know who among us might be a bloody informer. Talk like that in front of the wrong party and ye'll find yerself in the same predicament as those lads in Galway—swinging from a rickety gallows in a high wind."

"Aw . . . yer as feeble as a toothless widow, Danty Duff." Joe Donelly, equally wizened from too many days cutting turf in the sun, laughed and slapped his friend on the back. At the last moment Danty dodged the blow and Joe nearly tumbled from his stool. "Scared o' yer own shadow, ye are. 'Tis men o' action we're in need of . . . like them Captain Moonlight lads, raiding with torches and clubs. They'll gain us back our land, sure."

A cheer rose from the patrons, a hearty, raucous sound that filled the old pub from its low timbered ceiling to its rush-covered stone floor.

This was why the men gathered here at O'Manion's Pub day after day. It wasn't for the ale, which they could drink at home. It wasn't for the warmth of the fire or the fortitude of the mutton stew bubbling over the cozy blaze. It wasn't even for an afternoon's respite from their wives' clattering tongues or the antics of their rambunctious children.

They came to O'Manion's seeking the companionship of men who encouraged them to be braver than themselves, bigger and stronger, men who challenged each other to rise above their imposed poverty and strike a blow for freedom. So far they had dared only verbal blows in the form of curses, the bowel evacuations of the soul. But throughout history, passionate words had always wielded the power to stir the Irish heart to action. The day was coming for all of them. And they knew it.

"So, what have you done to wrench yer God-given land from yer landlord today, Joe Donelly?" Danty asked, clearly offended. "Did ye hold a torch to his arse and did ye kiss it as he rode by on his fine white horse?"

"Maybe he just kissed the *horse's* rump," Denis offered, then hunched down into the collar of his jacket when he saw the glare in Joe Donelly's eye. "Sorry, Joe, no harm 'twas meant, surely."

Old Joe had a reputation in the village as a man who brooked no guff from anyone. Only Danty, his friend since childhood, could insult him to his face and walk away without his nose bloodied.

"Here ye go, lads," said the barkeeper as he slid two mugs of ale beneath Joe's and Danty's chins. "How about a song from those golden throats to please the ears and lighten the heart."

Indignation melted in the face of flattery, and Danty and Joe instantly burst into a drunken rendition of their favorite ditty.

> "Her beautiful eyes
> Were a terrible curse!
> Three days in his grave
> She ran off with his purse.
> He gazed down from heaven
> On the love of his life.
> God help you, poor lad,
> She's another man's wife!"

The patrons settled down to serious drinking, the welcome bitterness of the ale cooling their throats. The rushlights flickered on each rough-hewn table and reflected in the cracked mirror behind the bar; the glass had been broken years ago in a ruckus between Joe and Danty.

Their souls momentarily cleansed by their curses, the villagers could set their troubles aside for a few minutes and enjoy the enthusiastic—if off-key—singing of their comrades.

But the peacefulness was short-lived. A sudden and violent commotion in the street brought them all to their feet, hurrying to the window to see what was astir. Angry shouts echoed down the street, feet pounded the muddy road, and they heard the whinny of a frightened horse.

"Lads! We've a landlord coming through and all hell is breaking loose!" Ryan shouted gleefully. "It appears he's to be taught a lesson."

Forgetting their song, Joe and Danty tossed down the remainder of their ales and rushed out the door, eager to be a part of the action rather than watch from the windows like their friends.

Their curses had reaped results even more quickly than the most believing among them might have hoped. Sir Geoffrey Hampton, owner of Hampton House, sat on the leather diamond-tucked backseat of his polished black carriage. And a handsome conveyance it was, with an equally polished driver wearing black-and-silver livery and a slightly pop-eyed expression. Both the driver and his master realized they were in a desperate situation.

The peasantry pressed around them, a motley unruly mob, bearing shovels, picks, and shillelaghs along with years of collective grudges. People whose clothing had seen too many seasons, people who had endured too many hardships and suffered too many heartaches.

The crowd swarmed into the road, blocking the

path of the carriage. The driver whipped the horse, which could only inch along as the mob grew thicker and angrier.

"Damn yer fat-bellied soul, ye bollixin' bastard!" yelled one woman.

The landlord folded his arms over the front of his blue velvet coat with its black silk lapels and glared at her.

"Yer a blight on the country that never belonged to ye!" shouted a hunch-shouldered farmer whose young son clung, weeping, to his thigh. The child was nearly naked and far too frail and small for his age. "Damn ye to hell in a hand basket!"

An old woman, having no shillelagh in hand, bent down, grabbed a rock from the ground, and hurled it at the coach. The stone knocked the landlord's black satin top hat off his head. It fell into the crowd, where it was promptly and thoroughly trampled by a dozen dirty bare feet.

Joe Donelly gouged his friend in the ribs. "Hand me yer weapon, Danty, and I'll shoot the gentleman dead meself."

"What weapon do you see me carrying, Joe?" Danty replied. "I don't have a weapon . . . unless ye'd fancy bludgeoning his honor with me clay pipe."

"Then I'll give the divil a bit of me own philosophy." Cupping his hands around his mouth, Joe shouted, "Landlord! Yer a sinner. Between yer lungs there's neither heart nor spirit, but the lump of yer own swallowed money bag!"

Pleased with himself, Joe elbowed Danty and chuckled.

"Ye've devastated the fella, Joe," his friend said with an approving nod of his head.

The words of the eloquent curse stirred the anger of the crowd, and they surged forward, closing the ring around the unfortunate landlord. The gentleman reached into the pocket of his velvet jacket and produced a small silver pistol.

Pointing it directly at Joe Donelly, he laughed when he saw the look of confusion and fear on the farmer's face. "Where's your courage now, old man?" he taunted.

A hush stole over the crowd. No one dared to breathe as the landlord's finger tightened on the trigger. Joe blanched but didn't flinch. He had always believed that a soul didn't depart the earth until the good Lord called him home. But he could almost hear that celestial choir calling his name.

In a fit of daring the woman who had thrown the stone stepped closer to the carriage. "If ye shoot ol' Joe, yer honor, we'll all kill ye dead where ye sit. Surely we will."

The landlord's eyes scanned the crowd, sizing them up. Then, in the last split second, he lifted the barrel of the gun ever so slightly and shot over their heads.

At the gun's report the horse lunged, yanking the carriage forward. Like wheat before the thresher, the peasants fell. Joe Donelly tumbled headfirst into the street, striking his forehead on an embedded stone.

"Ah, Joe, what is it ye've done to yerself, lad?" Danty bent over his friend, the escaping landlord and teeming throng forgotten. "Yer bleedin' bad, Joe."

Only the old woman who had thrown the stone noticed their plight. She offered her kerchief as a bandage and Danty wound it around the fallen man's head.

Joe's eyes flickered open, but conscious or not, he was obviously gravely wounded. "Get me home, Danty," he said, feebly clutching his friend's arm. "I must be at home with me sons when I expire."

YOUNG Joseph Donelly looked up into the sky and blessed the day. With the dodgy weather of the morning past, the late afternoon promised to be glorious, with the sun streaming through the white clouds in glimmering shafts that gilded the emerald fields with a gold patina.

As he rode his ancient donkey—the animal was reputed to have been one of Brian Boru's pack animals—down the dirt road, his mind held not a worry or a care. Life had presented Joseph Donelly with few challenges, and those that had come his way he had met with courage and success. As a result Joseph was well pleased with himself.

So far he hadn't done anything worthy of renown, but he hadn't gotten himself hanged either, and there was something to be said for that in times like these.

Turning a curve in the road, Joseph saw two girls coming toward him, baskets of eggs under their arms. One carried a small cage containing two guinea hens. The girls' faces glowed as brightly as the afternoon sun when they saw Joseph.

He returned their smiles, enjoying the effect the sight of his countenance always had on women. With his dark hair and a flirtatious, mischievous sparkle in his eyes, Joseph knew that he was handsome—exceptionally so. All the more reason why his self-confidence bordered on vanity.

The girls giggled as he doffed his hat to them and he flashed them the bright smile that had charmed half the females of the county. The other half had never looked upon Joseph Donelly.

"Good day to ye, lassies," he said as he passed them, hat still held high. "Yer beauty graces the road ye walk upon."

Tittering, the girls ducked their heads and cast him sideways glances from beneath their bonnets. Joseph bowed as low as possible, but his graceful gesture was cut short by his donkey's decision to trot. Joseph fought to keep his balance, barely hanging on as the donkey jiggled him violently down the road.

In that moment Joseph realized it was difficult to maintain one's dignity and seat at the same time. With his arms around the donkey's neck and his long legs around its distended belly, he shouted a curse into its ear. "Tattheration to ye, stupid creature that ye are. Destruction upon yer evil hide. It's a purse ye'll be before sundown."

By the time Joseph was sitting upright and the donkey slowed to a comfortable pace, the girls were far down the road and the damage to Joseph's ego irreparable. Their laughter still rang like the cackle of so many wild and crazy geese.

What did he care what they thought of him? They were only girls.

Ah, the wonder of females, he thought with a sigh. *They drive a man crazy, but the asylum would be a cold place without them.*

JOSEPH clip-clopped up the path toward the Donellys' humble cottage, the donkey barely under control. The tiny, stone structure with one window and a brightly painted red door sat in the middle of a field that sloped down to the craggy beach and the ocean. The plot of land appeared to have yielded an excellent harvest of rocks. Other crops were less evident. The cottage itself had been built with the same stones, mortared with a bit of mud and a great deal of sweat—Joseph's father's sweat. Joe Donelly had built this cottage at the beginning of his life, before the birth of his three sons, before the death of his wife.

Often, when Joseph rode or walked up this road, he felt a surge of pride that his father had built their home with his bare hands, simple though it might be. Last summer Joseph and his father had rethatched the roof, a devil of a task, but a fine job they had done of it. Joseph had poured a great deal of his own sweat, as well as a little blood, into this property, and he took joy in the knowledge that someday it would be his birthright.

Joseph felt less joy and pride when he spotted his two brothers, Paddy and Colm, in the yard, attempting to box each others ears. Big, slothful, and a bit drunk, they were pummeling the air more than their opponents.

"Look, Colm!" Paddy shouted, lowering his fists long enough to point at Joseph as he entered the yard. "It's God's gift to the universe."

"Sweetheart of a child." Colm's sarcastic tone belied his words. "Been cutting turf have you, Joseph?"

Joseph stiffened as usual at this taunting, which never ended. His brothers seemed to feel it their God-given mission to humble him, to "take him down a few notches" as they put it.

"How do you think the fire would burn if nobody cut the turf?" Joseph said as he hopped off the donkey and began to unload the bricks of dark turf from the two baskets that hung on either side of the beast. "The wise men say, 'Work as if there was fire in yer skin and ye'll never be without a fire in yer hearth.'"

His proverb garnered nothing but a round of laughter from his siblings. "Hear that, Paddy?" Colm said between whoops. "Our little brother's all full of wisdom!"

The donkey skittered and Joseph yanked at the rope around its neck. "Stand still, ye ugly animal," he hissed under his breath.

"Aye, he may be bustin' with wisdom, but he can't keep hold of his ass," Paddy said as Colm guffawed. Lifting his fists, he said, "Hold up yer face, courage. Give us something we can aim at."

Joseph shrugged them aside as he continued to carry the turf to the lean-to at the side of the cottage, where he stacked it in neat piles. "Shag off, both of ye. There's a goat over there. . . ." He nodded toward the pen behind the shed. "Improve your love life."

His brothers laughed, continuing to spar. "Come on, Joseph honey." Colm pranced around in front of him, blocking his path. "Just a bit of a nosebleed. That's all we're after."

Colm poked him in the ribs and the turf flew in a dozen directions, several bricks knocking Joseph on the shins. But the young man retained his composure.

Drawing a deep breath, he said softly, "I've no wish to fight ye." The moment the words escaped his lips, Joseph's fist flew out and slammed Colm in the nose, sending him reeling. The war was on!

Fists crashed into jaws, knees into groins, toes against shins, teeth clamped down on any available flesh.

"Try pummeling *me*, ye arrogant bastard!" Paddy complained as he received the full benefit of his younger brother's pent-up fury.

Joseph landed a solid right hook, which cracked soundly. "Bastard? And what does that imply about the ghost of our dear dead mother?" A hard left. "Ye son of a bitch!"

Despite his superior boxing skill, Joseph was clearly outnumbered. His persistence, though admirable, was suicidal, as his face soon sprouted the sought-after nosebleed. Sprawling in the dirt, he struggled to rise and come back for more.

"Accept defeat, ye fool," Colm said. "We've three quarters murdered ye now."

"I'll use whatever's left of me to slaughter the two of ye both." Back on his feet, though a bit unsteady, Joseph came after them again.

But the fight was interrupted by the sound of a wagon, clattering up the road at breakneck speed.

"'Tis ol' Danty," Colm said. "Where did *he* get a wagon?"

"And why is he movin' faster than he's moved in his life?" Paddy added.

"Something's amiss." Joseph started down the road, a pain forming in his chest that had nothing to do with the thrashing he had just received. "What is it, Danty?" he called with a premonition of dread.

"Lads!" the old man shouted back as he rumbled into the yard. "Come runnin'. 'Tis yer father. He's been sorely damaged."

"Took on the enemy with his bare hands, he did. Fifty of them, armed with hideous guns, and yer father smote them one by one." Danty stood at the foot of the pallet where Joe lay, attended by his youngest son. Drawing on his pipe, he blew the smoke to the rafters of the tiny cottage and continued, "I killed a portion meself, to tell God's truth, but—"

"Quiet, Danty Duff, for once," Joseph said as he twisted the rag over the bucket of water and placed it on the gaping wound in his father's head.

"—humble as I am," Danty continued under his breath, "I'll keep that part of the story . . . for later."

"How're ye feelin', Da?" Joseph asked.

Joe's eyes flickered open, but they had a vacant look as he gazed up at his son. "My soul's departin' me, Joseph," he said, every breath an effort.

With frantic haste Joseph reached over, stirred the turf fire on the hearth, and adjusted the kettle so that the water could come to a boil more quickly. The wound was a bad one and would need thorough cleansing before he stitched it with a darning needle and black thread.

"Ye mustn't talk that way," Joseph said, casting a helpless look at his brothers, who said nothing as they stood in the corner, arms crossed over their chests.

Joseph looked down at his father's ashen face and feared the old man was speaking the truth.

"I'll talk any way I please," replied Joe. "I'm dying, I tell ye. Don't give me a bloody argument."

"But ye can't die." Joseph squeezed the cloth and allowed the water to flow over the gash and onto the pallet's worn ticking. It didn't matter. Nothing mattered now, not with his father expiring before his eyes and no way for him to prevent it. "We love ye," he added. "We need ye here."

"Need me for what? I've given ye nothin', lads. A poor cottage on a broken bit of rock—and not even ours for all our labor. I'm glad to be gone, if the truth be known."

Joe closed his eyes and took a deep breath. Reaching beneath his father's neck, Joseph lifted his battered head to offer support, but it lolled drunkenly to the side. "All I ask . . ." Joe continued in a feeble voice, ". . . is a pleasant funeral, lads. 'Her beautiful eyes . . . '"

His song faded away and his chest ceased to rise and fall.

Colm and Paddy crept forward, peering curiously at the lifeless body that had been their father. Danty crossed himself. "God rest yer soul, Joe Donelly," he muttered.

"Da." Joseph cradled his father against his chest, a thousand thoughts and memories flooding his mind. His father teaching him how to fish, how to dance a jig, to plant praties and drink whiskey. A thousand remembrances. A thousand kindnesses.

Paddy and Colm bowed their heads but, after only a few seconds, sneaked a peek at each other.

"Sure, we'd be as well to sell off a thing or two, now that the old man's gone," Paddy whispered.

"His bed, for instance, might be worth a sum," Colm added.

"Is that any way to keen over the death of our father?" Joseph said, glaring up at them. "His body not cold and you two fools are already dividin' up his worldly goods."

"Misery's a personal matter, Joseph," Paddy said with an affected wounded tone. "We don't need instruction, thanks. He's left us with a big debt on the rent."

"We'll begin to settle our debts as soon as we harvest the land," Joseph replied.

Paddy snorted in disgust. "Bah! That's a God-long awful summer away."

"Grow the praties and pick 'em yerself, Joseph, ambitious lad that ye are," Colm said.

Joseph laid his father gently back down on the pallet. "Don't listen to them, Da. They're heartless and lazy and fat and they're about to join ye in yer grave."

Joseph rose to his feet and lunged for Paddy, who was the closest of the two.

"Aye, they're a couple of cows," the recently deceased Joe replied.

"Holy Jaysus," Colm cried. He, Joseph, and Paddy froze like three dead rabbits left on a December snowbank.

Danty's pipe dropped out of his mouth as the dead man's eyes suddenly popped opened.

"Da! Sweet Mary, Jaysus, and all the saints preserve us! It's alive ye are!" Joseph said, tears of joy replacing those of sorrow and anger.

"No, Joseph," the old man replied, "I've passed away."

"But yer talkin' to me, Da. And yer eyes are lookin' about."

Joe sighed. "Always an argument. I'm dead as a stone, I tell ye, floated halfway up to heaven's gates, I did. But then I remembered something I wanted to tell ye, lad."

"Me?" Joseph asked.

"Yes, you. Yer jackass brothers aren't worth coming back from heaven for. Now come close, me boy, and pay attention. I've a word I must say to ye."

Trembling, Joseph leaned near to his father. "Yes, Da?"

"The word is . . . land," he whispered.

"I didn't hear ye, Da." Joseph bent his head closer.

"*Land!*" he bawled. Joseph jumped back, his ears ringing. "Land, Joseph."

Joseph dropped to his knees beside his father. "I don't understand."

"'Tis all a matter of land. Ye must be understandin' me, lad . . . yer an especially . . . odd boy," Joe said. "I know yer mine, cuz ye've got me handsome looks, but I don't know what to make of ye, son."

Joseph leaned closer, a confused look on his face. "Ye've come back from heaven's gate to tell me that I'm odd?"

Joe shook his head sadly. "Ye've got all kinds of things flyin' about in yer brain. So did I when I was young as you. But dreams, lad, in this poor corner of the world, end up in a glass of ale."

"Not my dreams, Da," Joseph said. "Someday I'll own me own land and—"

"That's what I mean. A man can't have a dream without land. Without land ye can't build a house. Without a house ye'll never get a woman. And without a woman . . ."

"Yer pecker'll drop off," Danty interjected.

The two old pals shared a boyish laugh. Then Joe reached up with a shaking hand and grabbed his son's collar.

"When I was a lad like yerself, Joseph," he said, "I dreamed that in my lifetime the battle would be won—that my generation would take back the land that was stolen from our ancestors. I got old and gave up—but I'm passin' on me dream to you. If ye manage it, by God yer ol' da will be smilin' down on ye from heaven above."

Once more, quietly singing, Joe closed his eyes and died. Danty crossed himself and the sons repeated the gesture.

"God rest yer soul a second time, Joe Donelly," Danty said.

"May ye be over heaven's threshold at least an hour before the ol' horned fellow discovers ye've died," added Joseph as he bent down and kissed his father's cheek.

OUTSIDE the Donelly cottage a bonfire blazed, lighting the night sky with an eerie glow, beckoning the mourners to Joe's wake. In the small village the excitement and festivity of a wake was surpassed only by that of a wedding, and lately—thanks to the landlords, the Moonlighters, and a number of violent evictions—more folks had died than wed.

Smoke from the bonfire filled the air, but inside the cottage, behind the door that was crossed by a thick black ribbon, the smoke was even thicker. A good wake required plenty of food, poteen, and tobacco, and Joe Donelly's midnight vigil supplied a bounty of all three for the grieving survivors.

Women, draped in heavy woolen shawls, moved among the guests, plying them with fresh-baked cakes with butter and tobacco for their pipes. Beside the open coffin, Danty Duff puffed on his clay pipe and took a deep swig of poteen. The strong liquor with the strange smoky taste was loosing his already agile tongue.

"Died twice, he did," he told Father Nolan, the feisty old priest whose presence graced and enlivened every occasion. "Had a vision of paradise, described it

—— 15 ——

to me in detail: St. Peter, angels and the heavenly host, the whole kit and caboodle."

"It can happen," the priest replied solemnly with a nod of his silver-haired head. Many of his parish thought the father looked angelic with that shining hair that resembled a halo, especially when the morning sun shone through the church window, anointing him with a golden glow. Some less respectful folk suggested that the father stood in that particular spot for that very reason. But there was no proof of their theory. "I died meself, you know," he said, "the time they shot me through the heart."

Danty raised one eyebrow in reproach. "Now, Father, I won't stand for a lie. We all know they shot ye through the foot."

The priest shrugged. "Ah, but they were aimin' at me heart. You can be sure of that."

All conversation ceased as Joseph Donelly came out of the back room. The crowd parted and allowed him to pass as he walked through the room, a solemn expression on his handsome face. His eyes were red from weeping. The young man walked over to the coffin, touched his father's cheek for a moment, then ceremoniously placed a pipe and tobacco on a stool near the body.

From the opposite corner of the room, Colm and Paddy drifted over, a no-nonsense look on their faces.

"Joseph," Colm began, "there's a matter of business we need to discuss."

"Now is not the time," Joseph replied.

"But he's left us here with rent to pay, and we were thinking . . ."

". . . that we'd rather not," Paddy finished.

Joseph glared at them, his eyes full of Donelly fire. "Our debts will be settled once we harvest our land."

Colm smiled and puffed out his chest with self-importance. "Our ambition is a bit grander than that."

"We're goin' out in the world," Paddy said. "Taking roadwork. Leveling ruts and making the country smoother."

"Come with us, Joseph." Colm laid one hand on his younger brother's shoulder. "This land is blighted. A blind dog wouldn't piss on it."

"And it isn't ours besides," Paddy added. "It belongs to the landlord Christie of County Clare."

Joseph shook off Colm's hand. Everyone in the room held their collective breath, eager for the blows to begin. The Donelly boys held a reputation for settling disputes with their fists. This wake had enough food, drink, and tobacco. All that was lacking was a good head-busting affray.

"The day of the landlord is coming to an end. This land is my home," Joseph said with deadly calm. "I will stay upon it until the day I die. There'll be not another word spoken on the matter."

Joseph turned and performed the ritual of placing a plate of salt upon his father's chest.

Colm and Paddy glanced sideways at each other and each quirked an eyebrow knowingly. Joseph was daft as a goose. No doubt about it, he had gone mental entirely.

"Even the heavens are weepin' for ye today, Da," Joseph whispered as he walked along at the head of his father's coffin. Joseph Donelly was being carried to his final resting place by his three sons and his best friend, Danty Duff. The rest of his friends and neighbors followed along behind, a tattered crew of men, women, and barefoot children. The professional keeners, two women from a neighboring village, wailed in soulful agony, adequately demonstrating how beloved Joe Donelly had been and how much he would be missed.

A fine, cold mist fell on the funeral party as they traveled the road, and Joseph hunched down into the collar of his greatcoat, seeking the little warmth it supplied. But the chill went all the way through to his heart, and for today he was thankful for the numbness. Tomorrow he would feel the loss of his father, deeply and completely. But this morning he would keep the sorrow as far away as possible. It would catch up with him plenty soon enough, after they had laid his father in the grave, after Joseph had to face a day without the benefit of his father's smile and good humor.

Damn those landlords! This was their fault! Damn their filthy souls into the fiery furnace of hell!

Suddenly, in the distance, they heard the sound of hoofbeats, coming down the road hard and fast in their direction. From over a hill rode five soldiers, led by a darkly handsome fellow wearing a black coat, his coattails billowing in the wind.

Instinctively, the peasants lowered their eyes and continued to walk.

"Protestant enemy, lads," Danty said under his breath. "Say nothing to them. This country is ours. They don't exist."

The soldiers and the man in black rode up to the procession and pulled their horses to a halt in front of the coffin. "What dead man lies inside this box?" the leader demanded as his powerful bay pranced menacingly around the pine box. No one said a word. "You needn't answer. But hear these words," he continued. "I am Stephen Chase, and I represent the family Christie. By their authority you are hereby charged."

The man pulled his coat open, flashing a set of white pistols, and took out a piece of paper. "Rent on this property has not been paid," he said, "though warning has been given thrice."

Bending down in his saddle, he slapped the paper on top of the coffin lid. Then he wheeled his horse around and he and his soldiers thundered off down the road toward the Donelly cottage.

"What's it say, Danty?" Joseph asked, a hard lump of fear knotting in his chest.

Danty spoke the inevitable words: "'Tis a notice of eviction, lad."

"No!" Joseph released his hold on the coffin and began running down the road after the soldiers. "Damn ye, no!"

His long legs pumped and his heart throbbed. His ribs were aching before he reached the cottage, where the soldiers had already dismounted and had begun their work, carrying the family's few poor belongings out of the cottage and throwing them into a heap.

"Ye've no right!" Joseph screamed. "No right at all to do such a thing!"

Stephen Chase turned to face him. Flinging back his coattails, he placed his hands on his pistols. "Stand away," he said. "This land is to be cleared for grazing."

"But me father built this house!" Joseph said, fighting down the bitter sickness that kept welling up from his stomach. "He raised it with his own two hands, and now yer doin' such a thing as this with him hardly cold in his coffin. Have ye no heart at all, man?"

Chase smiled, a cold, hard smile that didn't light his eyes. "Be thankful that we waited until he died," he said with a sarcastic tone.

Joseph looked into the eyes and saw the hate, the bigotry that the aristocratic class held for people like himself. This man considered him less than human, less than a man. In this blue blood's eyes he was nothing more than a troublesome beast.

The fury in Joseph rose like bitter bile into his mouth and he spat at the aristocrat. His missile had been well aimed and it landed on the man's right cheek. In an instant Joseph found himself looking down the barrels of half a dozen rifles.

The man in black reached into his pocket and pulled out a lace-trimmed handkerchief, which he used to wipe his cheek. "This land," he said slowly as he tossed the kerchief to the ground with disdain, "and all improvements upon it belong to Mr. Daniel Christie. You're a trespasser here. Be gone before I lose my patience and have you shot where you stand."

One of the soldiers exited the cottage, a burning torch in his hand. Already thick black smoke was beginning to pour from the cottage's small window.

"No! God damn the lot of you," Joseph said, tears stinging his eyes. Two rifles were shoved into his ribs. He bit back his anger.

"There is no civilized way to deal with your kind," Chase said. "You must be treated like a savage because you *are* a savage." Taking the torch from the soldier, he walked over to the cottage and held the blaze up to the thatched roof. In seconds red-orange flames covered the dried grass, which curled into ten thousand tiny writhing black snakes.

Joseph turned his head away, unable to watch. Down the road he saw the mourners, as shocked and helpless as he. He saw Paddy's and Colm's faces, their expression of relief, of liberation; they were free. In that moment Joseph hated them. He hated the entire world.

Without a backward glance Stephen Chase mounted his bay and, with an uplifted hand, directed his soldiers to follow him. They galloped down the road, past the mourners and over the hill.

The pungent smoke filled Joseph's lungs and burned his eyes. Tears rolled unchecked down his cheeks. He turned to look back at the cottage and shuddered at the sight and sound of the thatch collapsing inward with a roar and a blast of heat that made his skin crawl.

His father was gone, and so was the home of his childhood. Inside those walls he might have relived some memories of his father, times spent before the winter fire, smoking or playing a tin whistle. But even the cottage was gone now, the last tangible reminder of his youth.

And like so many of the homes of his fellow Irishmen, it stood, an empty blackened shell. As empty as the people who would never again call it home.

This couldn't continue to happen across the green fields of Eirinn. It was an evil too dark, too hurtful. Something had to be done.

But what? Joseph asked himself as he turned away from the burning wreckage and walked back toward the funeral procession. For now he had to put the question out of his mind. For now he had to bury his father.

Two

J OSEPH stood, his face to the sea, his body braced against the cold damp wind that blew off the Atlantic. Many an hour he had whiled away on this bluff, his eyes searching the ocean, his mind spinning dreams of adventures and journeys he would take someday.

But today his dreams were less romantic. Today he planned a murder.

His handsome face wore a bitter expression; his eyes, which were usually bright, had the look of a lost soul. Too much had been taken from him too quickly, and his mind hadn't yet grasped the magnitude of his losses. Having eaten little and slept less in the past few days, he had only one thing keeping him going: the burning need for revenge.

He watched the kelp makers below on the shores as they gathered seaweed and heaped it on the fires to dry. Ankle-deep in the ocean, the harvesters stood, scraping the seaweed with long cross poles. It was a hard living, but it put praties on the table—if one had a table—and the occasional ale in the belly.

Among the harvesters, Joseph saw Danty Duff,

yielding his pole with less enthusiasm than the younger ones, but with more grace and skill. Danty had harvested seaweed since he was a lad and would undoubtedly do it until he dropped dead in his tracks there on the sand. Few people of Danty or Joseph's social stature had the opportunity to change their occupations and their lives.

Joseph had thought that one day he would change his life. Now that dream had been pushed to the back of his mind. Other things must be done first. Much more important matters. Matters of honor.

Joseph climbed down the cliff toward the beach, ignoring the girls who walked in front of him, baskets of seaweed on their backs, a seductive sway to their hips, their eyes bright with interest. They giggled and tossed their heads in his direction. For once he didn't care, and he strode past them without giving them so much as the twinkle of his eye.

Seeing Joseph, Danty splashed up onto the beach and thrust his pole into the sand. After giving the lad a hearty embrace, he said, "Girls, girls, Joseph. The world has girls in it. Bonnie, soft, cuddlesome girls. Have ye noticed?"

Joseph sniffed. "I've no commodity for girls, Danty. With neither land nor fortune to promise—I'll slip over girls in this life."

"Salt and pepper! Yer handsome as the devil himself." He patted Joseph's shoulder. "'Tis yer brain talkin', lad. Let yer pecker get a word in. Yer sorrow will pass and things will look different to ye someday. May it be soon."

Joseph turned and began to walk down the beach, his strides long, his head down, his hands buried deep in his pockets. Danty hurried along after him, huffing a bit to keep up.

"Danty, it's paralyzed I am in this place," he said. "Me brothers are gone gangin'. They're gettin' on with

— 23 —

their lives, but I see no future for me." He stopped so abruptly that Danty ran into his back. He whirled around on the old man. "Who is this landlord Christie? 'Tis justice I'm after. He must be payin' for what he did to me family."

Danty's eyes flickered. Standing on his toes, he whispered in Joseph's ear, "The answer is a simple one: Assassinate the gentleman. Lay him low in his grave, where him and the rest of his kind belong. Truth be known, I've been ruminatin' here in the seaweed about killin' him meself. But I wouldn't want to deny *you* any pleasure."

Joseph looked up and down the beach. No one appeared to be listening. *A man must be careful when discussing such matters as murder*, he reminded himself. *One spy with his ears on the stretch could hang a man, sure.*

"I must be truthful with ye, Danty Duff," he said. "I've entertained that very thought myself. But I'm in need of yer help if I'm to accomplish the deed."

"I love nothin' more than the glow of murder in a young man's eyes," Danty said as he and Joseph sat on the floor of Danty's shack amid the clutter of fishing nets and wooden barrels. "Does me heart good to know there's still a fire of courage ablaze in the sons of ol' Eirinn."

Joseph felt that fire flicker for a moment, blown by a strong gust of doubt and fear. "Till now, I've only killed chickens and pigs," he admitted.

Danty laughed heartily and slapped him on the back. "Well, not to worry. He's a pig and a chicken in one, this Mr. Christie. Takes in his rents and torments his horses. Give him a taste of death, lad!"

"But I've never seen his face."

"And it's lucky ye are. For that means he's never seen yers, and he won't know ye when ye go after him. He lives far and away from here . . . a hundred miles."

"A hundred *miles*, Danty? 'Tis the other side of the world!"

"No man becomes a hero, Joseph, sittin' on his arse in his backyard."

Danty rose from the floor, walked over to a barrel in the corner that bore the label J. REEVES, SAUCE AND PICKLE MAKER. With a small crowbar he pried it open. The smell of vinegar and cucumber wafted out, mingling with the fishy aroma of the shack.

"Thank ye, anyway, Danty," Joseph said, feeling a bit nauseated, "but I'm off me feed today. I don't care at all for a pickle at the moment."

"And it's not a pickle ye'll be gettin'."

Danty tossed the lid onto a pile of ropes and chains and reached inside the barrel. One after the other he began to pull out pieces of a decrepit rifle. Lastly he retrieved a leather pouch containing ammunition and dumped the lot onto Joseph's lap.

A wide smile split his wizened face. "There ye go, lad. Smuggled all the way from Birmingham, arrived at Ballyshannon. Is that a prize, I ask ye?"

Joseph tried to hide his misgivings and keep a straight face. "It . . . ah . . . it has a terrible go of rust on it, Danty. I hate to be so plain, but I could just as easily damage his head with a loy."

"A loy!" Danty was scandalized. "That's not the way a hero kills a fiend." He sat back down on the floor and began to assemble the gun.

Joseph suddenly perked with interest. "Would I truly be a hero, do ye think?"

"A hero? Why most certainly, lad. Ye'll be changing the course of history. 'Joseph Donelly!' people will say. The bards will be penning tunes to sing yer praises, the girls will swoon at the sight of ye—though many of them already do—and ye'll surely never pay for another drink in all yer life."

Slowly, with great dignity, Joseph rose to his feet and adjusted his dusty hat. "I could stand a bit of admiration. Sometimes I even fancy I was meant for somethin' grand."

Danty stood, the same pride shining on his face as he warmed himself at the fire of the young man's passion. "And yer father, Joseph. Don't forget him," he added, stoking the flame a bit. "He'll smile down upon ye from the heavens above." He handed him the gun. "Captain Moonlight," he said, his chin thrust forward, his shoulders squared.

"Aye," Joseph replied. "Captain Moonlight!"

Danty reached over and smacked him on the side of the head. "Ye don't even know what Captain Moonlight means, so stop pretendin' that ye do. 'Tis the rebel's code, and now that ye've heard it, yer to keep it to yerself. Ye mustn't breathe a word of it to a soul, Joseph."

"Aye, not a word, I promise." Bravely, Joseph hefted his weapon.

The barrel fell to the floor with a clatter . . . along with the better part of his courage.

THE villagers scurried out to meet Joseph as he rode through town on his skinny donkey. His saddlebags were packed, his rifle protruding.

"Captain Moonlight, Joseph!" shouted Patrick the cooper.

"Off to kill yer landlord, eh?" yelled O'Manion from the door of his pub.

"Quiet now," Joseph said halfheartedly. "No one's to know." It wasn't easy to discourage adoration when it had been such a long time coming and so well deserved.

"Blow the bastard's head off, lad!" cried the blacksmith from the field beside his forge, where he stood examining the shoe of a mare. "Plug him between the eyes! Butcher his livestock while yer at it!"

Joseph saw the admiration—even envy—in the men's eyes, and his heart soared. So this was what it was like to be a hero. Had he known what joy it could bring, he would have become one long ago. The tailor's wife and her daughter walked across the street in front of him and the pretty girl flashed him a coquettish smile as she tossed a flower at his donkey's feet. He replied by bowing low and doffing his hat.

Then he turned and saw Danty Duff wobbling out of the pub, a mug clenched in his fist. He raised the ale in a parting salute. "Slainte, Joseph child."

"Bless me, Danty," Joseph replied, suddenly needing the comfort of an older man's benediction.

"May the strength of three be in yer journey, Joseph, and may the door not slap yer arse till ye've returned to us safe and sound."

"Thank you, Danty Duff." Joseph kicked his donkey in the sides and held his head high as he left his village in search of his prey.

Still standing in the pub door, ale in hand, Danty looked down into the amber depths and sighed. "Ah . . . thirst is a shameless disease," he said, lifting the mug to his lips, "so here's to a shameful cure." Having drained the mug, he added, "Good-bye, Joseph, lad. Yer the spittin' image of yer father, may he rest in peace. May ye not wind up as cold and dead as he."

JOSEPH rode his donkey down the muddy rode past the burned-out shell that had once been his home. The sight of that collapsed structure did more to strengthen his resolve than all the adulation of the villagers. The landlord would die. And Joseph would take pleasure in killing him.

A little farther along he came upon a road gang, a tired, muddy knot of men leveling ruts in the road with shovels. Two of the mud-smeared faces were familiar to him. He sighed inwardly.

"If it isn't the avenging badger himself!" Paddy cried, pointing at the rider and the rickety donkey.

"And with a gun no less!" Colm's sarcastic smile grated on Joseph's already taut nerves. Damn them both. Who had ever been cursed with two brothers as worthless and ornery as these?

"Do you know which end to point at the gentleman's ear, Joseph?" Paddy leaned on his shovel and wiped the sweat-damp hair from his eyes.

Colm swaggered over to the donkey. "He'll shoot himself in the balls, I wager, and come hobblin' home in tears." He clutched his groin and the rest of the gang roared with laughter.

Joseph smiled down on his brothers with tarnished affection. "I've no wish to fight ye," he said quietly.

The old signal. This time his brothers were ready. They grabbed him off the donkey and promptly beat the devil out of him. The gang cheered, the skirmish being the social event of the month. Having thoroughly pummeled him, the brothers politely set him back on his donkey.

Joseph spurred the animal, which responded with a loud and fluttering fart. The laughter began all over again. Colm whacked the pathetic creature's rump and it trotted off while the battered Joseph clung to its scrawny mane.

"Good-bye, Joseph honey," Colm called after him. "See ye at yer wake."

Long after the sun had set behind the hills, Joseph continued to ride. Past stone fences, ruins of castles, churches, and round towers, the silent ghostly witnesses of Ireland's rich and violent history. Old Eirinn's sons had fought many battles against the Vikings, the Saxons, against famine and tyranny. Some of the battles had been won, many had been lost. The poets said that the fields were so green because of the red waves of human blood that had washed over the land.

Joseph found himself listening for the wail of those lost souls as he traveled the moonlit roads.

He turned left to cut across a broad field and shorten his journey, but before he allowed his donkey to step onto the tall lush grass, he checked his pocket to see if he had a bit of bread. This stretch of land was known as a "hungry field," a place where many people had died during the terrible famine that had been called the "Great Hunger." Traditionally, no one was to cross that field without at least a morsel of bread in his pocket, out of respect for the souls who had suffered and died of starvation on this very plot of land.

Joseph thought of those people, the men, women, and babies who had died here as the result of the callousness of their landlords. In that moment he felt a bond with those unfortunates, an affinity that he had never felt before. Soon he would strike a blow for freedom, for his father, and for those people. The bloody Englishmen would pay for their sins at the hand of Joseph Donelly.

His fancies of grandeur and heroism were interrupted by the sound of hoofbeats pounding in the stillness of the night. A rider was coming toward him, fast and hard.

He turned and looked behind him, and what he saw took his breath away. A beautiful woman, like a princess from an old Celtic fairy tale, sat upon a white horse, riding as though the devil himself were pursuing her.

Her unbound hair—he couldn't tell what color—shone like a cloud of spun silver in the moonlight as it flew wild and free in the wind behind her. Her skirts were pulled up above her knees and her long shapely legs hugged the horse's heaving sides. She didn't see Joseph, her eyes straight ahead, the movement of her body as fluid as that of the magnificent horse she rode.

Joseph's heart throbbed as he watched her. When she passed by, only a stone's throw away, he heard her laugh, a crazy, spontaneous laugh that made Joseph ache. He longed to be that free, to cast off all restraints like this moonlight goddess and race through the night with the wind in his face and the heart of an eagle. To feel that free, that unfettered by the world and its cares for only one moment.

As suddenly as she had appeared, she was gone. Only the echoing hoofbeats told him she had been anything other than a spinning of his own fancy.

"Someday I will feel like that," he said to his donkey, the only creature within earshot. "Someday I'll ride the night wind just like that girl."

The donkey snorted his disdain, then released another long gust of flatulence.

"I'll have a horse like that someday, too," he said, kicking the beast in the ribs, "and ye'll be underground where ye belong."

Maybe I'll have a woman like that of me own, too, he mused for the briefest moment. Then he shoved the thought to the back of his mind. Some dreams were out of reach, even for an imaginative, self-satisfied youth like Joseph Donelly.

Women like that didn't really exist. They only rode across moonlit pastures, their limbs bare, their hair blowing in the wind . . . and on a rare night they traveled the silvery, shadowed landscape of a young man's midnight dreams.

JOSEPH rode up to the door of the small tavern, dismounted, and after wrestling the cantankerous donkey who tried to bolt, tied the creature to the hitching post. As he entered the pub three of the locals glanced his way, then gave him a studied perusal when they realized he was a stranger.

"God bless all in this house," Joseph muttered, following the custom of blessing the dwelling. But his heart wasn't in it. He had more curses in his mind at the moment than benedictions.

"A hearty welcome to you," the tavern keeper said as he poured Joseph an ale. "I'm Kevin and those lads at the end of the bar are Peter, Matthew, and John. They're worthless, the lot of them, without a virtue to recommend them, but they've been known to buy a stranger's first drink in this village."

"I'll buy me own, but it's grateful I am to ye for the offer," he said.

"Ah . . . a man who turns down a free drink," commented Peter. "This is a stranger, indeed. Down from the north, are ye?"

"Or perhaps the west?" Matthew said.

"Or east of here maybe?" the third disciple added.

Joseph didn't answer, but continued to sip his ale.

"South?" said Peter. Joseph wished they would give it up. All he wanted was to sulk in peace and fill his belly with the cool dark ale.

"I prefer to keep me business to meself," he said, "if ye please."

"Wise, wise, very wise . . ." they said, shaking their heads in turn.

Joseph ignored their snickers and curious glances as they returned to their drinking, smoking, and gossip.

A few moments later the door burst open and a sturdy man about fifty years old barged in. He wore the fine clothes of a gentleman, though his boisterous manner suggested less than aristocratic breeding.

"God bless you one and all!" he roared, flinging his hat across the room. Obviously he had imbibed already this evening. For all of his energy, he was none too steady in his boots.

"How are you tonight, sir?" the tavern keeper asked as he hauled a bottle of poteen from under the bar and poured a generous portion into a tumbler.

"Oppressed is the word for me!" the gentleman complained good-naturedly. He gulped the powerful liquor with a deftness that made him the envy of every man in the pub, Joseph included. "I live in a house that's stuffy and dull. I've a headstrong wife who forbids me to drink and a daughter engaged to a fool. I crave adventure, boys! If I had wings, I'd fly to the stars!"

If he bolts another poteen like he did that one, he won't need wings to be flyin', Joseph thought as he watched the men raise their mugs in a toast.

"Slainte. Your health, Mr. Christie," said Peter.

Joseph choked and spat his ale onto the counter. Christie! That murdering, thieving, home-burning villain right here under his very nose. It was as though Providence had delivered the bastard to him straightaway!

Trembling with anxiety and fury, Joseph hid his face as Daniel Christie, his soul's enemy, swallowed another poteen and waited for the barkeeper to pour yet another.

Just when Joseph thought that everyone in the pub must be feeling his rage, Christie walked over to him and whacked him soundly between the shoulder blades.

"Liven up, lad!" the landlord said. "You're too young to be brooding in your ale. What places you in this small chapter of the world?"

When Joseph didn't answer—he couldn't, as his heart was pounding between his tonsils—the tavern keeper said, "He's keepin' himself to himself, that one."

"Then it's one of two things," Christie said with the tone of a philosopher. "Enterprise or love. And if it's love, God help your frailty. The outcome of love is doom."

Joseph gave Christie a bitter sideways glance. "'Tisn't love. Ye can be most certain of that."

"Then you're a man of business like myself. But I warn you. It's brought me nothing but misery. I'm lost in a fog of commerce and compromise. I'd trade it all away for fifteen minutes of freedom."

"Freedom's a rare thing in these parts," Joseph muttered into his mug.

"It is." The landlord shook his head solemnly. "It is indeed."

Christie held out his glass to Joseph in a salute. His eyes glimmered with mischief, like a boy whose body had grown into a man and whose spirit was still unwilling to follow.

For a moment Joseph was struck by the fact that this was a living, breathing human being. A man he intended to kill. Then he recalled the vision of his father's cottage consumed by flames, and his resolve hardened.

"To a long and happy life," Joseph said, looking straight into the landlord's eyes. He heard the sarcasm in his own words. He searched the landlord's face to see if he had heard it, too.

But the gentleman smiled, a warm, hearty smile full of generosity. "God bless you," he said. "It's clear you're a good lad . . . wherever you're from."

Two hours and a half a bottle of poteen later, the pub door flew open and the landlord Daniel Christie stumbled out. "Good night, boys!" he shouted with slurred speech as he staggered to his horse and tried to mount.

"Stand still, animal," he said. Missing the stirrup completely, he lost his balance and tumbled to the ground. "Ow, my head. Not that I ever use it anyway." As he regained his feet he massaged his forehead, which had contacted with the horse's hoof. "Come, horse. I'll spoil you this once."

He groped for the reins, found them, and led the horse away. But as they ambled down the road it was difficult to tell who was leading whom. The horse seemed practiced in the art of guiding his master, who experienced some difficulty keeping his boots beneath him.

A moment later the pub door creaked open. Joseph stepped outside and stood for a long time, watching the two figures as they disappeared into the darkness. Then, lifting his chin and squaring his shoulders, he walked over to his donkey, untied it, and mounted.

At a slow clip-clop he followed the landlord out of town. Finally . . . he was on the hunt.

JOSEPH watched from a safe distance as Christie walked on and on down the narrow, winding road. Where was his house, anyway? Joseph wondered after they had traveled what seemed like miles. He had decided to murder the landlord on his own property. It seemed only fitting. Yet his impatience soared by the moment.

Even worse, he had to endure the ear-bending racket of Christie's off-key singing as he wailed a mournful ballad.

> "Oh woman high of fame,
> For thee I shall not die!
> Though foolish men you slay,
> A better man am I . . . !"

Suddenly Joseph pulled back hard on his donkey's reins. Christie had stopped and wandered over to the side of the road. What was he doing? Joseph wondered. Had he noticed that he was being followed?

The landlord made a strange movement at the waist-band of his trousers. Was he pulling out a weapon?

No, it wasn't a weapon, Joseph realized with relief that nearly made him laugh aloud. His honor was unbuttoning his pants. Apparently the first wash of the poteen was demanding release.

Joseph slid off his donkey, reached into his saddle-bag, and extracted the gun. What better time would he have than this to do the deed? What better way to send a scoundrel out of this world and into the next?

"Hello, souls of the departed," he heard Christie say. "What a disappointment I must seem to you all . . ."

Lifting the rifle, Joseph looked down the barrel and sighted on his target, who was peacefully urinating at the side of the road. His hand began to shake so hard that he couldn't aim.

Desperately trying to gather his courage and steady his nerves, Joseph took a deep breath. But even that shuddered as it left his lungs. This was a *man* in his gun's sights. A flesh-and-blood being who would be dead in a few seconds. Murder. He was going to commit murder.

A landlord. He was a bloody landlord, deserving of death. Kill him, you coward, he told himself. Do it now!

Christie continued to relieve himself, gazing up into the heavens, talking to the stars.

> "Why should I expire?
> For the fire of any eye?
> Though foolish men you slay,
> For thee I shall not die . . . !"

A moment later he was buttoning his pants and returning to his horse. Joseph didn't know whether to curse or weep with relief. He did neither, but mounted his donkey and followed after once again.

He thought of the villagers who had cheered him

when he had left his home. He thought of the pride shining on Danty Duff's face when he had bid him Godspeed. He thought of his scornful brothers and their lack of faith in him. He thought of the burned-out shell of the cottage.

Then his mind took a turn and he thought of Daniel Christie's mischievous eyes and the warm way he had slapped him on the back.

No! He couldn't think of his enemy as a man. If he did, he would never be able to complete his mission. And complete it he must. How could he ever go back to the village, to Danty and his brothers, if he hadn't fulfilled his vow?

There was no other way. The landlord had to die. Tonight.

DANIEL Christie entered his estate, passing between a pair of beautifully sculpted shrubs, which marked the beginning of the labyrinth of hedges that lined both sides of the driveway leading to the big house, a graceful example of Georgian architecture, with strong gray walls, a steep slate roof, and white shutters.

Joseph followed him, agape at the splendor of the estate. Having seen only stone-and-thatch cottages, Joseph had no idea that such mansions existed in the entire world, let alone that people lived in them. His mind couldn't grasp the size and the grandeur of the house. It must have at least a thousand rooms, maybe ten thousand, he thought. A thousand rooms for only one man and his family.

Then a thought occurred to Joseph that sent a tremor through his body that settled in his stomach and made him sick with fear. There had to be more people living in a place like that. Other families besides Christie's, servants by the score and soldiers . . . there had to be legions of soldiers guarding a castle like that.

Who the devil did he think he was, anyway, coming after a man like this? An aristocrat who lived in a palace such as this had the power of a king, a king who could call out his armies with the flick of a wrist. Joseph wondered how he had ever thought that he, a simple peasant, could kill a man like this and get away with his life.

Danty's encouraging words echoed in his brain. "Ye'll change the course of history, lad. And ye'll never have to buy another ale for as long as ye live."

Words easily spoken in a poor fisherman's shanty. Words that were difficult to believe now, with this awesome mansion, the symbol of this man's power and wealth, towering over him.

Halfheartedly, Joseph gave the donkey a kick so that he could gain a bit of ground on the landlord. When he had drawn close enough to get a good shot, he dismounted and pulled out his rifle.

Soldiers or no soldiers, he had to do it. He had to avenge his father's loss and his own. It was a matter of honor. He would kill this landlord, the blight of the land. The gentleman would be knocking at the gates of hell any moment now.

Taking careful aim, Joseph wrapped his finger around the trigger and began to squeeze, just as Danty Duff had instructed him.

The landlord paused for a moment. Joseph could see the dark figure clearly in his sights. It would be a good, clean shot, right through the heart . . . or the belly. Joseph wondered what would happen in the following seconds. Would the landlord die right away, or slowly and painfully?

It doesn't matter, he told himself.

Would an army of soldiers pour out of the mansion and hang him on the spot?

It couldn't matter. He was a man with a mission. A man about to change history.

Count to three, he told himself. *Shoot on three. One, two*—stop shaking. *Ye'll never be able to hit the bloody devil if yer shakin' like that. One, tw*—Daniel Christie was a man, a flesh-and-blood, breathing—*two, thre*—

The gun was knocked from his hands as the donkey wheeled around, its rump knocking Joseph nearly off his feet. Then it took off running down the road they had come. He didn't dare shout at the beast, so he hissed. He hissed until his lips stung, but the donkey made a complete escape. Joseph's transportation was gone, along with all of his supplies.

He looked down the road at his prey, who was disappearing around the corner of the house.

"Damnation!" he cursed. Then he breathed a heavy sigh. "This is a difficult murder."

As the landlord rounded the end of the mansion and disappeared, relief flooded Joseph, warring with disappointment. He was alive, and he was likely to continue to live throughout the night. Unless he did something incredibly stupid, his body wouldn't be swinging from the trees come morning.

But on the other hand, he was a lowly peasant who would never change history, never have a song written about his illustrious deeds, a commoner destined to buy his own ale.

He looked up at the grand mansion, the symbol of all he would never have, never be. He thought of the boisterous, friendly landlord who had wished him good health and Godspeed. In light of it all, his great mission seemed trite and childish.

Tucking the gun under his arm, Joseph pulled his coat more tightly around him. The night felt much colder and much blacker than before without the fires of vengeance to warm him.

What now? he asked himself as he stood there shivering in the darkness. *What in the name of heaven is a man to do now?*

Three

_____

JOSEPH woke with a start and wondered where the devil he was. Looking up, he saw an unfamiliar roof, a roof much higher than the one in his family's cottage. With his nose full of warm, animal scents, and the sharp prickle of hay gouging through his shirt and pants, he realized that he was still in the Christie's barn, where he had sought shelter and a straw bed the night before.

He tried to sit up and found that every muscle in his body ached as though Cromwell's army had tramped over it. Looking down at the decrepit rifle that lay across his legs, he smiled wryly, recalling the shame of last evening. Ah, that he might have slept forever and never wakened to humiliation and despair.

With a start he bolted upright as the sound of hoofbeats rang out through the morning stillness. Grabbing his rifle, Joseph peered out through the slats in the barn's wall. His heart lurched when he saw that the rider who was barreling across the open field, riding hard for the yard, was none other than the long-haired moonlight goddess he had glimpsed last night.

But although she still rode at breakneck speed, she presented a much more dignified picture this morning in her tall hat, heavy riding dress, and boots. Instead of straddling the horse bare-legged as she had the evening before, she was perched demurely on a fine sidesaddle, where she sat with all the dignity due a young lady of the manor.

As she approached the house she reined in her horse, forcing the magnificent beast to a polite trot. She cantered by the house, and Joseph watched with fascination and awe at her poise and her horsemanship.

"Dignity, Shannon," cried a genteel, feminine voice from a second-story window of the house. "Dignity."

The older woman waved a dainty lace handkerchief at the girl. "Yes, Mother," Shannon replied.

Shannon, Joseph thought, savoring the word. *Her name is Shannon.*

It fit her, he decided when he thought of the beauty, yet the wildness, of the River Shannon as it flowed, graceful and free, to the sea.

"A lady must always be civilized," the woman called after her, "even when she rides."

"Yes, Mother," she replied.

"A lady never gallops."

"Yes, Mother."

"Cover your pantaloons, dear."

Sighing, the girl slid from the saddle with one fluid movement and primly led her horse toward the barn. Joseph plastered himself against the wall. If she saw him, he might as well tie the noose around his own neck. How would he ever explain his presence here?

Once inside the barn and out of her mother's sight, Shannon yanked off her hat and threw it away from her in a gesture that reminded Joseph of Daniel Christie the previous evening in the pub. Instinct told him this girl was Christie's daughter. Her eyes glowed

—— 40 ——

with the same life and light of mischief. They both seemed about to burst the unwelcome restraints that had bound them.

Defiantly, she shook out her hair, and Joseph caught his breath at its beauty. By moonlight it had appeared silver, but in the golden light of morning it shone a bright red, like a fine copper kettle Joseph had once watched the blacksmith craft.

With a smack on its rump she sent her horse into a stall. Then she sat down on a wooden box and loosened her clothing. Her pretty, heart-shaped face flushed from the exertion of her ride and the warmth of the morning sun. Joseph thought she was the loveliest vision he had ever seen, and he felt an acute awareness of her in every inch of his body, an awareness he had never experienced before.

"A lady must always be civilized," she said, repeating her mother's words with a degree of sarcasm, "even when she rides. Cover your pantaloons, dear."

Boldly, she reached down and flipped her heavy skirt up and over her knees. Joseph peeked through the crack in the wall, mystified by the miracle of pantaloons—the first he had ever seen.

Suddenly, as though sensing that someone was watching her, the girl looked around. She spotted a horseshoe lying on the floor beside her, and reaching down, she picked it up. Joseph pulled back and pressed against the wall, wishing he could be smaller somehow, wishing he had never set upon this fated mission.

"Hello?" he heard her say. "Is someone there?"

Who did she think it was? he wondered. A rat, or a lion, or the devil himself perhaps?

A moment later the horseshoe sailed through the air, bounced off the barn wall, off the partition, and landed directly at Joseph's feet, the end of it upon the toe of his boot. Cautiously, he bent down to move it away, when the wall right beside him splintered with an ear-shattering crash. The sharp prongs of a pitchfork jutted from the split wood only inches from his nose.

"Holy Jaysus!" He whirled around and ran, heading for the door of the barn, only to find his way blocked by the red-haired girl and her pitchfork, which she brandished with abandon.

"Stay right where you are," she said, her voice low and menacing. "Don't even flutter an eyelid or I'll puncture you through."

Even with a pitchfork waving in front of his face, Joseph had the presence of mind to consider how beautiful this girl was. In fact, the fire in her bright blue eyes and the courage with which she handled her weapon made him admire her even while his body awakened to her.

For the first time in his life Joseph noticed the subtlety of femininity, the rise and fall of her bosom, which showed demurely above her bodice, the flushed pinkness of her cheeks, the translucent perfection of her skin.

For a moment he felt insane, as though his senses had been stolen by this female—stolen, yet sharpened. He thought of all the comments he had heard from his father, Danty Duff, his brothers, and other men about the mystical charms of women, and every word suddenly took on new meaning. She was divine. And perhaps more important, her bright blue eyes were staring into his with a strange expression, which made him think that maybe she had the same sort of awareness of him.

He made a slight movement toward her, just a tiny raising of his hand. The fire of courage in her eyes dimmed and she screamed, "Father! Help! I've a desperate criminal in here!"

A desperate criminal? Him? The fears of last evening, horrible fancies about legions of avenging soldiers, flooded his mind. He was going to get himself hanged after all!

He made a dash for the door, but she lunged at him with the pitchfork, spearing him in the thigh.

"Oooowww!" he shrieked, and grabbed his leg. "Look what ye've done now, woman. Ye've lamed me for certain."

Shannon looked down at the wounds on his leg, which sprouted several red streams, and her flushed cheeks paled to a stark white. "Good heavens," she exclaimed, her hand over her mouth.

After throwing the pitchfork to the ground, she ran, screaming, from the barn. "Father, help! I've been all but raped and slaughtered!"

Daniel Christie and his wife ran from the mansion, the mistress's dressing robe fluttering about her, the master none too steady on his feet.

"What's all the fuss about?" Christie shouted. "What's wrong with you, child?"

"In the stable, Father! It's the devil himself! There!" Hiding behind her parents, Shannon pointed toward the barn door. Out hobbled Joseph, his leg bleeding, his old rusty gun in his hand.

Joseph looked around the yard at the girl, her mother, and her father . . . but no soldiers. Drawing a deep breath, he gathered his resolve. Providence had given him another chance to prove his heroism after all. Who was he to deny his destiny?

"Mr. Daniel Christie," Joseph said in a voice that surprised him with its strength and steadiness.

"Yes?" replied the landlord.

"Me name is Joseph Donelly. I'm of the family Donelly—that you pushed out of our land."

"What in God's name are you talking about? We were drinking together only last evening." Christie shot a quick glance at his wife; she was staring at Joseph's rusty gun. He pushed both women away from him, but they walked only a few feet, reluctant to leave his side. Again the girl hid behind her mother, peeking around at Joseph, an expression of fear mixed with amazement on her pretty face.

This was perfect, Joseph thought. Now he had a clear shot at the landlord without danger of shooting the women.

"Prepare to pay for your crimes!" he shouted.

"Stop him, Daniel," the woman cried. "He's come to shoot us all down."

"That's not likely to happen." Christie smiled wryly as he studied the lad. "He's waving his gun all over the place."

It was true, Joseph realized. If he didn't pull the reins in tightly on his fear, he would never be able to accomplish the deed.

He took a deep breath and tried to steady himself. Suddenly a power he had never felt before surged through him, a force he thought must surely be Destiny. The energy flowed through him and into his hands. His finger squeezed the trigger before he was ready. And what surprised him even more was the deafening explosion that followed.

Joseph's rattled mind had no time to assimilate what had happened as the blast hurled him backward against the barn. The fragmented gun fell, piece by piece, to the ground with a clatter of finality.

Pain coursed through his body as the dull realization dawned upon him that something had gone wrong. The landlord hadn't been harmed at all. He himself had been damaged.

In a trio the family rushed toward him.

"Captain Moonlight," he muttered as he sank to his knees. "Damn you, Danty Duff. Come all this way for vengeance and I've gone and murdered meself. . . ."

A moment later he pitched forward and fell on his face.

The last thing Joseph Donelly remembered was the gritty, earthy taste of dirt and dust in his mouth and the faraway sound of the girl's screams. Then a darkness blacker than midnight fell over him and the world disappeared.

SHANNON stood at the foot of her bed with its yards and yards of frilly white flounces, which were now stained with smears of blood from the young man who lay stretched across it. She held a bowl of water as her mother dipped a cloth and washed the lad's gunpowdered face.

"Look how black his fingers are, Mother," she said. She had also noticed that beneath the powder he was an extraordinarily handsome boy, but she assumed it would be best not to mention that fact to her mother.

"Never mind his fingers," Nora Christie replied. "He's a lowborn blatherskite of filth."

"Then why are you bothering to save his worthless life?"

Nora dropped the cloth into the bowl. She donned her most judicious face. "Because, my dear," she said, "our duty is to restore him to health and full remorse so that he can hear his own neck crack when he dangles from the hangman's noose."

"Of course," Shannon replied, feeling a little sick at the thought of this boy swinging from the end of a rope. He might have black fingers, but he also had beautiful green eyes. She would never forget that warm, tingling feeling she had experienced that moment in the barn when she had first looked into his eyes.

"To think they dare to claim against their betters," Nora continued. "This perfect world would crumble if they stepped above their station."

She lifted the edge of a linen sheet that covered the young man's body. "Now turn away, Shannon," she said. "Protect the innocence of your eyes."

Nora peeled back the bed sheet, uncovering Joseph's naked body. Shannon peeked through slightly parted fingers as her mother covered his genitals with an overturned empty saucepan.

"Of all the days to intrude upon our peaceful life," Nora complained. "The ladies are coming by this afternoon for tea and whist."

"The ladies?" Shannon uncovered her eyes. "Oh, no. Not the ladies." She passed a hand over her forehead. "I'm feeling sick."

"Mind yourself, Shannon. Those ladies are models of manners and behavior." With a pair of scissors Nora began to cut a length of snowy linen into bandages.

Suddenly the sound of breaking glass caused both women to jump.

"Good heavens," Nora exclaimed. "What was that?"

"Nothing happened!" shouted Daniel's voice from downstairs.

"Nothing happened, indeed," Nora replied as she dropped the scissors and bandages on a nearby table and walked from the room. "Your father is at the bottle again, Shannon. Whatever shall I do with that man?"

But Shannon scarcely heard her. All she could think of was the lad stretched across her bed, a saucepan covering his groin, and the fact that the two of them were all alone here in her bedroom.

What if he woke? What if he opened those green eyes and looked at her the way he had there in the barn? As she leaned forward and studied his handsome face, she found herself almost wishing he would. Fear battled with anticipation.

To maintain her composure she began to quietly

sing a little nursery rhyme. "Mary, Mary, Mary Nell, do you hear your wedding bell?"

Glancing toward the door and seeing no sign of her mother, she tiptoed closer to the bed. Gingerly she lifted the saucepan by its handle and peeked beneath. But in the dimly lit room none of the mysteries of manhood were revealed to her. "Will he love you, Mary Nell? Time and time alone will tell."

Continuing to sing, she held tightly to the pan's handle. Curiosity overwhelmed her. Never having been blessed or cursed with brothers, Shannon's inquisitiveness had remained unsatisfied throughout the years. Her parents, as excellent chaperons, had carefully guarded her virtue, making certain that she remained ignorant of such earthy knowledge.

Unable to control herself, she lifted the pan once more and nearly died when the lad stirred and his eyes popped open.

"You're having a dream," she said, sputtering. "This isn't really happening at all. And I'm not really here."

She clamped the saucepan down on his groin, much harder than she had intended to, and he yelped in pain—her first lesson in the vulnerability of certain parts of the male anatomy.

As though the handle had burned her hand, she released the pan and turned to run away from him. But before she could escape, he grabbed a handful of her hair and yanked her down onto the bed beside him.

"Let go, you heathen animal," she shrieked. "You aren't allowed to touch me. You're a peasant."

"Shut your noisy mouth, girl," he muttered, tightening his grip on her hair.

Her face was so close to his, she could feel the heat of his breath on her cheeks. His eyes were greener than she remembered, blazing with anger and a desperation that she had never felt or seen in another human being.

"You're a terrible man, aren't you?" she said, excitement and fear causing her heart to pound. Surely he could see her bosom pulsating beneath her bodice. "You're a lawbreaking murderer."

"The law means nothing to me."

"It'll mean something when the soldiers come. They're going to hang you by the neck."

"Help me escape," he said, "or 'twill be *yer* neck that's broken."

She laughed, but she couldn't stop the tremor that quivered through her body. She couldn't ignore the fact that he was lying so close to her. A man. A man with nothing but a saucepan to hide his nakedness.

His eyes closed for a moment and he shook his head. Shannon realized that he was fighting to remain conscious. A part of her, deep inside, understood and admired his struggle.

"I . . . I want . . ." he said, his voice weak and shaky as he fought to breathe.

She tried to squirm away, but he held her tightly, his fingers twisted in her red locks. "What is it you want, boy?" she asked, her voice as unsteady as his.

"I . . . want . . . my . . . land . . ."

As soon as he had uttered the words, the lad closed his eyes and his head lolled on the pillow. His hand released her hair, dropping to the bed beside her.

His land, she thought as she slowly rose from the bed. *He wants his own land . . . desperately. Almost as desperately as I.* A strange feeling crept over Shannon as she stood staring down at the lad. She sensed an odd kinship with him to hear her own dream spoken on his lips.

Could they have something in common, she and this ragged peasant? A sense of destiny and inevitability swept over her, leaving her knees weak. She had been fated to meet this young man . . . this peasant who seemed to share the same dream.

Then she thrust the thought from her mind. No, she must have misunderstood.

Peasants didn't have dreams . . . did they? They were as different from gentry as Kerry was from Connemara. There was simply no understanding a bog boy . . . even if he did have beautiful green eyes.

As Nora Christie descended the spiraling staircase she saw her husband attempting to stash a whiskey bottle beneath the skirt of a small table in the foyer.

"Daniel, whatever happened? We heard the sound of breaking glass all the way upstairs."

"Nothing happened." Christie wore the expression of a young boy caught with his trousers around his ankles and his bum bared.

"Nothing happened, indeed," she replied with a matronly, indignant tone of voice.

"A poor misguided robin has broken a window-pane."

"What a manufactured lie." She walked into the sitting room and over to the liquor cabinet, where a few bits of telltale glass shimmered on the highly polished wooden floor. The smell of whiskey filled the air.

Nora turned to her husband, who shrugged and raised one eyebrow. "I was merely dusting the liquor cabinet."

"As if a bottle in your vicinity stood long enough to gather dust," she replied sarcastically. She shook her head as though overcome with sadness. "Respectability, Daniel. You are a gentleman of title. When will you ever begin to act like one?"

"I inherited my title and I don't know what it means," he said with a confused, lost expression on his round face.

Nora held the scissors up and shook them in his face. "I'll not tolerate this behavior, Daniel Christie. Surely you know that by now."

"Yes, dear. Of course, my love," he replied in mock derision. "My only calling in life is to reach the high standard which my lady sets for me."

Nora stood, looking at him for a long moment, then snorted and left the room.

Christie followed her and watched as she climbed the stairs. The moment she disappeared a broad, mischievous smile split his face. He reached beneath the table and retrieved his whiskey.

"I crave adventure," he whispered as he uncorked the bottle and took a long draft. Wiping his mouth with the back of his hand, he said to the amber fluid in the bottle, "And someday I will have it. But for today you, my friend, will have to do."

Nora entered her daughter's bedroom just in time to see Shannon secure the bandage around the boy's leg. Studying the girl closely, Nora's trained mother's eye detected a certain flush to her cheeks, a reluctance to look her in the face.

"What became of the man I married?" Nora asked as she circled the bed, watching the girl's every move as she tied the final knot. "Some other man has replaced him and goes about with his name."

"Father's life is a hard one," Shannon said in his defense, still refusing to meet her mother's eye. "He would prefer to be an adventurer in the wildest, darkest Africa, or a pioneer in the deserts of America."

"Pooh. He's a man. He doesn't know what he wants." Nora glanced down at the boy, then back at her daughter's red face. "Any sign of revival, Shannon?" she asked.

Shannon, abject as a nun, took the scissors from her

hand and snipped the ends of the bandage. "None that I've noticed, Mother."

Nora shook her head and clucked disapprovingly. Shannon, like her father, was a dreadful liar. But Nora didn't bother to challenge the girl. There was no point in suggesting that a liar improve his art. Better that he or she remain clumsy in their execution.

At least Nora knew which way the wind blew . . . and whether it smelled like bovine manure.

In a formal white dress with a stiff lace collar and stays that pinched her ribs, Shannon sat beside her mother, her hand filled with cards, her pretty face pulled into a polite smile that did little to hide her boredom and irritation.

After this morning's excitement this card game with her mother and six of Nora's friends held even less appeal than usual . . . and usually Shannon feigned illness or any other lie she could devise on the spot to avoid participating.

Coiffed, perfumed, aristocratic, and chatty, they simply didn't fill Shannon's qualifications for stimulating company. Given the choice, she would have preferred to be hanging about the stables, listening to her father's lectures to the stableboy and groomsman about animal husbandry.

"We of the upper class must never tolerate the indolence of these savage natives," Nora said as she delicately fanned herself with her cards. "As the Protestant minority we must realize that our very lives are threatened by these heathens. We must never allow them to get the upper hand."

The woman to Shannon's right nodded her regal silver head. "They'd murder us in our beds if they had half a chance. Why that boy upstairs would like nothing better than to creep downstairs this very minute and slaughter us one by one."

The ladies gasped, then chattered in enthusiastic agreement. The thought occurred to Shannon that perhaps they—like herself and her family—might almost welcome this exciting interruption to their normally dull lives.

"You needn't be frightened," Nora assured them. "He's securely locked away."

One of the younger women at the end of the table sighed. "How disappointing. I've never seen a real authentic murderer before."

"You wouldn't want to see him," Nora replied. "He's the ugliest, most vicious creature I've ever set eyes upon. Isn't he, Shannon?"

Ugly? Vicious? Shannon thought of the lad's bright green eyes and shiny dark hair. Her mother's expression was turning colder by the second; she must say something. "Dreadfully ugly," she muttered.

"Did *you* get a look at him?" the silver-haired matron asked Shannon.

She thought of the saucepan, then smiled and studied her cards carefully with wide-eyed innocence. Again she felt her mother's eyes on her. "Yes," she replied demurely, "a peek."

As Daniel Christie clipped a stray twig from one of the perfectly groomed hedges that lined the road to his mansion, he heard the pounding of horse hooves coming fast. Without even looking up, he knew who it was: Stephen Chase. Chase was the only man he knew who never trotted anywhere. He always rode at full gallop, as though everything he had to do and everywhere he had to go were of the utmost importance.

Daniel sighed and considered ducking into the house. God help him, he really didn't like Stephen, though he had tried to. After all, the chap was engaged to his only daughter . . . thanks to Nora's matchmaking. Daniel only wished he was as happy about Nora's choice as she was. But when he looked into Chase's cold eyes and then at his daughter's vivacity, he simply couldn't summon the enthusiasm.

"Hello there, Stephen," he said when the young man pulled his horse to halt in front of him.

With a decorous military flourish Stephen waved his two deputies on to the stable. "We've come for your prisoner, Mr. Christie," he said with equally military austerity.

"Take your time," Christie said, resenting the eagerness in the man's voice. He reminded him of a giant vulture, sitting there on his horse, swathed in his black cloak. "The poor fella's upstairs dead, more or less."

Chase deflated slightly. "Very well, sir." He studied Daniel and the bush he was trimming with a raised eyebrow. "And what are you doing, sir, out here in the shrubs?"

With an impish twinkle in his eyes Daniel reached into the hedge and pulled out a whiskey bottle. He held it up to Chase.

"Join me?" he asked. "There's a gin and bitters in that rhododendron over there."

Stephen lifted his chin in haughty disdain. "Not when I'm working, sir."

As Daniel watched Stephen ride around the side of the house, he sighed again. More deeply this time. That lad was a cold fish, all right. How the devil was he ever going to warm him up? And would it be worth the effort even if he did?

Upstairs in Shannon's bedroom Joseph stirred and opened his eyes. For a moment he had no idea where he was or what had happened to him. Then he remembered and groaned.

His face ached. His hands hurt. His entire body felt

battered and bruised, as though he had been dragged over a half-dug field of turf on his belly.

Where was the girl? When he had last passed out, she had been lying beside him . . . right here on the bed. Remembering, he could hardly believe it had happened. That memory, too, had a dreamlike quality.

When would he wake from this devil of a nightmare?

With a great effort and even more pain, he sat up, slung his feet over the side of the bed, and forced himself to stand. He nearly cried out from the agony in his leg. Damn that girl anyway for stabbing him like that. He'd get even with her one way or the other.

For a moment he considered the possibility of kissing her rather than punishing her, but he banished the idea from his head. Other, more important, matters were at hand.

On unsteady feet he ambled over to the window and looked out. The height made him dizzy. His heart sank. The distance was far too great to make an escape. If he jumped, he would surely break whatever bones in his body remained intact.

Turning back to the room, he saw his clothing lying on a chair, and he realized for the first time that he was naked. Had he been exposed this way for the girl to see?

The thought embarrassed him and at the same moment made him feel as though the room had suddenly turned hot and stuffy. Faintly he recalled pulling her down onto the bed beside him, her body next to his. Surely he hadn't been naked then.

Once again he pushed all thoughts of the girl out of his mind. She was the reason he was here in the first place. She was the one who had lamed him, and this was probably her bedroom, judging from the frilly spread that covered the bed and the dainty pictures of flowers and animals that adorned the walls.

Gathering all of his strength, he gritted his teeth and pulled his clothes on. He had to get out of here. Now. Or he would be swinging in the breeze come morning.

But even in the midst of his fear, Joseph's mind drifted for a moment, and he wondered if he would ever see that red-haired girl again.

A pain shot through his punctured knee. "I'm hopin' not," he muttered bitterly. "And she'd better be hopin', too, because I'm not finished with that red-haired daughter of the old horned one. Not at all, at all."

Four

===

"AND where will you and your handsome Stephen live after the marriage, Shannon?" asked the snowy-haired dowager who sat across from her, staring down at her cards through silver-rimmed bifocals. "Will you move to a town, do you think?"

Shannon's throat tightened as always when she thought of her forthcoming nuptials. Living with Stephen. The thought should have filled her with joy and anticipation. She was terribly happy about her engagement . . . wasn't she? So why did she feel a little sick at hearing someone else speak the words?

"Towns are full of ruffians," Nora said with a decisive lift to her chin. "They're going to live here, with us, where they belong."

"What a lovely life you'll have," the lady crooned, placing one hand delicately over her prominent bosom.

"There's nothing grander than marriage," replied her neighbor to the left. "A woman needs a husband for security."

"With all the dangers in the world, young people

are better off with their parents," Nora said. "Sit up straight, Shannon," she added with a nudge of her elbow to Shannon's ribs.

"Yes, Mother," Shannon replied with weary submission.

Nora squinted at her daughter's neckline. "And what is your button doing there, dear?"

"It's choking me."

"Better to choke than be vulgar."

Shannon gagged as her mother reached over and fastened her topmost button tight against her throat.

From the front of the house they heard the sound of a door opening and closing. All the ladies jumped, nearly losing their grip on their cards and their composure.

"A noise!" said the blue-haired matron. "Nora, I heard a noise!"

"Let us hope it's Stephen Chase," Nora said.

Let us hope it isn't, Shannon replied silently. Then she pushed the unhappy thought from her mind. Stephen was her fiancé, her betrothed, her beloved. Surely she must be glad to see him at least a little.

With all the flourish of a military hero in the making, Stephen swept into the room, a dashing figure in black, tall and regal. The ladies sighed in unison.

"Ah," Nora said. "Speak of the sun and we see its rays. Ladies, may I present my daughter's fiancé, Mr. Stephen Chase."

Stephen bowed elegantly. "Good evening, ladies."

The women fanned themselves with their hands of cards, blinking up at him flirtatiously. Shannon supposed she should be proud of him; obviously women thought him handsome. But mostly she felt irritation in his presence. She wondered if he had ever noticed. She didn't think so. Stephen seemed to be the sort of man who saw only what pleased him.

"Stephen is a brilliant young man," Nora continued to gush. "Not only does he manage my husband's business affairs, but he's studying for the law."

"And we understand, Mr. Chase, that you're very handy with a gun," said one of the ladies.

"Unrivaled, he is, in marksmanship. He can shoot a sparrow at a range of a mile."

Shannon winced with embarrassment at her mother's effusive flattery. Even more embarrassing, Stephen appeared to be basking in the adulation.

"Now, now," he said soothingly. "Keep calm. You're safe and protected. Go back to your sinful cardplaying. Everything's going to be fine." Then he turned his attention to Shannon. "Good evening, my darling," he said in a voice that reminded her of molasses.

He walked over to her, took her hand in his, and placed a delicate kiss upon her fingers. The women giggled and pretended not to be watching.

"Your daughter is certainly a lucky girl, Nora," one of them said.

Stephen dropped to one knee beside Shannon's chair. "I've been so worried about you, darling," he said. "Did that ruffian frighten you?"

She leaned close and, lowering her voice to a whisper, said, "If there's anything to be frightened of, it's my mother and her frivolous friends."

He squeezed her hand companionably. "I'm here now. We'll endure their company together."

The ladies continued playing their hands as Shannon and Stephen spoke. "Is it true, Stephen," she said, "that he'll die for his crime?"

Stephen studied her suspiciously. "Do you really care? He tried to kill your father."

"But he failed miserably. I doubt he's got a brain in his head. He's hardly dangerous."

"The authorities will decide his fate. It needn't be your concern."

She placed her lips near his ear. "What *are* my concerns, Stephen? I feel trapped in this stuffy old house. And just look at my hair. It's pinned up so tightly that it hurts to blink my eyes. See?" She demonstrated, and he laughed softly.

"Shannon," Nora said, her tone gruff.

Shannon jumped. "Yes, Mother?"

"The ladies and I would like you to play the piano."

"No."

In shock the ladies turned their heads like so many ostriches.

Nora raised one delicate eyebrow. "I beg your pardon?"

"I'm not in a musical mood."

Nora's face registered a storm brewing on the horizon. Stephen, ever chivalrous, hastened to the rescue.

"Come, darling, play something for us. Something fanciful and nice."

Feeling betrayed, yet compelled, Shannon rose from her chair and shuffled to the piano. So . . . he wanted to hear something cheerful?

Placing her fingertips upon the ivories, she began to play the dreariest classical piece she could think of. It suited her mood. Perhaps she would use this dirge for her bridal procession. Somehow, at this moment, it seemed appropriate.

WHAT *a sad and mournful tune,* Joseph thought as the music filtered upstairs and into the bedroom where he was held prisoner. *I've heard cheerier melodies at funerals and wakes.*

But the music served a useful purpose, sorrowful as it was. For the past half hour he had been laboring to unlock the door, fearful that the sound of his rattling about might alert someone downstairs. But with this infernal racket no one was likely to hear his feeble efforts.

Fumbling with the doorknob yielded no results at all. Now was the time to try something else.

He looked around the room and spotted a book lying on the bedstand. It was a copy of *The Pilgrim's Progress* by John Bunyan.

With no conscience or even hesitation, he ripped off the cover and tossed the damaged book onto the bed. Books meant nothing to him. Joseph Donelly had never been granted the privilege of learning to read. Peasants were forbidden this luxury, and even the traditional hedgerow schools, where priests risked their lives to secretly teach the children of their parishes, were becoming more and more rare as time went on.

Joseph had a more useful function for the book cover at the moment. In seconds he had fashioned it into a tool, which he slid between the door and the jamb, trying to coax the latch to release.

For moments that seemed like eternities he jiggled, wriggled, and sweet-talked the lock. All to no avail. Finally, his patience exhausted, he threw the book cover aside, drew back his fist, and slammed it through the door. Having accomplished this, he reached through the hole he had made, grasped the lock, and opened the door.

In the hallway he paused, listening, but hearing only the pounding of his own heart, his own labored breathing, and the infernal music downstairs. No one came racing up the staircase. Apparently the piano noise had covered the sound of him crashing through the door.

Not knowing what to expect, he tiptoed down the stairs, being careful not to step too heavily and cause the wood to creak. As he reached the bottom of the staircase he caught a glimpse of the ladies seated at the table in the parlor. He saw Stephen, and a wash of bitter bile rose in his throat. That bastard again! Would he never be rid of him?

Then his eyes traveled over the rest of the circle and he saw Shannon, seated at the piano, looking beautiful in her white dress. For a moment Joseph forgot all about Stephen, all about everything . . . even to breathe.

Then, even his heart stopped. She was looking at him. Straight at him. Her blue eyes wide with shock.

He prepared to bolt. Would she expose him? Surely she would, as she had this morning. His eyes silently begged her to spare him. Just this once . . . please.

Suddenly she ceased the funeral dirge and burst into another song, pounding the keys in a raucous, rowdy tune that filled the house with its lively tempo.

"Shannon," her mother shouted over the din. "Whatever are you playing?"

"It's modern, Mother," she replied. "It's from America."

"Stop it. It's ghastly."

"It's called band music, Mother. It's the latest fashion in Boston, I've heard."

The ladies put their hands over their ears and grimaced. Apparently band music was not to their taste.

As Shannon's hands flew over the keys she glanced up once more and stared straight at Joseph. The unspoken words passed between them: hers, telling him that she was creating a diversion for his escape, and his, silently thanking her for his life.

He crept down the stairs, his glance darting between Shannon at the piano, the ladies in the background, and his nemesis, Stephen Chase, whose full attention was trained upon the pretty pianist. So intent was Joseph upon the people in the parlor that he didn't pay close enough attention to his footing. One misstep, his ankle twisted, and he tumbled headlong down the stairs.

No amount of music could cover the racket caused by Joseph's fall. The sound thundered through the house, a rolling rumble as he hit stair after stair, followed by a solid thud as he landed upon the hard wooden floor at the bottom.

"The terrorist has risen!" Nora screamed as she and Stephen rushed from the parlor into the foyer.

With additional pains now shooting through his body, Joseph crawled toward the door. He had to escape or hang at the end of this bastard's rope.

But as he reached for the door—Stephen Chase directly behind him—it flew open and in tramped Chase's two deputies, followed by Daniel Christie dogging behind.

"Careful, boy," Stephen said in his haughtiest tone. "Your life's worth little as it is."

"You're the bastard that burned my father's house," Joseph said, staring up at his enemy, hate burning like a slow hot flame in his green eyes.

"I've burned many houses in the line of duty," Chase replied. "Am I meant to remember yours?"

Joseph glanced quickly around the foyer, and the faces blurred. Only one stood out in his mind. Shannon. She stood in the entrance to the parlor, her hand clasped across her mouth as though she might cry out at any moment. The thought crossed his mind that if she did speak, it would be in his defense. But that was probably nothing more than a fanciful wish.

He looked back at Chase, hating his arrogance, hating his fine black coat, hating the polished pistols that he knew hung on each hip beneath that coat.

Joseph moved his hand to better support his weight and felt the tufted edge of a small rug . . . a rug upon which Stephen Chase was standing. His fingers curled around the fringe and he yanked as hard as he could.

The results were spectacular—better than he had hoped. The rug flew across the highly polished floor, Stephen's feet shot out from under him, and he landed on his pompous arse with a less than graceful plop.

In a second Joseph had struggled to his feet and walked over to Chase. He planted one boot firmly on the man's chest. "I'll give ye somethin' to remember, ye bollix—ooww!"

Pain crashed through his injured leg as one of Chase's men smashed the wound with the butt of his rifle. Then they both attacked him with rifle butts and fists. Joseph thought his time had surely come as the blows rained down on him. He flailed back at them, but the agony in his leg was so great that he couldn't concentrate and land the punches.

"Stop!" Chase shouted. Joseph heard the word as though it had come from far away, though a long narrow tunnel.

The beating ceased. Joseph felt himself supported on either side by the deputies, whose fingers bit into his upper arms.

Through eyes that were rapidly beginning to swell, Joseph saw Chase, who was now on his feet, reach down and wipe his boot with a snowy-white glove. Then, with great ceremony, he tossed it to the floor at Joseph's feet.

"Pistols," Chase said. "Tomorrow, at dawn."

At first Joseph's battered brain held no comprehension of what those words might mean. It wasn't until the deputies were dragging him—still thrashing—upstairs that he realized . . . he had been challenged to a duel.

The last time he had attempted to fire a gun, he had nearly killed himself. And Joseph had a sick, sinking feeling that this time Stephen Chase would finish the job, for sure.

JOSEPH paced, he cursed, he rattled the lock on the door, which had been boarded up since his last escape, but his efforts produced no results. He was as trapped as a salmon in a lucky fisherman's net.

Somehow he had to get out of this room. With dawn only a few hours away, he could almost hear the cry of the banshee, the harbinger of death. That son of a bitch would shoot him right between the eyes and not even flinch. And Joseph was determined not to give him the pleasure if he could help it.

As the hours wore on, his fear subsided a bit, and quiet determination took its place. Every man had to die sometime. At least he would depart this world like a man, facing his death head-on, chin up, as befitted a Donelly. After all, his father was waiting for him just on the other side. And maybe some bard somewhere would write a song about him. Perhaps pretty girls would sing that song when they were walking through the meadow, and thinking of him, they would shed a tear or two for poor Joseph Donelly, cut down in the prime of his youth.

Joseph sat on the bed for a moment to rest his wounded leg and enjoy the bittersweetness the fantasy evoked. He would be a hero, after all, and the only hero in Ireland who was more revered than a live one was a dead one.

Suddenly his daydream was interrupted by a clunking sound beside the window.

"What the divil?" Joseph muttered, rising from the bed and walking over to the window.

As he leaned out he found himself face-to-face with Shannon, who had propped a ladder beneath the window and was climbing it without hesitation, her long skirts drawn nearly up to her waist, her face shining with excitement in the silver moonlight.

He leaned backward and she poked her head into the room. "Shhh," she said. "I'm running away."

Joseph could say nothing. Why was she here? Already in the past twenty-four hours she had betrayed him, then attempted to help him; now what was she after? There was no reading the mind or intentions of a female.

He stood back and watched as she fairly tumbled into the room, landing with surprising grace on her feet. She straightened up, smoothed her skirt and her hair, and donned an expression of nonchalance. Something in her eyes betrayed her; Joseph sensed her agitation and excitement.

"Excuse me," she said as she walked past him to the dresser. "There's something in here I need."

Still, Joseph said nothing. But when he made a slight move toward her, she jumped like a mouse who had just spotted a rattlesnake.

"Perhaps you're wondering why I'm running away," she said as she pulled the dresser away from the wall, huffing slightly from the effort.

He knew she was waiting for his inquiry; he decided to let her wait a bit longer. There was no point in speaking your mind if you were already standing with one brogue in the gravedigger's hole. "Well, I'll satisfy your curiosity and tell you," she said impatiently. "I'm running away because I'm modern."

From behind the dresser she pulled a small jewelry box. Placing it on the bed, she began to rummage through it, pulling out photos, pamphlets with pictures of sailing ships, and a small red, white, and blue flag.

"I'm modern," she said, chattering on, "and I'm going to a modern place. You're not the only one who's trapped. If I stay here, my mother will turn me into one of her perfumed friends. No thank you! I'm very smart and I'm very modern, and that's all you need to know about me."

With studied deliberation she placed a pamphlet on the bed, adjusting it so that Joseph could see it clearly. At the top of the paper was printed one word, "LAND." Joseph refused to look at the paper, which meant nothing as the printed words were a mystery to him.

"Perhaps you're wondering where I'm running away to," she said. "Here, have a look at this."

She held the paper up before Joseph's eyes. He squinted at it and moved his eyes across it, pretending to read.

He saw the comprehension dawn in her blue eyes, and humiliation washed over him, leaving his face red. "You can't read! Can you, boy?" she said. Then she clucked her tongue in a way that made him furious. He didn't need or want her sympathy, damn her. "How pathetic." She pointed to the large four-lettered word at the top. "It says, 'Land.'"

"Land?" The word lit a fire of interest inside Joseph that he couldn't hide.

"Yes, land," she said, obviously delighted that he had finally spoken. "They've got so much of it, they give it away for free."

"Who does?"

"*They* do. In America." She studied him for a sign of understanding. He stared back at her blankly. "You have heard of America, haven't you? On the other side of the sea? It's very modern there and—"

Joseph reached out and snatched the pamphlet from her.

"Where did you get this?"

"A man with a mustache gave it to me."

Joseph snorted and tossed the paper back onto the bed. "That surely lends a lot of weight to the document. Yer daft, girl. No land is given away in any part of the world."

"In America it is," she said, retrieving the pamphlet from the bed and folding it carefully. "I can't own land here in Ireland, but over there I'll have a place of my own and I'll raise horses on it and ride them any way I please."

Joseph laughed at her. He had to admire her spirit, but obviously she had been touched by the fairies. "Ye'll never get to America. Look at ye. Yer all nothin' but ribbons."

She raised one dainty eyebrow and took one step toward him, her hands on her slender waist. "It wasn't a ribbon or a bow that stabbed you in the leg," she said with self-satisfaction that rubbed him raw and made the pain in his leg all the more intense.

"No," he said, "'twas a frightened little brat with a head full of blind ideas. Freedom? Land? Why do ye need land? Ye own half of Ireland as it is—took it, yer people did, never mindin' the bloodshed and the miseries ye caused."

"*I* didn't take it!"

"No, ye just lived here all fancied up on rent and broken backs."

He turned away from her, but from the corner of his eye he saw a look cross her face that looked a great deal like admiration.

A moment later she stepped closer to him and she raised her hand slightly as though she might reach out and touch his arm. But then she withdrew it and folded her hands before her. "If it's land you want, lad," she said softly, "come with me."

Joseph spun around and looked at her as though she had gone insane. "Come with ye?" he asked.

Adopting a businesslike manner, she walked over to the bed and picked up a picture of a ship, which she shoved under Joseph's nose. "Great ships sail out of Dublin and Liverpool," she told him, "but a woman dare not travel alone. I need your protection."

"What's a wild-headed squip like yerself need protection from? Just take that pitchfork o' yers along and ye'll be fine."

"It isn't that simple. Nine out of ten of the women on those ships are raped, and the tenth is murdered for resisting. You're brave," she said, not looking at him. "I've seen evidence of your courage myself. You shoot at men and step on their chests when you feel it's necessary. You could be quite useful to me."

"Useful? Could I?" The very thought filled Joseph with a sense of male importance. Already he could fancy himself fighting off any would-be attackers who might wish to do her harm. He would be her hero and she would be so very grateful and—

"Yes," she said, "you could be my serving boy."

Joseph's eyes narrowed and he shook his head solemnly. "I see. And would I be polishin' yer boots for ye, then?"

Shannon shrugged, then nodded. "They will need a polish now and again."

"And perhaps I could boil ye a cup of tea?"

"When teatime calls for it, yes."

Joseph reached out and grabbed her by the shoulders, drawing her to him. She gasped. "I'll throw the tea in yer face," he said, "and I'll piss on yer fancy boots before I'll serve the likes of you."

She stared up at him without flinching, though her eyes betrayed her fear. "I'll pay you thruppence a day."

He pushed her away from him. "Get out! I've an appointment come morning and I'm off honorin' it."

Scooping up her jewelry box, he shoved it at her.

"You'll never win this duel with Stephen," she said. "We've all seen how *you* handle a gun."

"I'd never have blown me head off if the gun hadn't been defective."

"Oh, be quiet. Even if you *do* win, you're sentenced

to hang for coming to kill my father. I'm giving you your freedom, boy."

In reply he pushed her toward the window. "I'm not goin' to a distant world. I'm of Ireland. And I'll stay in Ireland till I die."

With her jewelry box and papers under one arm, she gathered her skirts and climbed out the window. After taking two steps, she paused and in a tone that chilled Joseph's blood she said, "Until you die, you say? Well, dear boy, that will be in about five hours."

WHEN Shannon reached the bottom of the ladder, she gave it a kick, then grabbed at it, trying to keep it from hitting the ground with a clatter and awakening the household. All she accomplished was to bruise her shin and spill her jewelry.

"Hellfire and damnation!" she swore, enjoying the release of words that ladies were forbidden to speak.

Glancing around, she didn't see anyone astir. Even the window above was empty and she was somewhat grateful that the wretched bog boy hadn't seen her clumsiness.

After replacing the ladder in one of the outbuildings in the courtyard behind the house, she stashed the jewelry box and pamphlets beneath the straw in the stable near her horse. Then she made her way back to the house.

Tiptoeing through the kitchen, she discovered her father hiding in the pantry, enjoying a secret drink. She smiled, feeling a bond with him; they had both caught the other sneaking around. And it wasn't the first time. She had come by her mischievous spirit honestly, her father being as sly as she, and many times they had discovered each other in the midst of some prank or devilment.

She walked over to him and sat beside him at the

small table. The lamplight shone on her copper locks and on his thinning silver strands.

Covering his hand with hers, she said, "You're a lonely sight, Father. What in the world do you think about when you're sitting here all alone like this?"

"Fog," he replied in a distant voice, his eyes staring into space.

"Fog?"

"Aye, girl. My life is one long mollifying fog. The land I hold I inherited, and it manages itself with a foggy logic of its own. I knew nothing of that boy's family nor their eviction. I'm sorry for their pain."

Shannon reached for the flask, which sat on the table, and refilled her father's glass. Pushing the tumbler toward him, she drew a deep breath and said, "If I were to tell you, Father, that I might . . . go away . . . even though I'm promised to be married to Stephen . . . would you despise me for having such a thought?"

The old man's eyes twinkled enigmatically. He reached over and stroked her cheek once with his forefinger, his face radiant with parental affection.

"It was after the Shannon River that I named you, child," he said. "And if you journey upstream, you'll discover why. It roils and tumbles with a terrible passion, and a temper all its own."

Shannon's eyes misted over and she blinked rapidly several times. "I'm barely a woman, Father. I know that. But my appetite is huge."

Daniel Christie leaned forward in his chair, his eyes intent as they locked with his daughter's. His hand covered hers and squeezed tightly. "I have only a few words of advice for you, girl," he said. "Satisfy that hunger. Whatever you must do—satisfy it!"

Shannon gripped his hand, hearing not only his words but their meaning. As dearly as he loved her, as much as he needed and wanted her near, he was releasing her with his blessing.

The tears that clouded her eyes rolled down her cheeks. She didn't know what to say, so she said nothing. As they sat together in companionable silence beneath the lamplight, Shannon knew this was the last night she would spend in her father's house, as his child, under his protection. This was the last night of her girlhood.

And her heart felt as though it were breaking, even as it rejoiced.

JOSEPH sat on the side of the bed, elbows on his knees, hands clasped, his head bowed. He hadn't closed his eyes in sleep the entire night. Fear, raw and cold, had kept him awake. Fear of what he might see if he were to close his eyes. Fear of a condemned man's nightmare that might be worse than the reality that soon faced him.

Over and over he played the scene in his mind. Even if he survived the duel, even if by some kind intervention of fate he was able to shoot and kill that bastard Stephen Chase, he would have rescued himself from death by bullet only to face death at the end of a rope.

What would it feel like to have the hangman's noose tighten around his throat? he wondered, preferring to think about hanging rather than being shot to death. The possibility seemed a bit more distant at the moment. Would he be one of the lucky ones whose neck would break and death would be instant? Or would he, like so many others he had seen hanged before him, dance the macabre jig of the Irish peasant?

Would the red-haired girl—daft, crazy girl that she was—feel a bit sorry for him, or would she smile like that infernal Chase?

Hearing some shuffling footsteps outside the window, he sat up straight and strained his ears. In a moment he heard strange, rhythmic noises that seemed familiar, yet he couldn't quite recognize them.

Going over to the window, he stared out into the darkness. It would be dawn soon. Already he could see the pale gray light stealing into the horizon beyond the hills.

Far below him, in a field near the house, he could barely discern the silhouettes of two men. His heart froze in his chest as he realized who they were and what they were doing.

They were gravediggers. And they were shoveling the six-foot hole in the earth that would, undoubtedly, soon hold the remains of Joseph Donelly.

"I miss ye, Da," he whispered. "And I've been achin' to see ye. But I wasn't intendin' to do it quite so soon."

Suddenly the door behind him banged open. Chase's two deputies stepped inside the room.

"Come along, boy," one of them said, grabbing him roughly by the arm. "We're to take you downstairs and feed you a hearty meal. Your last one, that is."

HALF an hour later the same two deputies led Joseph outside, to the field behind the house where he had seen the gravediggers at work. The fog, damp and chill, hung so low and heavy that Joseph felt he was walking through a nightmare from which he would never wake.

From out of the fog to his right, Daniel Christie stepped, a bit tipsy and unsteady on his feet as usual.

"'Morning, son," he said. Joseph was surprised to realize that he was speaking to him. "How was your breakfast. Was everything satisfactory? The sausage? The scones?"

Joseph could see that his concern was genuine and he felt a moment of kindness toward the landlord. A brief moment. After all, it was this man's fault that he was about to die. "It was as fine a meal as I ever ate in me life," he said sincerely.

"Good," replied Christie, nodding his head approvingly. "Well . . . I'm to serve as your second in this barbarism."

"I appreciate that, sir," Joseph said, though he had no idea in the wide world what the man meant.

It didn't matter. It sounded like another offer of kindness, and right now Joseph needed all the help he could get.

FROM the parlor window Shannon watched as Joseph disappeared in the thick fog. A sick feeling uncoiled in her belly. He was going to die. There was no doubt of that. The only question was: Would it be quick and merciful, or long and painful?

"Are you frightened for him?" asked a voice behind her.

She spun around to see her mother standing behind her. "Him?" she asked.

Nora laid her hand on Shannon's shoulder in a comforting gesture. "Of course you are. But Stephen is a man of honor, and by honor our class has stood and survived." When Shannon didn't answer, Nora patted her soothingly. "There now, don't fret. In a few minutes that dirty savage will have a bullet between his black little hideous eyes. . . ."

But Shannon didn't hear the rest of her mother's speech. The only words in her heart and mind were: His eyes aren't black or hideous. *They're as green as a field of shamrock and beautiful besides. And soon they'll be closed, and he'll be gone.*

But the thought that bothered her most was that after this morning she would never see Joseph Donelly again.

BENEATH a large oak tree, one of Stephen Chase's deputies, serving as his second, opened an ornate wooden case. Inside lay two long pistols.

"We of the Protestant minority in this superstitious land," Chase began in a rich oratorical voice, "stand cultured against the indolence of these savage natives—"

"Just get on with it, lad," Christie said. "This isn't a time for speechmaking."

Chase hesitated only a moment. "These weapons belonged to my father's father," he told Joseph, who stood beside him, trying not to be ill at the sight of the guns, the likes of which he had never seen in his life.

Daniel Christie leaned over and whispered in Joseph's ear. "His father's father was an ass. Believe me, I knew the man."

The second extended the box to Joseph, and he realized that he was being given the first choice of weapon. Little good it did him. He might as well be coming against Goliath with a slingshot for all his skill with firearms. At least this was a handsome piece of gunsmithing and wasn't likely to explode in his face.

He chose the gun closest to him, lifted it from the box, and pointed it directly at Stephen's face.

They stared into each other's eyes for a long moment, then Chase said, "I'd prefer to be civilized, boy, and follow the rules."

Though he had no idea what the rules were or how to follow them, Joseph snapped the gun away from Stephen's face and tried to don an equally arrogant expression.

"Count away fifteen paces apiece," said the deputy who was serving as Chase's second.

Christie turned Joseph by his shoulders, steering him into the fog and trying nervously to stay out of the line of fire.

"I want you to know, boy," the old man muttered drunkenly, "I knew nothing about your family's eviction. Nothing at all. I'm truly sorry for their pain. I understand why you came to murder me, son. I don't blame you for it at all."

Joseph heard the words as though from far away, and they held little relevance for him. He knew that the landlord was apologizing, and a dull, half-asleep part of his brain knew that the reason why the landlord was apologizing was because he knew that Joseph would soon be a dead man. Ten more paces. And Christie didn't want a dead man on his conscience.

It occurred to Joseph that he should speak some word of forgiveness, but there wasn't time. Ten more steps. Five more. One more. No more time.

"Turn!" the second shouted. "Each man turn and fire!"

Christie dashed away. Joseph whirled around. And panicked.

"I can't see anything!" he yelled. "Wait a minute! I can't see a thing through this bloody fog!"

"I can." The words reached him through the cold murk. In seconds a bullet would, too.

Frantically he waved the gun around, seeing movement in the fog, but no target. He waited for the shot, his body tense and shaking, ready to be torn by the bullet. But none came.

Gradually he became aware of a sound coming toward him, the clatter of wagon wheels, muted by the thick fog. From out of the white haze burst a two-seated cart drawn by a huge black horse, driven by Shannon. Her red hair was streaming down her shoulders, as wild as the first night Joseph had seen her riding through the moonlight.

As she clattered up to Joseph and reined the horse to a stop, he saw that the back of the cart was piled high with luggage and trunks.

"Assess your stupidity, lad," she said in a tone that irritated the devil out of him. "All the land in the world . . . or a bullet in your brain?"

"Get away from me, woman!" he shouted back.

She shrugged. "As you wish."

She lifted her whip to crack it across the horse. Turning, Joseph saw Stephen and his deputies emerging from the fog, grim determination on their faces as they charged toward him.

"Wait!" he cried. Dropping the pistol, Joseph dived for the wagon, hampered by his wounded leg.

As Joseph struggled aboard, Stephen Chase reached the wagon, where he hesitated, looking up at Shannon, his grim expression turning to bewilderment.

"Shannon," he said quietly. "We're endeavoring to fight a duel."

She stared at him, a look of sadness on her pretty face. "Good-bye, Stephen," she said.

"Good-bye?"

Shannon turned to Christie, who stood several paces back, gazing at her with pride in his eyes. "I crave adventure, Father," she said.

He simply smiled in return and nodded once.

Shannon lifted the whip, cracked it, and the buggy lunged forward, tumbling Joseph—who wasn't yet seated—into the back atop the luggage.

"Stop them!" Nora screamed as she ran out of the house, hands fluttering, skirts flying. "Stephen, don't just stand there, boy. Your fiancée is leaving you. Daniel, do something! That bogwater boy came here to murder you and now he's kidnapping your daughter!"

"Alleviated the tedium of this stuffy place," Daniel replied quietly, "was all he did."

Nora returned her attention to Stephen. "Are you just going to stand there, looking as though lightning has struck you?"

Stephen, still stunned and completely baffled, made no move. Nora ran up to him, grabbed his pistol, and fired once into the air.

The fog swallowed the roar of the blast, rendering it nothing more than a muffled pop. Joseph never heard the sound of the gun or the angry shouts. He heard only the clatter of the cart as they sped away and Shannon's laughter, as crazy and uninhibited as that night in the moonlight. The laughter of a spirit set free.

A moment later Joseph heard himself laughing, too, and he sounded as crazy and free as she.

LATER—as the fog began to lift and the Irish country-side unfolded before them, gold and green in the sunlight—Joseph came to his senses. He turned on the wagon seat and looked at the girl beside him. Her hair stood out in every direction, her cheeks were flushed bright pink, and her eyes shone like someone who had lost her mind entirely.

"God in heaven," he muttered, as though coming out of a deep sleep. "What am I doing with ye?"

"You're in my service, shoneen, whether you like it or not. Be silent and obedient—and leave the scheming to me."

"I don't like it at all, madwoman," he said. "We were born to be enemies."

"You're coming to America with me. As my servant. There's nothing more to be said on the matter."

"I'll never serve you. Yer the blight on me country. A foolish female who's nothin' but fancy—"

"Ribbons again, am I? I saved your neck, you ungrateful bog boy. You owe me your allegiance and servitude. It's the least you can do after I risked my life for you."

Joseph considered this for a moment in silence. Finally he shook his head and stared at his hands in his lap. "Don't look down on me now, Da," he whispered. "I've betrayed ye . . . and all of Ireland, too. Heaven help me now."

Five

On the deck of the magnificent schooner Shannon Christie and her fellow first-class passengers sat beneath festoons of fluttering ivory canvas, sipping afternoon tea and champagne, listening to the music of twin violinists, taking their fill of the ocean air.

Cigar smoke drifted across the decks, scenting the salt sea breeze as gentlemen discussed their business interests in America and Europe. Ladies, shielding themselves from the sun with lacy parasols, chatted about the latest French fashions as they nibbled crumpets and sweetcakes.

But the grace and leisure of the afternoon was lost on Joseph Donelly, who stood behind Shannon's chair, imprisoned in a coat and necktie, holding a teapot in one hand, a snowy linen napkin draping his other arm.

With aristocratic delicacy she tapped the edge of her cup. Feeling like a well-trained busker's dog doing tricks at the local hiring fair, Joseph leaned over and refilled her cup.

"Thank you, boy," she said.

"Don't call me boy." He bumped her elbow slightly as she raised the cup, causing her to slosh a bit into the saucer.

"Sugar," she said.

He plunked the teapot down belligerently. "I know."

With even less skill and grace he tossed a teaspoonful of sugar into the cup.

"Two," she said in a tone that made him want to bop her on the side of the head.

He added the second spoonful and dropped the spoon onto the saucer. The clatter caused several of the ladies seated nearby to glance their way, then lower their voices to whisper behind spread fans.

"You might display some gratitude, considering the price I paid for your passage. *I* paid, let me emphasize."

"I can't be showin' gratitude if I'm not feelin' any."

"A servant, as part of his duty, *pretends* to be grateful, Joseph. What you *feel* is irrelevant."

Joseph looked down at his pert little nose, turned up so arrogantly. One little pop . . . less than half of what he had given his brothers . . . and she'd lose a bit of that bloody haughtiness.

Joseph stifled the thought. He had never hit a woman in his life, and he wasn't likely to start now, no matter how much she deserved it.

"I gave me word I'd do this till we're across the sea," he said, "but this bloody ocean, it never ends. It surrounds us like a jail."

Shannon laughed and twirled her parasol. "You and I see things so differently. To you the ocean is a jail, but to me it's a highway to the future: majestic, welcoming, courteous, kind—a benevolent friend."

"In that case ye'd be makin' us both happy if ye'd go for a swim."

His insult was wasted, because at that moment a dapper gentleman with a dark, pointed beard strolled by. Immediately Shannon's attention riveted upon him.

"Forgive me if I'm intruding," the man said, "but I wonder if you'd enjoy a gentle stroll around the deck."

Joseph bristled. "She's drinking her tea."

"There's no need to state the obvious, Joseph," she said in a condescending tone.

The man smiled, flashing rows of white teeth, and bowed. "My name is McGuire. Of Boston, Massachusetts."

"You're American?" Shannon asked, obviously enraptured.

"Irish born. I went back for, well, personal reasons. But now I'm moving forward again."

Shannon rose to her feet. "A stroll would be delightful, Mr. McGuire."

Slipping her arm through his, Shannon walked away with him as Joseph watched in silent fury.

First she asks me to protect her from the surly sorts aboard, he thought, *then she goes walkin' off with one, holdin' on to his arm as though she's afraid he's goin' to get away. Well, she asked for protection, and that's what she's goin' to get.*

Joseph hurried and caught up to them, walking only a pace behind. Shannon, obviously annoyed, tried to block him out with her parasol. The lace fluttered in his face, making him even more angry. The woman was impossible.

"America *is* a step forward, isn't it, Mr. McGuire?" she said in a simpering voice that made Joseph even more nauseated then he had been the first few days out to sea. "I mean in my imagination, it's a wonderfully modern place."

"Modern as modern can be," McGuire replied with an irritated glance over his shoulder at Joseph, who was nearly breathing down the collar of his dandy suit. "The people, the culture, the industry: everything is a celebration of hope and prosperity."

Joseph brushed the parasol out of his face. "What about the land?"

"I beg your pardon?" McGuire asked.

"This girl's got it in her head that they're intendin' to give away land for free."

"That's true. Oklahoma Territory. The west is opening up."

Shannon cast a self-satisfied glance at Joseph. "I told you, boy."

"Well . . ." He sniffed. "It can't be *good* land."

"It's the finest in the world," McGuire said. "Seeds flourish in it, and the cattle that graze upon it are fat as elephants."

Smugly, Shannon eclipsed Joseph with her parasol again. "How do you get it, Mr. McGuire? Is it there when you step off the boat?"

"No, you'll have to travel, a thousand miles or so. But don't lose time in Boston. As soon as you can, purchase horses, a wagon, and supplies." He paused, noticing her petulant face. "I'm sorry. Have I upset you?"

"I never expected it to be so complicated," she said with a sigh.

"Any difficulty can be overcome with money."

Suddenly cautious, Shannon stopped and turned around. She glanced up and down the deck to see who might overhear. "Joseph," she said, "I would like to speak with Mr. McGuire alone."

Joseph's eyes narrowed. What was this, anyway? She asked for his help, then waved him away like an old mule after the plowing's finished.

"Why?" he asked indignantly.

"Because I *choose* to speak to him alone, just as you *chose* to be my servant."

Joseph stared at her for a long moment. Then he

shook his head. "Why didn't I just fight that duel and be done with it?"

He turned and walked away. Grumbling, he ripped off his necktie. A man and woman walked by him, their pert noses in the air as well. Their nostrils ascended two notches when they saw him. Joseph dangled the tie in front of them like a snake. Regarding him suspiciously, they quickened their pace.

With a flick of his wrist Joseph tossed the tie overboard.

Curse that girl, anyway. Her ancestors had tied ropes around the necks of his grandfars for centuries. He'd be damned if he'd allow her to do the same to him.

SHANNON watched Joseph walk away, thinking how immature men could be sometimes. With his lower lip protruding like that, he looked like a pouting child. Quickly she turned her attention back to Mr. McGuire, whom she had already decided could be of use to her in the days ahead. He was certainly affable enough and appeared to have a vast knowledge of America.

"Mr. McGuire," she said, leaning her head closer to his. "I do have money, but it's in the form of spoons."

He stared at her quizzically for a moment. "Spoons?"

"Ancient spoons, made of silver. I plan to sell them in Boston as soon as I arrive."

McGuire nodded approvingly. "I can recommend a couple of shops that will treat you honestly."

"I'm very obliged to you, sir."

"The pleasure is mine."

McGuire bowed politely. What a gentleman he was, she thought. Not at all like that ruffian she had dragged aboard with her. Remembering Joseph, she decided it was best not to leave him alone too long. Heaven only knew what mischief he could get himself into.

"Excuse me, Mr. McGuire," she said, laying one hand lightly on his forearm. "Our conversation has been most pleasant and enlightening, but I must return to my table."

"Thank you for your company," he said as he doffed his bowler.

Ah, the joys of speaking with one of her own kind, she thought, walking across the floor to the table where she had been having tea. But her pleasant mood evaporated when she saw Joseph sitting in her chair, his tie discarded and shirt unbuttoned. Worse yet, he was eating the piece of chocolate pie that she had left behind. With his hands.

"May I ask what you are doing, sitting at my table?" she demanded, quickly looking around to see who might have witnessed this disgrace.

"Eating yer chocolate pie," he replied without apology.

The arrogance of this common bog boy! She fought down her temper. "I see. And what have you done with my father's necktie?"

"It was gagging me throat. I flung it into the sea."

With studied deliberation Shannon closed her parasol and sat on the chair across from him. She slid a fork toward him, hoping he would take the hint and use it. He didn't.

"You're just upset because everything I've told you about is turning out to be true," she said, trying not to sound too smug, but unable to stop herself.

He snorted and shoved another bite of pie into his mouth. "Cattle as fat as elephants? I know what that man's after, even if yer too stupid to know."

"What do you mean?"

He lifted the tablecloth and pointed to her feet. "Ye could at least take the bother to keep yer ankles covered."

She laughed. He was jealous. Somehow she found

his reaction touching and a bit flattering . . . even if he was a lowborn peasant.

Reaching across the table, she patted his hand. The clean one. Without the chocolate all over it. "We're sailing to a place of hope and promise, Joseph. We'll each find happiness there. You'll find yours and I'll find mine . . . when we go our separate ways. . . ."

She had meant the words to encourage them both, but she found that speaking them only made her feel sad. This was silly. Why should she feel melancholy about the thought of saying good-bye to a servant?

It didn't bear thinking about.

Once again she nudged the fork closer to Joseph. This time he noticed and stared down at the utensil for a long moment. Then he looked up at her, his green eyes full of anger and rebellion.

Picking up the pie, he shoved the rest into his mouth.

How revolting, Shannon thought as she watched him chew it openmouthed. *But what else can one expect from a bog boy?*

"For heaven's sake, you're among polite people here," she said, casting an uneasy look right, then left. "Use your manners."

"You don't need manners to get the food into your gut," he replied with a chocolate-smeared grin.

"Joseph—" She reached out and stuck his hand with a dinner fork.

"Oww! What's the great and grand importance of forks to ye, woman? It's mortally wounded, I am."

"Oh, shut up. You're fine. Every eye is upon us now, thanks to you."

"Excuse me. . . ."

Shannon turned toward the deep, authoritative voice to see the steward standing at her left shoulder. The stern look on his face indicated trouble on the horizon.

"Yes?" she replied demurely.

"You're traveling first class, I presume?" The officer's sarcastic tone rankled Shannon. Joseph simply smiled up at him as he wiped his mouth with his sleeve.

"Would a lady of my breeding travel any class but?" she asked, trying to sound indignant.

"And the gentleman?" He nodded toward Joseph.

"He's no gentleman. He's my servant." Shannon saw Joseph's instant scowl and felt a moment of satisfaction.

"I'm nobody's servant," he replied indignantly, pushing the pie plate away. "Least of all yers."

That's it. It's all over, Shannon thought. *That stupid peasant has ruined everything.*

As though in a daze, she watched the steward nod briskly to a couple of waiters, who hurried to his side.

"May I see your tickets, please, ma'am?"

With a sinking feeling Shannon looked over at Joseph. Maybe he would have a flash of insight. Some brilliant idea might come to mind. Perhaps with his wit and charm he could rescue them from the horrible fate that seemed inevitable.

But Joseph didn't seem to have much of a plan after all. He was frantically stuffing lamb chops into his pockets.

BELOWDECKS, in the belly of the great ship, the peasant families huddled in seasick, frightened knots. Without benefit of the fresh air, champagne, and fiddle music of the first-class passengers, their trip was an ordeal to be endured rather than a pleasant excursion.

The incessant creaking of the ship mixed with babies crying and the trembling voices of the children. Soothing words from mothers filled the stale air in a dark space that no kerosene lantern could illuminate.

An old priest sat in the center of the room, fingering his beloved prayer beads. "Heavenly Father," he prayed, "preserve the lives of these poor sinners on their journey—"

His supplication was cut short by the opening of the hatch. Rose-golden light from the setting sun poured in for a moment, along with a gust of fresh saline air. A second later two young people were hurled down into the hold. The hatch slammed shut.

Shannon rose first, looked around at her dismal new surroundings, and moaned. "Down into the bowels of hell," she said, kicking at Joseph's shin with the toe of her boot. "Thanks to you. I had them all completely fooled."

"Bollocks. 'Twas only a matter of time. At least I had the sense to fill my belly and pockets. He reached into his jacket and extracted a greasy lamb chop. "I've robbed the gentry blind."

Shannon ignored him, looked around the large room, and spotted her luggage near the stern. Carefully, she wove a path among the pallets, hammocks, and knapsacks, not to mention her new fellow travelers. The smell of human waste and seasickness made her gag, but she forced down the taste of bile that kept regurgitating into her throat.

"To think I saved your life," she said over her shoulder as Joseph caught up with her and passed her, striding toward the luggage. "I sacrificed the luxury of first class to buy your ticket. All I get in return is rudeness."

Grabbing his arm, she yanked him back behind her. "Don't walk ahead of me. Trail along behind, where you belong."

He grabbed her shoulders in a grip that hurt, but she refused to cry out, to let him know. "I've told ye, woman," he said. "I'm not yer serving boy."

"No? Then you might explain to the holy father over there just who in the world you are."

Her voice was loud enough to carry to the priest,

who raised one eyebrow. Many of the passengers suddenly grew quiet, obviously listening to the newly arrived entertainment.

"We're brother and sister," Joseph said, flashing one of his famous smiles toward the father.

"Brother and sister? Our blood's not even the same temperature."

Joseph stopped abruptly and whirled around to face her. "You want these people to know you're Protestant?" he said in a low hiss. "They'll pitch you into the sea."

She glanced around, evaluating the situation. Promptly she favored the nearest group of travelers with her sweetest smile.

As she and Joseph approached the pile of luggage that was hers, they both broke into a run. They hit the pile together, plopped down upon it, and jostled for space, a dear commodity in such close quarters.

Grinning at her, Joseph unfastened yet another button of his shirt. "I'm glad to be rid of yer father's tie," he said triumphantly. "The bloody thing was choking me to death."

"Good. At least it served *some* purpose."

Around them the passengers were shedding their clothes and spreading threadbare blankets, preparing to sleep. Shannon thought of the comfortable berth she had slept in last night in her luxury cabin and she sighed. Life had certainly taken some nasty turns for the worse since she had met this peasant.

Slowly she began to unbutton her dress. "Don't look at me," she told Joseph when she saw him cast a furtive sideways glance in her direction.

"I'm not," he replied. "I'd rather watch a pig wallow in a mud puddle than to watch the likes of ye. But that bloody bastard over there . . ." He nodded his head toward a man with a scruffy beard. "He's watchin' ye. Gawkin', even, I'd say."

"Let him gawk," she said, enjoying his obvious display of jealousy. "His flirtation is the only way I have of gauging my appearance—since I didn't pack a mirror. Now turn your head, like I said."

He half turned away, and she decided to make the best of the circumstances. Shielding herself with her cloak, she removed her dress, then rolled it into a ball for a pillow and covered herself with the cloak.

Such misery. She couldn't help thinking of her feather bed with its freshly ironed linen at home. Oh, well, dreams didn't come for free. One had to pay a price for an aspiration as lofty as hers.

Joseph settled uncomfortably close to her, using his jacket for a pillow. He had no cloak. She thought of offering him the use of half of hers, but reconsidered. Already she found herself far too aware of the nearness of his body. Even though they were several inches apart, she could feel the warmth of his leg radiating through their clothing to hers.

Sometimes, when he moved, she noticed how his thigh muscles swelled against the fabric and she wondered if they were as hard and rounded as they looked. Of course, as soon as she thought such things, she shoved them out of her mind. No lady would think about matters like that. And certainly not about some lowly peasant with dirt under his fingernails, who ate chocolate pie with his fingers, who didn't even know how to read.

Besides, if it weren't for him, she would be in her comfortable berth upstairs, where she belonged with the rest of her kind. Not down here in this hellhole with the peasants who stank and probably had vermin in their hair.

Something moved near her foot, and she looked down, expecting to see some loathsome rat. Instead, she found herself looking down into the large round eyes of a little girl. The child's face was dirty and her hair uncombed, but she had a sweet smile full of childish shyness. She had merely been changing sleeping positions with her brother and had bumped Shannon's foot.

For a moment Shannon felt ashamed of what she had just been thinking about these peasants. Perhaps the little girl wasn't so lowly, or smelly, or vermin-ridden. Beneath the dirt, only a bath and scrubbing away, was a lovely child who would have graced the parlor of any aristocrat.

Just as Shannon had begun to readjust her thinking, a couple in the corner began to make love. With only a thin blanket thrown over them, little was left to fancy.

Red-faced, Shannon turned away, pretending not to see this blatant display of vulgarity. Had they no shame? In all her life Shannon had never even seen her mother and father kiss on the lips. But here were these peasants rutting like animals for all to see.

Glancing quickly at Joseph, she saw that he, too, seemed embarrassed and uncomfortable. As they listened to the muffled sighs of passion, the steady rhythm, the labored breathing and soft moans, Shannon found herself more and more aware of Joseph's nearness. The covering of the cloak made her too warm, but she dared not cast it aside and expose her underclothes.

The unfamiliar sounds frightened, yet excited her—mysterious, scary, yet erotic. They seemed to go on forever. She and Joseph didn't move. They scarcely breathed as they pretended nothing was happening.

Finally the couple finished. And not a moment too soon for Shannon.

"Can't you move over a bit?" she said irritably.

"There's no room with all this luggage," he replied with equal vexation.

He tossed several of her bags aside, almost burying

her. At that moment the ship pitched, throwing her over on top of him.

"Get off me!" he shouted, shoving her away.

As though she had wanted to be near him, to feel their bodies touch! Who did he think he was?

Suddenly the claustrophobia overwhelmed her.

"I'm out of patience with this fiendish boat!" she cried. "This ocean is endless. And I want the chocolate pie that *you* ate!"

But instead of a word of sympathy, he laughed at her. A hearty, belly laugh that echoed through the hold, embarrassing her until she felt her face turn as red as her hair.

I really could begin to hate him, she told herself.

In a display of temper she kicked him once in the shin. Instead of howling with pain, he laughed again. That was the moment when she decided . . . she already despised him. Cursed bog boy.

PETER, Matthew, and John stood at the edge of the road, staring across the open field at a strange sight—a man sitting beneath a tree at a small writing table, scribbling furiously.

"There's a sad example of what happens to the upper class," Peter commented philosophically. "That young man was the finest marksman in Ireland once. Full of promise he was."

"Aye, he could shoot a sparrow out of the sky blindfolded," Matthew added.

"Times are changing. Rioting and killing and such. Protestant rule is coming to an end, some people speculate." John sucked air through his teeth and donned a quizzical, thoughtful expression. "Did he eat those sparrows, I wonder. A bird that size would be blown to pieces I'd think."

"Typical of the upper class, that man," Peter said. "With no honest work of their own to do, they must come up with all kinds of things to occupy them-selves."

"Aye, if someone would pay me some rents, I'd try my hand at shootin' sparrows," John said.

"Ah, there goes the landlord himself." Matthew nodded toward a figure on horseback that had left the road and was headed toward the man under the tree. "He'll take care of the situation, sure."

"True, true. He'll put it right."

"Nay," said John. "Nothin' under heaven's sun will put that one right again. 'Tis a blitherin' idiot he's turned."

Out of earshot and therefore without the benefit of their observations, Daniel Christie rode across the meadow, through the herd of shaggy sheep that grazed, unconscious of his presence as they nibbled at the lush green grass. Slowly Daniel made his way toward the center of the field, where a large oak stood, tall and splendid, as it had since the days of the druids.

Beneath that tree sat a strange figure, one whom Daniel had studied for several minutes, hoping he wasn't seeing what his eyes insisted was true.

But as much as Daniel wanted to deny it, this was Stephen Chase sitting at the table, his head bent over his paper, writing as though his life depended upon it.

Such a peculiar vision. Daniel shook his head. The man had surely lost the wits the good God had given him.

As he rode up beside him Daniel reined in the horse and said, "I . . . ah . . . hesitate to ask how things are going, Stephen."

Stephen looked up from his writing. His long dark hair—usually combed and held back with a bit of ribbon—was tangled, his customarily impeccable attire rumpled, his eyes tormented.

"I'm writing your daughter a letter, sir," he said.

"Though I don't know where to mail it." He picked up the paper and held it high above his head. "Fly! Fly away!" he shouted, a maniacal gleam in his eye. "Fly away words, to my true love's heart!"

He tossed the pages into the air and they scattered in the wind.

Christie watched, an incredulous look on his face. Without a doubt the lad had lost his mind. A few too many doves fluttering about in his cote to be sure.

"You're seriously agitated, son," Daniel said. Then, searching for any gesture of solace, he reached into his saddlebag. "Here." He tossed it to him. "I brought you an apple."

Stephen allowed the apple to fall to the ground at his feet without making any effort to catch it. He stared at it vacantly. "Adam and Eve ate an apple," he said with great gravity. "And that was the end of paradise."

"True." Daniel nodded his head as though considering the words carefully. "But after that they got on with their lives, lad. And you must be doing the same."

"She trampled my heart." To illustrate his point the young man placed his heel upon the apple and squashed it into pulp.

"Aye, but she didn't snuff it out entirely." Leaning over, Daniel placed one hand on the young man's shoulder. In that moment he felt more compassion toward Stephen Chase than he had ever entertained. Perhaps the lad had a heart after all, if it could be broken. "I can't bear to see a person young as yourself all ravaged and distraught. The sun is shining. Let's go to the pub and drink," he added, offering his own panacea for life's ills.

But Stephen ignored him, his tortured eyes searching the horizon. "Where is she, Mr. Christie? I'd follow her if only I knew."

"We haven't received a word."

"My spirit will not rest until I've taken her in my arms." Picking up his pen, he resumed his writing on a fresh piece of paper.

Daniel turned his horse around and headed for the pub alone. There was nothing left for him to do for the lad. The boy's mind was gone.

Strange, he had always thought Stephen Chase so strong, invincible, even formidable considering his young age. Ah, but love had broken much stronger men, Daniel reminded himself.

"Oh, woman high of fame," he began to sing.

> "For thee I shall not die!
> Though foolish men you slay,
> A better man am I. . . ."

An hour and two shots of poteen later Daniel Christie reached into his pocket and withdrew a tattered letter. Looking around the pub and seeing no one except the barkeeper and himself, he unfolded the paper and spread it on the bar before him.

He read if for the hundredth time in only a few days.

My dear father,
To you alone I write and no one else. If I hide this letter in the rhododendron, you will find it soon enough.

Daniel smiled and blinked away a tear as he continued.

I am traveling out to Boston, and to you I'll admit my fear. But you've always spoken of freedom, and freedom is the thing I crave. I will miss you, Father,

*but I will carry your spirit with me, when I step out
into America, and all my dreams come true. . . .*

> *With greatest affection,*
> *Shannon*

Daniel refolded the letter and placed it inside his breast pocket near his heart. How he missed her already, her bright smile, her beauty and charm. It was as though a light had gone out of his life, the brightest light.

Daniel picked up his glass and bolted back another shot of poteen, enjoying the smoky hot burn as it trailed down to his belly. He might miss her more than life itself, but he also loved her. And Daniel Christie loved his daughter enough to rejoice in the knowledge that her spirit was finally free.

Six

═══

THE ship arrived on American shores amid a thunderstorm that rumbled through the Boston Harbor with black clouds, flashing lightning and driving rain.

Hours later the soaked and thoroughly chilled passengers stood in endless queues inside the Immigration Center, their luggage in tow, their spirits only a bit more dampened than their soaked garments.

Joseph struggled in line behind Shannon, trying to drag her endless luggage along as the procession inched forward. Finally, when he felt certain that his arms would pop out of their sockets from the weight of the bags, it was their turn to face the immigration officers.

"So, Shannon, where is yer dear friend Mr. McGuire?" Joseph asked, his heart pounding in his chest.

What if they were turned back? What if those stern-looking officials found them unworthy in some way to enter America? Where would they go from here?

"I think that honorable gentleman had deserted us entirely," he said, not bothering to hide his sarcasm or contempt for the dandy on board who had promised

Shannon that he would guide them through this confusing maze of bureaucracy.

Shannon didn't answer him. Instead, she stood preening, attempting to tuck her unruly curls into a bun at the nape of her neck.

"Keep up, woman," he warned her. "Hurry along now."

"I want to look presentable when I talk to the officer. Appearance is important, you know."

Joseph looked around and saw at least six men staring at Shannon. His temper flared.

"Are ye mad entirely? Ye've got those men all gawkin' at ye. Move along, I say, unless yer gaugin' yer appearance again."

"There," she cried, pointing at one of the windows at the far end of the room. "There's Mr. McGuire. He's waving to us. Come along, Joseph; we must hurry."

"Cursed woman," Joseph muttered as he fought the mountain of luggage and followed her to the end of the row of windows where McGuire stood with an immigration officer who wore a blue uniform studded with brass buttons and a decidedly grim frown beneath his handlebar mustache.

"Shannon, Joseph," he called to them. "Where have you been? I've got you documented. Tell this man your last name."

"Donelly," Joseph said breathlessly as he flung the luggage at McGuire's feet.

"Mr. and Mrs.?" the officer asked, jotting something on the paper in his hands.

"No!" Shannon cried. "Don't write that down!"

"They're brother and sister," McGuire quickly interjected, exerting a gentle pressure on Shannon's forearm.

"Wait a minute. We're—"

Suddenly another tide of immigrants surged forward and Shannon's words were lost in the cacophony of voices. The officer shoved two cards into Joseph's hands—the precious landing cards.

McGuire was already off and running with Shannon close on his heels. Joseph sighed, looked down at the luggage, and cursed all women . . . along with his own stupidity for finding himself in this demeaning station. Surely he hadn't been born into this world just to be a servant for some giddy redhead. Surely, in this land of opportunity, he would find his destiny.

And when he did, he would tell that prissy female to carry her own luggage . . . to hell and back.

ONCE outside the Immigration Center, Joseph felt bombarded by a thousand sights, smells, sounds, and sensations. Cold rain lashed at his face, stinging his skin and running down into his eyes. The crowd jostled against him as he attempted to follow Shannon and McGuire down the street that teemed with bewildered immigrants, as well as runners and vendors who preyed upon their confusion.

One peddler shoved some pamphlets under Joseph's nose. "Maps here! Maps to jobs! Maps to hotels!"

Another danced in front of him, waving all sorts of hats and caps. "Hats! Get yourself an American hat! Don't want to look like you just stepped off the boat. Hats for sale!"

When Joseph, who had always fancied owning a fine hat, stopped to consider the man's wares, McGuire shouted back at him, "Follow me, children. I know the games of these predators. They'll rob you blind if you don't beware."

McGuire plowed through the crowd, dragging Shannon along with Joseph in their wake. Joseph couldn't help noticing that, even soaked to the skin, her hair streaming down her face, Shannon was a pretty sight with her cheeks all flushed from the excitement and the chilling rain.

"I'm here in America, Joseph," she said as though in a happy daze. "I finally made it. I've arrived."

Joseph simply grunted, shifting the weight of a particularly heavy bag higher on his shoulder.

"You certainly have arrived," McGuire said as they neared the outer edge of the commotion. "And you'd do well to remember that the pace is much quicker here. Come along now, Shannon. I'll get you to a suitable hotel right away. Just leave everything to me."

A small, ratty-looking boy who appeared to be in his midteens approached McGuire and tugged at his sleeve. The thought occurred to Joseph that he hadn't seen anyone looking so ragged or dirty in all of Ireland. This boy's grime wasn't the result of a day's hard labor cutting turf. This lad's skin hadn't reaped the benefit of water and a washcloth in months or years.

Joseph felt a surge of both pity and aversion. What kind of people were these Americans?

The boy skipped along beside McGuire, hanging on to his sleeve. "Hey, mister," he said, "need a job? I can take you to the ward boss."

McGuire jerked his arm in an attempt to rid himself of the lad. "Go fleece somebody else, boy. Away with you now."

But the lad held fast. Reaching out with his other hand, the boy grabbed Joseph as well. "How about you, mister? Work? Lodging? Can't get nothing without the ward boss. He's the biggest man in Boston!"

The boy lost his balance and fell to his knees, but he wouldn't relinquish his hold on either man. Joseph had to respect his determination as he swung between them, his knees dragging in the mud.

Finally McGuire stopped, grabbed the boy by the throat, flung him in the gutter, and steamed ahead, as though the lad had been nothing more than a minor irritation.

Joseph looked back as the boy picked himself up out

of the mud and immediately turned his attentions to the next group of immigrants within his reach. Joseph shook his head. He certainly had to admire the boy's tenacity and zeal.

When Joseph turned back to McGuire and Shannon, he noticed that she was gazing at McGuire, glassy-eyed, like a lovesick cat.

"Thank goodness for you, Mr. McGuire," she said in a breathy voice as she clung to the man's hand. "Whatever would we do without you to guide us."

"Whatever would we do . . ." Joseph repeated in a sarcastic, singsong tone as he glared at the two of them.

They turned down a street that was far less crowded, and Joseph was enormously relieved when McGuire slowed his pace a bit. The street, like the lad who had solicited them, appeared dirty and unkempt, as though no one cared, no one loved this corner of the earth.

Joseph stared in wonder at the smut-blackened walls, the litter of paper, rags, and scraps of rotting food that clogged the gutters along the sides of the streets. Even in the poorest communities in Ireland there was a love of the land, a respect for every road and wayside. Even the most destitute of homes had their doors freshly painted in bright colors of red, robin's-egg blue, or green.

But these people, the ones who huddled against the buildings, trying to escape the chilling downpour, seemed full of despair. Too tired to care about the streets, the houses, or even themselves. All of them were wet and cold; many appeared hungry. Some were hopelessly drunk and carried bottles half full of gin in one hand, a bundle of humble belongings in the other.

This wasn't right. A bell of warning sounded in Joseph's brain. Wasn't this the land of golden opportunity? Why were there so many homeless people if land and homes were given away for free?

He glanced over at Shannon to see if she were as uneasy as he. She turned toward him and he saw his fear and misgivings mirrored in her blue eyes.

For a moment he considered speaking a word of consolation in her ear, trying to convince her that they would make it, no matter how difficult it was in this confusing new world.

Then he bit his tongue. She was a proud one. Far too proud for her own good. She would never admit to being afraid, and she would only make him feel like a fool. Why bother?

Let McGuire soothe her if she were in need of comfort. After all, he was already holding her hand, wasn't he?

Suddenly McGuire stopped, frozen, staring straight ahead. Joseph squinted, trying to see through the rain. Two thugs stood in the middle of the road, blocking their path. These fellows made the young lad in the gutter seem well groomed. And the expressions on their faces reminded Joseph of wild dogs who killed for the sport of it rather than for food.

"McGuire," one of them said, taking a step toward them.

McGuire released Shannon's hand. Instinctively, Joseph dropped the luggage and reached for her, pulling her behind him.

"Yes?" McGuire answered carefully. Joseph could hear the fear in his voice.

"Welcome back," the other hooligan said, but the sneer on his ugly, scarred face belied the hospitality of his greeting.

Before Joseph could move or even breathe, they pulled pistols from beneath their jackets and both fired point-blank at McGuire. He grabbed his chest, crumpled, and fell facedown onto the street.

Shannon screamed and grabbed Joseph's arm. "Joseph! Oh, my God, do something!"

Joseph's mind raced. A dozen potential actions entered his mind, then fled. There was nothing to be done for McGuire; he could see that clearly as the dead man's blood flowed into the streams of water racing down the street.

The killers vanished in less than a heartbeat, and in even less time at least half a dozen of the nearby vagrants sprang to life and attacked the body like vultures. Ripping his coat apart, they scavenged the corpse as Joseph and Shannon stared down at them, paralyzed by horror.

"My spoons!" Shannon screamed as the silverware slid from McGuire's torn pockets and fell with a clatter and splash into the street.

She hurled herself into the mud, grabbing for them. Joseph followed her lead, jumping into the melee, knocking a few of the vagrants aside. But the thieves, skilled in their sordid craft, were much quicker. In less than two seconds every piece had been snatched and the human vermin scurried away like rats returning to their holes.

Wearily Joseph lifted himself up from the mud and vainly tried to brush away the grime from his face with his sleeve. "Come away, Shannon," he said, offering her his hand.

She simply lay there in the mire, staring up at him in shock and disbelief. "My spoons," she said. "They stole them from me. I have no money now. God is punishing me, Joseph."

Grabbing her hand, he pulled her to her feet and supported her with his hands on her shoulders. She was trembling violently.

"Why? Why is the good God punishing ye, lass?" he asked in a gentle tone . . . far more gentle than he had ever used with her before.

"I . . . I . . ." she sobbed, clinging to him. "I stole them from my mother the morning I ran away."

As though determined to add to their misery, the rain began to fall at least twice as hard as before. The crowds pushed past them, and horses nearly trampled them as they stood there, their arms around each other.

A protective, animal instinct rose in Joseph. He was the man. He had been hired to protect her. Now was the time to take action. But what?

His eyes combed the crowd, searching for possibilities. He spotted the boy whom McGuire had thrown into the gutter standing at the edge of the crowd, watching them with a wary eye.

The motley child wore the expression of one trying to appear tough, but when Joseph pointed a finger at him, the boy jumped.

"You!" Joseph shouted through the noise of the crowd and the driving rain. "Come here."

"Don't trust him, Joseph," Shannon said fearfully. After her loss some of her buoyancy and self-confidence had eroded. Joseph ignored her warning and continued to beckon the lad over.

Reluctantly, the boy strolled toward him, shuffling along with a belligerent swagger, his hands stuffed deep into his pockets. "Yeah, what you want?"

"What's yer name, lad?"

"Dermody."

"Well, I'm Joseph Donelly and this is Shannon . . . Donelly, my sister," he added as an afterthought. Shannon scowled through her tears. "I have some questions to ask ye, so yer ears best be on the stretch."

"What you wanna know?"

"Just two things. Who's this ward-boss fella and where can we be findin' him?"

THICK smoke, dim lights, the stench of stale beer and sweat, and the roar of a crowd. So this was a den of evil, Shannon thought as Dermody led her and Joseph into the social club full of drinkers, dancing girls, and bloodthirsty Irish-American spectators who were gathered around a pair of bare-fisted boxers who stood toe to toe, battering each other in the center of the enormous hall.

"That's him there," Dermody told them, pointing to the big, burly fighter who was pulverizing his opponent to the delight of the rowdy crowd. "That's the ward boss. Mike Kelly his name is. And the man he's fighting is named Gordon. They're both fearsome boxers."

With his hand on her arm Joseph tried to lead Shannon away from the fighters toward the other side of the room. "Shannon, ye'd better wait for me over here."

She pulled her arm out of his grip. "Don't shield me, Joseph. It's only a boxing match. I've read all about this sport. Barbaric, but fascinating nevertheless."

Shannon was feeling much better than she had when lying in the muddy street, and her spirit had revived. She was determined to absorb every element of her new surroundings with relish, inviting all novel experiences. Elbowing her way to the front of the crowd, she watched, enthralled as the skilled boxer whom Dermody had identified as the ward boss, Mike Kelly, landed another blow on his opponent's already scarred and swollen face.

"I had no idea ye were knowledgeable about such things," Joseph muttered dryly.

"There are advantages to being able to read," she said smugly.

A second later she felt something warm and wet spray her face. Appalled to think it was the man's sweat, she pulled out her handkerchief and wiped her face. But it was a red ugliness that stained the linen.

Blood. She had been showered with Gordon's blood.

She screamed and the strength drained from her legs.

All eyes turned toward her as she released the bloodcurdling screech. Even the fighters turned to look. Mike Kelly stared at her in amazement. Gordon's beefy fist shot out and smashed into Kelly's jaw.

Kelly dropped to his knees, gazed at Shannon for a moment through dazed eyes, then fell like a tumbled elm to the floor, where he lay, not moving.

Gordon knelt beside him, more worried than jubilant. "Sorry, Mike," he mumbled as he shook the big man's shoulder.

An unnatural hush descended on the room, a silence pregnant with fear. In unison the men all turned and stared at Shannon. Confused, she glanced at Joseph—who looked as perplexed as she—and then at Dermody.

Dermody shrugged and smiled a crooked, anxious smile. "Ah . . . Mike isn't happy when he loses," he explained.

A round-bellied bartender walked over to the fallen fighter and dumped a bucket of water on Kelly's face. Everyone stepped back. The big man groaned, raised himself onto his hands and knees, and crawled past the lines of boots until he was only two feet from Shannon.

She shrank back ever so slightly, but stood her ground, refusing to be intimidated, though she was shaking violently.

"You distracted me," he said with a bloody snarl as red ooze crept down his chin from the corner of his mouth.

Shannon didn't know what to reply, and before she could think of an answer, Joseph had pushed himself between her and Kelly.

"*Ye* weren't concentratin'," Joseph replied in a matter-of-fact manner.

Several of the men, including the bartender, gasped at this audacity. Apparently few men spoke their mind to Mike Kelly, the ward boss.

. Kelly stood and Shannon caught her breath. Her eyes searched Joseph's face, but she took heart when she saw no trace of fear on his handsome features. She felt a momentary swell of pride that he was her escort.

Kelly reached into his mouth, extracted a tooth, and carelessly flicked it away. "A scrappy Connemara man," he said, scrutinizing Joseph from head to toe, "fresh off the boat. Follow me."

He dragged himself to his feet and limped away with Joseph close behind. When Shannon followed Joseph, Kelly whirled around and said, "Not you, woman. You cost me a tooth."

Shannon pulled herself up to her full height and lifted her chin. "If *he* gets to go, then *I* get to go . . . wherever it is you're going."

"I am Mike Kelly," the ward boss barked at her. She jumped. "Nobody argues with me." He turned to Joseph. "What is this bit of snit—your wife?"

"Certainly not!" Shannon said, indignant at the very thought.

"Then just who the hell are you, lass?" Kelly said, "coming into my club?"

Shannon opened her mouth, but nothing came out. She cast a helpless look at Joseph, who was smiling.

"She's my sister," he said.

Kelly shook his head and laughed. "Tell me she isn't a pain in the ass," he said with a snort. Then turning to the rowdy, crowded room, he shouted, "Settle your bets, gentlemen."

Kelly strode away. Joseph started to follow, but Shannon grabbed him by the arm. It was time to put an end to this foolishness before it got out of hand.

"Will you *please* stop telling people that I am your sister," she said. "I have no wish to claim kin to a bog boy like you."

Joseph bristled. Lowering his head to hers, he whispered, "Shannon, these are me own kind of people in here. And *our* kind has no fondness for *yer* kind. In fact, these people hate everything about ye."

Shannon cast a furtive glance around. This unruly mob was hardly a crowd whose anger she would wish to incur.

"Now," he continued, "for some reason which I can't figure, I'm willing to stretch the truth a bit on yer behalf. I can lie for ye, or we can be tellin' them right now that yer a rich Protestant . . . whichever ye like. It might be sportin' to watch what they'd do if they knew."

For the first time in her life Shannon felt like an outsider, hated and outnumbered. It wasn't a feeling she liked very much.

But Shannon was sensible, if nothing else. A survivor with the strength and common sense to do what was necessary under the circumstances.

"No, Joseph," she whispered in return. "We don't need to tell them any such thing. For the moment you will be my brother."

A look of triumph crossed his face, a look of temporary victory over her, a look that made her want to slap him silly.

"So stay put," he said. "And keep yer fancy mouth shut before it gets us into trouble again."

As she watched him walk away she vowed that someday she *would* slap him for that. Hard. And then she would feel a lot better.

As Joseph walked away from Shannon to follow Mike Kelly, he couldn't help feeling a bit smug. It was rather nice to have the upper hand with that cursed woman for a change. Here in America, at least in this tavern tonight, *his* people had the authority, and *she* was the powerless one.

As he walked past an old battered piano, Joseph's eye was captured by three young women wearing little more than fancy bloomers and tight corsets. At the sight he nearly fell over his own feet. Never in all his days had he seen such a display of bulging bosoms and bare limbs.

Not only were they sorely in need of modest covering, but these females were smoking cigarettes as well. This sight was equally novel to Joseph and he had to fight the urge to gape in astonishment.

His brothers had whispered tales about such women who strolled the back streets of Dublin and Limerick, stories that had haunted Joseph's nights as he lay on his bed, recalling each erotic, though sketchy, detail.

One of the girls, a brunette with an enormous pair of breasts that threatened—or promised—to spill over their lacy confines at any moment, winked at him and pursed her lips in a pouting fashion that he had never witnessed before, but he didn't require an interpreter.

Heat, liquid and hot, rushed to his groin, and he found himself instantly uncomfortable. Maybe his father had been right to warn him about this sort of female. She certainly did look like a woman who could lead him into the fires of hell . . . if the heat in his britches was any indication.

"Don't spend your money before you've earned it," Kelly said with a chuckle as he turned back to Joseph. "I haven't found you a job yet."

Leaving the girls and temptation behind, Joseph walked over to the table, where Kelly sat, a ledger spread before him.

"What do you call yourself?" Kelly asked without looking up when Joseph sat across from him.

"Joseph Donelly," he replied proudly.

Kelly didn't appear to be impressed as he scribbled into the ledger. "This is my doomsday book, Donelly," he said. "Once your name goes in, you belong to me. You get in trouble, you come to me. Give me trouble, I come to you. Understand?"

Joseph didn't like the sound of that, but he didn't appear to be in a negotiating position at the moment with no money, no roof over his head, and no job.

"I'm not settling in Boston. I'm going out west for land."

Before Kelly could reply, a roar of laughter echoed through the room and Joseph heard a familiar female voice shriek, "Away, or I'll claw your eyes out!"

Across the room he saw that Shannon had been surrounded by a flock of drunkards led by big Gordon the boxer. Gordon and his friends laughed lasciviously as he flicked the hem of her dress with a pool cue.

Amid the guffaws he sang,

> "'Twas a lady who took to the street,
> Her name was Biddy McMack.
> She makes a handsome living now,
> A-laying upon her back. . . ."

In a heartbeat Joseph had crossed the room and grabbed the pool cue from Gordon's hand. He waved it threateningly in front of the big man's face.

"I'll ask ye to leave this woman alone," he said, nodding toward Shannon, who was still bent backward over a pool table, her face white, her blue eyes wide.

"So go ahead and ask," Gordon replied sarcastically.

"I've no wish to fight ye," Joseph returned.

Gordon snorted. "He's no wish to—"

With a crash of fist against flesh, Joseph's knuckles slammed into the boxer's jaw. The fight was on.

In a swarm of cheering and betting men Shannon covered her eyes as Joseph took a severe punch in the face. But he absorbed the shock and returned the jab, then another and another.

In only two minutes it became obvious to all observers that Joseph possessed the greater agility and boxing skill . . . not to mention the meaner temper.

"Come on, ye ugly mule," he taunted the older man. "Give me something I can aim at."

With inspired and practiced expertise Joseph hooked and jabbed Gordon across the room. The crowd was ecstatic. This newcomer's boxing style was completely different from any they had seen before. Using the Marquess of Queensbury rules, fighters normally stood toe to toe at the scratch mark, throwing body punches until a knockdown, which ended the round. They jabbed at the face, especially the nose and mouth, trying to avoid the rest of the head, so as not to break their knuckles. Their punches were straight and cutting.

Each fighter had his own style, but none ever dodged a punch. However, Joseph wove back and forth, circling his opponent, jabbing and ducking beneath Gordon's punches.

At the edge of the circle of spectators Dermody and some of the other boys boxed the air, trying to emulate Joseph's movements.

Finally Joseph forced a weary and confused Gordon back against a beer keg. Another blow from Joseph and the boxer fell into the keg, arse first, his boots sticking high in the air.

Joseph whirled around, jubilant at having defeated his opponent, his fists raised to take on more if necessary. There stood Mike Kelly.

"Well now," Kelly said, stroking his chin thoughtfully. "You knocked the piss out of the man who knocked the piss out of me. I'm not sure how I feel about that." Then, to the crowd he shouted, "Settle your bets, gentlemen."

The men crowded around Joseph, everyone talking at once, elated over the excellent bout of boxing they had just witnessed, amazed at this newcomer and his strange technique. Joseph swelled with pride.

From the corner of his eye he saw the buxom brunette ooze off the stage and stroll in his direction, trying to get a closer look.

His feet wouldn't allow him to stand still. This was simply too wonderful. All this attention! All the adoration! He danced around in a jubilant victory jig.

Even Shannon, miserable wench that she was, wore a newfound look of respect, even worship on her face. With her head high she strode over to Gordon, who was still stuck breech position in the barrel.

"That'll show you," she said, poking him in the chest with her finger.

Gordon began to rise up out of the keg like a whale surfacing for air. With a small squeak Shannon scurried back to Joseph and clutched his arm.

"Dermody!" Mike Kelly shouted into the crowd.

The skinny lad appeared instantly. "Yes, sir, Mr. Kelly!"

The ward boss tossed him a coin. "Time to make the rounds," he told him. "Grab the luggage. We'll take this scrapper and the girl here and lodge them at Molly Kay's. . . ."

Lodging? A roof over his head, and it was only his first night in America. Joseph smiled broadly. Yes, indeed, this was the closest thing to a perfect moment he had ever lived on God's good earth.

Seven

WITH all the pomp and circumstance worthy of a ward boss, Mike Kelly strode down the street, his entourage in tow.

"'Evening, boys. Howdy, Tim!" he shouted, greeting his constituents with wide grins and bone-crushing handshakes. "Good to see you, lads!"

In a position of honor directly behind him followed the newest hero of the Irish boxing circle, Joseph Donelly himself. Shannon still clung to his arm. Little Dermody dragged along behind, lugging the massive burden of Shannon's luggage.

"You sure can box, mister," Dermody said, panting slightly. "Where'd you get your training?"

Joseph swelled with pride, straining the buttons across his shirt, which already seemed to have shrunk since this morning. "Me brothers beat the bloody hell out of me in Ireland," he explained. "I never had the honor of fightin' only *one* man before. And I never tasted sweet victory till today."

Kelly turned and said over his shoulder, "Victory's the only flavor going in this place, Donelly. A first-class scrapper like you is bound to get ahead. You wouldn't consider boxing for a living, would you?"

Joseph considered the offer for a moment. The glory, the money, the buxom beauties struggling for a better position on stage just to get a better look at him. Then he shook his head. "No thanks. It's not in me nature to be fightin' men for money."

Shannon, who had already been quiet for an unnatural length of time, could hold her tongue no longer. Joseph had been getting enough attention and it was certainly her turn. "*My* plan, Mr. Kelly," she said, "is to go out west for land."

"Shannon." Joseph glanced down at her disapprovingly. "Don't be botherin' the man about that."

Ignoring him, she continued. "I'm going to get a ranch, breed horses on it and raise them."

"You? Ya pioneering piece of fluff!" To her humiliation Kelly waved her aside without even a glance in her direction. "Better stick with your brother. He's got the hard black hands of a man who knows the soil. It's his kind that's gonna open this country up. Say, Jake, how ya doin'."

Seething, Shannon looked up at Joseph to see him beaming at the flattery. She yanked her arm out of his and pushed away from him in a huff. That insufferable braggart, that arrogant bog pig, that . . . that egotistical plebeian. Her mother had been right about his type all along. They didn't deserve the air they breathed or the ground they walked upon. They served no purpose but to ease the lives of the aristocracy.

From the corner of her eye she watched as Joseph surveyed the dirty streets, the dingy, run-down buildings with wide-eyed fascination. "What a city this is, eh, Shannon?" he said. "'Tis excitin' and lively with things movin' everywhere yer lookin'."

"Hmmph," she grumbled. Her upper lip curled with disdain.

Suddenly a trio of Irish youths burst out of a nearby alley, chased by four swarthy teenagers who were cursing and threatening them in Italian. Shannon squealed and grabbed once again for Joseph's arm.

In an instant Mike Kelly had thrown himself into the middle of the race. "Outta here, ya bollixin' I-tyes!" he shouted to the Italian boys. Flailing his arms and stamping his feet, he was a formidable presence, and the pursuers fled back into the alley.

"Bloody Italians!" Kelly said, spitting onto the street. "Flooding in by the boatload and taking Irish jobs! Boston's an Irish town—and I plan to keep it that way!"

Joseph and Shannon watched this display of temper with a mixture of admiration and dread. What power this man wielded! What a formidable enemy he would be, and how lucky they were to have him befriend them.

As though taking off one mask and donning another, Kelly continued down the street and stretched out his hand to the first man he met, a broad, winning smile replacing his scowl.

"Hi, Frank! Howdy, boys . . ."

Joseph and Shannon followed, like children trailing after the mythical piper.

"He's a mighty strong man, that Mike Kelly," Joseph whispered in Shannon's ear. "And he likes me, he does. Called me a scrapper, he did."

"Hmmph."

Surely this couldn't be their destination, Shannon thought as Mike Kelly led her, Joseph, and little Dermody—still toting her luggage—to the door of a dingy, dilapidated building. Once it had been an attractive lodging house, as evidenced by the ornate scrollwork and gingerbread along the rafters and over the door. But the house's glory days had long passed, and with its peeling paint and sagging shutters, it was merely a tarnished version of its former self.

Kelly reached for the door, but at that moment it flew open and a middle-aged woman appeared. Like the house she lived in, this woman had passed her prime, but the reminders of her beauty remained. With faded golden hair and bright blue eyes that bore a tracing of wrinkles at the corners, she appeared to have smiled more than she had frowned.

Shannon quickly appraised the woman's gaudy clothing and wondered at the propriety of wearing scarlet and purple satin. But Shannon's assessment came to a halt when she saw what the woman was carrying in her hand. She held an enormous dead rat by its tail. The thing was hideous, its beady black eyes still open, its teeth bared in a death grimace, its mangy coat matted with blood from the trap.

Shannon's heart stopped, then she shrieked and nearly swooned.

The men laughed at her, adding humiliation to trepidation.

The woman lifted one eyebrow and said sarcastically, "This is just as unpleasant for me as it is for you, dearie."

With a flick of her wrist she flung the limp creature into the street.

Was this what American women were like? Shannon thought with alarm. It was one thing to be modern, but a woman should remain a lady above all else. And no lady touched a dead rat, let alone tossed it carelessly into the street.

Mike Kelly stepped forward into the house without waiting for an invitation. Joseph looked as though he might follow, but Shannon held him back. Under no circumstances was she going to step into that dismal building that housed rodents of that magnitude.

"Got a fine young couple here, Molly," Mike Kelly said, pointing to Joseph and Shannon. "They need a room."

Molly surveyed them both with a practiced business eye. Her gaze seemed to linger on Shannon's figure, evaluating. "You're in luck," she said. "We had a suicide just this morning."

Shannon's already ailing stomach did a flip-flop. They were to have a room where some poor wretched soul had just killed himself? This would never do.

"Come along," Mike Kelly said, waving them inside. "Haven't got all day."

Molly held the door open, obviously expecting Shannon and Joseph to follow.

"I'm *not* going in there," Shannon hissed to Joseph.

He bent his head down to hers. "What is it yer talkin' about? Why not?"

"There are . . . rats . . . in there, and she looks like a . . . woman of ill repute."

"There are surely bigger rats in the ditches and characters of murderous reputations in the alleys of this town, and that's where we'll be spendin' the night if ye continue this foolishness.

Shannon considered his words for a moment, thought about the streets through which they had just passed, and decided he was right. Dear Lord, how she hated him for being right so often.

Reluctantly she allowed him to drag her through the front door and down a dimly lit hallway. Smoke—thick and stale—filled the air, making it difficult and most unpleasant to breathe. Other sour, human smells made Shannon even more queasy. What a miserable place this was. It wasn't at all as she had imagined her first American accommodations to be. But then, so far, nothing in America had turned out as she had expected.

Molly led them toward the back of the house, and Shannon couldn't help noticing the tattered paintings on the walls. They depicted scantily clad women whose figures were far more robust and rotund than her own. She blushed at the sight and tried to avert her eyes. Instead, she saw Joseph eagerly scanning the paintings, and the anger that welled up inside her made her want to elbow him in the ribs.

"When this house was first built," Molly said, "it was used as a brothel."

Again Shannon noted Joseph's piqued interest and her anger soared. Two doors opened as they progressed down the dark hallways, and in those doorways stood girls whose attire made Molly appear matronly and modest. One wore only a dirty chemise and drawers, the other a thin dressing gown.

"A brothel?" Joseph remarked, his eyes fastened upon the girls, who were obviously enjoying his interest. "Is it so?"

"Yep," Molly replied. "And still is."

Shannon nearly swallowed her heart, which bounded into her throat. These girls were . . . prostitutes? Good heavens, if her mother knew where she was this moment, she would surely die on the spot of heart failure.

In her distress Shannon looked up at Joseph, hoping to find comfort in his handsome face. He had been her savior once already today. Perhaps he would come to her rescue again.

But, to her horror, he appeared to be quite content with their lot . . . even happy.

"Any gentlemen up here, girls?" Kelly asked the young women in the doorways. "How's business tonight, ladies? Dermody, make an announcement."

Dermody took a deep breath, threw back his head and screamed, *"Waaarrrdd Booosss!"*

Suddenly men began spilling out of the rooms, tugging their trousers up and stuffing in their shirt-tails. More women in states of undress appeared with them, and none sumed to have the slightest bit of shame about their attire or their occupation. Shannon's humiliation was complete.

Molly reached out and placed a restraining hand on Kelly's arm. "You're not campaigning now, Mike, not in my house at my busiest hour."

"Relax, Molly," he said. "Politics are more important to these men than sex."

Molly snorted and tucked a stray golden-silver lock behind her ear. "That'll be the day," she returned. Then she turned to Joseph and Shannon. "I apologize for the sinfulness, children," she said with half sincerity. "I'm not proud of my sordid life but . . . my husband left me for a seamstress."

The thought occurred to Shannon that Molly's remorse appeared to be questionable at best, but for once she kept her mouth closed.

They watched as Kelly grabbed a decrepit chair from inside one of the rooms, climbed upon it, and struck a stately pose.

"God forgive you," he called out. "'Evening boys. Do I see Jimmy Dunne there?" The fellow in question cringed in the doorway as he adjusted his suspenders. "Hello, Jimmy. I was chatting with your wife just today."

As Kelly pontificated, embarrassing one man after another, Molly drew Joseph and Shannon down the hall. Joseph smiled broadly at the whores, who devoured him with their smudgy eyes. Shannon fumed, barely able to contain her fury.

Molly pointed to a door that was badly scuffed, in need of paint, like the rest of the house. "In there is the bath," she said. "But don't linger in it too long. It's the only one in the house. And this is your room here."

Molly nudged another door open, and Shannon's panic began to bubble up into her throat.

"You're not suggesting that we *share* this room, I hope," she said, dreading the reply. Everything else had gone wrong since they had stepped off that cursed boat. Why should this be any different?

"Of course not," Molly replied. "You won't have to share it, dear. You'll have it all to yourselves."

"No, no, no! We need *two* rooms," Shannon said, trying not to scream.

"I've only got the one. But it's enough for a nice young married couple starting out."

"We're not married!"

Morally offended, Molly blocked the door. "Then you listen to me. Not *all* my scruples have fallen by the wayside. If you want to live in my house, you'd better find yourselves a priest."

Joseph chuckled, put his arm around Shannon, and gave her a fraternal squeeze. "I'm afraid ye don't understand, Molly, dear," he said in his most beguiling tone. "Shannon's me own sweet sister."

Molly smiled, obviously relieved. "Ahhh, and so close in age, you've probably squabbled from the moment you first set eyes upon each other. Well, children, you have no choice but to tolerate the curse of family, I'm afraid."

Shannon fought down her panic. "But . . . but I *must* have my own room. You don't understand."

"I've only got the one." Molly turned around and yelled down the hall. "Mike! What did you bring me here? She's bellyaching about the—"

Joseph grabbed her arm and spun her back to face them. "The room is fine, Molly," he said. "We'll take it. And 'tis mighty grateful we are indeed," he added with a pointed glare at Shannon.

Instantly Molly succumbed to the Donelly charm.

—— 118 ——

"I'm glad to hear that." She leaned closer to Joseph. "Your sister was spoiled, I'd say."

Spoiled? Her? Shannon waited for Joseph to come to her defense, but he didn't. He just stood there smiling down at that . . . that . . . strumpet.

"Well," Shannon said with a haughty toss of her head. "I never—"

"That," Molly interrupted her with a chuckle, "I believe. But if you stick around this place, you will before very long . . . just like the rest of us girls."

Molly spun on one heel of her boot and sashayed down the hall, swinging her hips and casting one irritatingly self-satisfied grin over her shoulder at Shannon.

"Did you . . . did you hear what she said to me?" Shannon sputtered, tugging at Joseph's arm. "I think she meant that someday I might . . . I might . . ." She couldn't bring herself to say the word. She couldn't even think of the word. In fact, she was wondering if she had ever even *heard* the word.

"Ah, I wouldn't fret so," Joseph said, wearing a half snicker on his face as he opened the door and ushered her into their new abode. "She probably didn't mean a thing by it. Women say all kinds of silly things, ye know."

Before she had the opportunity to become indignant over his comment about women, she caught a glimpse of the room that was to be her home, and her breath left her in one whoosh.

The tiny chamber was horrible, far worse than the lodging of the most lowly servant on her father's estate. Why, even her horse had enjoyed better accommodations than this.

The room contained only two pieces of furniture, a rickety dressing screen that bore faded pictures of still more scantily clad women, and a broken, crooked bed that resembled an old dog who barely stood on three legs, the fourth having been gnawed off in an unfortunate bout with a larger mongrel.

The walls—once covered with rose-and-lilac-spangled paper—was stained and the plaster exposed where the paper had been torn away or was blistering and peeling. The one window had been cracked and what glass remained was so grimy that only a dim light penetrated the filth. The roof bore a large dark circle with a hole in the center where rain had leaked through.

Shannon turned to Joseph, expecting to see her own horror reflected on his face. But to her shock he appeared ecstatic.

"This is grand!" he said, walking over to the bed and touching the warped iron footboard. "Quite grand, indeed. Needs a bit of patchin' up here and there, but me brothers and meself shared a room that wasn't half this size back in Ireland."

Crossing over to the window, he proudly adjusted a tattered gray curtain. "Look," he said. "We have our own window. What a luxury this is, eh, lass?"

When Shannon didn't reply, he turned his head and gave her a searching look. "Ah, 'tis disappointed ye are." Then he turned his back on her and stared out the window. "Why don't ye just get back on that boat and head on home? 'Tis clear enough that this isn't yer fancy cup of tea. But for me, America suits me fine. *I'm modern.*"

Shannon bristled. "Don't aggravate me, boy. If you're implying that I can't endure a little temporary hardship, you're terribly mistaken. Fetch my bags and unpack. I'm going to the bath to wash my face."

With her head held high, the picture of determination, she stomped out of the room, slamming the door behind her. Equally resolute, she strode down the hall, ignoring the snickering prostitutes whose eyes raked her as she passed.

She jerked the bathroom door open and glided inside with the grace of a princess. But once in the room with the door closed, her courage instantly dissolved. Amid steaming kettles and hanging underwear, she collapsed on a bench and covered her face with her hands, whimpering like a little lost puppy.

"Oh, my God, what have I done," she wailed. "What have I gotten myself into? And how will I ever get out?"

This was the worst moment of her life. Finally, after years of hoping and planning, she had found her dream. And her dream was a nightmare.

Then, over the sound of her own violent weeping, she heard another sound . . . that of water slopping. She ceased crying immediately and peeked through her fingers at the large copper bathtub against the far wall. A man . . . a big, ugly man . . . a big, ugly *naked* man chomping on a cigar was rising out of the tub.

"Hi, sweetie," he said, eyeing her lasciviously. "You're a cute little piece of baggage. Have I had *you* yet?"

Grinning hungrily, he continued to rise out of the water, leaving little to the imagination concerning his intentions.

Shannon couldn't scream; she was far too frightened and had no air in her lungs. Uttering one tiny, terrified peep, she fled for the door.

This time she paid no attention to the whores as she fled down the hall to her room. She didn't even see them. All she wanted was to be away from that horrible, naked man and with Joseph again.

Once inside the room, she slammed the door closed and flattened herself against it. Joseph looked up at her from where he knelt beside the bed, fixing its broken leg.

"Aye, hello again," he said with a smile that made

her feel far better than she would ever want to admit. "Short visit." He straightened up and dusted the palms of his hands. "What do ye prefer," he said, "the bed or the floor?"

Shannon didn't even stop to think. "Why, the bed, of course."

He grinned, reached over to the bed, and captured a bedbug between his thumb and forefinger. With studied nonchalance he squashed it and flicked it away. "I was hopin' ye'd say that."

JOSEPH lay on the floor, his only bedding—the blanket that covered him. But the blanket had no holes and the roof wasn't leaking at the moment, so all in all, his situation had vastly improved over his days in Ireland. Shannon lay on the bed across the room, and instinctively Joseph knew that her body was as tense and stiff as the boards he lay upon. He thought of that fine feather ticking and the linen sheets in her fluffy bedroom in Ireland and chuckled to himself. Spoiled brat that she was—time she learned a lesson or two.

He was pretty certain that tonight had been the first time in her life that Shannon Christie had undressed in the same room as a grown man. To be honest, it was the first time *he* had undressed in the same room as a woman.

They had devised a system whereby he had faced east while she faced west and, supposedly, neither had peeked. Of course, Joseph's male curiosity had gotten the better of him, but just as he had thought he was glimpsing something of interest, she had dived beneath the covers.

Several times since they had put out the light, he had attempted conversation with her, but to no avail. Now he was pretty sure that she was asleep. He couldn't even consider sleep, so excited was he with all that had happened to them today. His body was a bit sore from the fight in the club, but overall he was deeply satisfied with himself and his lot in life.

Then he heard a sound that disrupted his spiritual tranquillity . . . the creaking of bedsprings just beyond the wall in the room next door. Accompanying groans began to work on his nerves, disturbing him even more than the drunken sounds of shouting and fighting in the street below. He thought of Shannon, so close and yet so far away, so soft and pretty, yet so haughty and cold. He gritted his teeth and squeezed his eyes tightly closed, trying not to see the mental images—vague, yet disturbing—that played across his imagination.

A gunshot rang out and the shouting in the street ceased temporarily. He heard Shannon jump and draw a quick breath.

"Shannon, are ye awake?" he asked, eager for conversation. Anything to drive this inexplicable urge from his mind and body.

"No, Joseph, I'm sound asleep. What do you want?" she asked, sounding both irritated and frightened at the same time.

He tucked his arm beneath his head and stared up at the water-marked ceiling. "I think I like America," he said, allowing himself to be vulnerable for a moment.

"Do you now."

"We've only been here a day and look at the welcome we got. Would ye like a job? Here ye go. Would ye like a room? Here ye go. How about some land? Get a horse and help yerself."

"So now you believe me about the land, do you?"

Her self-satisfied tone didn't aggravate him, so happy was he about his new home.

"Well, if they're throwing it away, I wouldn't mind a piece of it," he admitted.

"Mr. Kelly made it sound as if it might be difficult."

"For you, but not for me. He took a likin' to me, that fella did. Maybe this is me destiny. 'Tis a farmer I am, after all. On his deathbed me own father spoke to me of land. I'm wonderin' if his spirit might be near this minute, guidin' me along."

He heard her sniff with contempt. "If he bumps into Mr. McGuire up there, tell him I want my spoons back."

Joseph laughed softly and sat up, holding the blanket around his bare chest, modest about his own nakedness.

"Imagine me," he said, "Joseph Donelly, standing on me own plot of land. What would I be plantin'? I wonder. Oats? Corn? Potatoes? God no, not praties. Maybe wheat. Oh, Shannon, I'm dreamin' about it now: great fields of wheat as far as the eye can see."

"Ambitious plans for a bog boy," she said, spilling cold water on his aspirations. "How do you intend to accomplish this?"

"Me father was always tellin' me to save a penny a day. We never had a penny to spare, so it didn't work, but America seems like a place where it might. To get land we need a buggy and horse. If we put our earnings together—"

"No."

Her abrupt rejection offended him. "I was just tryin' to save time," he said with a wounded tone.

She turned over to her side, and by the dim light that filtered through the cracked window, he could see her condescending smile. "What you say is practical, Joseph," she said ingratiatingly. "But only within the limited boundaries of your lowbred mind. A penny a day is progress to you, but I'm going to find a shortcut."

Joseph laughed bitterly. "Ye spoilt, pampered little brat. Ye think Lady Fortune is just gonna walk right up and sit herself down in yer lap?"

"I know she will."

He sighed with impatience. "Good night, Shannon Christie, and dream, dream, dream away. Ye'll *still* be dreamin' months from now, and where will I be? This lowbred boy'll be standin' on a plot of land as far as the eye can see."

"Ah . . . bottle up your bragging. If it weren't for me, you wouldn't be here."

"And if it weren't for me, ye'd have died outside in the street, or those drunken bullies would have had their way with ye in the club tonight."

Enraged, she threw her pillow at him. "Bogwater boy! I don't need *you* to survive. And as for Oklahoma land—which was *my idea* in the first place—I'll have my share of it long before you've even learned how to read a map!"

"We'll see about that!"

"Give me back my pillow."

"Not in a hundred years." Angrily Joseph stuffed the pillow under his head and turned his back to her.

With equal fury Shannon turned her back on him. The only sound in the room for the next few minutes was the huffing and puffing of their breath.

Unfortunately, the rest of the house wasn't so quiet. The old brothel continued to groan, creak, rattle, shake, and thump with the sounds of copious copulation.

"Damnation," Joseph muttered into his pillow as he tried to cover his ears. "Cursed female."

He recalled that more than once his father had told him, "There are three kinds of men who fail to understand women: young men, old men, and middle-aged men."

Well, there was one thing to be said about this woman he had been afflicted with—her tongue would surely never rust or gather moss. He just wished to hell that she weren't so pretty, didn't have such soft-looking red hair, and wasn't lying nearly naked in a bed right beside him.

And the thing that made him angriest of all was she thought she was too good for him, a mere bog boy as she called him. He'd known a lot of women who were gentler, more kindly spoken, and prettier. Well . . . maybe not prettier. She just might be the prettiest thing he had ever seen. But she was certainly the contrariest.

Damn, he wished those women and their customers would stop that infernal racket next door.

He recalled Danty Duff's observation, "Without a woman yer pecker'll drop off."

As Joseph twisted and turned on his pallet, fighting the needs that raced, hot, through his bloodstream, Danty's words didn't seem so funny anymore. They seemed all too true.

Eight

THE Christie mansion seemed strangely desolate with only a few lights burning at the windows and without the usual score of servants bustling about. Once the mecca of the county's social events, the house stood silent and dreary.

Nora Christie, far more sedate than before, sat primly on a diamond-tucked maroon velvet chair, her knitting in her lap, her needles clicking away. Daniel sat opposite her in his leather chair, his boots propped on a footstool, a book open before him. He hadn't turned a page in half an hour.

"This book is irritating me," he said, rising from his chair.

He walked over to the shelf and traded his novel for a hunting guide. Hidden behind his sporting collection stood an already-poured cocktail. With his back toward his wife, he quickly downed the drink, then sauntered back to his chair.

Nora continued her knitting without breaking her rhythm. "Do you actually think you're fooling me, Daniel?" she asked, not bothering to look up.

He stared at her wordlessly for a long moment. A dozen responses, most of them denials, raced through his brain. But in the end he discarded them all. There was no point in lying to Nora. The woman had eyes in the back of her head. Eyes that could bore straight through a man.

"Would you prefer," he said, "that I proclaim my independence and drink in the open?"

Nora paused in her knitting and considered carefully before answering. "No, I rather like the system we have now."

She resumed her knitting, the needles clicking away even faster.

Daniel watched her, concerned at the cold emptiness she had exhibited since the departure of their daughter. He much preferred the old days when she had been constantly harping at him about his irresponsible behavior, when she had ruled their roost like a spirited little bantam hen instead of this tired old chicken with her feathers dragging in the mud.

"What are you making there?" he asked, pretending to be interested.

She sighed. "I have no idea. It began as a sock, evolved into a sweater, and now it's a hybrid of both. The truth is, I'm just passing the time until somebody cuts my throat."

Christie's bushy eyebrows flew up. "You don't mean me, do you?"

"The tenant farmers, Daniel," she snapped. "They're gaining power, taking the land for themselves. All the politics, the violence. The world feels unsteady to me now, as though it might all crumble down."

"I'm surprised to hear such things from you, Nora. It's not like you to be threatened and afraid."

Suddenly her facade crumpled and her lower lip began to tremble. For a moment Daniel caught a glimpse of the young girl he had loved and courted so many years ago in Galway. A lass much softer and sweeter than the cranky women he now lived with.

"How can she be so cruel, not to send us any word?" she said, fighting back her tears. "I'd rather hear the worst than suffer this uncertainty."

Throwing her knitting to the floor, she reached into her pocket and extracted a lace-trimmed linen handkerchief. Daniel watched sadly as she dabbed at the corners of her eyes.

It was time. He had to tell her. He simply couldn't allow her to go on suffering this way.

"She's in America, Nora," he said softly.

Nora looked up from her handkerchief in surprise. "What? Whatever are you talking about?"

Christie left his chair and walked over to the piano. Lifting the lid, he extracted a small packet of letters, which he handed to his wife.

"You've hidden these from me?" she asked, not meeting his eyes, the hurt obvious in her voice as she studied the postmarks.

"At Shannon's request," he admitted. "Read them now. . . ." He saw that her hand trembled as she unfolded the first one and began to read. Again a wave of tenderness swept over him, compassion and empathy for her pain. "Though they may not bring you comfort," he added with a whisper.

OUTSIDE in the darkness, shadows moved in the courtyard. A slight rustling of black figures gliding quickly through the night, a murmur of hushed voices, the labored breathing of men whose blood pounded in their veins.

The door of the stable swung open with a loud creak and the groomsman walked out. He barred the door and stretched, his arms above his head. A moment later a gloved hand reached around him and covered his mouth. A club descended on his head and he collapsed onto the cobblestones.

Seconds later a dozen torches, like tiny fireflies, emerged from the hedges and fluttered toward the back of the mansion. The pungent smoke from their kerosene-dipped tips polluted the sweet night air.

The men who carried the fiery clubs wore cloth masks over their faces. Converging around the leader, they listened to his whispered instructions.

With all directions given he muttered the code word, "Captain Moonlight."

They dispersed and surrounded the mansion.

"DANIEL, did you hear something?" Nora sat at attention, Shannon's letters still spread across her lap.

"Like what?" Daniel asked, puffing on his pipe.

"I'm not certain. It's just that I could have sworn that I heard a—"

The window directly behind her exploded, raining glass all over her. Throwing her hands over her head, she screamed.

"Nora!" Daniel jumped up from his chair and started toward her. She stood and the letters fluttered to the floor.

A split second later a torch sailed through the broken pane and landed on the letters. The paper burst into flame. Falling to her knees, Nora tried to gather them up, but Daniel grabbed her by the arm.

"Come, Nora, quickly!"

They fled down the hall, but at the end of the corridor they ran up against a wall of flame that blocked the door. In terror they raced to the back of the house and into the kitchen. The moment they entered the room another torch crashed through the window, setting that room as well ablaze.

From all over the house they could hear the breaking of glass, the roar of the fire, and angry shouts.

"My God, Daniel!" Nora screamed, clutching at her husband's shirtsleeve. "Whatever can we do? We'll burn alive!"

"Not yet!" he shouted with more confidence than he felt. "Not bloody yet!"

Suddenly, over the commotion, they heard the galloping of hooves on the cobblestone courtyard behind the house. More angry shouts. Gunfire. The pounding of feet in retreat.

Daniel looked around frantically as the fire closed around them. It curled along the ceiling, over the cupboards, and snaked along the floor at their feet. The heat singed their skin. The smoke grabbed at their throats, stealing their breath away, choking them with its black, deadly vapors.

"Come on, in here!" he shouted, pulling his wife by the arm into the pantry.

They slammed the door behind them and huddled in the corner. Second by second the heat and the smoke grew thicker.

With his arms wrapped tightly around his wife, Daniel had time to think over the reckless life he had lived. Many times he had walked up to death and shaken its skeletal hand, and Daniel had always believed that he would die young as a result of his own foolishness.

But not this way! Not roasting like a Sunday pig on a spit in his own house!

"Daniel, I think I'm dying," Nora gasped, her mouth close to his ear.

"Don't say that, love. You mustn't think it, let alone say it."

"But it's true. I can hardly breathe."

Before Daniel could offer further reassurance, the door crashed open and they saw a tall, thin figure outlined against the glare of the blaze.

"Fire!" Nora screamed to the welcome intruder.

"Indeed," came the sardonic reply.

"Stephen!" Daniel shouted. "What a pleasure to see you, lad! Get us the hell out of this inferno!"

"Follow me."

The young man grabbed them both roughly by the shoulders and hauled them to their feet. He half led, half dragged them through the kitchen, where he picked up a chair and hurled it through a window.

Pushing them toward the opening, he shoved first Daniel, then Nora out. Servants' hands eased them to the ground. Then Stephen himself burst headfirst through the window just as the room behind him exploded into flames.

They stumbled away from the house and fell onto the grass at the edge of the lawn. The Christies lay there and watched, unbelieving, as their house crumbled before them into a fiery heap of burning timbers.

"Those bloody bastards," Daniel said as he watched, tears streaming down his cheeks. "That was my father's house, and his father's before him. Damn those bloody bastards."

Then, in a moment of regret, he recalled that boy's words, something about how Christie's men had burned his father's cottage.

Daniel closed his eyes against the sight of his own house's destruction. But behind tightly squeezed lids he saw the burning of a humble cottage, and his tears flowed even more freely down his face.

THE next morning Nora, Daniel, and Stephen emerged from the stable to face the rising sun, which illuminated their worst fears. The house lay in charred ruin, the heavy stench of smoke hung in the air, and an eerie quiet surrounded the scene that had been chaos and turmoil the night before.

Nora picked some straw from her hair, which, for the first time in years, hung limply around her face.

"Dear God in heaven," she murmured. "Just look at what those heathens have done to our home."

Daniel appeared dazed, his eyes sightless as he stared at the carnage.

Stephen slicked back his hair with one hand and adjusted his tie with the air of a survivor who had every ounce of his dignity intact. "All your life collected and destroyed. I'm truly sorry for your loss," he said with a more gentle tone than Daniel Christie had ever heard him use.

"Does this mean we're finished?" Daniel asked him. "Are we impoverished now?"

Stephen shot him a skeptical look, and for the first time in his life Daniel considered the fact that he knew nothing of his own fortunes, that this lad knew more about his estate than himself. And it occurred to Daniel that, perhaps, he had been irresponsible with his wealth in the past.

"No, sir," Stephen explained, carefully patient. "You aren't exactly impoverished. You still have the land and your holdings."

Stephen walked into the courtyard and picked up one of his pistols, which he had dropped in the melee the night before. With the practiced ease of a soldier he tucked it into his belt.

But he drew it again when they heard a groan from behind the stable. He hurried in that direction, Daniel and Nora at his heels. They found a man lying near a trough, his black hood still on his head.

Stephen pointed his gun as though preparing to shoot, but Daniel held out a restraining hand. "No," he said. "There's been enough destruction already. Let's find out who my enemy is."

Kneeling beside the man, Daniel tugged off the man's hood. The rebel was the kelp maker Danty Duff.

"How did we do?" Danty mumbled as he shook his head, striving for consciousness.

Daniel Christie looked up at Stephen, at his wife, and then at their ravaged home. "I'd say you were successful, renegade," he said dryly.

Nora turned and walked away from the men with a light of purpose replacing the sorrow in her eyes. As she strode over to the ruins Daniel called after her, "Where are you going, woman? Be careful there, you'll step on hot cinders."

"Mrs. Christie, please wait," Stephen added, going after her.

But Nora was oddly focused as she searched the smoldering wreckage, kicking aside the debris.

"Ah-ha," she said as she pulled her handkerchief from her pocket, folded it several times, then used it to pick up a small steel box. Gingerly she flipped open the lid, which burned her fingertips. Gold coins sparkled inside, untouched by the fire, as bright and promising as the day she had placed them inside the chest.

"What is it you have there, love?" Daniel asked, picking his way through the black timbers and ash.

"Our future," she said. Straightening up, she surveyed the horizon. For the first time since her home had burned, Nora's eyes clouded with tears. "This is no longer the Ireland of my birth, the beautiful emerald land of my girlhood. Everything has changed now. All the beauty, the grace, the nobility . . . it's all gone."

"I know, love. I know." Daniel walked up and placed his arm around his wife's shoulders, offering comfort.

But her face suddenly shone with the light of courage and resolve. "Our daughter has fallen into perilous ruin, Daniel. We must go to her now."

"Shannon?" Stephen stood at the edge of the ruins, a bewildered expression on his face. "You can go to her? You know where she is?"

Without meeting the young man's eyes Daniel gave him the information which he had been withholding for so long. "She's in Boston these many months, lad."

But instead of being indignant for having been kept in the dark, Stephen smiled broadly, his eyes glowing like a man whose soul had awakened with inspiration. "Then we shall find her there."

Daniel looked at his wife and saw the same optimism and resolve. "Yes," he said, "we've nothing to keep us here any longer. We'll leave for America straightaway."

For the first time in her life Shannon Christie had a job. To earn one's living by the sweat of one's brow . . . a romantic idea, but a fantasy that faded in the face of reality.

She stood in an assembly line along with dozens of other women with kerchiefs on their heads and a number of ragged children, plucking the feathers from dead chickens. Her skin itched miserably from the irritation of the feathers, the chickens stank abominably, and the perspiration trickled down her face, dripping off her pert nose.

Disgusted, she paused for a moment to mop her face with her sleeve.

"Get to work!" shouted a harsh voice only a few inches from her ear. The foreman rapped her head with a pencil.

Biting her tongue, she returned to the chickens, who seemed more smelly and ugly by the moment. The limp, clammy bodies hardly resembled the golden fried chicken their cook had served at her father's mansion. Now she didn't believe she could ever eat another drumstick in her life without thinking of these loathsome carcasses.

Glancing down the assembly line, she saw Joseph, who worked with a group of other men, boiling the chickens in a huge vat. She could hear their raucous laughter and bawdy joking, and their good humor made her feel even worse. How dare he have a good time in such wretched circumstances.

"Every man in the world has a pecker, right?" said one of the men beside Joseph. "Line all them peckers up and how far do you think they'd go?"

Joseph considered the question thoughtfully. "That's a hard one."

The men roared with laughter and Joseph looked obnoxiously pleased with himself.

"My guess is they'd go to France," another man said.

"And have one hell of a time there, too," Joseph added.

Shannon blushed, embarrassed and infuriated at his earthiness. Wasn't it just like a lowbred bog boy to make such vulgar jokes within her hearing.

"Look at the women," Joseph's neighbor said. "Under each of those aprons there's all kinds of activity."

"Aye," Joseph replied, "the breasts alone are worth a visit."

The men enjoyed a good laugh. One of them who had been eyeing Shannon all morning said, "I think the prettiest girl of the bunch, the one with the prettiest eyes and the prettiest hair, is Joseph's sister."

Instantly, Joseph turned on the man as though he had spoken treason. "Watch yerself, lad. I don't fancy ye talkin' about me sister behind me back."

"Behind your back?" The man lifted one eyebrow. "I'm right here in front of you, Joseph."

"So quit yammering on about it!" Joseph shouted, his face flushing with anger.

The men all laughed again and several of them threw handfuls of feathers at Joseph. Shannon watched the exchange with interest, trying to ignore the coarse, common women, Olive and Glenna, who plucked on either side of her.

"Men have all the pleasure in this world," Glenna said. "Even in bed they satisfy themselves and fall asleep."

"In the case of my husband, with a trumpet of flatulence," Olive added.

The women cackled. Shannon grimaced; these women were so crude, so crass. What a pity that she had to spend her days in such company. For a moment the boring card games in Ireland almost seemed welcome.

Offended by Shannon's haughty expression, Olive and Glenna held up dead chickens to her face and made vulgar gestures. Shannon squealed and turned to run away, but the foreman shoved her back into line.

"Get to work!" he yelled, pinching her arm with his fingers.

"Take your filthy hands off me, you ugly animal!" she shouted.

The factory fell silent. Dozens of eyes turned her way and Shannon felt her face grow red and hot. The foreman pointed his pencil at her throat. "That cost you a day's wage."

She opened her mouth to speak.

"Go ahead," he said. "Insult me again."

In a tiny voice she whispered, "Pig."

"There goes tomorrow," he said with a sarcastic smile. "Done?"

Shannon glanced around again. From the other end of the line Joseph was watching. Their eyes met and he gestured with his thumb for her to return to work. He was right, of course. They needed the money desperately.

But her pride and temper got the best of her.

"Take Friday as well," she shouted. "You spineless little fraction of a man."

Furiously she returned to work. With rage to inspire her she worked twice as fast as before. And Olive and

Glenna seemed to be watching her with a wary eye . . . and a great deal more respect. It might cost her the job, but by God she was glad she had stood up to that swine.

After all, she was a Christie, and Christies didn't take that sort of business from anyone.

But then, Christies didn't have to work for a living either, so she wasn't so sure where she stood in this strange new world. Everything, it seemed, had changed. Even she.

SHANNON trudged along the muddy street, nearly too tired to place one foot in front of the other. However, Joseph ambled along cheerfully as though he had all the energy in the world.

Curse him, she thought, wishing she knew some really good profanity that would express her frustration. Why did he look so fresh and full of vinegar when she felt as though Cromwell's army had tramped over her body?

Joseph chuckled to himself, adding to her irritation. "Yer a corker, Shannon Christie," he said. "What a corker ye are. Ye don't have the dimmest idea about how the world is run."

"If this were Ireland, I could have that wretched man shot." She picked a feather from her hair and flicked it off her finger.

"Wasn't it grand when ye called him a pig! Yer the entertainment at the factory. 'Tis a pity. We'll be missin' ye when ye lose yer job."

"I *hate* that job! I wasn't meant to be slathered in chicken fat. I wasn't meant to *work* in this lifetime at all, let alone at a horrible place like that."

Joseph donned his philosophical face, which irritated the devil out of her. "Nothin' comes without workin'," he said, as though speaking to an idiot or a very young child. "Look at that man there."

He pointed to a fellow who was smeared with coal dust, carrying the tools of a chimney sweep. The man led a handsome horse by the bridle as he strolled down the street. "How do ye think he got that beautiful horse? Sir, how much does a horse like that cost?"

"I don't know," the man replied. "I stole it."

Shannon didn't bother to hide her smugness. As they watched the man mount the horse and ride away, Shannon picked another feather from her hair. "I could be talked into thievery," she said dryly.

Joseph reached over and laid a hand on her shoulder. "Ye'll have a horse of yer own someday, lass. Don't fret so."

Shannon sighed. "To think I had a *barnful* of them once."

They entered the lodging house to find the stairs and hall packed with prostitutes and their customers. One of the girls lifted her skirt and showed Joseph her knickers.

"Payday, Joseph?" she asked.

Joseph stared, mesmerized.

Shannon grabbed his arm and dragged him down the hallway and into their room. "What's wrong with you, boy?" she asked, her hands on her hips, her blue eyes blazing. "Didn't your mother ever warn you about the wiles of evil women?"

Joseph shrugged. "Don't remember me mother. Died when I was born, she did."

Shannon was momentarily taken aback. "Oh, well, if she had lived, she would have told you to avoid wicked females like those in the hall."

"But she was showin' me her knickers. How's a man supposed to resist such a sight, I ask ye?"

"A *decent* man would have turned his head."

"A *decent* man like that fool you were engaged to?"

"Stephen wasn't a fool. But he was a gentleman, and

yes, he would have averted his eyes and avoided such temptation."

"Well, I'll be tellin' ye this, Shannon Christie. If a girl wants to show me her knickers, I'm goin' to be lookin'. I don't figure that hurts anybody. At least she's a friendly sort, not all haughty and puttin' on airs like yerself, afraid someone might see somethin' ye've got when ye undress at night."

"I've seen you peeking at me. Don't think I don't know what a degenerate you are."

"A degenerate? What the bloody hell is that?"

She tossed her head. "If you don't know, I'm not going to tell you."

He crossed the room and grabbed her by the arm. "Yer not goin' to call me a name and not tell me what it means."

"It means that you're a depraved wretch with vile appetites."

He thought for a long moment. "Oh. Well, ye'd better be careful what ye say from now on. I've heard just about enough bad words out of yer mouth directed at meself. I don't throw curses at you, at least not within yer hearin', and I'll expect the same courtesy from you in the future."

Shannon opened her mouth to retort, but reconsidered. In fact, he hadn't cursed her to her face. All things considered, he had been treating her rather well lately. Much better than she had been treating him.

"Now," he said. "If ye don't think one of those wicked women in the hall will grab me and drag me into hell, I think we should take our clothes into the bathroom and give them a bit of a scrub."

Shannon looked down at her dress. She couldn't remember ever wearing anything so filthy in her life. What if her mother could see her now?

She pushed the thought out of her mind. Her

mother must never, never know how her daughter was living.

For a moment Shannon considered ordering Joseph to wash her clothes for her. But she bit back the words and began to gather up her laundry. She knew how hard he had worked today in the factory, and she simply couldn't bring herself to demand it of him.

"So, come along," she said, trying to sound authoritative.

But as they walked down the hall on the way to the bathroom, she couldn't help feeling inadequate and a little afraid. How in heaven's name did one wash clothes?

Nine

INSIDE the steamy bathroom Shannon bent over the tub, delicately swishing her clothes in the now lukewarm water. Joseph draped his last sock over the line, where his other shirt, pants, and socks hung, dripping onto the floor.

Having completed his task, Joseph turned to study Shannon as she leaned over the edge of the old claw-foot tub, her hair hanging down onto her face in tiny locks, curled tighter by the steam that rose about them. He thought about what the man in the factory had said about her being the prettiest woman in the place. It was true, of course. No doubt about it. Too bad she had to be the most cussed, too.

She looked up and saw him watching her.

"What are *you* looking at?" she demanded.

Embarrassed to be caught staring, Joseph searched his brain for an excuse. "I'm just tryin' to figure out what yer doin' there."

She blew a tendril of red hair from her forehead. "It's obvious what I'm doing. I'm cleaning my clothes."

"I see. Do ye ever wonder why it takes ye so long,

Shannon? *My* clothes, if ye notice, if ye look about, are washed and hung. Done."

"You're very talented," she replied sarcastically, returning to her swishing.

Joseph walked over to her and nudged her in the ribs with his finger. "Move over. If ye want to clean yer clothes, lass, ye have to be gettin' yer hands wet."

He grabbed the bar of lye soap and demonstrated. "Ye take the soap like so, and the clothes like so, and ye plunge and scrub. Plunge and scrub, and plunge and scrub. Plunge and scrub and lift."

He held the blouse up for her inspection. All signs of chicken fat and soil had magically disappeared. "See? And if they're still not clean, then ye have another go at it. Plunge and scrub, and plunge and scrub. Ye keep right on plungin' and scrubbin' till all yer plungin' and scrubbin' is done."

He removed his hands and shook them, flicking some soap in Shannon's direction. With more enthusiasm than he might have anticipated from her, she leaned over and grabbed the soap and the nearest skirt.

"Plunge and scrub," she said, imitating his motions. "Plunge and scrub. Plunge and scrub."

"Too fancy," he said. "Too dainty. Put a little elbow into it."

"How important is it to *say* plunge and scrub?"

"Very important, indeed, while yer learnin'. Essential, I'd say."

Putting all her strength into the job, Shannon plunged and scrubbed with amazing vigor. Joseph laughed, enjoying her enthusiasm and the fact that *he* had been able to teach her something for a change.

Maybe she wasn't so bad after all, once you got used to her, he thought. He leaned over to help her by washing her chemise but, at the last moment, thought better of it and grabbed an apron instead.

"Plunge and scrub," he said, laughing, delightfully aware of the closeness of her shoulder against his as they worked together. She wasn't really such a bad sort.

"Plunge and scrub," she replied, and returned his smile.

THEIR cramped bedroom reflected their working status, cheaply decorated with a few spare coins saved from their weekly pay. New curtains made of gingham, a cheap blanket, various trinkets, and two new mirrors adorned the walls.

Behind the flimsy partition that bore a new coat of whitewash instead of the lewd pictures, Shannon peeled off her dirty clothes that were soaking wet from doing the laundry.

Bone-tired, every muscle in her body aching, she couldn't fight the wave of depression that swept over her. "When I was in Ireland," she said, more to herself than to Joseph who was puttering about the room, performing his nightly routines, "America was a twinkling in the distance, a marvelous modern place. I imagined myself going around, enjoying art, dining out or retiring to my beautiful ranch to ride. Instead, I'm plucking dead birds in a chicken factory and the nearest ranch is a thousand miles away from this wretched place."

"Aye, well, I'm goin' to cross that thousand miles while yer complainin'—penny by penny with every chicken I pluck."

"But your kind was bred to do things slowly and never get ahead. I'll find a quicker way to make my money, just you watch." A sneeze tickled at her nose. "Oh, those feathers. Ah . . . ah . . ."

"Go ahead, sneeze," he muttered beneath his breath as he pulled a small clay crock out from under the bed. "Blow yer silly head off for all I care."

—— 144 ——

He sat down on the bed, the crock between his legs, and began to drop his week's earnings into it. "Thirty, forty, forty-five . . ."

Shannon peeked around the partition at the sound of clinking money. "My, my, Joseph," she said sarcastically. "You could be a banker with your ability to count."

"Thanks for the compliment. But I'd rather till the land."

Don't let her get to ye, lad, he told himself. *She's only tryin' to get a quarrel outta ye.*

His counting finished, he tucked the crock back under the bed and began to get undressed.

"I don't suppose you've calculated what the journey will cost," Shannon said. He could hear the curiosity in her voice. She wanted his opinion but was too haughty to ask for it.

"If I barter, I can get a buckboard for under twenty-five. It's the harness that's costly: bit, frame, collar, tongue, reins."

"I think I'll skip the buckboard part. I'm happier to ride."

"Ye'll be needin' a whopping saddlebag to carry yer supplies."

She said nothing for a long moment and Joseph sensed her agitation behind the partition. "What supplies?" she asked at length.

"Food, clothes, soap, water, ammunition, gun."

"Why would I need a gun?"

"To hunt. And defend yerself. A woman all alone is bound to be robbed now and then. Or a tribe of Indians chases ye, ye'll want to discourage a few."

His eyes sparkled with mischief as the silence behind the partition stretched into long moments. There, scare her a little. Served her right, the spoiled little brat that she was.

Then he heard her sigh dreamily. "Whenever I think of guns," she said, "I remember Stephen Chase."

Instantly the grin disappeared from Joseph's face. "Aye, yer lucky to be rid of that piss-headed snob."

"I suppose. But I miss his courtesy at times. There wasn't a puddle of mud he didn't lay his coat upon for me to walk across."

Suddenly furious, Joseph flung his trousers at the wall. "That man burned the house where I was born! I will not allow ye to speak his name in me presence."

"Stephen," she replied. "Stephen, Stephen, Stephen, Steeee-phen."

"Shannon!"

"You can't tell *me* what to say and not say—just because we're lashed together in this closet of squalor, boy! Am I to squelch my memories of when I was adored? He *adored* me, Stephen Chase did."

Joseph snorted. "What he found adorable in the likes of you, I'll never know."

"You wouldn't recognize my qualities if they were staring you in the . . . the . . . oh, these blasted feathers! Achoo!"

She sneezed so violently that the partition suddenly fell forward. The two of them stood there, perfectly naked, staring at each other's body in shock.

Joseph was the first to find his breath. "Bless you," he said reverently, surveying her curves with hungry eyes.

Snapping to consciousness, Shannon screamed and dived for the bed, burying herself in the covers. Joseph, suddenly aware of his own nakedness, yanked one of the curtains from the windows and wrapped it around his hips.

Without looking at her, he extinguished the light and hurried over to his pallet on the floor. Settled beneath the blanket, staring up into the darkness, his heart was still pounding.

Dear God in heaven, she was beautiful. He had thought her lovely in her knickers that day in the barn. But the sight of her perfect body, bared before his eyes, was a vision he would never forget.

He wondered if Adam had felt that way the moment he had realized that Eve was naked. No wonder he chased her all over the Garden of Eden for a second look.

Damn. Now even more fuel had been added to the fires of torment that he must endure every night. He lay there listening to the squeaking and creaking of the mattress next door and his body burned.

In a feeble attempt to block out the pictures that flooded his mind, Joseph imagined himself boxing, just like Mike Kelly, pounding the snot out of some poor sap. Yes, that was exactly what he wanted. More than anything else, Joseph Doneliy wanted to hit somebody to release some of this frustration and anger that was building in his body.

Anybody would do.

Two hours later Joseph stepped out of their room and into the hall, quietly closing the door behind him. Though the house was less rambunctious than before, several of the prostitutes were still plying their trade in the various rooms. The creaks, squeaks, and moans of lovemaking still permeated the old building. It was enough to drive a man mad.

He made his way to the bathroom, where he washed his face in the old rusty basin. The cold water helped a bit, but it made him long for the swimming hole near his village where he, his brothers, and the other lads had gone dipping in the summers. That cold, invigorating water would help cool him down . . . but it was so far away.

For a brief moment he felt a pang of homesickness, a longing for the sweet, fertile smell of Ireland, the emerald fields so green they hurt your eyes to look upon them.

Then he thought back over the many adventures he had experienced in the short time he had been in America and decided that he preferred this new land to his old home. There were so many possibilities here, so many opportunities for a young man in his prime.

And Joseph Donelly's body was forever reminding him that he was definitely in his prime.

He walked out of the bath, drying his face with a towel, and nearly ran into Molly as she exited a room with a fistful of dollars.

"You're up quite late, Joseph," she said, her voice soft and solicitous.

"I'm having trouble sleeping."

She peeled off a couple of bills. "Can I treat you to a girl?" she asked matter-of-factly.

Joseph marveled at this candor. In Ireland a lass pretended to not even know of such things. Here in America, the women appeared to take these matters in stride and speak of them openly. He wasn't sure which he preferred. On one hand, talking to a woman about sexual matters provided a certain excitement. But on the other, a simple Irish lad like himself found his face blushing bright red and his tongue tripping in front of his eyeteeth until he couldn't see what to say next.

"Well," she said, "how about Sally Mae there?" She nodded toward a pretty little brunette who was walking down the hall in their direction. "She's had her eyes on you since you arrived. I'm sure she'd help you release some of that pressure you're about to bust with."

Joseph watched the girl walk, her hips swaying enticingly. Her eyes were friendly, her smile open . . . not like someone else he could think of right now.

Tempted, he considered the thought for a few

heartbeats, then shook his head. "Thank you, Molly, no. I'm just . . . restless is what I am. I'm in a hurry, I think, to get ahead."

"Ah . . . ambition."

"Aye. I want to be someone who's done a thing or two in his time."

Molly laughed softly. "Men pin their hopes entirely on their accomplishments. It's their frustration, I suppose, that I make my living by."

Her openness encouraged him to confide in her. Maybe, since her business was men and women, she could help him understand what was going on in his head and body.

"Molly, what's it mean when a woman drives ye mad? I'm thinkin' of a girl I knew in Ireland once."

"Did you drive *her* mad?"

"I believe I must have. Everythin' was a contest between us. Her eyes turned red whenever she looked at me."

Molly nodded knowingly. "That girl was a girl who wanted to be kissed."

Joseph's eyes widened in astonishment and he felt as though someone had just punched him in the stomach—a good, solid belly jab. "Kissed? Not by me, surely."

"Who else? Those red eyes were the flames of a fire that was kindled and lit by you. I'm sorry that you left that girl behind. Love is available less than people think. There's nothing sadder than an opportunity come and gone and missed."

Molly smiled compassionately and headed downstairs. After watching her go in stunned silence, he shuffled down the hall to their room. On the way he had to pass Sally Mae, who gave him another come-hither look. She smiled deliciously and he couldn't keep his eyes from wandering to her cleavage and her naked legs beneath the ruffled drawers.

As though running from the tempting serpent, he scurried on down the hall. He heard her laughter as he closed the door.

He walked over to the bed where Shannon lay and stared down at her, noticing how her hair glimmered in the pale light of the street lamps that filtered through the window.

A girl who wants to be kissed? Couldn't be so. He could swear that on any given day she'd much prefer to slap him than kiss him.

With his eyes he traced the soft roundness of her cheek, like a little girl's, with her long lashes gently sweeping them. But her lips were those of a woman, full and sensual. He allowed himself the luxury of fantasizing how it might be to kiss those lips. Of course, it would have to be while she was asleep, because if she were conscious, she would no doubt try to murder him if he even tried.

Finally he turned away from her, walked over to his pallet, and lay down; he stared up at the ceiling as he had so many nights before.

To his surprise she spoke. "Joseph, am I beautiful at all?"

His heart raced. He decided to answer her honestly, but when he replied, his tone was glib and defensive. "I've never seen anything like ye in all me livin' life."

"Good."

She rolled over with her back to him, and in moments he heard her deep breathing, which told him she was asleep again and he was alone. Arrogant Protestant brat!

He lay there, his body in misery, a bomb waiting to explode. This wouldn't do. It simply wouldn't do at all, at all.

He jumped up from the pallet and ran to the door. He had to be away from this woman. Now! Before he did something to her that they would both regret.

He didn't dare consider what he would do. Just . . . something. Something terrible or wonderful. At this point he couldn't decide which.

He ran out of the house and through the city streets, the night air cool on his face, his feet pounding a brisk cadence on the cobblestones. He sprinted all the way to the social club without slowing and charged through the door.

Joseph plowed his way through the crowd of late-night carousers who were cheering a boxer who had just won a fight. In their midst little Dermody squawked, "Settle your bets, gentlemen. And if we have another challenger, please step forward!" The boy knelt on the floor and chalked a new scratch mark.

Pushing through the crowd, Joseph ripped off his shirt and barged up to the boxer.

"Toe the line, gentlemen!" little Dermody shouted. "No kicking, no gouging, no biting, and no hitting below the belt!" Then, to Joseph, he said, "Put your foot on the line."

But Joseph ignored the mark and the rules. All the pent-up frustration exploded through his arm and fists and crashed into the fighter's jaw.

The hall erupted with cheers and betting. Joseph heard the roar of the crowd as though from far away. He threw punch after punch, landing each one on his stunned opponent.

"Go after him, scrapper!" From the corner of his eye he saw Mike Kelly standing inside the circle of spectators, punching the air, sparring with an unseen adversary.

The club had never witnessed such a brutal fight. Dermody watched, jumping up and down like an excited rabbit. Grace and the dancing girls leered from the stage. And Mike Kelly didn't stop shouting and punching for the remainder of the fight.

Joseph's attack was unskilled but full of long-suppressed fury and frustration. By sheer will he finally knocked out his opponent. The man hit the floor facedown, his nose bloodied, his left eye already turning black.

"Settle your—" Dermody's screeching voice was lost in the roar of the crowd, ecstatic with the violence of the exchange they had just seen.

Joseph, jubilant with his success, danced around, holding his fists high while at least two dozen well-wishers slapped him on the back. Kelly pushed his way through the fans, grabbed Joseph, and dragged him aside.

"You clobbered the fella's brains out, lad! What a fight! Congratulations to you." Then he turned to the adoring women. "You," he yelled to Grace. "Get up the burly-que."

The piano player suddenly sprang to life, filling the hall with the tinkling, half-flat notes from the out-of-tune piano. Grace, with a hungry look toward Joseph, led the other dancers onto the stage where they began to kick and twirl to a risqué cancan.

Kelly grabbed Joseph by the arm and pulled him over to the ward boss's private table. Joseph felt his chest swelling with pride by the moment. He had done it! He had beaten that man with almost no trouble at all, and now he was a hero. Minutes ago he had been lying on his lowly pallet, feeling despondent and frustrated because of that cursed redhead. And now he was on top of the world. What a wonderful place this America was!

Another man who looked vaguely familiar strolled up to their table and sat down. The fellow wore a splint on his nose.

"Gordon, give this scrapper something to smoke," Mike said, then, turning to Joseph: "You remember Gordon, don't you, lad?"

Suddenly Joseph recalled that this was the boxer he

had beaten his first night here in America. "Ah . . . aye, I remember having the pleasure of a bout with ye."

"I'll have to breathe through my mouth for the rest of my days," Gordon replied bitterly as he handed Joseph a cigar.

"I have a good life, don't I?" Kelly said, gesturing toward the hall, the customers, and the dancing girls. "All it takes to succeed in this country is hard work and a dash of corruption."

Joseph gave him a skeptical glance. Kelly slapped him on the shoulder. "I'm joking, scrapper. I haven't worked hard at all!"

Kelly laughed and tossed a handful of coins onto the stage. Joseph watched, red-faced, as the dancers obscenely stuffed the coins down the fronts of their skimpy costumes. Grace danced up to Joseph, stopped directly in front of him, and kicked up her leg.

Joseph's eyes widened with astonishment at such a brazen display of bare limbs, and she was close enough so that he could have almost touched her. She danced away, coyly peeking at him over her shoulder.

"Hey, lad, look sharp. There's a gentleman here you must meet," Kelly said, gouging Joseph in the ribs with his thumb.

A fat-gutted man in a fancy suit was waddling toward them, a pompous swagger to his walk. Something about him made Joseph's skin crawl. In spite of the man's expensive, well-tailored clothes, he had a sickly, unhealthy look about him.

"Who's your boy there, Kelly?" the man asked as he walked up to them. "He's a helluva battle-ax."

"This is Joseph Donelly, Mr. Bourke. He's a stout-hearted Galway lad. Shake this gentleman's hand, Joseph. His name is Mr. D'Arcy Bourke: member of the city council."

Reluctantly, Joseph extended his hand. "I'll shake

—— 153 ——

yer hand, Mr. Bourke, but I'm not in a friendly mood. I came here to fight, and there's fight left in me."

Bourke sucked on his stubby cigar and laughed. "He's a lively one, Kelly." He turned to Joseph. "Would you box an Italian if I scared one up?"

An Italian. The very thought thrilled Joseph. In his short stay in Boston he had become all too aware of the rivalry between the Irish and the Italians. The Irish, firmly rooted in Boston for decades, had recently seen their jobs and their housing taken over by the newly immigrated Italians. Tempers ran hot between the factions, both well schooled in the art of feuding and vendetta.

What Joseph didn't realize was the political significance of Bourke's suggestion. If Bourke could pit an Irishman against an Italian and win, his popularity would soar among his constituents . . . not an unwelcome development just before elections.

"I'll box any man you put in front of me," Joseph replied with cocky confidence. The intoxicant of his latest victory still flowed hot through his veins. "Especially an Italian."

No sooner had he spoken the words than Dermody came skidding up to their table.

"We've got another pug, Mike!" he shrieked in his high irritating voice.

Kelly plugged his ears. "Jayzus Christ, Dermody—when's your voice gonna change?"

Joseph sprang to his feet. "I'm ready to box again! Bring him on!"

"And I'll put money on you, lad!" Mike shouted.

"The boy's got an appetite for it, Kelly," Bourke said with an approving nod.

A crowd quickly formed around them, then split apart as another boxer approached, even bigger and meaner than the last. But Joseph didn't care. One by one he'd take them all. This one would fall just as easily as the first. And in the end he'd be a hero and feel better to boot. Not a bad arrangement.

"Place your bets, gentlemen!" Dermody shouted.

Joseph lunged at his new opponent . . . punched, swung, and jabbed . . . and felt a fist as hard as Connemara marble slam into his jaw.

Maybe this one wouldn't be so easy after all.

SHANNON stole quietly down the stairs, not wishing to wake anyone in the rooming house. The last thing she wanted was a conversation with one of these dreadful women or their frightening customers. What she did want was to see if she could find Joseph. He had wakened her long ago when he had stormed out of the room, and though she had been lying awake for hours, there had been no sign of him.

Downstairs, in what had once been the parlor of the old house, Shannon saw Molly sitting at a cluttered little desk, counting money and sorting receipts. She glanced up from her work as Shannon entered the room.

"Molly, do you know where Joseph is this night?" she asked, trying not to sound too anxious, dreading what she might hear.

What if Molly told her that he was visiting one of those awful women? What if some of those groans and creaks she had been forced to listen to had been his? The very thought of him doing those awful things with those horrible women made her want to grab a gun and put a bullet between his eyes . . . and the woman's, too.

Though she couldn't imagine why she cared what that stupid bog boy did.

"He flew out the door like his trousers had caught on fire," Molly said with a half smile.

"Oh . . ." Shannon walked over to the window and glanced outside. The streets were bare and dawn was beginning to break. She saw the lamplighter, a little man on stilts, going from lamp to lamp, extinguishing the lights. "I don't care what he's doing, of course, but he has to work in the morning . . . in just a few hours, that is."

"So do you, dear," Molly said with compassion. "Go to bed. If he blows off a little steam, it won't do any harm."

Shannon left the window, but lingered beside the desk. The high stack of currency was impressive. She thought of the pittance she earned each week at the chicken factory, and she recalled a sermon in which the minister had said that sin didn't pay. Apparently he had been mistaken. It appeared that sin paid very handsomely, indeed.

Tnen, beside the piles of money, Shannon spotted something else. A familiar pamphlet. She picked it up and read it.

"Wanted: Strong, healthy men and women. Every citizen of the United States is entitled to one hundred and sixty acres of land." She studied the other woman thoughtfully. "Molly?"

Molly glanced around secretively and lowered her voice. "I've been a whore all my life," she admitted, "and I'm sick of it. I want to change my life for the better."

"An admirable ambition," Shannon said, feeling for the first time a bond between herself and this woman. Maybe she wasn't *all* bad even if she was a whore . . . though Shannon would never have suggested such a thing to her mother.

Shannon studied the pamphlet wistfully. Thoughts of what Joseph had said about Indians floated through her mind. "I wonder what it's like out there, so far from civilization."

"Ah, don't worry. Joseph will look after you."

Shannon's chin shot up. "No, he won't. I don't want company. I came to America to be independent."

Molly laughed. "What a silly idea."

"It's a *modern* idea, Molly. I'm surprised you don't think that way, being an American woman and all. Besides, Joseph and I drive each other mad."

Molly peered at her curiously. "Do you, now? Would you say that the two of you quarrel a lot?"

"All the time. Every minute we're together."

"I see. And would you say that sometimes his eyes turn red with anger when he's yelling at you?"

"Well . . . yes. That's exactly right. How did you know?"

Molly chuckled and shrugged her shoulders. "Just a lucky guess. Now, why don't you go on upstairs and get a bit of sleep before you have to go to work. Your wayward . . . brother will be home soon. I know about that sort of thing, too."

Trying to believe Molly's words, spoken with such authority, Shannon turned and started back up the stairs.

Safe home, Joseph. Safe home and around the fairy forts, she thought, trying to send the words of the old Irish blessing from her mind to his. Then she silently added, *And if you're doing anything you shouldn't . . . with some other woman . . . when you get back, I'll kill you.*

AN hour later Shannon was still pacing the floor of their room. She had worn a path to the window, to the door, and back. Then, on her two-hundredth trip to the window, she heard footsteps in the hall. Faltering footsteps. And raucous singing. Fully clothed, she dived into bed and rolled over on her side, pretending to be asleep.

The door opened and she heard a female voice say, "Steady now, Joseph."

—— 157 ——

So much for feigning sleep. She shrieked and jumped out of bed, ready to commit murder with her bare hands.

But one look at Joseph's face froze her in midstride. He was so battered that his features were hardly recognizable. His eyes nearly swollen closed, his lips cut, his nose bleeding, and a purple knot rising on his forehead.

"Joseph!" she shouted. "Oh, my God—what happened?"

Joseph teetered, unsteady on his feet. He said nothing but stared vacantly at her through the slits that had been his big green eyes.

As Shannon's stunned mind grasped the frightening reality that he had been badly beaten, she realized another equally disturbing fact: He was clinging to an extremely voluptuous brunette who was wearing a spangled costume that made the prostitutes' outfits seem demure by comparison.

"Help me get him into bed," the brunette said, struggling beneath Joseph's sagging weight.

Instantly, Shannon moved to his other side and grabbed him around the waist. Together they wrestled him over to the bed and laid him across it.

Shannon's gaze darted back and forth between Joseph's battered face and the woman's obscenely large bosom, most of which spilled over the top of her low-cut bodice.

Pulling her attention away from the other woman, Shannon focused on Joseph. "Joseph, you're covered in blood! Who did this to you?"

"He's been boxing, but he'll survive," the girl said with a shrug. "I've seen them a lot worse than this before and they lived. He had a charge of gunpowder in him that needed to go off."

"And who might you be?" Shannon fixed her with a cold, haughty stare.

"I'm Grace. I work at the social club."

Joseph smiled up at the brunette and said in a groggy voice, "I won . . . didn't I . . . ?"

"You beat 'em all, Joseph," Grace said, brushing his hair away from his forehead. The gesture wasn't lost on Shannon, who scowled. "But don't talk now. Get some sleep."

Grace turned and left the room, gesturing for Shannon to follow. Once outside in the hallway, Grace shut the door behind them and turned to Shannon.

"You're his sister, right?" she asked.

"Mm-hm."

Grace leaned closer and Shannon could smell the scent of cheap perfume and cigar smoke that permeated her clothing. "What kind of a man is he?" Grace asked. "I mean, besides tough and handsome as the devil."

Shannon's eyes cut downward to Grace's enormous breasts. "He's extremely moody."

Grace nodded. "I believe that. Full of spit, isn't he? And passion."

Shannon lifted one eyebrow slightly. "Not really. He's fairly dull."

"Dull? I don't know what sort of men *you're* used to, but he's anything but dull! And the build on him . . . me and the girls got swollen eyes from gawking at his bum. Best bum in Boston, we decided, and believe you me, it's a subject we girls know about."

Shannon tossed her head and turned her back on the woman, her blood boiling. "Good-bye, Grace." She reached for the doorknob.

Grace laid a restraining hand on her forearm. "Tell him I—"

"Nice to meet you." She shook her hand away and opened the door.

"I just want to give him a—"

—— 159 ——

"Good night."

Shannon slammed the door in the brunette's face and fantasized that maybe . . . just maybe . . . she had also slammed it on those huge breasts and flattened them down to size.

She turned back to Joseph, who was snoring loudly on the bed. So at least she knew where he had been all night and with whom.

After giving his cuts and bruises a cursory cleansing with a clean cloth and cold water, she walked over to his pallet on the floor and lay down. But she still couldn't sleep. Every time she closed her eyes, she saw Joseph's pummeled face, and worse yet, the way he had been clinging to that cheap dancing girl.

Finally, as she drifted into a fitful sleep, she dreamed that she was standing by, watching Joseph being beaten by a big, ugly man whose fists were the size of Christmas hams.

Then the dream changed and she found that it was she who was fighting. Punch! Jab! Duck and punch again!

To her surprise she was enjoying herself, feeling the thrill of victory over her opponent with every well-laid blow.

But it wasn't the ugly boxer she was fighting. It was that floozy brunette with the big bosoms. She was beating the bloody devil out of her . . . and enjoying every minute of it.

Ten

═══

UNCONSCIOUSLY, Shannon ran a hand through her hair, tidying the wild nest of unruly curls. After only an hour of sleep it was time for her to go to work. But before she left, she supposed she should do something about attending to Joseph's wounds more thoroughly. Last night she had been too angry to give him the attention he had needed.

Summoning her dignity, she walked over to the dresser, dipped a cloth into the chipped porcelain bowl, and squeezed most of the water out. Then she sat on the edge of the bed and began to wipe Joseph's face with a cloth.

He stirred and peeked at her with one swollen eye. "That was Grace who brought me home," he mumbled through split and bleeding lips.

"So she said," Shannon replied coolly, continuing to bathe his wounds.

"She dances at the burly-que."

"Yes, well, never mind her now. Lie still. I'm going to allow you to continue to use the bed . . . at least for today while I'm at work."

"Thank you, Shannon. 'Tis grateful I am to ye."

Shannon stood and walked back to the dresser, rinsing the bloody cloth in the water. She felt a bit squeamish at the sight and tried not to think about the fact that this was Joseph's blood or how terrible his face must feel right now.

"And I'll tell them at the factory that you'll be missing a day or two," she said, trying to think of anything she could do to make him feel a little better. She walked back to the bed and laid the clean cloth across his forehead.

"Just tell them that I'm never coming back," he replied.

"Don't be so pessimistic, Joseph. You're beaten, but you aren't going to die."

"I'll not be needin' to go back, Shannon. Look in me boot down there."

Puzzled, she lifted his cuff and found money tucked in his shoe. "Four dollars!" she exclaimed, pulling out the bills. "That's more than we'd make plucking chickens in a month!"

Joseph reached down and took the money from her, clenching it in his fist. "I won it, all by meself. And now 'tis the champion I am, till somebody knocks me out, that is."

Shannon's eyes widened and her mouth fell open. No . . . he couldn't mean . . .

"You're intending to do this again?"

He nodded. "I'll have me horse-and-buggy money before the winter comes."

Shannon looked unbelievingly at his pummeled face, unable to comprehend how anyone could suffer this sort of abuse and then return for more. No matter how much money was involved. If his face hurt even half as badly as it appeared to, it must be agony.

She stood and began to pace the floor, her agitation building by the moment at the thought of him returning to this room, night after night, in this condition. It simply wasn't acceptable. It wasn't moral.

Besides, the competitive side of her nature flared and she found herself jealous that he had made so much money in only one night . . . even if he had to be beaten for it.

"This isn't fair at all, Joseph," she said with a pout.

Joseph smiled. "I was quite admired."

"Well, *I* don't admire you. Here I am assimilating, subjecting myself to the world of manual labor, and you're going to *fight* your way to Oklahoma?"

"*You* suggested a shortcut."

"For *me*, not you. I'm a class above you, you black-fingered bog. I don't know *how* to work. Get out of that bed."

"What is *wrong* with you, woman?"

"You're sleeping on the floor, where you belong."

She yanked at him, but he held on and pulled her onto the bed beside him. Their faces were so close together that she could feel his warm breath on her cheek. He laughed softly.

"I'll tell ye what's the matter with ye, lass. It's jealous ye are. I'm goin' up in the world and ye've plummeted. High and mighty. Ye can't stand it."

"Jealous! Jealous? Me? Of you? Now, there's a silly notion if I ever heard one." She bounded off the bed and began to pace the floor again. "I'm jealous of you because you have the stupidity to get your face flattened in a brawl. What a vivid imagination you have, Joseph."

Joseph grinned knowingly. "Aye, must have been me imagination, 'tis all."

"Yes, of course it was. I'm glad you realize that." She continued to pace, thinking fast and hard. "Joseph, there are other ways of getting to Oklahoma," she said, trying to keep the emotion out of her voice as she appealed to his logic. "Look at you, boy. They've beaten you up. You're a mess."

She walked back to the bed and grabbed his hand, as though she could somehow restrain him and force him to do as she wished. "Stay away from that club, Joseph Donelly. It's a terrible place."

But Joseph just grinned through his cuts and bruises. "Ye should've heard them, Shannon, cheerin' me on. Somethin' is changin' for me now. 'Twas a grand and glorious night."

He waved his money happily, and Shannon could see that he was, indeed, obnoxiously proud of himself. He *was* going to fight again. And there was nothing she could do to stop him.

What if the next time he were beaten even more badly? What if those animals crippled or maimed him? What if they even killed him?

A sick feeling rose up inside her, and try as she might, she couldn't force it down.

"Excuse me, Joseph," she said as she left the bedroom. "I'm going to go wash up and get ready to go to work. I'll be back in a few minutes."

She took the bowl of bloody water with her and walked down the hall toward the bathroom, fighting the nausea that welled up from her stomach.

Once inside the bath, she threw cold water on her face and wiped it dry with a towel. She stood there for a moment thinking of how happy Joseph had looked, grinning through his bruised and bloody face. She stared at her reflection in the mirror and saw the one expression that she should have seen on Joseph's face, but hadn't. She saw fear. Cold, white fear.

A fist that felt as though it had a freight train behind it slammed into Joseph's jaw. His knees nearly buckled beneath him. He felt as though his limbs were weighted down with lead, too heavy to hold him up any longer.

"Go after him, scrapper!" Mike Kelly shouted from the ring's edge.

Kelly, Gordon, Dermody, and more than half of the crowd at the burly-que screamed their encouragements, some cheerful, some threatening, as Joseph swung again and again at the big Irishman who was fresh off the boat from County Kerry. The man had taken a brutal beating, but refused to hit the floor.

A lot of money rode on this fight, and Joseph knew it. He had to win, had to maintain his championship, had to get paid because he had already squandered last Saturday's pay and it was only Sunday evening.

Gathering all his strength, determination, and rage into one punch, he landed a firm right cross to the man's chin. The big Kerryman's eyes rolled backward in his head and he tumbled forward.

"Settle your bets, gentlemen!" Dermody shouted.

Kelly caught Joseph, who was ready to collapse. He wouldn't allow him to sit down but kept propping him up. "Come on, lad," he said, shaking him. "Perk up. The night's young yet."

Gordon chugged over to them. "We've got another pug, Mike."

"I've fought three times already tonight," Joseph protested feebly.

"Are you still cutting turf in Ireland, boy, or climbing up in the world?" He turned to several men standing nearby. "Pour gin on his face and toss him out there, boys!"

Joseph was promptly doused with gin and yanked to his feet. There, standing with his toes on the chalked line in the center of the room, was his next opponent, looking as though he were hungry and eager to eat Joseph for supper.

"Place your bets, gentlemen!" Dermody shouted.

And Joseph was hurled into the fray.

SHANNON trudged down the hall toward her room, dragging her feet, every muscle in her body aching. Feathers pricked at the back of her sweaty neck, her hands itched, and she knew she smelled abominably. This working-for-a-living business wasn't all it was proclaimed to be. Independence, she was finding, didn't come cheap, even in a modern country like America.

At the end of the hall the door opened and she saw Joseph strutting out of their room, wearing a new coat, a fancy little blue cap perched jauntily on the side of his head. Another hat. By God, he must be spending all his earnings on hats, she thought, despising him, yet savoring the sight of him.

These days she saw precious little of him. He fought at the club evenings and nights and slept in the day. She worked at the factory all day and spent her evenings alone in their room. She found that she missed him terribly . . . even if he were a pain in the backside.

"Howdy-do, ladies!" he said, tipping the hat to a knot of prostitutes gathered in one of the doors.

As he and Shannon met in the hall he gave her the same flashing smile and tip of his hat. For a second she wished that he would stay and talk to her a while, then she quickly discarded the thought. Better that he and his silly hats were out of here as soon as possible. She certainly didn't want to have to contend with his bragging and swaggering all night.

"'Evenin', Shannon," he said as they passed.

"Good evening, Joseph," she replied.

The whores ogled and tittered, making a big fuss over him. Shannon tried to ignore the women, but she couldn't help hearing their words as she walked past them to her room.

"He's a handsome catch, that Joseph Donelly is."

"If he can keep his knuckles up night after night, imagine what his willy can do."

They screeched with laughter as Shannon strode by. Entering their room, she slammed the door behind her. But it did little good, considering the old building's thin walls.

She flopped down on her bed and lay there . . . still listening to their giggling and their speculations on the fitness of Joseph's "willy."

Good heavens, but her life had changed. Only a few months ago she wouldn't have known a single word to describe a man's private parts. Now, thanks to her fellow tenants, she knew several.

She tried to summon an appropriate portion of contempt for the women on the other side of the door, but all she felt was burning jealousy at their remarks about Joseph.

Lately she had found herself less and less shocked by their behavior and their occupation. Although her mother had always told her that such women were wicked, horrible creatures, she had actually found them to be rather nice . . . when they weren't teasing her about Joseph.

Shannon had tried diligently to cling to her disgust, as her mother had taught her, but day by day she felt it slipping away. These women were human after all, whether Nora had thought so or not.

And, perhaps, in some ways they weren't so different from herself, Shannon thought with unsettling recognition.

Lately, she had been spending more and more time wondering about those things that an unmarried girl her age had no reason to even think about. But the very fact that she wasn't *supposed* to think about them made these matters all the more attractive. She simply couldn't *help* thinking about them; her body wouldn't allow her to stop. Maybe she was just as bad as those women in the hall.

And what made her even more miserable was that, sometimes, when she caught Joseph looking at her in that funny sort of way, she had the distinct feeling that he was thinking those things, too.

Maybe Nora had been wrong. Maybe people weren't so different after all.

"Ah . . . that was an ugly punch if I ever saw one," Mike Kelly said as Joseph's latest opponent landed a nasty blow to the side of his head.

Another jab and Joseph went reeling and spinning through the rambunctious crowd. At the end of his fall he pitched forward, face-first, against Grace's famous bosom.

The room exploded with laughter.

Grace lifted his face and smiled brightly at him. "Keep fighting, Joseph," she said. "There's nobody better than you."

She planted a big, wet, lipsticky kiss smack on his mouth, then turned him around to face his opponent.

The crowd went mad.

Joseph swelled with confidence, then bounded toward his fellow boxer . . . and knocked him flat.

With winter on the way the city of Boston seemed even grayer than before to Shannon as she walked home with her two workmates, Olive and Glenna. The soot-darkened buildings, only a few shades darker than the sky above them, seemed to close around her, and she found herself fantasizing more and more about the ranch she would own someday.

There would be color everywhere. Green fields with snowy-white fences. A bright red barn. A yellow house with a blue roof and a yard full of chickens, geese, and ducks of every hue.

The dreams helped to dispel the gloominess of the city and the feeling that she would live and die in this place, never fulfilling her dream.

"The winters here are wicked, Shannon," Olive said, noticing that she was shivering in her thin dress. "You need to buy a coat."

"I can't afford a coat," Shannon replied, thinking of the closetful of warm woolen garments she had left behind in Ireland.

"She's become a thrifty thing," Glenna commented. "And works so hard she puts the rest of us to shame."

"I find the work is easier, the harder you go at it," Shannon said, kicking a small pebble along the cobblestone street as she walked. Her boots were rapidly wearing out, too. She could almost feel the hard roundness of the cobblestones against the soles of her feet. "I hate the factory," she said, "and that nasty little foreman, but plucking the dead chickens doesn't bother me anymore."

The women paused before a store window that featured the latest fashion: a mauve satin dress with billowed sleeves and padded shoulders.

"Look at the sleeves, all bunched up. From Paris, France, it says. Can you imagine ever owning a dress like that?" Glenna said wistfully.

"Own it? I'd like to just once *wear* that sort of dress," Olive said. "Think how elegant it would feel to put on such a wonderful dress and dance around the room."

She swished her worn, soiled skirt from side to side and hummed a tune.

Shannon listened to her friends with a sense of shame that she couldn't quite understand. Back in Ireland she had several wardrobesful of dresses like those, and she had always taken them for granted.

Somehow, it had never occurred to her that for most other girls in the world, wearing such a dress was only a dream.

At that moment a well-dressed woman walked by, her nose in the air, leading a poofy poodle at the end of a red leather leash.

"Imagine being that rich and having everything you want," Glenna said.

For the first time in her life Shannon felt a surge of irritation toward someone she would normally consider one of her own kind. This woman was no different than her mother, her mother's friends, and . . . to be honest . . . like Shannon herself had been not that long ago.

But now the woman's demeanor didn't seem dignified or elegant; she appeared haughty and cold. Shannon found that she much preferred the warmth and candor of her newfound friends. Although her mother would have considered Olive and Glenna "lower class," Shannon found them kind, generous, and much more fun to be around than her more socially acceptable friends in Ireland.

"Even her dog is putting on airs," Shannon muttered, echoing her friend's sentiment. "The stuck-up little mutt."

Across the street a bell tinkled as a shop door was opened. Their attention shifted to the handsome young man who was exiting the store.

"Look, Shannon," Olive said. "There's your famous brother."

"Good grief." Shannon shook her head. "He's bought himself another hat."

Joseph sauntered out of the hat store, pausing to study his reflection in the front window and adjust the brim. The girls chuckled at his vanity.

"He's all dappered up for the church-social Sunday," Glenna said. "Will you be coming, Shannon?"

"I don't think so."

"Ah, come on. You've got to live a little bit." Glenna slapped her on the back. "After all, it's Thanksgiving!"

Shannon looked confused for a moment. "It is? Oh, yes, I suppose it is."

She wasn't sure what Thanksgiving was, but apparently it was some sort of American holiday that she should be observing. She felt at a loss in this new country that didn't celebrate most of the Irish holidays she was accustomed to, and honored others she had never heard of.

"See you tomorrow," Glenna said as she and Olive turned the corner and headed toward their own lodging house. "Don't eat too much turkey."

Turkey? What did turkeys have to do with anything? Shannon wondered as she walked across the street to where Joseph still stood in front of the window primping.

She tapped him on the shoulder. "You look like an idiot," she said good-naturedly.

Joseph turned around and grinned, not at all offended by her insult. "Oh, yeah? Well, let's get some other opinions."

Taking her arm, he led her down the street. He flashed his breathtaking smile at everyone they met, and women, children, and old people alike were completely charmed.

"That's a fine hat, Mr. Donelly," called the fruit vendor as they passed his stand. "And a fine fight last night as well."

"Glad ye enjoyed it, Connor," Joseph replied.

To Shannon's disgust the vendor tossed him a peach.

"Okay, okay," she said. "You've made your point. You'd better be careful, Joseph. You're becoming vain."

He took the hat from his head and pretended to dust

it with his sleeve. "No, surely 'tisn't true. Me? Not at all, at all."

She laughed at his antics, then happened to look down and see an enormous pool of mud at her feet. "Oh, dear, a mud puddle."

"I'd lay down me coat," he said with playful sarcasm, "only—I don't want to get it dirty."

Instead of a display of gallantry, he grabbed her arm and jumped her over the mud. They landed on the other side, giggling.

"You know, Joseph," she said as they continued down the street. "You have far more charisma than any one person should ever be blessed with. Too bad you're such a conceited arse."

"Arse? Did I just hear the perfect, well-bred Shannon Christie herself utter a profanity? My, my, what is the world comin' to, I wonder?"

"My mother would die," Shannon admitted, but without much remorse. "It's the bad company I've been keeping."

They walked along in silence for a while, past the bakery that scented the air with the savory smell of freshly baked breads and rolls, past the butcher shop where legs of lamb and turkeys hung in the window along with a sign that read: GET YOUR THANKSGIVING BIRD HERE!

"Do you like me hat, Shannon? Tell me, for I want to know."

She could hear the vulnerability in his voice and it touched her. But she couldn't bring herself to give him the satisfaction of hearing that she thought he was terribly handsome . . . with or without a new hat.

"You're a regular Bostonian," she said. He seemed pleased with the diluted compliment. "Joseph," she added thoughtfully, "do you ever miss Ireland?"

"Yes and no. I'd like to see people's faces if they saw how successful I am. But goin' back to that poor, poor poverty: I shiver at the thought o' that." He looked down at her searchingly. "What about ye, Shannon? Yer soundin' homesick tonight."

"I miss my parents, even my dreadful mother. And my horses. And my servants. And my books. And my shoes. And my bathtub and my soaps and my brooch and my quilt and my music box."

"Perhaps you should go back."

"Never. In Ireland everything was done for me. I want to prove to myself that I'm independent."

"Well, yer certainly provin' that, lass, day by day."

She beamed with pride at his praise and decided to broach a subject she had been wanting to ask him about for a week. "You're going to this function on Sunday, I suppose?" she asked as they passed another hat shop boasting the prettiest bonnets she had seen for a long time. Oh, what she wouldn't give for any one of them. But first things first. Right now she couldn't even buy herself a coat.

"Aye," Joseph said. "I can't let the people down. Joseph Donelly will attend, yes indeed. Perhaps I'll even dance a jig or two."

He stopped and did a little two-step there on the sidewalk. Several passersby stopped to watch with delight.

Shannon tried to be embarrassed by his behavior. After all, he was behaving like a busker, a tinker man who did tricks at the hiring fairs in Ireland.

But she couldn't summon her indignation. Joseph Donelly might be a black-fingered bog boy, or more recently, a common brawler-for-hire in taverns. But at moments like these he was absolutely charming. There was no denying that.

"Come on," she said, laughing as she took his arm and led him on down the sidewalk. "You're impossible."

"'Twould do ye a world of good, lass, if ye were to cut loose once in a while."

"I don't have time for such nonsense right now. I have a dream of tomorrow to fulfill."

He nodded thoughtfully. "Dreams of tomorrow are important, to be sure. But ye mustn't lose yer todays on the way."

His words had the ring of truth, and Shannon filed them away to ponder them later.

"So will ye be goin' to the church social yerself, Shannon?" he asked.

"Absolutely not. You won't catch me at a Catholic Mass, mumbling Latin and such."

Joseph's smile faded and he looked down at her sadly. "Yer makin' yerself unhappy, lass, and for no reason at all. Come along, now. The party'd do ye good."

Stubbornly, Shannon shook her head. She stared down the street, at the people bustling in and out of the shops, collecting the necessities for their evening meal. So many people, and she didn't recognize one face. Worse yet, no one recognized hers.

"The picture I had of America," she said, "was nothing like this. I'm used to a little attention, but here I'm all but invisible."

Joseph wrapped his arm around her shoulders and gave her a hearty hug. "Ye don't have to be. Yer a pretty lass, and that counts for a lot, back home or here . . . or so I'm findin' out. How would ye like me to buy ye a brand-new fancy hat?"

His generosity made her smile in spite of herself. "I don't want any favors from you, Joseph, but thank you all the same."

"Is it certain ye are? 'Tis a wonder what a hat can do when yer feelin' gloomy-glum."

She laughed. He saw life so simply. A hat could cure all woes and soothe all sorrows.

Donning what she hoped was an indifferent face, she asked the question that was making her crazy. "Will Grace be there on Sunday?"

"I hope so," he said without even a decent interval of thinking it over. "I like Grace. She compliments me all the time."

"She's got an awfully large chest to be going to church. I've never seen such a disproportionate figure in all my life."

"Ah . . . I wouldn't fret about it too much. All chests are equal in the eyes of God. Besides, 'twould be difficult for her to leave it home," he added with a teasing grin, "but I'll be sure to tell her that ye thought she should have."

"You'll tell her no such thing."

To her irritation he threw back his head and laughed heartily. She couldn't help enjoying his spirit. But she also couldn't help wanting to slap that grin off his face.

And she couldn't help feeling jealous when she thought of her own well-rounded but hardly voluptuous chest. All bosoms might be equal in the sight of God, but it wasn't God's sight she was wondering about.

For some reason that she couldn't comprehend, she found herself wondering what Joseph Donelly thought and saw when he looked her way.

Eleven

As Joseph and Shannon approached the lodging house they saw an ominous black carriage sitting in front of the building. As they drew nearer to the closed-in coach the door opened and Mike Kelly climbed out along with a few of his thugs.

"There's my boy," Kelly shouted joyously, "looking fit and dandy! How are you, scrapper, you rascal of a holy terror?"

"Never better, Mike. Hello, lads!"

The thugs nodded and smiled. Kelly walked up to Joseph and began to spar with him.

"You're my pride and joy, Donelly." Mike led him toward the carriage. "Come, lad, Mr. Bourke would like to have a word with you."

Shannon, feeling completely ignored, watched as Kelly steered Joseph over to the carriage. The other coach door swung open, revealing the rotund figure of D'Arcy Bourke, who remained inside. His small porcine eyes raked Shannon thoroughly from head to toe, then he turned his attention to Joseph.

"So, Donelly," he said, "still undefeated, huh? How's

it feel having every eye upon you full of hate and envy?''

Joseph laughed and ducked his head at the flattery. "No one hates me, Mr. Bourke."

"Don't kid yourself. No man enjoys another man's success. There's fellas on every corner just dying to knock you down."

Joseph drew himself up an inch or two and puffed out his chest. "They're welcome to try if they've money in their purses."

Kelly and the thugs laughed, and Kelly slapped Joseph on the back. Shannon, tired of Joseph's arrogance and even more tired of being ignored, turned on her heel and marched into the lodging house, slamming the door behind her.

Bourke watched her and smacked his lips. "That was a long-legged piece of strawberry tart," he commented lasciviously.

"Mind yer mouth, Mr. Bourke," Joseph snapped. Bourke, Kelly, and the thugs were stunned into silence. No one spoke to D'Arcy Bourke in this manner and remained healthy.

"This *is* a whorehouse," Bourke observed, "am I wrong?''

Joseph still bristled. "That girl is a decent sort, and I'll be askin' ye to treat her so."

Bourke's round face flushed with anger and Mike Kelly cleared his throat nervously. "Now, Donelly," Mike said, "you don't talk to Mr. Bourke that way."

"Let it go, Kelly," Bourke said. "This is business, and the boy's our stock-in-trade. Now listen to me, lad. There's a man I want you to box. He's Italian, and I want you to spill his blood."

Joseph glanced quickly from Bourke to Kelly, alert with interest. "I'll box and I'll win." He lifted his chin so high as to threaten the position of the new hat on his head. "But ye boys don't own me, Mr. Bourke. No one owns Joseph Donelly. I box for meself alone."

—— 177 ——

He turned to walk away from the carriage, but Kelly hurried after him and dragged him aside. "What are you doing, lad, pissing against the wind? D'Arcy Bourke is a powerful important man in Boston—a man whose connections I need."

"I'm not gonna kiss the back of his trousers just cuz the rest of ye do."

Kelly leaned closer and lowered his voice to an ominous whisper. "You like your suit, Joseph? You like having a roof over your head? You like having the price of a beer in your pocket? Well, without me, you're nothing but an ignorant mick. Cross me and you'll never box again. I'll throw you in the street and every door you knock upon will slam in your face. Do you understand me, lad?"

"Aye," Joseph said grudgingly.

Kelly slapped him on the back and turned him around, displaying him for Bourke. "It's gonna be a grand fight, Mr. Bourke," he exclaimed. "A grand fight indeed!"

WHEN Joseph entered the lodging house, he couldn't believe what his eyes were seeing. Shannon sat playing band music on the piano, with Molly and several of the prostitutes. They were hanging all over the piano, complimenting her on her playing and laughing raucously.

"Shannon?" Joseph said, still not comprehending the vision before him.

She turned to him and flashed her brightest smile. "Hello, Joseph. I'm drunk."

Joseph shook his head in disbelief. "How can ye be drunk? Ye just left me side not minutes ago."

"She's working her way through a jigger of rye," Molly explained, pointing to the bottle that sat beside Shannon on the stool.

"And when I finish it," Shannon said with an affected slur, "I may or may not have another."

She grabbed the bottle, took a sip, and made a wry face. Then she swallowed the mouthful and with a shudder said, "Mmmm . . . good."

"Well, ye came to America to be modern," Joseph said philosophically. "'Tis glad I am that everything's workin' out for ye."

He turned and headed up the stairs. Shannon, having failed to shock him with her pseudo-drunken performance, downed another swig of whiskey, choked, and when she had caught her breath, marched up the stairs after him.

Once inside their room, Joseph hung his new hat carefully on a peg on the wall, the latest edition in what was becoming an impressive collection. Shannon quickly followed and stood uneasily on her feet, surveying him and his collection.

"You have changed, Mr. Donelly," she said.

"Improved, ye mean."

She cocked her head to one side thoughtfully. "No. Changed. Look at all those silly hats. You'll never get to Oklahoma. You've spent all your money."

Joseph laughed and raised one eyebrow, looking very self-secure and proud of himself. "At the rate I'm goin' now, they'll bring the land to me."

"You've turned into a snob."

"A snob?" He bristled. "Now isn't that the pot callin' the kettle black? Since when would ye be noticin' another snob . . . even if one walked up and bit yer arse?"

Shannon opened her mouth to eply, but another feminine voice called out from the street below. "Joseph!"

There was a delicate pause in their conversation before Joseph turned away from her. "Excuse me a minute . . . drunkard," he said as he walked over to the window and lifted the sash.

"Jooooooseph!" the woman's voice called again.

Joseph leaned out the window and saw Grace standing on the sidewalk below. She gave him a vigorous wave.

"Hello, Joseph," she called. "Will I be seeing you in church tomorrow morn?"

"Sounds divine and holy, Grace," he replied with equal enthusiasm. "We can share a pew, you and me."

"Toodle-loo."

"Same to ye."

He nearly fell out of the window waving good-bye as Grace threw him a kiss and sashayed away.

When he closed the window and turned back to the room, Shannon stood, glowering at him.

"That was . . . ah . . . Grace," he said.

"No kidding. I'm sure the entire neighborhood knows that was Grace."

He grinned, enjoying her obvious jealousy. "Grace is a friendly lass, she is. Loved by one and all."

"I don't doubt it. If she goes in the confession box, she'll never come out, the little tramp." She tossed her head in what was undoubtedly meant to be a haughty demonstration of her contempt, but in her delicate state she nearly lost her balance and fell sideways.

"Grace isn't a tramp," Joseph said indignantly. "She's a dancer in the burly-que."

"Ha. That isn't dancing. That's kicking her knickers up. And I suspect, if you asked her to, she'd kick her knickers *off* as well."

Joseph grinned and gazed into space as though fantasizing. "Maybe she would, indeed," he said thoughtfully.

"Has she?"

Again, he contemplated at length. "Hmm, let me see. I'm tryin' to remember."

"Think hard," she said sarcastically. "If there's any brain left in your head. Look at you. They're making a fool of you, the ward boss and his friends."

"They respect me," Joseph said, his temper rising. How dare she try to belittle his newly found prestige just because she was jealous of him.

"They do not. You're money in their pockets and nothing more, Joseph. You've let them pickle you like a piece of pork."

"Enough out of ye. Button yer lip, woman, now!"

Something inside him snapped, some hidden thought or fear that there might be an element of truth in her statement.

He stomped over to her and scooped her up in his arms.

"Joseph! What are you doing?" she cried as he carried her out the door.

She smacked him in the face with her palms and punched at his chest as he carted her down the hall, kicking and screaming.

"Put me down, Joseph!" she screamed. "Damn you, bog boy, put me down this minute!"

As they charged up to the bathroom door Molly and the girls came up the stairs and hovered nearby, listening.

"The sparks are flying tonight," Molly said with a smile.

He kicked the door to the bathroom open and carried her inside, where he unceremoniously dumped her into the tubful of water.

"*That*," he said with satisfaction, "is for callin' me a snob."

"You *are* a snob," she said, sputtering and fuming. "A Galway rock-picking boy you were, but now you've cabbaged your face and risen in the world and you think you're the cat's meow!" She struggled to rise out of the tub, but he pushed her back in.

"Tell me that ye like me hat," he demanded.

"What? You aren't *wearing* a hat."

He held her down while she splashed and thrashed. "Say ye like me hat! Why can't ye say ye like me hat? Why can't ye say ye like me suit? I've earned this. I've done well for meself. Why can't ye give this to me, woman?"

She paused in her struggles and lay there glaring at him for a long moment, then she lunged at him and tumbled out of the tub. Grabbing for the first thing she could lay hands on, she hurled a kettle at him. He ducked and it clattered against the wall.

He took a step toward her, but she seized a shaving mug and brush, threatening him with it. "Don't touch me, Joseph," she cried, brandishing the mug. "Go fondle that slut with the runaway tits, if she isn't stuffing her face with a pie, that is!"

Tossing the mug onto the floor, she stomped out of the bath. A dozen whores had gathered around the door, and they divided like the Red Sea to let her pass. Joseph hurried after her, skidding on the wet floor.

"'Tis jealous of me ye are, Shannon," he yelled as he ran after her. "I've made more money than ye and I've almost got me land, I have!"

"I can make money as fast as you," she called back. "Just watch me—'scrapper'!"

She charged into the room and slammed the door in Joseph's face. He rattled the lock, then swore and punched the wall.

"Why don't you just fook her and get it over with?" asked a sarcastic, teasing voice behind him. He whirled around to see Molly standing there, her hands on her hips, a smile on her face.

The prostitutes stood behind her, wearing the same knowing grins on their faces.

"She's me sister!" he cried.

Molly snorted. "Sure she is. And I'm your mother."

They all laughed heartily. Joseph blushed bright red . . . and hit the wall again.

LATER that evening, their tempers cooled for the moment from the earlier tempest, Shannon and Joseph were sharing a quiet hour in their room before Joseph had to leave for the social club.

He sat in the corner on a rickety chair, which he had found broken and discarded in an alley behind the social club. After gluing the thing back together, he had proudly brought it home and presented it to Shannon. At the moment she had been thrilled with his acquisition. It was only later, after she had thought it over, that she had considered how far she had sunk in the world to be ecstatic over a broken-down barroom chair, and she had refused to use it.

But night after night, before he left to go to the club for his fights, Joseph sat in that corner with a children's book in his hand, struggling to learn to read. In the beginning she had helped him a great deal, but now he preferred to labor alone.

Tonight as he read, she folded clothes on the bed. In a lighthearted mood, she hummed a little tune to herself.

He glanced up from the book and studied her for a moment, then said, "Shannon . . . about next Sunday . . . would ye consider goin' to that church social with me?"

She smiled briefly, as though flattered by the offer, then shook her head. "No, thank you. Like I said, it's a Catholic Mass. I'd feel terribly uncomfortable sitting through something like that. I wouldn't know what to say, or do, or when to do either."

He shrugged his shoulders. "Suit yerself. I just thought I'd ask."

He resumed his reading, scowling at the words, his forehead crinkled with concentration, his lips silently

— 183 —

forming the words. Shannon continued folding the clothes.

"Even if I wanted to go . . ." she said, "which I don't . . . I haven't a thing to wear."

He brightened. "Ye brought tons of dresses with ye from Ireland. At least it felt like tons when I was luggin' them around."

Shannon went over to one of her trunks and pulled out a green dress trimmed with ivory lace. Then she dropped the dress back into the trunk. "I can't wear them anymore," she said.

"Why not?"

She gave him a contemptuous look reserved for men who had no fashion sense at all. "They're out of style," she explained.

"Oh, I see. Well, we mustn't be seen in somethin' that isn't fashionable," he said, imitating her arrogant tone.

"Joseph."

"Aye?"

"Shut up."

ALL over the city the bells in the church tower pealed, calling the worshipers to Mass, and the larger portion of the Irish citizens of Boston responded. Many of them walked cautiously, taking each step with care, as though too vigorous a movement might cause their heads to burst apart at the seams. Saturday nights were important social events on the Irish calendar, and hearty celebrating with ale, dance, and song took its Sunday-morning toll with hangovers and sore feet.

Joseph and Shannon walked among the throng that filed down the street toward the church. Shannon clung nervously to Joseph's arm, dreading this experience. What if her mother were to see her now? A good Protestant girl attending a Catholic Mass.

Shannon wore the green dress she had brought

from Ireland. But the skirt was less full and the sleeves now were billowed and the shoulders padded. The recent stitching was hardly the work of a professional seamstress—quite the contrary. But it was fashionable . . . and that was all that counted.

Later, as they sat straight-backed in the pew, Shannon felt her shoulder pad slipping down to her chest. She reached inside her bodice and quickly shifted it back into position.

"I won't be taking Communion, Joseph," she whispered, leaning over toward him.

"I don't care what ye take," he replied.

Familiar faces filed by as the worshipers went forward to take the Holy Communion: Mike Kelly, little Dermody, Molly, Olive and Glenna and other factory workers, as well as men from the social club.

Shannon felt a rush of anger and jealousy as Grace strutted by and smiled down at Joseph. To Shannon's added fury, Joseph returned her bright smile.

"That was Grace," he informed her.

What did he think she was? Stupid? "I know. I recognize the chest."

Joseph slid out of the pew and walked up to the altar. Shannon watched as Grace deliberately knelt beside him.

"*Deus qui humanae substantiae . . .*" the priest intoned.

Checking her shoulder pads, Shannon left the pew and hurried up front. Without bothering to excuse herself, she wedged between them.

"Scoot, Grace," she said, nudging the woman aside. "You're taking up half the church."

The priest worked his way down the line with the sacrament. Shannon wondered if taking Communion under these circumstances would damn her eternal soul. But after a sideways glance at Grace's bosom, she decided that God would understand.

"Dignitatem mirabiliter . . ." The priest droned on, holding out the wafer.

Shannon grimaced and stuck out her tongue.

THE church banquet hall was filled with music, drink, food, and chaos. The solemnity of the Mass a thing of the past, the spirited Irish celebrated with nearly as much abandon as the night before. The musicians—an accordionist, piper, and a drummer who played the traditional Irish bodhran—provided the lively rhythm for the dancers and singers, while a bevy of women mixed bowl after bowl of fruit punch generously laced with imported Irish whiskey.

Shannon downed her third glass as she watched Joseph fill two more.

"Grace is really a good lass," he said. "She's always complimentin' me and cheerin' up me spirits when they drag down."

"I don't care how supportive she is of you, Joseph. Any woman who dances for a living is a tramp. And I can't understand why you're so friendly with her . . . or maybe I can."

"All I'm doing is taking her a glass of punch."

"I hope she drowns in it or spills it down her cleavage," Shannon muttered, already feeling a bit tipsy from the sweet, fruity drink.

Joseph chuckled softly as he walked away from Shannon. She was drinking that whiskey punch as though it were spring water and he could already picture himself carrying her back to their room, slung over his shoulder like a sack of Irish potatoes. Women . . . especially spoiled Protestant ones . . . never could hold their liquor.

He took the cup of punch in his hand to Grace, who batted her eyelashes at him flirtatiously and trailed her fingers over his as she took it from him. He glanced back at Shannon to see if she was watching. She was. With red eyes.

Molly's words about her being a girl who needed to be kissed crossed his mind. No . . . couldn't be. She might be a bit jealous from time to time, but that wasn't because she gave a fig about him. It was only because she was a vain, prissy little brat who couldn't stand it if every man's eyes weren't trained on her.

Though in this room, this afternoon, that wasn't much of a problem. He noticed with niggling irritation that most of the lads were eating her alive with their eyes. He had half a mind to black those eyes for them and put an end to their leering.

"Joseph . . . I asked if you're enjoying yourself," said a soft but impatient voice.

Joseph snapped himself back to attention. He had been ignoring Grace shamefully. "Oh . . . aye . . . a grand time. And yerself?"

"I already told you that I was a little bored with no one to dance with, but you seemed to have something . . . or someone . . . else on your mind."

Joseph glanced over at Shannon, who was downing another cup of punch while at least four lads descended on her with offers of yet another. "That's fine, Grace," he mumbled. "I'm glad yer enjoyin' yerself."

A big, heavy hand slapped him on the shoulder and he turned around to see Mike Kelly, smiling broadly around his ever-present cigar. "Come here, Donelly," he said. "Mr. Bourke has a bit of business to conduct with you."

"I've nothin' to say to that . . . gentleman," Joseph said, slurring the last word to show his contempt. "He insulted me sister the last time we spoke, and I haven't forgiven nor forgotten it just yet."

"Listen, lad, when a man has a sister who looks like yours, he's gotta expect that sort of thing from time to time. Besides, she's not exactly behaving like a shrinking violet over there."

He nodded toward Shannon, who was leaning

drunkenly on one fellow's shoulder while flirting shamelessly with another. Joseph tried not to notice, tried not to grit his teeth or clench his fists, or imagine how nice it would be to feed those two blokes their teeth.

"Joseph, my boy," Bourke called as they approached. "How nice to see you and that pretty sister of yours here today."

"Hmmph," Joseph returned. Kelly poked him in the ribs.

"I'm in the process of setting up that Irish/Italian fight for you," Bourke said. "I'll expect you to be in . . . excellent form." His eyes left Joseph and slowly traveled the length of Shannon's figure as his voice caressed those last words. "Yes, excellent form, indeed," he added lasciviously.

"I'm not fighting yer battles, ye tub o' lard!" Joseph said. "Go a few rounds yerself if ye choose, and land up on yer fat arse."

Bourke's little black eyes flared. Kelly grabbed Joseph by the arm and yanked him away into a corner. "What are you doing? I told you to never talk to him like that again. He's one of the most powerful men in Boston. He carries the south and the west, for heaven's sake."

"He can carry the north pole for all I care. No man *tells* Joseph Donelly to fight."

"I'm your bread and butter, lad," Kelly said, lowering his voice ominously. "Snap my fingers"—he demonstrated right under Joseph's nose—"and you'll never box again. I'll throw you in the street, and every one in this city will forget you ever lived."

Equally angry, Joseph opened his mouth to respond when a disturbance erupted in the middle of the room. Shouting, laughing, and clapping hands, a circle of rowdy observers had crowded around a particular performer who was invisible, buried in their midst. But Joseph had a sinking feeling.

He left Kelly and pushed his way through the throng. There she was, standing in the center of the circle, her skirts hiked up, dancing a jig and singing a song. "Mary, Mary, Mary Nell! Do you hear your wedding bell . . . ?"

Joseph charged out of the pack and grabbed her by the arm. "Shannon!" he yelled into her face. She looked at him with curiosity and vague recognition.

Then she snapped to attention and pulled her arm out of his grasp. "Don't you touch me, Joseph Donelly!" she said with inebriated indignation. "Go slobber over that whore with the overstuffed chest."

The room rocked with laughter and Joseph flushed bright red. "Stop yer mouths," he shouted, "all of ye!"

"Yes, you'd better watch yourselves," Shannon warned sarcastically. "This is Joseph Donelly himself, the boxing man known far and wide for knocking other men unconscious and getting his own face beaten to a pulp. Such a grand celebrity he is these days . . . admired by men and desired by women."

Her shoulder pads askew, her riotous curls flying wild around her face, she reeled away from Joseph, who followed after her. She stumbled, her foot striking a spittoon that rolled into Joseph's path. He promptly tripped over it, cursing her as he went down.

Once again the crowd roared with laughter.

"Will he love you, Mary Nell . . . ?" she sang. "Time and time alone will tell. . . ."

Joseph looked up from where he lay on the floor and saw her dancing for the wild-eyed men who had been leering before, but were now being treated to an eyeful.

Worst of all, D'Arcy Bourke had elbowed his way to the front of the crowd and was standing there with his belly sticking out, wetting his lips with his tongue.

Skirts lifted, ankles and a bit of lacy pantaloons showing, Shannon danced up to him and ran her fingers seductively through his scant hair.

Bourke, completely enchanted, reached into his pocket and pulled out a dollar, which he shoved down the front of her bodice.

Laughing, she danced away from him and over toward the dessert table. One misstep sent her sprawling, and in her drunken state recovery was impossible. She fell face-first into a custard pie, her petticoat over her head, her drawers exposed for the world to see.

Joseph's temper exploded. Enough was enough!

He bounded up off the floor, lifted her, and threw her, kicking and screaming, over his shoulder. Then he carried her from the room and out of the building into the street.

"Put me down. Put me down this minute!" she cried, pounding on his back with her fists. "You low-down, worthless, bog boy."

He did as she asked, unceremoniously dumping her in the gutter. "Ye've got a lot of nerve, callin' me names, girl!" he shouted back. "After the way ye showed yer hind end to everybody in that room! 'Tis ashamed I am of ye, ashamed I even know ye, let alone that I'm yer brother."

"You're *not* my brother, and don't you forget it. And as far as those men back there, I hope they *did* get an eyeful. It was nice being admired for a change. And that rich friend of Mr. Kelly's liked my dancing so much that he put a dollar in my shirt."

Joseph looked down at her and shook his head slowly. "And ye say *I'm* bad, talking to harmless little Grace."

"Grace is a slut."

"Oh, really?" Joseph raised one eyebrow and turned his back on her. As he walked away he said, "'Tis you who's lyin' in the gutter with the dollar in yer shirt."

Twelve

MOLLY sat on the porch of her lodging house in a rocking chair that was hidden in partial shadow. Many times in the evening she sat here, watching the passersby who were unaware of her presence, studying the peculiarities of human nature.

This was her private time, a pause in the busy day when most of her customers were at home, dining with their families. She and her girls could take a rest, knowing that within an hour or so the men would leave home, giving the excuse of going to the local pub for their evening pint, not mentioning that this would be by way of the brothel.

Molly preferred to think that her whorehouse provided harmless entertainment for lonely single men in need of female companionship. As long as she concentrated on that aspect of her work, she felt as though she were doing the world a service.

She didn't like to think about the married men or the lies they told their wives and children. That was the part of the business that goaded her conscience and drove her to sit out here on the porch, contemplating the changes she would like to make in her life.

In the midst of her reverie, her daydreams were interrupted by the sight of Joseph Donelly strolling down the street toward the house with a young woman clinging to his arm.

Right away Molly knew that he wasn't escorting Shannon. This woman was shorter and much fuller of figure, and she was hanging on to Joseph in a possessive way that Molly had never seen Shannon doing. Molly pulled further back into the shadows.

"Thank you for dinner, Joseph," the woman said, sidling even closer to him as they neared the front door. "I don't know *how* to thank you for the evening."

"Ah, yer company and fine conversation was payment enough, Grace," Joseph said as he bent down and placed a discreet peck on her cheek.

"Oh . . ." The woman was clearly disappointed. "Well, I thought you might invite me in for a while. You said that your sister would still be working at this hour . . . and I thought that perhaps you and I could . . . could . . . you know."

"Aye . . . well." Joseph cleared his throat. In the shadows Molly smiled. "'Tis going to be a rough night ahead for me, Grace. I think I'd best be gettin' some rest before I fight. But I thank ye for the offer, nevertheless."

"But Joseph, I—"

She reached for him, but he slid neatly out of her grasp. "Sorry, Grace, but I must be off now. See ye at the club this evenin'."

Without another word he disappeared inside the house, leaving the woman standing on the porch. Molly watched, feeling the girl's sadness. God knows, she had been rejected often enough herself.

"It isn't your fault, dear," she said.

Grace jumped and whirled around, peering into the darkness.

"Over here," she said, leaning into the light. "I'm Molly, and I run this house." She held out her hand.

The girl walked over to her and grasped her hand in a strong handshake. "I'm Grace, a friend of Joseph's. I dance at the burly-que where he fights."

"Yes, I remember seeing you one night when you brought him home after his first bout."

Grace sighed. "For all the good it did. I don't think he notices any of my kindnesses toward him."

"Ah, he notices. It's just that his eyes are focused elsewhere."

Grace's interest piqued. "Oh, and where is that?"

"On that girl he calls his sister."

"Do you mean she isn't his . . ." Grace puzzled for a moment. "Oh . . . I see. That makes sense. That's why she slammed the door in my face that night and why he . . ."

Molly watched with compassion as the realization dawned on Grace's face. "I'm sorry, dear. I hate to be the one to tell you, but you're better off knowing the truth than wasting your time barking up the wrong tree."

Molly glanced up and down the girl's ample figure with a practiced eye. "You know . . . if it's male companionship you're after, I could give you a job here. With a shape like yours you'd never be lonely and I can guarantee you'd make a lot more than you're earning dancing in the burly-que."

Grace smiled and shook her head sadly. "No, thank you. I may be a dancer, but I'm not a wh— I mean . . ." She flushed with embarrassment.

"That's all right, dear," Molly said, rescuing her. "I know exactly what you mean."

"I don't mean that I'm too good to . . . do it," Grace explained clumsily. "It's just that I don't believe in charging money for it."

"You needn't explain. Once I felt the same way, but

circumstances were such that I found myself . . . oh, well . . . it doesn't matter."

"I have to go now. Thank you for talking to me about Joseph, and thanks for the offer." Grace stepped down off the porch and started to walk away, then she paused and turned back to Molly. "You might be wrong . . . about Joseph and that girl, I mean. She might really be his sister, and he might just be very fond of her."

"I might be," Molly said. "If it gives you comfort, just forget everything I said."

The girl brightened slightly as she walked away, but Molly noticed with sadness that her shoulders stooped and her step had no bounce.

"Men and women are my business," she whispered to the departing figure. "And you'd better find another tree to bark up, 'cause those two are in love . . . even if they're too stupid to realize it yet."

"GET to work . . . get to work . . . get to work." The foreman strutted up and down the aisles between the lines of workers who were furiously plucking chicken after chicken, then flinging the carcasses aside. Occasionally he punctuated his orders with the jab of his pencil to their ribs or the sides of their necks.

Shannon tried to ignore him, but her fury grew by the minute. Who did he think he was anyway, abusing people like that? She recalled that her father, although he was master over hundreds of people, never wielded his authority in an unkind manner.

"Always be kind to your inferiors, dear," her mother had told her many times. "Benevolence is the mark of a true gentlewoman. Just because God has set us above our fellowman, we should never use our station to abuse others."

Well, obviously this foul-smelling, ignorant foreman's mother had never told him such things. And he certainly was no gentleman.

"He smells worse than usual today, did you notice?" Olive said, leaning over and whispering in her ear as they both reached for another chicken to pluck. "I don't think he's changed that sweaty shirt in the past month. Just look at those gray circles under his arms."

"True," Shannon replied. "I didn't think anyone would be able to pollute the air in a poultry factory, but he stinks more than the chickens."

On the other side of her Glenna snickered. "He asked me to go to a dance with him the other night . . . mentioned that if I didn't, I might not keep my job."

"I'd rather dance with this fellow here," Shannon said, stretching the wings on her chicken into a dance pose, "than with an old rooster like him."

All three girls collapsed with giggles, then quickly regained their composure when they saw that the "rooster" in question was glaring at them from half-way down the line.

"Huh, oh, we're in trouble now," Olive said, plucking with added vigor.

Shannon finished her chicken and reached up to hang it on the overhead hook to be conveyed on down the line. But a big, burly, hairy hand reached out and grabbed the bird.

"Just a minute," the foreman said, breathing down her neck, the stench of his sweat rancid in her nose. She tried to breathe through her mouth instead. "You call this chicken plucked?"

"No, I call him Frederick," she replied with a sarcastic grin, "and he's a marvelous dancer."

Olive snorted and covered her face, trying to hide her smile. Glenna developed an instant coughing fit.

The foreman ignored the remark and continued

with his speech. "I see one, two, three, four . . . at least five feathers left."

He thrust the chicken at her, shoving it into her breasts. The lecherous grin on his face was her undoing. She took the chicken from him. "Five feathers you say? This chicken has *five* feathers left on it. You're harassing me on account of *five* lousy feathers?"

"Go on. Get to work."

Splat! Shannon slapped him across the face with the limp carcass. The entire factory came to a halt and no one spoke a word as he and Shannon stood glaring at each other. Tense seconds ticked on.

Then she slapped him again, and again, backing him across the factory.

"You little mouse of a man!" she screamed in his face as she hit him with the clammy gray bird. "You've got nothing to hide behind but a pencil and 'Get to work!'"

"Get to work!" he screamed, his face scarlet, his temples pulsing.

"Yes, sir," she replied. "I certainly shall. And what is my work?" She took another step toward him. "To hit you with this chicken, that's my work."

The stunned workers came to life and began cheering her with every blow as she slapped him again and again. Finally he tumbled backward into a bin full of feathers and lay there sputtering and snorting, bits of fluff drifting down around him like giant snowflakes.

"I've had it!" Shannon cried as she threw her weapon into the bin beside him. She reached up and ripped the kerchief off her head. "I *quit* this bloody work!"

MOLLY was sitting at her desk, counting money, tallying the month's profits, when Joseph came hurrying down the stairs, a worried look on his face.

"Molly, Shannon didn't come home from work today. Have you seen her?"

Molly shook her head and stuck her pencil inside the mass of blond curls piled on her head. "No, I haven't, and I've been sitting right here for hours. I'm sure to have noticed if she'd come by."

The door banged open and Dermody came skidding into the house. "Joseph, it's you," he said, looking enormously relieved. He had the urgency about him of a man on an important mission.

"'Tis meself, indeed," Joseph replied. "And 'tis yerself besides. What an observant lad ye are."

Dermody hurried over and grabbed Joseph's arm, attempting to pull him toward the door. "Mike Kelly is looking for you. Tonight's the fight, the big fight! The place is crawling with I-tyes."

"Let go of me, Dermody." Joseph shooed the boy away. "Ye tell Mike Kelly I'll fight when I'm ready and not a minute sooner."

Dermody's eyes widened in fear and he shook his head. "I'll not tell Mike Kelly a thing like that. He'd hang my hide out to dry if I did. You have to come along and tell him yourself."

"I haven't the time for this, lad," Joseph said. "Now scramble. I'm off to look for Shannon."

Dermody brightened. "She's there."

"Where?"

"At the club. She's dancing in the burly-que."

"The burl—"

Joseph plowed Dermody aside and dashed out the door with the boy on his heels.

Molly pulled the pencil out of her hair . . . and smiled knowingly. Joseph Donelly was certainly the most devoted "brother" she had ever known.

Molly watched him from her window as he hurried down the street with the boy, and she enjoyed the

—— 197 ——

view of his broad shoulders and nicely rounded backside.

Shannon was a lucky girl, indeed.

THE moment Joseph charged through the doors of the social club, he could feel the anger and tension in the smoke-filled atmosphere. Irish and Italians, scores of them, milled about, shouting and shoving. Nationalist tensions ran as freely as the beer, and here, in this bloodletting sport of bare-fisted fighting, each faction hoped to prove its superiority over the other.

But Joseph gave no thought to the political and sociological factions represented in the crowd tonight. He only cared about one thing—finding Shannon.

"Hey, scrapper!" Mike Kelly shouted as he rushed toward him, a relieved and enthusiastic grin on his ruddy face. With the club packed and betting running rampant, Kelly couldn't be happier. Tonight's fight would make him an even richer man than he already was. And if there was anything Mike Kelly wanted, it was to be richer.

"Outta me way!" Joseph said, pushing Kelly aside. He plowed through the crowd and up to the stage.

Sure enough, there she was, wearing a skimpy little outfit, vivid makeup, brightly painted red fingernails, and spangles in her red hair. To his astonishment and horror she was bumping and grinding with the other three dancers, one of whom was Grace.

A group of Italians in the front tossed some coins onto the stage and Shannon fought Grace for them, scooping them up off the wooden floor and stashing them down her corset.

"Shannon! Stop this! Where's yer dignity, woman?" Joseph shouted up at her.

She paused in her dancing long enough to give him a scathing look down her nose. "Mind your business,

Joseph Donelly! You get your brain smashed in every night. What's the difference?"

"There's a world of difference. Boxing's a noble profession and this kind of work is for whores."

One of the dancing girls stomped across the stage and knelt down by Joseph. "I'm not a whore!" she said, slapping him soundly across the face. "*I'm* an actress!"

Before Joseph had a chance to reply, Mike Kelly grabbed him and pulled him away from the stage toward a crowd of Irishmen who were shouting his name, fists raised defiantly. Apparently the whiskey had been flowing just as freely as the nationalist tension in the club tonight.

In the middle of the throng Joseph saw D'Arcy Bourke, and his blood boiled even higher. He tried to hang back, resisting Kelly.

"Come on, Donelly," Mike said impatiently. "These I-tyes are tearing the place apart."

"Yeah," Bourke said, sucking on his cigar, "get in there and box. I've got a hundred dollars bet on you tonight."

"Then it's a good-bye kiss ye'd best be givin' it," Joseph said. "I'm not in the mood for fightin' this evenin'."

In a surge of bodies the Italians pushed their way over to Joseph, carrying their champion on their shoulders, shouting, "Carlo! Carlo! Carlo!"

The Irish responded by chanting Joseph's name.

With much pomp and circumstance the Italians set their boxer on a table right in front of Joseph. Sneering down at Joseph, he ripped off his shirt, showing an impressive display of muscle and sinew. His thighs, encased in red tights, bulged and his waist was encircled by a belt with golden stars and moons sewn on it.

He said something in Italian that Joseph didn't

understand, but his meaning didn't need translation. He was describing the damage he was intending to inflict on Joseph's body in just a few minutes.

He taunted Joseph, shadowboxing and spitting on the floor.

"Aye, yer fighter is ugly and has bad manners as well," Joseph muttered to the nearest Italians. "He's deservin' of a good thrashin'." He turned back to Bourke and Kelly. "But it won't be me that'll be givin' it to him. Not tonight."

Bourke studied him for a moment, then said, "I'll make it two hundred—and I'll split the winnings with you."

With a note of desperation Kelly added, "I'll match that offer."

Suddenly, like a calming wave, silence swept across the hall. It was a stunning proposal, unequaled in the history of the club. Joseph stood, his eyes darting from Bourke to Kelly, unable to believe what he had just heard. The music had stopped, and Shannon and the other dancers stared down from the stage.

"Two hundred," was whispered through the hushed ranks of Irish that lined one side of the hall and the Italians who filled the other.

The suspense gathered thicker and thicker until someone had to say something.

"Take it, Joseph." Shannon's voice filled the hall.

Joseph turned and looked up at her. "Why?"

"You'll have it. Horses, wagons, everything," she said, her voice brimming with excitement. "Don't let your stubborn pride destroy this chance. You've boxed for nickels gladly, but this will get us out of here."

"Us?"

"Well, you, I mean. Whatever."

All eyes turned to Joseph. He turned to face the Italian champion. The boxer jumped down from the table and the two men stood facing each other.

Little Dermody scrambled to chalk a scratch mark on the floor between them.

Joseph smiled but shook his head. "I have no wish to fight ye."

In less than a heartbeat Joseph fired the first blow and the second. Caught off guard by his ferocity, the Italian hesitated long enough for Joseph to land a short-arm blow to his neck, followed by punches to the ribs.

Recovering himself, the Italian returned with a sledgehammer right, and the crowd exploded with cheers and boos.

"This is a fight to the finish, gentlemen," Dermody shouted with his earsplitting shrill voice. "Side-betting is allowed and a knockdown terminates a round!"

Money flew back and forth. The Italian punched and jabbed, landing the occasional blow. But Joseph was better. He fought with a fury, raising a lump under the Italian's eye, a bad cut in his lip and numerous black bruises along his ribs, and belly.

Once the Italian struck near Joseph's belt and cries of "Foul!" echoed through the Irish sector. Kelly cautioned him, and the fight continued with Joseph clearly in control of the battle.

On the stage Shannon watched, wincing with every blow Joseph took, cheering with every one he threw. He glanced up at her for a moment, then newly inspired, he delivered a battery of brain-shaking jabs. The Italian fell to the floor. The crowd howled.

"End of round one!" Dermody yelled as he tied a green sash, the color of the Irish flag, around Joseph's waist.

"This is no contest, Kelly," Bourke said, puffing twice as fast as usual on his cigar. "Let's put up another hundred each."

Kelly swallowed hard but nodded his head. He hurried up to Joseph. "Keep it up, scrapper. Bourke's got me betting my way to the poorhouse. Damage the fella."

Joseph shook his head, wiped the sweat from his brow, and charged back into the battle.

"I smell victory, Kelly," Bourke said. His gaze slid over to the stage where Shannon watched, punching and kicking the air as Joseph battered his opponent. "I'd enjoy my success even better with a piece of strawberry tart." He pointed his thumb at Shannon. She saw the gesture and instinctively backed away.

Kelly walked up to the stage and crooked his finger, beckoning her closer. Reluctantly, she complied.

"Mr. Bourke would like a little company," he told her.

She glanced over at Bourke, at his potbelly and piggy little eyes. "I'm not especially attracted to Mr. Bourke," she said carefully.

Kelly reached up and grabbed her ankle. "You came to me for help," he said. "Let's show some manners here."

Joseph continued to fight, but watched from the corner of his eye as Kelly pulled Shannon down from the stage and pushed her toward Bourke.

Joseph was distracted for a second, long enough for the Italian to land a solid punch. The Irish gasped.

"Concentrate, lad!" Bourke yelled, his arm tightening around Shannon's waist. "I want to see that bastard with his teeth knocked out!"

Throwing one more haphazard punch at the Italian, Joseph turned his attention back to Shannon, who was being pulled down upon Bourke's knee. The Italian swung, Joseph ducked, and Joseph landed another blow to the man's left jaw.

Abandoning the fight, he turned from his opponent and stomped across the room toward Bourke.

"Just what the hell do ye think yer doin', Mr. Bourke?" He reached down and shoved Bourke's shoulder, nearly knocking both the rotund politician and Shannon off the wooden chair.

Bourke spat his cigar onto the floor. "Damn you, boy. Nobody does—"

Before Bourke could finish his statement, the Irish crowd grabbed Joseph, lifted him, and hurled him across the room. He was tossed on the stormy wave of arms and shoulders until he was thrown directly into the Italian's right cross.

The fight resumed with a vengeance as Joseph took another hard punch in the jaw. He reeled from the blow and tried to fight back, but the Italian had the advantage.

Again, and again, and again, he hit Joseph, returning the hard blows that Joseph had scored earlier. Until finally, unable to withstand the onslaught, Joseph fell to his knees. A second later he saw the floor coming up at him and it hit him, plunging him into a darkness filled with exploding stars.

Kelly ran over to Joseph, who was fighting to stay conscious. "Get up, scrapper!" he yelled, shaking him. "Get up!"

Shannon wriggled away from Bourke. When he grabbed her and tried to pull her back down on his lap, she kicked his shin. "Joseph! Joseph!" she yelled as she ran over to him.

Kelly grabbed her arm and jerked her away from Joseph. "You get back over to Mr. Bourke. Your brother's cost me enough embarrassment. See what you can salvage."

"Let me go!" she yelled, attempting to kick him, too.

Kelly shoved her in Gordon's direction. "Get this little tramp out of my way, Gordon," he ordered as he knelt, rolled Joseph over onto his back, and slapped his face. "Get up! You've got less than a minute to get back to the scratch line or it's over! Get up, I tell you!"

Joseph's lids fluttered open for a second, but then

his eyes rolled back in his head and he passed out again.

Cheering, the Italians hoisted their champion onto their shoulders. A large Italian flag was unfurled and waved above their heads in triumph.

Bourke limped over, his florid face red with fury. "What kind of club ya running here, Kelly?" he demanded. "The boxer won't box and the tart won't tart." Turning on his heel, he hobbled up to the bar. A nervous bartender scurried to fetch his drink.

Angry, Kelly beckoned two burly bouncers from opposite sides of the hall. "Get this loser out of my sight," he yelled, pointing to the prone Joseph, his voice thick with disgust. "Take him outside and throw him in a ditch."

One bouncer grabbed the front of Joseph's shirt, the other his feet, and they hauled him across the floor toward the door.

"Joseph!" Shannon struggled against Gordon, who held her with her arms behind her. "Don't! You leave him alone, you big bullies!"

Kelly spun around and slapped her hard across the face. The sound cracked across the room. "You shut your mouth, you little troublemaking tramp."

She glared at Kelly, her eyes blazing. Then she looked around the room at the other men standing there. None came to her defense. Most stared down at the floor. At the church social these men had called themselves Joseph's friends. Where were his friends now that he had lost a fight?

All around the club men began arguing as they attempted to collect their bets. Italians demanding payment, Irish paying or showing empty pockets.

A group of Italians climbed onto the stage and tore the Irish flag, bearing a harp, from its place of honor on the wall. Instantly a dozen fights erupted.

"You're all a bunch of pigs," Shannon screamed, her

voice lost in the cacophony as she tried to free herself from Gordon's grip. But his hands tightened around her wrists, cutting off the circulation of her hands. "Let go of me, you overpaid thug. I've had enough of this foul place. I'm leaving."

Kelly walked over to her and patted the cheek he had just slapped. "Not just yet, girl. Mr. Bourke requested the honor of your company . . ." He jabbed a thumb toward the figure at the bar. "And by God, as a favor to me, you're going to keep him company. Do you understand?"

"Never," she said.

"Don't be so sure, girl," Kelly said, his charisma melting and a cold-blooded anger taking its place. "Never's a long time."

Hours later Joseph lay, still watching the constellations that swirled through the blackness of his unconsciousness. As though from far away, he could hear a woman's voice calling to him. His name sounded sweet on her lips and he could hear her concern for him in her voice.

"Joseph, Joseph, wake up. Open your eyes for me, please."

Shannon. She was here beside him, calling him from death into the land of the living. He struggled to come back to her.

Blinking his eyes open, he tried to lift his head. "I've died . . ." He couldn't summon the strength to say more. Looking up at the woman, he thought her hair seemed more chestnut than copper in the faint light. Her face was little more than a blur as he squinted through swollen eyes.

She replied, "No, you haven't died, Joseph."

He looked around the dimly lit room and realized that he was lying on a bench in a small, cozy Irish pub.

"It's passed away I am, and me soul has ended up in the bosom of Ireland herself."

"No, it's late at night and you're in Boston."

Unconvinced, Joseph argued with her. "Me father died like this, passin' back and forth between the livin' and the dead. I believe 'tis himself drinkin' lager over there. Da? Is it you truly?"

The woman leaned over to dab his wounds with a damp cloth, her warm, full breasts pressing against his arm. "Lie quietly, Joseph."

"Whatever ye say, Shannon," he replied wearily, giving in to the delirium that muted the suffering in his body.

The woman's hand paused for a moment and Joseph closed his eyes. Then she continued to cleanse his wounds.

"Do you love me, Joseph?" she asked, her voice strangely full of pain.

Joseph smiled a crooked little half smile. "Love? How can ye call it love when all we do is fight? Every day, every night, sparks are flyin' between us, Shannon. I think we must hate each other."

She laid the cloth aside. "You're mistaken, Joseph. Those aren't the sparks of hate."

Leaning forward, Grace placed a kiss on his forehead and left him without another word.

Joseph allowed himself to slip back into darkness, but not so deeply as before. Rather than the void of unconsciousness, this blackness contained dreams. Dreams of a beautiful red-haired woman with soft, comforting hands. A woman who obviously cared for him, but was afraid to speak of her feelings.

Love. Hate. So many feelings. So many questions.

His mind couldn't take it in right now. For now, he simply wanted to sleep. Sleep and forget about the pain he was going to feel and the questions he would still have when he awoke.

A few hours before dawn Joseph stumbled groggily out of the pub. The fog rolled down the street and between the buildings, cold and gray, lending a dream-like quality to the scene. One lone figure walked the cobblestones—uneven footsteps that echoed through the heavy silence.

Joseph looked down the street and saw the lamp-lighter, high up on his stilts. The man was young, but his eyes were old, cynical, world-weary. His motions were stiff, without animation, reflecting only lethargy.

"What time is it that yer lightin' the lamps up there?" Joseph asked, feeling as though he were caught in a netherland of dreams and fancies.

The fellow chuckled. "It's a never-ending job. Takes all night to light the lamps and all day to snuff them out."

Joseph put a hand to his swollen face and grimaced at the pain. Only the aching of his jaw seemed real in this misty dreamscape, where fog floated in ghostly wisps, obscuring sight and muting all sounds.

He limped away, taking the long way home by way of the docks. Until tonight he had been fond of his job, too. Quite satisfied indeed. But then he had been a champion. Undefeated. The toast of the town.

Tonight he had been thrown into a gutter, tossed out like rotten garbage.

So much for fame and fortune.

As he wandered along the dark harbor he passed the homeless families huddled by fires, trying to warm themselves on the chilly autumn night. Walking by them, he overheard fragments of their conversations.

". . . Oklahoma . . . land there is given free . . ." one man said.

"Have to pay your own expenses, though. . ."

"I don't believe it's true. It's too good. It can't be true."

Abruptly, Joseph turned a corner and saw a sight that made his blood freeze in his veins. A man stood there in the dim light, a man dressed all in black. Joseph felt as though he had walked into a nightmare.

Stephen Chase. There was no mistaking that tall, slender figure, that black cape, and the arrogant stance. It was his old enemy, here in America, in the flesh.

"What about you, mister?" Stephen asked him, turning from a knot of people whom he had been speaking to.

Joseph stood, stunned, unable to speak. Finally he found his voice. "Me?"

"Have *you* seen her?" Chase asked impatiently. "She's about your age. Shannon Christie is her name."

At first Joseph was astonished that Chase didn't recognize him. Then he realized that his wounds provided a welcome disguise.

"I said, have you seen her?" Chase repeated.

Joseph shook his head. "I don't think so. I don't know."

"Are you sure? I've combed the city. If you hear of her, her family is in Jefferson Court, number six."

"I told ye, I don't know," Joseph said. The tone of his voice—a distinct note of aggravation—gave him away. He watched his enemy's face and knew the instant he recognized him.

"You!" Chase shouted.

Joseph turned and fled. Weaving his way through the camp, he leaped over bonfires, sending sparks into the sky, scattering ashes and coals everywhere.

Stephen raced after him, past barges, knocking over barrels, stumbling through the darkness. The race continued through the North End tenement streets and through the graveyard at Copp's Hill, and through trash heaped in alleys.

Joseph expected to be shot at any moment, to feel

the sear of hot lead ripping through his body. And all the time, he kept thinking, *If Chase is here in Boston, it's all over, it's all lost.* His time with Shannon was done. She would be his no longer.

He didn't have time to wonder about the strange sadness that flowed over him even as he ran for his life through the darkness. He would think about it later . . . if he survived.

Pouring every ounce of his energy into a final burst, he was able to pull ahead of Chase, far enough ahead to have time to hide. He climbed up a tenement fire escape and crouched down by the wall.

In a few seconds Chase raced into the alley. He stopped right below Joseph's fire escape and looked everywhere. Once he even looked straight up, as though he were peering directly into Joseph's eyes. Joseph didn't dare to breathe.

"Give her back!" Chase shouted, his voice echoing through the alley. "I've come with her mother and father. She belongs to her own class, do you not understand? You can't climb to her station. You're lowborn, boy. You can only bring her down."

He paused as though waiting for an answer. Joseph said nothing as the man's words cut into him like a cold knife.

"Hand her back to her own kind," Chase continued. "We can keep her and care for her. Otherwise you'll destroy her life . . . if you haven't done so by now."

Chase waited, listening, looking. Finally he turned and left the alley, his boots echoing on the cobblestones until the sound disappeared in the distance.

Joseph sat for a while, crouched against the wall, trying to gather himself back together. He felt fragmented, blown apart by the words he had just heard.

He thought of Shannon, dancing on that infernal stage in that bloody awful costume, her beauty exposed for all those rough men. He thought of her on Bourke's lap, that slimy creature putting his arms around her, pulling her against him.

Shannon! Bourke!

She was still in the burly-que, and God only knew what was happening to her. He leaped from the fire escape and began running down the streets toward the club. With only the thought of rescuing her in his mind, Joseph forgot about the pain in his body.

For the moment he even forgot Stephen Chase.

Thirteen

THE crowd at the social club had thinned out. Only the diehards sat, watching a tired comic as he pulled flowers from his hat, scarves from his ears, and chased the dancing girls around the stage, trying to pinch their shapely derrieres.

Shannon stood beside Mike Kelly's table, her hands on her hips in what she hoped like hell was a defiant, confident stance.

"Just pay me what you owe me, Mr. Kelly, and I'll go home and leave you alone," she said.

"You haven't earned it yet," Kelly said, without even looking up from his ledger.

Fear gripped Shannon. She had danced, hadn't she? She had debased herself by putting on this atrocious garb, which made her look like a prostitute, and had strutted her feminine charms for all to see, just as he had asked.

What more could he want?

She didn't dare consider the implications.

"I need my money, Mr. Kelly," she said, hoping that a bit of female pleading might soften his heart. "Please."

"Then earn it, tart," he said.

"I'm not a—" She bit her tongue. Now was no time to give free rein to her temper. The last time she had done that she had lost her job. "I danced for you. What is it you want from me?"

He looked up at her, his eyes blank, unreadable. "You told me you needed fast money," he said. "Well, it's time you worked for it. Mr. Bourke is waiting for you behind the stage."

Shannon felt her knees go weak. She could still remember Bourke's arms around her waist, his fat, pudgy hands trying to take liberties as she slapped them away. Her stomach did a somersault in her belly.

"I'm afraid that Mr. Bourke isn't my type," she said. "I've told you already that I don't wish to—"

"Men!" Kelly snapped his fingers, and two burly thugs appeared instantly.

Shannon didn't have to think twice to know whom she had rather wrestle with . . . these two or Bourke. If all else failed, maybe she could outrun the portly politician.

"All right," she said. "I'm going . . . I'm going."

Joseph rushed into the social club and cast frantic glances in every direction, searching for that familiar pretty face, for a woman with hair as fiery as her temper. But the only occupants of the hall were Mike Kelly, Gordon, and a few other men who were counting their losses at Kelly's table.

"Where is she?" Joseph demanded.

Kelly looked up from his money counting and, when he saw Joseph, slammed his fist down on the table. "You're banned from this place. Get the hell out of here!"

Joseph ignored him and ran up to the empty stage. "Shannon!" he yelled. "Shannon, are ye here, lass? Come out this minute if ye are!"

Kelly snapped his fingers and his men attacked. Joseph socked Gordon, knocking his splint half off. The man howled with pain as he grabbed his nose. The other men, seeing Gordon's agony, backed off temporarily.

"Shannon!" Joseph shouted again.

This time he heard the welcome response. "Joseph!"

He leaped up onto the stage, trying to peer into the dark wings. "Shannon? Where are ye, girl?"

"Joseph, help me. I'm back here behind—"

He heard her scream, but the sound was muffled, as though someone was holding his hand over her mouth. Rushing behind the stage sets, Joseph had to dodge the two thugs who had followed him on Kelly's orders.

In the dimness backstage Joseph could barely make out two struggling figures stretched across an old sofa. He ran toward them and saw that Bourke had Shannon pinned beneath him.

Even through rage-blinded eyes, Joseph could see that some of her clothing was torn open. She was fighting him with her fists and trying to kick at him with her feet, but he was a large and heavy man and he had her thoroughly pinned.

With a roar of fury Joseph charged toward them, aching to feel that animal's soft, fleshy face break beneath his fist. But Bourke reached inside his jacket and pulled out a pistol, which he pointed directly at Joseph's face.

"Stop where you are, lad," Bourke said with deadly coldness, "or I'll shoot you dead."

Joseph grinned, but the smile didn't reach his eyes. "This close to election?" he asked sarcastically. "Just think how it would look on the front of the news sheets."

After taking three more steps toward Bourke, Joseph reached out with lightning speed and swiped the gun from his hand.

He glanced down and saw that some of the fear in Shannon's eyes instantly abated. "Come along, lass," he said, trying not to sound too self-satisfied. Undoubtedly it had been a long time since she had been rescued from the clutches of shame and death so gallantly.

"Wait, Joseph," she said, climbing out from under Bourke. "I have a little gift for Mr. Bourke."

With that she slammed her knee full force into Bourke's groin. Even Joseph cringed as the man curled into a tight, groaning ball and fell off the sofa onto the floor, clutching his crotch with both hands.

From behind them Kelly and the two thugs scrambled around the set. Joseph waved the gun . . . with a great deal more confidence than the last time he had held a firearm.

"Hold it right there, gentlemen," he said. Grabbing Shannon by the hand, he pulled her with him as they backed away from Kelly's entourage and made their way off the stage and toward the back door. "Ye must excuse us," he called as they exited the hall, "but we must be off and runnin'."

They ducked out the door and raced down the dark alley, Joseph dragging her by the hand, Shannon stumbling along on flimsy heels. Choosing a side street, they wove a zigzag path through the neighborhood, hoping to lose any pursuers who might be following.

Finally, not hearing any footsteps behind them, Joseph stopped and pulled Shannon into a dark alcove. "We can't be stayin' in Boston any longer, Shannon," he said breathlessly. "'Tisn't safe now."

Shannon clung tightly to his hand and he could feel her body trembling against his as they huddled together. "Then where can we go?"

Joseph thought long and hard before he spoke. "Ye could return to yer family, lass. I'm sure they'd welcome ye with open arms."

"No! I'm not going back to Ireland. I'm not giving up on my dream."

Joseph reached out and wrapped his arms around her, drawing her closer and trying to give her some of his body's heat. "Are ye sure, Shannon? Are ye absolutely certain of that?"

"Absolutely sure. I'd never forgive myself if I were to quit now."

Her declaration soothed his troubled conscience . . . but not much. Stephen Chase's words kept echoing through his mind. Truly she wasn't his kind. They were worlds apart. And since he had come into her life, she had suffered nothing but trouble and danger.

But he couldn't bring himself to tell her that her family was right here in Boston. He opened his mouth to speak the words, but they wouldn't come out.

"Then it seems our only choice is to travel west and put our money together," he said matter-of-factly.

"But I'll be nothing but a burden to you out in the wilderness."

He laughed. "That's probably true."

She pulled away and looked up at him through her tears. "How can you be so mean to me when I'm sobbing in your arms?"

He patted her hair, smiling down at her with emotion and affection. "We're cast away again, Shannon. It seems we're meant to be together—I mean, to have to put up with each other. So it's partners we are, all the way."

"*My* portion isn't very much, I'm afraid," she admitted, staring down at the ground.

"Ah . . . I wouldn't be so ashamed, if I were you," he said, hugging her closer. "Eighteen dollars is a tidy little sum."

Abruptly she pulled away from him. "Joseph! You snooped!"

"And ye didn't do a bit o' snoopin' yerself?"

She hesitated, then smiled broadly. "You had sixty-seven dollars and fifty cents at five this afternoon."

They looked at each other with arithmetic in their eyes. They arrived at the total at the same moment.

"It's enough," Shannon said.

"Let's make tracks."

PULLING Shannon after him, Joseph raced all the way to the lodging house. When they entered the building, they nearly ran Molly down in the hallway.

"Good heavens," she exclaimed, regaining her balance by grasping a nearby door frame. "The two of you are running as though your backsides were on fire."

"Not on fire, but in a sling if we don't move sharpish," Joseph said. He thrust the gun into Molly's hand. "Here, Molly, guard the door! Don't let anybody in!"

Leaving the stunned madam standing in the hall with the gun in her hand, they scrambled into their room and slammed the door behind them.

Frantically, they glanced around the room with no idea of where to start.

Shannon turned to Joseph, fear and confusion in her eyes. This had been a difficult night for her, and although she had been rescued from that fate worse than death and she was terribly grateful, the night wasn't over yet.

Joseph pulled the crock out from under the bed and dumped it on the bed. She bent over and shook coins out of her corset. He stared at her, his green eyes wide with astonishment and appreciation.

"At this point I'm beyond modesty," she said without emotion.

The door opened and they both jumped. But it was only Molly. "Are you going to Oklahoma?" she asked.

"The door, Molly," Joseph said with a nod toward the open doorway. She turned and closed it.

"One horse," she said, "one buggy, tackling, and supplies: ninety-four dollars and ninety-five cents."

"Thank you, Molly," Shannon said with a respectful tone.

Molly nodded and, her information dispensed, left the room.

Shannon turned to Joseph. "We've got easily that much, Joseph."

"Then let's pack up and go."

They began to grab their clothing and meager belongings and throw them into Shannon's luggage. Joseph's clothes he rolled into his blanket.

Joseph paused in his packing and watched Shannon for a moment. Her face was flushed with excitement, her beautiful locks hanging in her face and swirling unbound around her shoulders. She still wore the skimy outfit from the burly-que, which showed off her trim figure to perfection.

"Will we be able to stand each other, do ye think?" he asked with a smile.

She looked up from her suitcase and studied him briefly. "Nope," she replied.

They both laughed and resumed their packing.

DOWNSTAIRS, Molly stood guard. Against whom or what she had no idea. The prostitutes leaned on doorjambs and sprawled across the parlor furniture, looking bored with the ordeal. In this house a few raised emotions and anticipation of trouble were nothing new. They did little more than quirk an eyebrow when Mike Kelly and Gordon and at least eight thugs arrived and charged through the door.

Molly lifted the gun and pointed it at the throng that

had invaded her house. "Stop right there, Mike," she said. "Just what is this anyway? A raid? If it is, you'll have to drag at least a dozen of your friends out of here."

"It isn't my friends that I'm after tonight, Molly," he said, "and I think you know it. Now, move aside before you get yourself hurt."

Molly aimed the gun directly at him. "I said, wait right there."

Mike took a step toward her. "If you're going to shoot somebody, Molly," he said, "shoot me. I'm the one who can shut your house down."

With that he swatted the gun out of her hand. It fell to the floor with a clatter.

"Come on, boys," he said, waving them on. "We've got some housecleaning to do."

Joseph glanced quickly around the room. Shannon was throwing the last of her things into a trunk. In minutes they would be on their way. It appeared they were to make a clean escape after all.

But at that moment the door crashed open and a wave of men flooded in, led by Kelly.

"Grab them," he ordered.

Two of the thugs nabbed Joseph while two others took hold of Shannon's arms. Joseph tried to free himself, but they held him fast. The others began to rip their luggage apart.

"No!" Shannon screamed as her lingerie and personal items were tumbled to the floor.

"Shut up, tart," Kelly said, "or I'll slap you like I did earlier tonight."

Slap her? He had already hit her once tonight? Joseph's fury soared. This man had pretended to be his friend, then he had struck his woman when his back was turned.

For the briefest moment Joseph considered why he

had thought of Shannon as his. What a foolish thought. One that might bear reconsideration at a more convenient time.

As the club toughs continued to shred their belongings, Kelly walked over to the bed and scooped up the coins and bills.

"Oh, please," Shannon said, "not our money. We'll go away. We'll do anything you say, but you can't take our savings from us. We've worked so terribly hard for every cent and—"

"There isn't a penny here that didn't originate with me," Kelly said. He walked back to the door and yelled down the hall, "Molly Kay! Come here this minute, girl."

Molly appeared instantly as though she had been standing right outside.

"These two are banished," he said. "Shelter them even for a night and I'll shut this whorehouse down. Do you understand?"

Molly looked from Shannon to Joseph with sad eyes. She hung her head. "Yes, Mike. I'm sorry, children."

On Kelly's orders his men dragged both of them down the stairs and out into the street. They were tossed onto the sidewalk, both of them landing on their backsides.

Angrily Joseph jumped to his feet, fists swinging, but Gordon and the others pinned his arms behind him.

"You're done, scrapper," Kelly told him, his face close to his. Joseph resisted the urge to spit at him. They were in enough trouble already. "You won't work here, box here, nothing here," Kelly continued. "It's a shame, to be sure, but I saw it coming the day you walked in off the boat."

Joseph was still struggling, but Kelly's words caught his attention. "Ye saw it then? How?"

"The girl." Kelly nodded toward Shannon, who lay on the ground, tears running down her pretty face, but her chin held high as usual. "She had 'Protestant landowner' written in her eyes. Her kind and ours never mingle, lad. It's from their tyranny we've all escaped."

Gordon released Joseph and shoved him down onto the ground beside Shannon. Then Kelly and his men turned around and walked away without a backward glance. Joseph watched them go, along with his boxing career, which had been full of glory but all too short, along with his dreams of grandeur and hopes for tomorrow. He wanted to shake a fist at heaven, but it would do no good; what was gone was gone.

And *everything* was gone.

He looked over at Shannon and saw that she was gently sobbing, her hands over her face.

Reaching out, he pulled her hands away and looked into her tear-swollen eyes. "Ah, girl, please don't cry. Me heart is heavy enough without seein' yer tears."

"They took everything. All the money we worked so hard for. Even our clothes. We have even less now than when we landed here. We have absolutely nothing in the world."

He put his arms around her and rocked her, trying to quiet the frightened child within her as well as the one within himself. In all his living life Joseph couldn't remember feeling such despair. He knew he should be strong for Shannon. "Ye still have yer pretty red hair," he said, "and I still have me wit and charm."

His attempt at humor fell short of his intention. Shannon wept even harder. "A lot of good red hair and charm will do us," she said through her sobs.

He patted her head and placed a discreet kiss on the top of her hair. "We'll be all right, Shannon, truly we will," he said. He only wished he could believe his own words.

IN the lace-curtain district of Boston, where the wealthy Irish settled, hansom carriages rolled by the dignified brownstone town houses, driven by coachmen decked out in colorful livery, drawn by high-blooded horses with plumed headgear. A freshly fallen blanket of snow covered the buildings and trees with glistening white radiance, making even the older, drabber architecture look pristine.

Inside one of these town houses on Jefferson Court, Nora Christie removed her hat, gloves, and muffler, stamping the snow from her kidskin boots onto the foyer rug.

"Bring in the groceries, Danty, if you can manage it . . . you imbecile," she called to the coachman, who still sat on the driver's bench in the carriage below.

"Whatever ye say, Mrs. Christie," the old man muttered under his breath.

"What was that?"

"I said, I'll bring them in straightaway."

"Good." Closing the door, she turned and handed her coat to the maid, who quickly disappeared with it, then returned with a delicate lace shawl.

Nora walked into the library and found her husband shoving a bottle of gin beneath some logs in the fireplace. Looking far too nonchalant, he strolled over to his wing-back chair and sat down. He propped his feet on a stool and picked up the copy of the *Police Gazette* from the floor, where he had dropped it when he had heard her enter the room. With his left hand he attempted to hide the cover of the paper, which bore an alluring picture of a young woman wearing only a corset and knickers.

"Polluting your mind and your body, I see," she said as she strolled over to her own chair and picked up her knitting.

"Just taking a bit of relaxation," he replied indignantly. "Can't a man escape his troubles in the bosom of his own home."

"And what troubles are you trying to escape, Daniel?" Her needles began to click together furiously. "I hadn't noticed you taking on any particular challenges lately."

"More than you might think, dear," he said with a wounded tone. "Stephen and I were out all morning, combing the harbor for Shannon."

The needles stopped clicking for a moment. "Any luck?"

"None at all."

"Oh." She resumed her knitting, a frown furrowing her brow, which had once been unlined, but the creases appeared deeper ea h day.

"And how about you?" he asked, trying to sound cheery. "Did you have an adventure while you were out?"

"Not if you mean queuing up behind half the population for a pork chop the size of a shilling. I question the efficiency of city life. In the country you simply step out the door and kill an entire pig."

"You mean have someone kill it for you," he reminded her.

"Of course that's the real issue. What I miss most about Ireland is I don't have the proper staff."

At that moment Danty entered the front door and tramped down the hall, groceries piled high in his arms. As he passed the library door he slipped and fell, scattering the supplies across the floor.

"Snow," he mumbled, explaining his fall.

"Never mind the groceries," she told him. "It's chilly in here. Light the fire."

Daniel cast a furtive glance toward the fireplace, but there was nothing to be done for it. To his dismay

Danty promptly went to work, piling more wood into the fireplace, further burying the hidden drink.

"Nora, I have a question to ask you to do with money," he said, trying to hide his distress with the casual question.

"Having to do with money?"

"Yes."

"What is it?"

"Do we have any?"

She sighed and shook her head. "Yes."

"Ah, good. I was getting worried."

"Don't worry, Daniel," she said, replacing her yarn in its basket. "I'm taking care of you, just as I always have. But it's a tiresome job, to say the least. I'm going upstairs for a nap."

Daniel brightened as she walked out of the room. When she had disappeared up the stairs, he hurried over to Danty, who was picking up the groceries in the hall.

"Did you get it?" he whispered with a glance up the empty stairs where Nora had retired.

Danty reached inside his jacket and pulled out a bottle of clear liquid. "I surely did, yer honor, though it wasn't easy. Ballyshannon poteen, just smuggled in."

Christie took the bottle and pressed it to his lips affectionately. "Ah, Danty Duff. Fortune smiled upon us both the night you burned my house and sacrificed your freedom. Come along and share the bounty with me, old lad."

They tiptoed into the library and up to an oak cabinet. Daniel unlocked it and reached into the depths, extracting two glasses, which he promptly filled.

"Ye say"—Danty swigged the fluid then wiped his mouth with the back of his hand—"she knows ye drink. I've never grasped the arrangement ye have with yer missus."

"Neither do I, Danty, neither do I. And we should never try. Marriage is the most intricately complicated idiosyncratic concept God ever concocted. It's a mystery and should stay that way."

They lifted their glasses and bolted down the liquor, which momentarily took their breath away. Eagerly Daniel poured seconds. But before they could drink it, the door opened.

Daniel shoved the glasses and bottle back into the cupboard and turned around to see that it was Stephen. The young man walked into the library and Daniel noted that he looked more tired than usual. Dark circles ringed his eyes and his pallid complexion seemed sickly white.

"Stephen, any adventures?" Daniel asked. "Any word on her?"

Daniel knew better than to expect an affirmative answer to either question. No one ever had any adventures these days, it seemed, even in America. And they had been searching for Shannon for weeks without success. Why should today be any different?

Stephen drew a deep breath. "I have news of Shannon."

Daniel's heart did a double thump. He surveyed the young man's downcast eyes. "Not good news, I see." *Please, God*, he thought, *don't let it be the worst news. I couldn't bear it*.

"She was living, I'm afraid, in a house of ill repute. I'm so sorry to have to tell you that, your honor. I can only imagine what pain it must bring you."

"With the boy?" Both Daniel and Stephen turned to see that it was Nora who had spoken. She stood on the stairs, her hands clasped tightly before her, her face whiter than Stephen's.

"Yes, with the boy," Stephen said.

—— 224 ——

"And are they still there?" Nora asked, lifting her chin as though steeling herself for more painful information.

"I'm sorry, no. I hate to bring further sadness to you, Mrs. Christie, but all who knew them say they've disappeared. Some believe they're here in Boston. But no one really knows. . . ." His voice trailed away as he stood there, staring down at the highly polished wooden floor.

"A house of ill repute," Nora murmured. "My Shannon in a place like that. The boy should be horsewhipped, then hanged. Even that would be too good for him."

"Dear." Daniel walked up the stairs and took her hand. "You must have faith in her, in the standards and integrity which you taught her all those years. I don't believe that our Shannon would do anything that would—"

"Oh, shut up, Daniel," she said, throwing his hand aside. "You don't know what she's done and neither do I. There's no telling what a young girl would have to do in this city just to stay alive."

Nora turned and started back up the stairs. "But I'll tell you one thing. It's that bog boy's fault, and I swear he will die for what he's done to my baby."

Daniel and Stephen stared after her, sadness and defeat showing on both their faces. "She's been through hell and back, and she still holds her head high," Daniel said with admiration.

"Your wife is a fine lady," Stephen agreed. "And I swear to you now, it will be my privilege and my honor to execute that miserable bastard who caused her this sorrow. I've made it my life's mission to find your daughter and bring her back alive and safe . . . right after I put Donelly in his grave."

SHANNON walked by Joseph's side along the street that ran with mud and icy rain. Well-dressed people in

— 225 —

sturdy carriages rode by, splashing even more mud on them. Other folk hurried by, sheltered by large umbrellas, shopping packages tucked under their arms.

Shannon couldn't help feeling bitter, remembering her family's three magnificent carriages and the fine coats and parasols she once owned. And it seemed a lifetime ago since she had enjoyed the frivolity of going shopping.

The city of Boston didn't seem so friendly or exciting anymore since they had been thrown into the street. Where had the warm summer days gone? she wondered. And why, with winter upon them, had fate been so cruel as to cast them out into the wind and weather? Then she reminded herself that fate hadn't cast them out; Mike Kelly and his henchmen had. And she hated them for it.

Thinking of how those thugs had robbed them of their hard-earned pennies, she conjured all sorts of gruesome fantasies about how she would murder them, given a chance. The fury that blazed inside her brought her warmth, so she fanned the flames with even more memories and more fantasies.

They rounded a corner and saw a crew of men and women excavating a ditch. Standing in mud up to their knees, they heaved one shovelful after another out of the ditch while a supervisor, wearing a heavy coat and carrying an umbrella, barked orders to them.

"Get a move on there! We gotta dig this mud before it freezes again. Get a move on, I say!"

As they walked by, the man noticed Joseph and shouted, "Hey, you. We need strong men here. Sign up and grab a shovel. The pay is good."

Without hesitation Joseph turned to Shannon. "Find shelter out of the rain, lass. I'm intendin' to buy our supper tonight."

She walked over to huddle in a doorway while he hurried back to the supervisor. "I'm yer man," he told him with exaggerated confidence. He grabbed a shovel, jumped down into the ditch, and began shoveling away with twice the energy of any man or woman there.

"All right," the supervisor said, "but I need your name." He hauled a ledger out from under his coat.

Joseph knew it was the dreaded doomsday list and he knew that Mike Kelly had scratched him off it long ago. "Me name doesn't matter," he said, continuing to shovel. "I'm diggin' and that's enough."

"Dig all you like. But you don't get paid if you're not on the doomsday list."

"But I'll do more work for ye than any ten of these men, just wait and see if I don't."

The supervisor shrugged. "Talk to the ward boss. There's nothing *I* can do."

Joseph lowered his voice and glanced around surreptitiously. "I'll do the work of ten men . . . for half the pay."

The supervisor considered his proposition carefully. He, too, looked around to see if anyone was listening. The other workers seemed absorbed in their own cold, wet misery.

"Carry on," the supervisor said as he walked away.

Joseph resumed his shoveling and Shannon crouched in the doorway, watching. Never in her life had she seen a man work the way he did, digging, lifting heavy shovelfuls of mud and rock, heaving larger rocks out by hand. Joseph was working for their dinner. More importantly, he was working for *her* dinner.

He owed her nothing. He had paid his debt for his passage long ago. This he was doing because he was her friend and because he cared about her.

Shannon decided, standing there in her warm, dry shelter, that she cared too much for him to allow him to do it alone.

Determinedly, she left the doorway and hurried over to the ditch. Grabbing a shovel, she jumped down beside him.

"Shannon?" he cried when he saw her. "What are ye doin'? Ye'll get yer feet wet."

She looked down at the mud, which was oozing around her shins. "Too late," she said. Then she laughed and began to dig.

"No, Shannon," he protested. "Ye can't do this work. Yer a fine lady, and ladies can't dig a ditch."

Her shovel bit into the muck and she struggled to lift her first shovelful. "Oh, yeah," she said, gritting her teeth with the effort to keep them from chattering. "Just watch me."

Joseph watched her for a moment as she tackled the muck. His eyes shone with tears of guilt, guilt for what his association with her had wrought in her life. But those green eyes also glimmered with admiration. Covered with mud, performing the manual labor of a commoner, she had never appeared more noble to him.

DOWN by the docks, those unfortunate enough to have been caught by the winter cold without a roof over their heads huddled around makeshift fires beneath the bridge, trying to absorb a bit of warmth. Among the homeless vagrants Shannon and Joseph had found a home and more acceptance and kindness than they would have ever thought possible. Already they had been offered some tattered clothing, a cup of soup—watered down, but soup nevertheless—and a few sticks of firewood.

Joseph broke the wood into smaller pieces, crashing it over his knee, while Shannon shivered miserably nearby. He was worried about her. Never, not even after a hard day at work in the factory, was her face this strange shade of gray. For the first time since they had met, she was saying nothing. He found that he actually missed her incessant chatter.

"This fire will be roarin' soon, lass," he told her. "And then ye'll be toasty warm."

She didn't reply, but nodded her head slightly. Then she began to cough, deep, racking spasms that seemed as though they might tear her apart. Yesterday morning the coughing had begun and now it seemed much worse. He wasn't surprised after that day of digging in the rain. He cursed himself for allowing her to have done that. It was little wonder she was so sick.

Joseph had heard that sort of coughing back in Ireland. He had also seen people die who were coughing like that, people whose faces were gray, listless people who shivered all the time. His concern was growing by the moment.

He had to get some food for her. Good food, not this watered-down soup with only the occasional carrot or onion floating in it. Also, he had to get her out of this cold dampness and under a warm roof.

But to do all those things he must have money. And money was a scarce commodity here on the docks. He had combed the harbor for days trying to find work, only to be turned away. There seemed to be a building prejudice against the Irish, and many establishments displayed signs that read, NO IRISH NEED APPLY.

His mind raced, considering a hundred possibilities, ways he could come to her aid and rescue her from this terrible existence. The most obvious way—taking her to her parents on Jefferson Court—kept running through his brain, but time and time again he dismissed the idea.

He tried to tell himself that he was helping her fulfill her dream. But this was no dream. This was a nightmare, and he couldn't see an end in sight.

"Your girl there is lookin' pretty puny," an old

fellow said as he sauntered over to Joseph and tossed him another piece of wood.

"Aye." Joseph cast a sideways glance at Shannon, who had slumped over against a half-rotten wooden crate. "She's led a charmed life up to this point, and she's not well acquainted with hardship."

"Well, it appears she's getting to know the gentleman now," the old man observed, rubbing his bristly chin with gnarled fingers.

Shannon began coughing again and Joseph cringed. The stranger reached over to his own pack of threadbare clothes and pulled out a moth-eaten blanket. He handed it to Joseph. "Here, cover the girl with this."

Gratitude overwhelmed Joseph and tears sprang to his eyes. "Thank ye," he said. "And God bless ye. May ye always have a clean shirt, a clean conscience, and a bob in yer pocket."

The old man smiled a toothless grin. "I'd love to have all three this minute," he said before he turned and walked back to his own fire.

Joseph struck a borrowed match, and with much care, sheltering it from the wind with his hands and body, he coaxed it to a flame, which caught the kindling. Then he turned to Shannon.

"Look what I have for ye, lass," he said, holding out the blanket. "That kind fella over there offered it to ye and we mustn't offend him by refusin'. Come along now."

He walked over to her and gathered her in his arms, pulling her closer to the fire. When he had her settled in place, he wrapped the blanket tightly around her, tucking in the ends for warmth.

"There ye go," he crooned as he wrapped his arms around her. "Isn't that much better now?"

She nodded, snuggling against him, and he was reassured. Maybe she was going to be fine after all.

And maybe he wasn't the selfish bastard his heart was telling him that he was.

As the warmth from the blanket and the fire relieved some of their misery, Shannon became more alert, looking around at the people who milled about. One woman passed with a small baby in her arms. Neither the woman nor the baby had any blanket or coat to cover them. The child's face was turning blue and the young mother was rubbing its thin arms and legs to restore circulation.

Joseph watched, his heart going out to her. He was just about to offer his coat when Shannon pulled the blanket from around her shoulders and handed it to the young mother.

"What are ye doin', lass?" Joseph asked. "Ye needed that blanket with ye so sick and all."

Shannon shrugged. "They needed it more," she said without emotion.

Joseph looked down at her, feeling a surge of affection and admiration for her. Maybe she wasn't as spoiled and selfish as he had thought.

She glanced up at him and saw him staring at her. "What are you looking at?" she snapped.

He grinned. "I didn't say a thing. Not me."

Suddenly a dozen whistles began to blow and they heard the shouts of police, the curses of the male vagrants, and some women's screams. They were being rousted . . . again.

Big, burly Irish cops raided the scene, kicking down the makeshift tents, scattering the poor fires, and knocking some of the vagrants over the heads with their clubs.

"Away! Get away from here!" they shouted. "You can't stay here, you filthy vagabonds!"

Joseph pulled Shannon to her feet. Taking off his coat, he wrapped it around her shoulders. "Come along, lass," he said gently. "It appears we aren't to find shelter here either. Aye . . . me father was right. There's no rest for the weary."

"Get out of here!" one of the policemen yelled in his face.

"And where do ye suggest we go?" Joseph asked, too tired for sarcasm or anger.

"That's easy," the cop replied. "Go to the devil."

Fourteen

JOSEPH leaned into the cold wind and pulled Shannon along behind him as they fought their way up the street. At the end he could see a sign that read, HELP WANTED, and he decided it might be worth a try. The freezing blast cut right through his thin shirt. But rather than fearing for himself, he was worried about Shannon. Although she was wearing both her coat and his, it wasn't enough to keep a healthy person warm, let alone someone who was coughing the way she was.

They reached the shop and hurried into the small alcove in front of the door, trying to escape the wind.

"I see no point in it, Joseph," she said.

He heard the fatigue and despair in her voice and fought his own feelings of hopelessness that threatened to overwhelm him. She was probably right. There was no reason to go in here, just to be turned away again. But he had to try. He had to do everything he could.

"Come along," he said. "At least ye'll be out of the cold for the time it takes for him to send me packin'."

They entered the shop, ringing a small bell that was

attached to the doorknob. The store smelled of meat and spices and soup; their mouths watered and their stomachs growled.

The shopkeeper who stood behind the counter looked up at them warily. "May I help you?" he asked doubtfully.

"We'd be happy to take whatever work it is yer offerin'," Joseph said eagerly, summoning all his strength to appear hardworking and worthy.

The shopkeeper hesitated and Joseph thought they would be thrown out like so many times before. But the man drew a deep breath and said, "The girl doesn't look like she's in any shape to work, but you might be able to do the job. Let's have your name."

Joseph's heart thumped against his chest. More lies. These days his soul felt as black as bog oak. "John Smith," he said.

The shopkeeper consulted a long scroll of paper. "Ah . . . here's a John Smith. Middle name?"

Joseph knew he was caught this time. He couldn't possibly guess the middle name on that list. Looking over at Shannon, he saw that her pale cheeks had turned red with fever and her eyes looked glazed as she stared at him, her face expressing the fear he was feeling.

He turned back to the shopkeeper, determined to try honesty for a change. Perhaps the good God would reward him.

"Sir," he said, "we're not on the doomsday list. But we're desperate, sir. We would work for food alone. Please, sir."

But the man shook his head. "I'm very sorry. I'd like to help you, but . . ."

"I told you there was no point," Shannon said as he led her back out into the cold. "We're never going to survive this winter."

"Don't ye be sayin' such a thing, lass," he said,

angry that her words were echoing his own thoughts. "We're Irish, by God, and we Irish don't die that easily. Hold yer chin up now, and let's see what yer made of."

With what must have been an enormous effort she lifted her chin, and for a moment Joseph saw the feisty young girl who had attacked him with a pitchfork. And that small but heroic gesture did more to touch his heart than anything she had ever said to him.

"We'll make it, lass," he said, putting his arm around her shoulder and hugging her against his side. "We aren't done for just yet."

THE snow was falling so heavily that Shannon and Joseph could hardly see as they wandered the dark streets, headed nowhere in particular and not likely to arrive. The wind had died down, but the air had become even colder, if possible.

As they stumbled along, Shannon clinging to Joseph's hand, she couldn't remember ever being warm before and she had the horrible, sinking feeling that she would never be warm again. Her hands had gone beyond pain, to the point of blissful numbness, but her body still ached and her lungs simply couldn't pull in enough of the frozen air. She felt as though some cruel giant were squeezing her chest between his fingertips, and the pain was growing worse by the moment.

Finally her legs buckled beneath her, and she could go no farther. She collapsed against a large iron gate, her thighs and calves jerking in spasms, her breath coming in ragged gasps.

"Joseph, I can't . . . I can't go . . . on." Each word was an effort that hurt. The air was so cold that it made her head, her nose, and her throat ache.

"I know, lass," he said, kneeling in the snow beside her. "But we must keep goin'. If we stop to rest now, we may freeze up harder than the hobs o' hell."

"I don't care," she replied, meaning it. Death almost seemed welcome now. At least she wouldn't be cold anymore and her chest wouldn't hurt.

Joseph looked around them, peering through the heavy curtain of snow that fell silently around them. The lamplight glittered on the flakes, and they sparkled like thousands of falling stars as they drifted down. Ordinarily, the scene would have been beautiful, but now it represented a struggle between life and death.

"We have to take shelter somewhere, Shannon," he said. "I'll carry ye there if I must, but we must get warm soon or we'll both surely die."

Shannon looked up at the gate and its ornate ironwork, then through the snow at the outline of the large houses with their stained-glass windows lit with cozy light that spilled out onto the snowy streets.

"These are fancy houses, Joseph," she said, feeling a bit better at the thought that they might have shelter soon, though she couldn't guess where or how.

Joseph wandered out into the street and pointed to a nearby house that was dark with no light shining from its windows. "That's the one," he said.

Minutes later Shannon stood, leaning against the back door, her ear pressed to the cold wood. She heard the breaking of glass. He was in. After a short wait the door opened.

"Welcome to me fine and fancy house," he said, beckoning her inside.

She entered nervously and glanced around. The house was dark and silent. Whoever owned this lovely home was apparently out for the evening. At least she certainly hoped so.

The house was warm, much warmer than outside, and within minutes she began to feel her limbs thawing with many pricklings and tinglings. She also felt her lungs loosening as she breathed in the warm air gratefully.

They groped through the house, in one dark room and out another, stumbling over furniture, tripping over scattered rugs.

"I can't find a lamp," Joseph said.

"Me neither." She ran her hand along a shelf and her fingers and her hands closed around a small box. She rattled it and was pleased with the sound. "I've found some matches," she said enthusiastically.

There was a brittle pause. "Ye say ye found matches?" Joseph asked with a sarcastic tone.

"Yes."

"Well, strike one."

She lit the match and the light illuminated their faces. They stared at each other, transfixed by the ghostly pallor on the other's face.

"My God, you look like the very devil himself," Shannon said.

"And ye look like his wife," Joseph retorted.

She struck a second match and Joseph found a lamp on a nearby table. Shannon lit it. In an instant the golden glow flooded the elegant parlor, revealing a large tree in the corner, decorated with bows, bells, candles, and candy canes.

They stared in wonder at the sparkling ornaments.

"It's Christmas, Joseph," Shannon said as tears sprang to her eyes. "How could we have forgotten Christmas?"

"We've had a few other things to be thinkin' about . . . like keepin' life and body together."

Joseph lifted the lamp and began to search the house. Shannon followed after. Everything the light revealed captured her imagination, and she was awestruck. Smoothing her hand over the beautiful highly polished tables and over the satin brocade chairs, she reveled in the splendor and wealth.

With a more practical mission at hand Joseph searched out the pantry. Moving blocks of ice aside, he greedily stuffed his pockets while cramming handfuls of food into his mouth.

"Shannon, here . . . take some. Ye need food. Take," he said.

But Shannon had seen something which he hadn't—a big, plump, roasted goose sitting on a sideboard.

"I want to dine," she said.

He held out a handful of bread and cheese to her. "Dine, dine," he said, still chewing.

"No, I want to sit down and dine, Joseph. Like a human being, not an animal. The way I used to do at my mother's Christmas table. Bring me that goose."

With pomp worthy of a princess she glided to the dining-room table and sat down. Nervously, Joseph grabbed the goose and followed her. He tossed the bird onto the table, where it landed with a splat.

"It belongs on a platter," she said with a lifted eyebrow.

He breathed a sigh of exasperation. "Shannon, we're burglars. They'll be hangin' us if we're caught."

"Carve, please."

Joseph ripped the goose apart with his bare hands. "Here, have a leg," he said, thrusting the drumstick toward her.

"I'd prefer light meat if I—"

"Damn it, woman! Eat the bloody leg!"

He threw it down on the table in front of her. Shannon jumped and shrank back in her chair. Trembling, she looked as though she were about to cry.

"Please, Joseph, humor me. My body doesn't need to be nourished as much as my pampered soul. Pretend with me. For fifteen minutes pretend this lovely house is ours."

Her fragile invitation, delivered with such sincerity, touched Joseph. "Ours?" he said.

"We'll never have these beautiful things, except in fantasy. Pretend that you're my husband. Sit down and dine with me."

His eyes locked with hers in an intense gaze filled with unspoken emotion, Joseph sat down beside her. The golden lamplight shone on his face, revealing the play of mixed emotions that he felt.

Neither of them ate.

"And what would we do together . . . married . . . you and I?" he asked, his voice husky and soft.

Shannon blushed a pretty shade of pink and leaned a little closer to him. "I suppose you'd have to be nice to me . . . and love me now and then."

Her words made them both blush and they stared down at the uneaten goose.

"I have no experience in love," Joseph admitted. She could tell by the tone of his voice and the expression on his face that he spoke the truth. She thought of Grace and felt relieved. He hadn't been in love with the other woman after all.

"You've never even dreamed of it?" she asked, thinking of all those nights when they had slept together in the same room, so close, yet so distant.

He shrugged. "Perhaps."

His answer made her bolder. "In books I've read a man and woman fall in love . . . and kiss."

She could hardly utter those last two words. Her heart was pounding so hard she was sure he must be hearing it, and she trembled so violently that she had to clasp her hands tightly together in her lap to keep them from shaking.

To her delight and amazement she saw that he was trembling, too.

"We can't pretend to kiss each other," Joseph observed quietly. "It's either a kiss or it's not."

"That's true."

She leaned toward him and he met her halfway.

— 239 —

Puckering her lips, she touched them to his for the briefest moment. But in that instant she had time to think how warm his mouth was, how full and sensual. And she realized she wanted to kiss him again . . . as soon as possible.

But she had to behave like a lady, so she suppressed her desires, and she wondered if he were trying to do the same.

"Oh, Joseph," she said, "why has fortune passed us by? Was I so blind in Ireland to believe I'd flourish here? Feel my hands." She held them out to him and he took them in his. "Poverty has broken them and made them as rough as yours."

She clutched his hands, holding on to him, trying to draw the strength she needed so badly. Unfortunately, his hands were as warm and sensuous as his lips and she felt her desire heat again.

"Ye had a life of comfort until ye ran away with me. I feel as if I failed ye," he said, staring down at her hands, which were chapped, red, and broken by the cold and hard work.

"How did you fail? I'm the one who's hopeless at adventure, and you've looked after me every step of the way. Without you God only knows what would have become of me."

They sat for a quiet moment, looking into each other's eyes. The sparks that had kindled the first day they met suddenly flared into flame. Shannon could no longer hold back her desire. It came flooding over her, hot and molten.

"Pretend you love me," she said.

"I pretend I love you," he replied.

They hurled themselves at each other, lost their balance, and tumbled off the chairs. With their arms still around each other's neck, they hit the floor.

Shannon landed on top of Joseph, her hair spilling

down into his face. His hands moved up her back and burrowed into the softness of her curls.

"Ah, lass . . ." he murmured as his lips found hers.

The kiss he gave her was much longer than the first and his lips even hotter. She forgot about restraint, about being a lady and guarding her virtue as Nora had lectured her so many times. She forgot everything but the feel of his arms around her and the passion his kiss was stirring inside her.

So, this is what it feels like to be kissed by a man, she thought as his mouth moved over hers and she responded in kind. *It feels like heaven.*

Suddenly he rolled her over and reversed their positions so that he lay over her. She felt the blissful weight of his body pressing her into the thick, plush carpet, and she reveled in the hardness of his body against her softness.

"Joseph," she whispered. There was no time to think of social differences now, of the fact that he was a common bog boy and she an aristocrat. He was Joseph, her partner, her closest friend . . . and at the moment, her lover.

"Yes, love?" he said, pulling his mouth from hers and continuing to kiss her cheeks and neck.

"I want . . ."

"What is it ye want, love?"

"I want you to . . ."

"Yes?"

"I want you to . . . touch me." There, she had spoken the forbidden words. She had gone against everything her mother had ever taught her, but the request had seemed so natural, the thought so welcome and right for the moment. She wanted to feel his warm, strong hands caress her like a lover. She wanted it more than anything in the world.

"Are ye sure?" he asked breathlessly, his hand

moving around her waist, his fingers splayed across her ribs.

"Yes, I'm sure."

He didn't ask again. Slowly his hand moved upward, then hovered over the fullness of her bosom. "Ah, Shannon," he whispered. "What a beauty ye are. How long I've wanted to touch yer softness and tell ye with me hands how I cared for ye. But I thought ye hated me."

"I never hated you, Joseph. I always thought that *you* hated *me*."

He lowered his hand and gently cupped the roundness of her breast. "Ah, so soft," he whispered reverently. "Softer than in me dreams." He looked into her eyes and she thought he had never seemed so handsome to her, so masculine and yet tender. "I thank ye, Shannon," he said. "I thank ye for this honor and privilege."

Unfastening the top button of her bodice, he pulled back the fabric and placed a soft kiss on the swell of her breast. She tangled her fingers in his thick hair and kissed his forehead.

"I never hated you, lass. Not for a minute. In fact—" He froze, then lifted his head and looked around.

"What is it, Joseph?" she asked.

"Shhh, I thought I heard somethin'."

A loud crash resounded through the front of the house and a man's deep voice called out, "Who is that? Is someone in here?"

Jumping up, Joseph blew out the lamp. Shannon scrambled up off the floor and grasped his hand. Their hearts pounded as they heard footsteps, heavy footsteps, echoing through the house.

"Come on, let's run," Joseph whispered to her as he led her through the darkness. She bumped into a large, heavy object and something glass shattered on the floor.

"Halt," boomed the voice. "Who goes there?"

They saw the light of a lamp behind them, coming closer as they tried to find their way through the dark rooms.

"Where's the bloody door?" Joseph whispered.

"There. It's over there." Shannon pulled him toward it.

They fumbled for what seemed like an eternity with the knob while the footsteps grew louder and closer.

"Stop! Stop right there, thieves, or I'll shoot you both!" roared the man.

A blast of cold enveloped them as they burst out of the door and onto the porch. Joseph half pulled, half dragged Shannon down the steps and into the thick snow that covered the back garden.

"Hurry! Hurry, Shannon!" he shouted at her.

She tried her best, but her skirt tangled around her legs and she pitched face forward into the snow. She felt Joseph's hands beneath her arms, lifting her up, and she was on her feet again.

An explosion roared across through the yard and a bright, white light flashed. Shannon felt a searing pain in her back, than a hot wetness spilled down her ribs.

"Joseph," she cried, falling into his arms. "I think I'm shot!"

He scooped her up and carried her to the fence. As they reached the gate they heard another blast and saw a second flash. "Halt! You bastards! I know I got one of you!"

But Joseph darted out the gate, holding her tightly against his chest.

"Don't worry, darlin'," he said. "I'll take care of ye. We'll find help, don't worry."

But Shannon wasn't worrying. She wasn't thinking anything at all except that Joseph's arms were around her and how sweet and warm the darkness was that was closing in on her.

* * *

"Someone help us, please!" Joseph cried as he carried Shannon through the dark streets. The snow piled higher and the wind was picking up again, cutting through his thin shirt, carrying his words away the moment they left his mouth.

Past one elegant iron gate and then another, he struggled, carrying his precious burden. He cried out again and again, but no door opened and no one came to the lace-covered windows.

"Joseph," Shannon murmured.

Her breath felt warm against his neck, her hair soft against his face. He clutched her more tightly to him. "Yes, lass. I'm here."

"Am I meant to leave you now?" she asked in a faint voice.

Fear shot through Joseph. She couldn't leave. Not now, when he felt as though he had just found her. "Fight, girl," he said, pressing a quick kiss to her forehead. "Fight to keep yer spirit in this world."

She raised one hand and laid it against his cheek. He was shocked to feel how cold it was. Could anyone remain alive, shot in the back and so very cold?

"I was starting to . . ." she said weakly, ". . . to go beyond pretending. I was beginning to fall . . . in love with you. Truly I was."

Joseph listened to the words that his heart had longed for, but that he had never thought he would hear. Could it be true? How could she—a wealthy, Protestant landowner's daughter—love a simple peasant like himself?

And yet the old wives said that a dying man never uttered a lie. He feared she was, indeed, dying there in his arms. Could she be finally speaking the truth?

He buried his face in her hair and closed his eyes for a moment, savoring the joy of hearing her declaration.

But his happiness was short-lived. She lifted her face to his, her eyes full of pain.

"It hurts so badly, Joseph," she said.

He felt a tremor run through her body. "I know, lass. I'd take it all away if only I could. Surely ye know that."

"Yes," she whispered. "I know."

He looked around again at the windows where golden lamplight shone warm and bright. If he could get her inside, out of the cold, and if somehow they could find a doctor.

"For God's sake, someone help us!" he cried, but as before, there was no response.

"I . . . I can't stay awake any longer, Joseph," she said, closing her eyes. Her hand fell from his cheek and her body went limp in his arms.

"No, Shannon, no . . ."

He staggered on down the street, trudging through the drifts of snow crusted with ice. Tears raced down his cheeks and he sobbed with abandon.

Then, up the street a ways, he heard the whinny of a horse. It was a carriage, a big, black coach with lamps hanging from each corner. He stumbled up to it, peering through the snow, searching for the silhouette of the driver.

"Hey, boy," a man's voice said. "What have you got there?"

Joseph looked down at Shannon, her beautiful face revealed by the light of the coach lanterns. Her eyes were closed and she looked asleep. But Joseph knew this was no ordinary sleep.

"'Tis me own sweetheart," he said, continuing to weep. "And I'm afraid she's just died in me arms. Could ye have mercy, sir? God knows, I'm in need of a kind heart and helping hand."

The driver climbed down from the seat of the coach

and hurried over to Joseph. He looked down at Shannon's face and shook his head.

"My, my, what a shame. And she was such a pretty thing, too. What can I do for you, boy?"

"If ye could give us a ride in yer coach, sir, I'd like to do what I should have done long ago."

"And what's that?"

"She never belonged with me. I want to be takin' her home where she belongs."

STEPHEN Chase sat in the Christies' parlor, staring into the blaze on the hearth. His long, aristocratic face wore no expression—as usual—but his gray eyes revealed the depth of his despair. He had looked for Shannon for so long, anticipating the day when he would snatch her from that wretched peasant, saving her from herself.

Oh, she might resist at first. He had to prepare himself for that. After all, she had willingly run away with that bastard. But if he could only bring her home, here in the bosom of her family she would be restored to sanity, and in the end she would thank him.

A house of ill repute. The very thought of her in a place like that seared his heart. Had she already been sullied, his pure dove? Had rough scoundrels used and abused her?

He cast the thought from his mind. It was simply too heinous to be considered. No, he preferred to think that his darling would have found a way to resist the temptations of the flesh. Somehow the virtue in her would win over any sinful weaknesses.

Stephen Chase was a man of honor, and he simply couldn't conceive of dishonor in someone he adored. And he did adore Shannon Christie. Even though she had spurned his affections and left him with another man—his sworn enemy—he couldn't wait for the opportunity to forgive her and welcome her back.

As he sat in the leather wing-back chair and toyed with the fob of his grandfather's gold watch, he imagined himself bursting through the door of some seedy establishment, pistols drawn, ready to shoot any lowborn rogue who tried to stand in his way. He imagined how Donelly would try to throw himself between them, and Stephen savored how it would feel to squeeze the trigger and watch the bastard fall to the ground, dead as he deserved to be.

Then he would scoop Shannon into his arms and return her to Mr. and Mrs. Christie, cementing his relationship with them forever. They would never forget how he had brought their precious daughter home.

Daniel Christie would undoubtedly make him—or any sons he and Shannon might conceive—his heir. And Stephen, as overseer of the Christies' finances, knew better than anyone how much Daniel Christie was worth.

Imagining the wealth that would someday be his, Stephen smiled. It was an unpracticed mannerism and appeared strange and awkward on his handsome face. And there was no warmth to it.

He rose and walked over to the fireplace, where he took a poker and stoked the flames. Lifting his head, he listened carefully, thinking he had heard a strange sound outside . . . perhaps the whine of the wind, or maybe someone crying out.

It was quite late and the streets had been deserted for hours. Daniel and Nora had long ago retired to their bedrooms upstairs. Surely no one could be out so late and in this terrible storm.

About the time Stephen had decided that it must have been the moaning of the wind, he heard it again. This time there was no mistaking a human voice, a man's voice. Though Stephen couldn't understand what he was saying, the tone left no doubt that the person was in distress.

Stephen hurried to the window and brushed the frost away with his handkerchief. There on the street below, he could make out the silhouette of a large coach, and a man. The fellow seemed to be holding something in his arms.

Chase hurried to the door and opened it. From this vantage point he could clearly see the man below, and his heart raced with fury. It was Donelly. As bold as day, standing right there.

Reaching into his jacket, Chase searched for his pistols. But he had already put them aside for the evening.

"Donelly," he called. "You son of a whore, get off this property or I'll—"

At that moment Stephen saw what . . . or rather whom . . . Joseph was holding, and he froze. It was Shannon. And she looked very ill, or maybe even dead.

"Ye must help," Joseph said, taking a step toward him. "Please, for her sake, not for me own."

Stephen, a man of action, couldn't move or speak. He just continued to stare at that limp form.

"Quickly," Joseph said. "Bring us in from the cold. 'Tis more dead than alive she is."

The young man's eyes were frantic with urgency. Suddenly Stephen snapped to attention like one of his well-trained soldiers. "Bring her here," he said, opening the door wider and stepping back inside.

Joseph hurried up the porch stairs, taking two at a time.

"Oh, Shannon," Stephen said when he looked down at her face, which was a deathly shade of bluish gray, "what kind of damage has he done to you, my darling?"

Joseph winced, then quickly said, "There's no time

to waste. Besides bein' half-froze, she's been shot in the back. She needs a doctor straightaway or she'll die, surely."

"Shot! Oh, my God!" Stephen opened the coat she wore, looking for the injury.

"Stephen . . . is that you?" asked a sleepy female voice from the stairs.

"Yes, Nora, it's me. You and Daniel, come quickly!"

Joseph saw the two figures descending the staircase. He looked down at Shannon, pain contorting his handsome face. "Yer safe in a beautiful house of yer own now, Shannon," he said. "Rest, sleep . . . mend."

Then he handed her into Stephen's arms. "Ye must love her to have followed her over the sea. Take care of her. Restore her to the life she left. She belongs with you, not me . . . and please . . . treat her tenderly," he added, tears streaming down his face.

Holding Shannon in his arms, Stephen watched as his enemy turned and fled, down the stairs and into the street. In only a few heartbeats he had disappeared in the storm.

Fifteen

JOSEPH ran as hard as he could through the snowstorm
without looking back, knowing that if he didn't get
away from the Christies' house—more precisely, away
from Shannon—he would never be free of her, or she
of him. They had nearly destroyed each other. He
knew that more clearly now than ever before. Everyone had said that her kind and his didn't mix, and
they were right. Trying to be together had almost cost
them their lives.

For all he knew, Shannon was dead this very minute
because of him. He would never know if she survived
the night, if they had found a doctor in time, if he had
been able to save her.

Joseph stopped in the middle of the dark street, his
fists clenched at his sides, his sweat icy on his brow.
He couldn't go on. He had to know. If he left this place
now without knowing, she would haunt him for the
rest of his days.

Turning around, he began to run back to the house,
retracing the tracks he had just made in the snow.

As soon as he found out, he would leave. That he
promised himself . . . and her.

* * *

HE stood behind a fence across the street, staring at the house. Hours ago he had seen a servant leave the house and run to a neighbor. He had heard the boy ask for the doctor, and an elderly gentleman had hurried back with him to the town house.

Now Joseph waited and watched the shadows that passed before a window on the second story. He could only guess what was happening in that bedroom and picture the doctor digging the bullet out of her back.

Several times he walked up to the door, only to change his mind and hurry back to his hiding place behind the fence, where he stomped his feet and beat his hands together, trying to stay warm.

Sooner or later the doctor would have to come out that door, and when he did, Joseph intended to ask him about her condition.

It was later, rather than sooner, nearly dawn before the elderly gentleman walked out of the house, his black bag in his hands, a weary slump to his shoulders. Having gone numb from standing in one spot for hours, Joseph's legs wobbled as he ran across the street and grabbed the man by his coat sleeve. The doctor looked frightened and pulled away.

Joseph realized what a sight he must be, all ragged, dirty, and half-frozen. "Don't worry, sir," he said. "I'm not intendin' to rob ye. But there's somethin' I must know."

"What is that, boy?"

"Ye must tell me if the girl is alive or . . . passed on."

"She's alive," he said with a tried sigh, "though not by much."

"And will she recover, do ye think?"

Something in Joseph's eyes seemed to touch the doctor because he reached out and put a hand on the young man's shoulder in a comforting gesture. "Oh, yes. She'll mend just fine. She's a fighter, that one."

"Aye, she's that all right." Joseph smiled sadly. "In some ways she's more of a scrapper than meself."

Joseph watched as the doctor returned to his house across the street. Then his conscience reminded him of his promise, and he, too, began to walk away in the opposite direction.

I'll never see her again, he told himself, overwhelmed by the melancholy the thought evoked. *I'll never come back to this place again. I promise.*

JOSEPH couldn't keep his promise. Early spring found Boston still covered with snow, daffodils and crocuses pushing up through the still-frozen ground in the gardens of the affluent neighborhoods, and Joseph standing behind the same fence across the street from the Christies' town house. The sun shone brightly in a clear azure sky, and the white covering of snow was beginning to melt in spots.

Astonished, Joseph watched as two men exited the house, snow shovels in hand, and began to scoop the snow and melting ice from the walkway. One he recognized instantly as his old enemy Daniel Christie. The other he identified as well, but he couldn't believe what his eyes were seeing.

"Her beautiful eyes were a terrible curse," the man sang, and Joseph knew it was Danty Duff himself, his father's best friend.

But the old scoundrel was shoveling snow with the landlord and singing as though they were old drinking buddies.

"Three days in his grave," Christie chimed in, "she ran off with his purse."

"He gazed down from heaven upon the love of his life. . . ." Danty tossed a bit of snow in the landlord's face and they both snickered.

That rotten traitor, Joseph fumed from his hiding place behind the fence, *consorting with the enemy like that!*

"God help you, poor lad, she's another man's wife," Christie finished with a flourish.

An upstairs window opened and Joseph ducked further behind the fence. A woman whom he recognized as Mrs. Christie leaned out of the window and called, "Daniel! Stop embarrassing yourself and let Danty do the work. You're supposed to be a gentleman."

Danty and Christie winked at each other and chuckled like mischievous schoolboys.

"I'll be right up, dear," Christie called.

As soon as his wife closed the window, he bent down, grabbed a handful of snow, shaped it into a ball, and hurled it at the window, striking the sill. Both men collapsed in fits of giggles.

"I'd better do as she says, old lad," Christie said, slapping Danty on the shoulder. "She's mean as the devil himself when she's crossed."

Christie hefted his shovel over his shoulder and begrudgingly trudged back into the house.

The moment he was out of sight, Joseph whistled softly. Danty looked up from his shoveling, a curious expression on his face.

"Who's there?" he asked.

Joseph whispered as loudly as he dared, "Danty! What calamity has linked *you* to the Christie family?"

Puzzled, Danty put down his shovel and crossed the street, following the sound of the voice. "My God!" he exclaimed when he saw Joseph. "Joe Donelly's son."

Seeing the stormy scowl on Joseph's face, Danty turned to bolt across the street. But Joseph grabbed him by the collar.

"Come back here, rebel," he said, spinning him

around so that they were eye to eye. "Ye sent me off to kill that man and now yer *singin'* with him?"

"I . . . I'm . . ." Danty fumbled for the words, trying to explain himself before he received a thrashing. "I'm a prisoner, I am, captured in battle, subdued I was into slavery, martyred I was—"

Joseph shook him until his teeth clattered. "Shut up with yer lies and excuses. Just tell me one thing . . . their daughter . . . Shannon . . . is she alive and well?"

"Aye," Danty said warily, "but keep away from her, Joseph. She hates ye, lad."

"Hates me? Why?"

"They all do. I'm strictly forbidden to mention yer name or any word that rhymes with it."

Across the street the front door of the house opened and the one person whom Joseph hated most in the world, Stephen Chase himself, walked out. "Danty, where are you?" he called, his prim, aristocratic voice grating on Joseph's already high-strung nerves.

Welcoming the interruption, Danty scurried away from Joseph, who ducked back behind the fence.

But then he saw her. Walking out of the house on Stephen's arm, decked in furs and velvets, she was a vision more beautiful than the one that had played through his fantasies these long winter months.

"Shannon," he whispered. And her name had never tasted sweeter on his lips.

But there was something wrong with her, with her walk, her posture. Where was the bounce in her step, the sparkle in her eye? Never in all the time they had been together, even in the miserable, hard times, had she appeared so downcast or dispirited.

There was a frailty about her that seemed to come more from a debility of the soul than the body. Joseph almost regretted that he had come to see her at all. He had promised himself that this would be the absolute last time he would see her, and he didn't want to remember her this way.

Had the bullet done this to her? Somehow he didn't think so.

"Danty, where have you been?" Chase asked, but without waiting for a response, he added, "Open the carriage. We're going to a piano recital and you're to drive us."

Danty rushed to obey with an obedience that made Joseph's blood boil. Stephen handed Shannon into the carriage and Danty closed the door behind them. After one look in Joseph's direction he climbed up onto the driver's seat and drove the carriage away.

Joseph watched until they disappeared around a corner in the distance, his heart aching inside. Yes, he was very sorry to have seen her again.

"Ah, Shannon . . . what has happened to ye, lass?" he whispered as he pulled his coat more tightly around him, thrust his hands deep into his pockets, and turned his back on the house and its occupants, who had never been and would never be a part of his life.

INSIDE the carriage, Stephen took Shannon's hand in his and squeezed it gently, trying to get her attention. He had attempted conversation several times with her already on the ride to the concert hall, but to no avail.

"You're looking well, Shannon," he said in his most solicitous tone. "Can you afford a smile?"

She looked up at him and gave him a halfhearted, lopsided grin. "Oh, Stephen, I'm sorry I'm not very good company today. You've cared for me so patiently, even when I've been a brat."

"You needn't thank me, dear." He lifted her hand and gallantly placed a discreet peck on her knuckles. "Caring for you isn't difficult, not when I love you so."

Shannon looked down at her hands, enveloped in his. "My hands are rough from poverty," she said. "They won't let me forget."

"Time will make them delicate again, my darling."

Shannon looked up at him, anguish in her eyes. "How is such cruelty possible," she said, tears brimming, "that he would abandon me in such a way. Throw me away as though I meant nothing to him."

"Life has no value to a man of his low class, Shannon. How many times have your mother and I told you as much? If I hadn't found you, you would have died in the ditch that night."

She began to weep softly. He pulled her head over onto his shoulder and stroked her hair. "But I thank God that I did find you," he said, "and returned you to the arms of your loving family. I don't know how I could have lived without you."

"Thank you, Stephen," she said, accepting his comfort. "Thank you for saving my life."

"ALL set? Okay, fire on three. One . . . two . . . three!"

On the foreman's order the workmen depressed their plungers, and the mountain shook with a series of blasts. The roar of falling rock drowned out the cheering of the railroad crew as smoke and dust rolled out of the tunnel entrance.

As soon as the rumble had died away and the clouds of dust had cleared, the laborers hurried into the tunnel and began hauling out wheelbarrows full of debris and carts filled with rock.

Joseph worked with them, harder than most, sweat pouring down his brow, tracing muddy paths in the dust that had settled on his forehead.

Most of the men wore distinct expressions on their faces, looks of fear or excitement, or agony from the backbreaking work. But Joseph's face was vague, his eyes blank, as though his mind were somewhere far away . . . in another time . . . another place.

"I love ye, Shannon. And I'm not just pretendin' either," he said in his daydream as they sat in the dining room of that fine home in Boston on Christmas Eve, their stolen goose on the table before them.

"I love you, too, Joseph," she said, her eyes shining. "I always have. I'm sorry I've been so unkind to you and called you awful names like bog boy. I never meant to hurt you."

"And I didn't mean to be unkind to ye either when I dunked ye in the bathtub that time. If I hadn't carried ye down the hall and half drowned ye, God knows what I would have done to ye. God knows what I *wanted* to do to ye."

She leaned closer to him, her lips soft and full, her face flushed with the same desires that he felt. "And what was that, Joseph? What was it you wanted to do to me that night?"

"This. This is what I've wanted to do to ye every night since the moment I laid me eyes on ye." He reached out and laid his hand against her cheek, marveling at the velvet texture of her skin.

He kissed her gently at first, then with more and more fervor, and she returned his passion with no hesitation or reluctance. Encouraged, he allowed his hands to roam over her hair, her face, her neck, and eventually, down to her full breasts.

"Ah, Shannon . . . touchin' ye brings me such joy."

"Not only you," she said. "It's wonderful for me, too. But . . ." Her lower lid trembled.

"What is it? Should I stop?"

"No, don't stop. It's just that I . . . I want more."

Joseph couldn't believe what he was hearing, but

the invitation seemed undeniable. "How much more?" he asked, speaking each word carefully.

"Everything," she whispered. "I want to do it all . . . with you."

Without another word Joseph rose from his chair, scooped her into his arms, and carried her into the parlor. Gently lowering her onto the couch, he began to unfasten the buttons on her bodice, revealing the perfect ivory skin beneath. He marveled at her beauty and at the fact that she would allow him to touch her, enjoy her in this way.

"Shannon, I want ye to know that I truly lov—"

"Take cover, men! Here she goes!" Joseph's speech of love was cut short by a harsh voice that boomed in his right ear. All around him the railroad crew scurried to find shelter.

The crew boss counted down the explosion. "On three . . . one . . . two . . . three!"

The plunger descended on count. Covering their ears, the men ducked and waited for the blast that didn't come. Silence. No explosion, no rocks raining down. Nothing.

"Damn!" The foreman tore the hat off his head, threw it down, and stomped it. Then he turned to his crew, who wore an expression of dread on their faces. "Men—you know what this means. I need a volunteer."

No one moved.

"Come on, now. Haven't got all day, for Christ's sake."

Finally Joseph rose from where he was lying on the ground. With a dead, empty look in his eyes he strode toward the foreman.

"Someone has to go in there," he said. "Might as well be meself."

"Thank you, Joseph. I'll make sure there's a bit of a bonus when you're paid this Saturday."

"Aye, he's a brave fellow, going in there after an unexploded charge," one of the crew members muttered as Joseph walked toward the tunnel entrance.

Another man shook his head. "I don't think bravery has anything to do with it. I think he's a young man with a sorrow that hurts so bad he'd do anything to get away from it. Even die."

ONCE inside the tunnel, Joseph climbed over the broken rocks, dirt, and debris, following the dynamite wire. Somewhere, something had gone wrong and it was his job to find the problem, remedy it, and get out of there before the mountain caved in on him.

"'Tis a bloody fool I am," he said, and no one was there to argue with him. "A fool over a woman . . . and that's the worst kind of fool on God's green earth."

Once again, the fantasy took over his thoughts, the past crowding into the present, even though his life was in jeopardy and his concentration necessary to complete his task. No matter where he turned he saw her lovely face, the pink roundness of her cheek, her flawless skin and bright blue eyes.

Again, his mind wandered back to that house in Boston—only this time the house was even grander than before, and this time he and Shannon weren't tattered beggars, thieves who had broken in. They owned this splendid mansion and every luxurious furnishing in it. From the brocade sofa, to the Oriental rugs, to the crystal chandeliers and heavy velvet draperies . . . it was all theirs, his and his lady's.

Instead of their threadbare rags, they wore splendid clothes. He was decked out in a fine suit with a golden fob and a dandy new bowler on his head. Shannon looked exquisite in a lace-and-silk frock that was the same shade of sapphire as her eyes. Her beautiful copper hair was piled on top of her head and fastened with diamond-studded hairpins. The gems caught the light from the hand-painted china lamp when she moved and sparkled like glistening stars.

"What shall we do this evening, my dear?" he asked her in a cultured voice that had been stripped of all traces of Irish peasantry. "Would you like to attend the theater or perhaps a concert?"

She walked across the parlor and reached out her hand to him. On the ring finger of her left hand an enormous diamond glittered. Her wedding ring. One of five . . . he had given her all five on their wedding day . . . just because he was so rich and could afford to.

"I don't think I want to go out tonight, Joseph, dear," she said, running her hand up the front of his stiffly starched shirt.

"What would you prefer, sweetheart?"

In a heartbeat she grabbed him behind the neck and pulled his face down to hers. With an intensity of passion that took his breath away, she kissed him, her lips devouring his as though she would never get enough.

"Oh, Joseph . . . I want you," she said, her hands tearing at his clothes, baring his chest, and then going to the buckle on his belt. "Now!"

"But perhaps we should go upstairs, darling, and get into bed properly."

"To the devil with propriety. I want you here and now, and by God I'm going to have you."

"Oh . . . all right," he groaned as she dragged him to the floor and began tugging at his pants.

Outside the tunnel the crew waited, hardly daring to breathe. They looked at one another nervously, then back at the tunnel. The foreman pulled his watch from his pocket, then studied the sun, which was beginning to sink behind the mountain.

"He's been in there a long time, sir," one of the men said to him.

"I know that, you fool."

"But something must have happened to him. Some rocks might have fallen on him and he might be lying in there broken and bleeding."

"So what are you saying?" the foreman snapped. "Are you volunteering to go in there after him?"

"Well, no, I wasn't exactly saying that. Maybe we should wait for a few more min—"

A blast shook the ground and the men hit the dirt, belly down with their hands over their heads.

"Holy Jaysus!" yelled an Irish worker. "He's sure to be with his Maker now!"

Smoke and dust belched out of the tunnel and they could hear the fatal roar of falling rock and debris. Joseph had set off the charge, all right. But at what cost?

"Poor bastard," the foreman said. "I hope it blew him to bits and it was all over quickly."

"He may be trapped in there, under rocks and dirt."

"So let's go get him."

No one moved.

"Hey, look! It's himself!" The Irishman pointed at a dark figure that was stumbling out of the tunnel, his clothes hanging on his body in shreds, his face black with dirt and grime.

They all rushed forward to congratulate him, but before they could reach him, he yelled something strange that no one could understand.

"Damn that woman to hell and back. She'll be the death of me yet!"

Then he keeled over backward and fell flat on his back.

THAT night the rail workers lined up at the stew pot, collecting their portion of the evening meal, which consisted of whatever had been left from the day before, a handful of barley, some potatoes, and some unrecognizable vegetables.

With their bowl in one hand and their daily cup of coffee in the other, they separated off into groups and huddled around the campfire like moths hovering in the amber light of a flame.

They swapped stories of the day's work, talked longingly of the women they had left behind—women who grew more beautiful and lusty with each passing day of absence—and they commiserated over their aching bones and muscles.

But Joseph, hardened by loneliness, sat away from the others, eating his stew, staring into the flames. Several times one or two of the men would walk by him and throw out some gambit of conversation. But a coldness in his response turned them away every time.

"He's a strange one, that Donelly fella," one of the workers told his companions. "Sure doesn't have much to say to anyone about anything."

"Ah," replied the fellow to his right, "he just prefers his own company to any of ours. And considering how you smell tonight, O'Manion, I don't blame him at all."

The group laughed, slapping each other on the shoulders and poking the other's ribs.

Joseph watched them from his solitary refuge. He saw the sideways glances and knew they were talking about him. He even assumed they were laughing at him.

But he didn't give a tinker's damn.

Joseph Donelly didn't give a damn about anything at all these days.

"C'MON any ya, sons-a-bishh!"

Joseph stood in the middle of the saloon floor, his

fists raised, his legs weaving beneath him. He stumbled around the room, flailing at first one and then the other of his fellow crew members.

It was Saturday night . . . payday . . . and the workers had gone into town to blow off a bit of steam. Joseph, however, was puffing like a locomotive.

"Sit down, you drunken shit," his boss said, giving him a push toward a chair.

Clumsily Joseph swung at the man. He easily ducked and pushed Joseph into the wall. The back of his head cracked hard against the solid surface, but he didn't even blink. Gathering his resolve, he lifted his fists and wobbled across the room toward another worker.

"I's once the grestesht boxer in Boshton . . ." he said. "I was."

His boss walked over to him and grabbed him by the collar and the back of his trousers. "Well, I tell you this, you crazy mick. Whatever inspired you then, you sure ain't got it now. Come on, Charlie," he said to a fellow standing nearby. "Give me a hand here."

A moment later Joseph was being thrown out the front door by the seat of his britches. Fortunately, he passed out an instant before his face hit the dirt.

THE tunnel having been blasted and cleared, the crew found themselves laying track for the next few days. The metallic cadence of the hammers hitting spikes echoed through the green valley, creating a strange music of its own. Steel hitting steel with a cold, sharp ring, punctuated by the curses and occasional moans of the workers.

Joseph lifted his hammer, feeling the muscles knot in his arms and back. Swing, strike, lift, swing, strike. The hammer struck the head of the spike, and the force reverberated through his hands, arms, shoulders, and through his body until he was numb from his hair to the soles of his feet.

Not far away a ragged procession of horses and wagons slowly trudged by, migrating west. An old man near Joseph leaned on his hammer and watched the wagon train with envy in his faded eyes.

"Oklahoma fever, boy," he said. "They're all headed for the Cherokee Strip." He sighed and wiped his brow with a blue kerchief. "I'd be goin' with 'em if I was young and strong as you."

Joseph sniffed and continued to hammer. "Doesn't interest me," he said contemptuously.

At that moment the crew boss walked up to them and the old man resumed driving the spikes with renewed vigor.

"I'm looking for damn fools," the boss shouted. Up and down the track men paused. The ringing ceased with an eerie suddenness.

"Here's one, sir," a fellow said, pushing his friend toward the boss.

The foreman ignored him. "Any damn fools around here? We're shipping men down Galveston way to work on a goddamned bridge." He hesitated, looking around. "Where's that Irishman? Where's that crazy mick?"

Joseph chucked his hammer aside. "I'll go, sir," he said without emotion. "It's all the same to me."

JOSEPH lay on the floor of the bunk car, his jacket rolled up beneath his head for a pillow. The rhythm of the train was lulling him to sleep as it rolled along, metal groaning as it clanked along over the tracks.

As though from far away he heard the voices of his fellow workers, immigrant workers of several nationalities, as they sat in a circle around an oil lamp, playing cards and discussing their hardships in broken English.

"Had a woman, didn't want me, cuz I had no money, see?" said one fellow as he threw down his hand, giving up all claim to the pile of matches, straws, and broken twigs that made up the small fortune that had accumulated during this hand.

"That's America," another said. "Unless you're rich, you're nobody. Shoulda never come to this place."

Joseph's eyes grew heavy and he closed them, hoping for a dream that would be more pleasant than his present reality.

As it had many times lately, his soul decided to visit Ireland—his father's farm, to be exact. The blessed old place looked the same as when he had last seen it, and though part of his mind told him he was dreaming, he marveled at the forty shades of green that fed his hungry eyes, and the sweet, sweet smell of old Eirinn.

"Joseph," he heard a familiar voice call from behind him. "Joseph, my boy . . ."

He spun around to see who it was, but knowing in his spirit. Off to his right he saw a stone fence, that blessed old fence he had vaulted so many times as a boy. Atop the stone wall stood his father, staring out to sea, his eyes trained on the gray horizon. Without the dreadful gash in his head, he looked as fit as a fiddle at a crossroads dance.

"Da? Is that you?"

"Aye, it is," Joe said. "Ye called for me, did ye not?" He jumped down from the fence and walked over to Joseph, who reveled in the sight of him. Joe looked his son up and down and scowled. "All muddled and lost ye are, ye handsome divil."

"I'm a sight better than ye, Da," Joseph said with a grin.

His father shook his head and muttered, "A sight better than ye, he says. Always eatin' the skin o' me. Come along. Ye'd better be followin' me."

"Where are we, Da?" Joseph asked.

Joe didn't reply but continued to walk on as Joseph

followed. Suddenly, out of the haze of the dream, other figures began to materialize. Joseph stared at them, puzzled.

"O'Dwyer, O'Donovan, Doyle . . ." Joe spoke each name as he nodded to the strangers. "MacRannal, O'Farrel, O'Keane . . ."

"Da . . . who are these people here?" Joseph asked.

"Walk along and be nice, you. These are yer ancestors."

"Ancestors?"

A crowd of people was springing up all over—men and women of the past, farmers, mothers, warriors, tradesmen. Some of them nodded at Joseph. Others argued among themselves.

"Look here, Joseph," his father said, pointing to a strong Aran fisherman who was busy lifting heavy nets. "Give this fella a nod. Ye get yer love of honest work from him."

Joe grabbed Joseph's sleeve and pulled him toward an old woman with a shawl about her shoulders, leaning on a blackthorn cane. "And see her?" Joe said. "From this woman comes yer sweetness, when ye choose to be sweet, ye gob."

The old woman smiled kindly at Joseph and nodded. But before Joseph could return her greeting, Joe had dragged him over to a couple of twin brothers who were dressed in soldiers' garb. "And what are these two?" Joe said. "You wonder where you got your fight? Look at 'em now!"

The two brothers began to argue and then to grapple with one another. Soon they both hit the dirt and rolled about, kicking, scratching, biting, and pommeling each other.

"And this man . . ." Joe said, pointing to a magnificent Norseman with a long golden beard. "He's a Viking or some such; wanderer he was, exploring the world like yourself, looking for God knows what."

Joseph heard the sound of piping behind him and turned to see a cheerful fellow blowing a merry tune. He wore a brightly colored pair of pants and a mischievous grin.

"And this rascal here," Joe continued, "is O'Mally of Mocharabuiee. 'Twas he that gave ye the twinkle in yer eye."

O'Mally began to dance a little jig, and Joe joined him along with the others. A spirited group, they quickly became rowdy and boisterous. Finally, Joe stepped away from them.

"All right," he said. "Enough. I'm talkin' to me son." With a wave of his hand Joe dismissed O'Mally and the others settled down.

Joseph watched his father, his heart swelling with joy to be with him again, just to see his face and hear his voice. "I've missed ye, Da," he said affectionately.

"Aw, away wit' ye," his father said, shrugging off the sentiment.

Joseph glanced down the hill and saw the beloved old cottage standing whole, not burned or tumbled as he had last seen it.

"Da . . . have I come home?" Joseph asked with a choked voice.

Beside the cottage stood a woman. She was dressed in a bright red dress, her long dark hair pulled back in a tidy braid.

"That woman there, Joseph, is yer mother, she is," Joe said, the emotion showing in his voice although he tried to hide it. "Ye never knew her, lad; she died in the year you were born. I must go to her now, and I must bid you good-bye, my son."

Joseph watched the woman in the cottage door, his eyes filling with tears as she smiled and waved to him. Joe walked away from Joseph, heading toward the cottage, then he turned back. "Joseph . . . yer an odd boy," he said. "I always said ye were, but now I understand ye, lad." He gestured to the crowd of spirits around them. "Yer a composition of miracles: a bit of this and a bit of that, taken from all of us here. But our time has passed, and yers has only begun. We've given ye all that we can."

"Da—" Joseph wasn't ready to say good-bye yet, but his father continued to walk toward the woman and the cottage.

"Go, son," Joe said, waving him away. "Follow yer road, boy."

"Me road? What road do ye mean?"

"Follow yer road, Joseph, and fulfill yer destiny."

THE train came to an abrupt halt, jarring Joseph awake. Sunlight stung his eyes as he struggled to consciousness with a thundering in his ears. At first he thought the sounds were within his own befuddled head, then he realized the noise was coming from outside the train car.

Pulling himself up off the hard floor, he rushed to the window and looked out. In his entire life he had never seen anything as incredible as the sight that greeted him. The trickle of settlers journeying to Okalhoma had swelled to a migration of massive proportions. Horses and wagons by the hundred followed the road, disappearing on the distant horizon.

So many people, so many courageous spirits, so many dreams being pursued.

And somewhere . . . out in that sea of hopes was his dream. His dream that had been misplaced somehow along the way, but not lost. Never really, truly lost.

Something in Joseph caught fire and kindled into a hot blaze. But beside him, other workers stared out the window at the exodus with faces that reflected their bitterness and defeat.

"Fools," said one grizzled fellow. "There's not enough land to go around. One in a hundred'll stake a claim. The rest of 'em are idiots."

The train began to slowly pull out. The fire inside Joseph flared, until all he could feel was the heat of its blaze and all he could hear was the roar of the flames. Unable to stop himself, he tore away from the window and charged through the bunk car.

Reaching the back of the car, he hesitated only a second, then leaped off the moving train and tumbled into the dust beside the tracks.

"Hey, mick!" the crew boss shouted to him. "Where ya think you're going?"

Joseph flashed him a bright smile and waved to the workers hanging out the windows. "Sorry, lads," he cried. "But I was on the wrong road!"

Sixteen

*R*OME *may not have been built in a day*, Joseph thought, recalling one of his father's old sayings, *but this town sure looks as though it was.*

Here, in the middle of the prairie, a town made of canvas had sprung up, teeming with noise and excitement, people rushing from tent to tent, which housed dry-goods stores, gambling joints, saloons, and brothels . . . all thrown up overnight.

The vibrancy, the hopes of these people ignited the air, old and young men, women and children of all ages, prosperous-looking sorts along with ragged bums. All gathered here at this time and place to stake out a new life for themselves. And all eagerly anticipating a chance to seize their dreams.

But Joseph had no eyes for all this commotion. He strode past them, his own dream burning with urgency. He was a man on a mission who couldn't afford distractions.

"Hey, good-looking!" a young woman wearing a red satin dress and black stockings called to him from the front of one of the larger tents. "Like fifty cents' worth of love?"

He walked on by. "I don't want a penny's worth."

He pushed through the crowded square in the middle of town, where men sat on wooden crates in front of a clapboard hotel and a blacksmith forge. In the distance a long line of people waited to register at a tent that bore the sign LAND OFFICE.

Joining them in line, Joseph stood with the rest in the blazing sun. Several dropped out to escape to the saloon across the way for a cold beer, but Joseph refused to leave his post.

Finally it was his turn and he stepped up to the door, where an officer was handing out stakes and giving instructions. "Each quarter section is marked," he told him as he handed him the stake. "You run for land, remove the marker, and drive in your stake. The race starts tomorrow at noon. Next!" As Joseph walked away, his precious stake in hand, he could hear the man instructing the next person in a mechanical singsong voice. "Each quarter section is marked. You run for land . . ."

Joseph walked over to a corral, where a group of men sat around on crates, chewing tobacco and swapping stories.

"Where can I get meself a horse?" he asked. "I've got a pocketful of railroad money for anyone who'll sell me a horse."

One wrangler whose face was lined from too many days riding the range in the bright sun, rose from his seat and brushed the dust from his britches. He adjusted the splint of wood in his mouth and talked around it. "You're a little late, cowboy. The pickin's are slim."

Joseph held out some cash and the wrangler snatched it from him and shoved it into his pocket. "Got two horses here." He nodded to the animals in the corral. One was sedate, the other a wild bucking stallion.

"This here horse is broke. That horse there is green-broke. You know the difference?"

Joseph nodded. "I think I can see it."

"A broke horse is a dependable horse," the wrangler told him. "But that green-broke horse, why, he's faster."

"The faster the better."

The cowboy sucked air around his toothpick and donned a thoughtful expression. "Maybe so, maybe not. No telling what he'll do. A fella could wind up in Canada on that green-broke horse. But whatever you say. Whoa, stand back!"

He yanked Joseph away from the fence just as the stallion kicked with lethal power, smashing a corral board in half.

Joseph waited for a second until he had caught his breath and his pulse had slowed a bit. Then he said, "I'll be takin' the dependable horse."

Proudly Joseph led Old Dependable—the first horse he had ever owned—back into town and tied him to a hitching rail near the forge, where dozens of other horses were tied. At that moment the blacksmith, an old man with a beard, happened to toss a horseshoe into the street. It landed, *plink*, at Joseph's feet, one edge just touching the toe of his boot.

A superstitious feeling crept over Joseph. The last time a horseshoe had been thrown at his feet, he had looked up and seen . . .

There she was, coming out of the hotel. She turned and walked down the street and into one of the tents, disappearing before his eyes had had their fill of her.

Shannon. Here of all places. Why the devil did she have to follow him? Wasn't it enough that she haunted his dreams every night when he laid his head down and tried to get some sleep.

Of all the women on God's green earth, why did it have to be her?

Joseph reached for the hitching rail and clung to it, steadying himself.

"I'm cursed!" he muttered. "I'm cursed."

As soon as he had recovered his breath and a bit of his composure, Joseph strolled down the street in hope of catching another glimpse of her. Instead, he spotted Danty Duff coming out of a tent marked DRYGOODS, with a pound of flour, which he threw onto a buckboard.

Joseph kept an eye on the tent that Shannon had entered as he hurried over to the buckboard and grabbed Danty's arm.

"Danty, ye ol' divil," he said. "Fancy meetin' up with ye again so soon."

Danty cast a quick glance up and down the street. "Oh, 'tis ye again, lad. Seems yer forever poppin' up where ye aren't wanted."

"I saw her . . . the daughter . . . down the street. What's she doin' here?"

"Same as ye, I suppose," Danty said. "But ye must keep away from her or that fiancé of hers will shoot ye dead."

"Fiancé? Then they aren't married yet."

"They plan to be, but not till they stake their claims. Unmarried, they can take a quarter section each."

Joseph smiled wistfully. "So she's never given up her dream for land."

A group of men and women came out of the dry-goods tent and Danty's mustache twitched nervously. "She's a schemer, that girl is," he admitted. "She's dragged the family west, the whole kit and caboodle . . ."

At that moment they both caught sight of a red parasol leaving the tent down the street. Shannon was walking toward the wagon, her parents and Stephen on either side of her.

"Holy Jaysus," Danty said, pushing Joseph behind

the wagon, "get the hell out of here, lad, before ye stir up a hornet's nest."

"I'm not leavin' till I've spoken to her," Joseph said as the group drew closer to the buckboard.

"Yer daft, lad. She doesn't want to talk to ye, I'm tellin' ye, truly."

Joseph watched from the rear of the buckboard, waiting to be discovered, as Daniel helped Nora into the wagon. Shannon was close, so close he could nearly touch her as Stephen handed her in as well. Halfway up, she dropped her parasol. Chase bent down to retrieve it, but Joseph was too fast for him. Leaping out from behind the wagon, he scooped the parasol off the ground and offered it to Shannon.

She took it, her blue eyes widening with shock. Then she recovered herself and whacked him soundly over the head. "Coward!" she screamed at him.

"Coward . . . ?" he replied, astonished at her reaction.

Rough hands pushed him aside as Stephen Chase vaulted into the wagon. "You heard the lady," Chase said. "She wants nothing to do with you. Get out of here before I blow your head off."

"Wait, Shannon, I must talk to ye."

"She's nothing to say to you," Nora said. "Leave my daughter alone, you black-eyed boy! You dragged her down into dance-hall squalor and all but murdered her!"

"That isn't true!"

Nora grabbed her daughter's parasol and swiped at him.

"Go back, lad," Daniel said. "You've harmed her too severely ever to make amends."

"Then let her be the one to tell me so."

Joseph tried to see Shannon's expression, but she had turned away from him, burying her face in Stephen's shoulder.

"Don't deny it," Stephen said. "You threw her away. If she hadn't been found, she'd have bled to death in the snow."

Outraged by the lie, Joseph shouted back, "And who's the one who found her in this story you've contrived? Yerself, I suppose."

"That's true."

"Are ye so threatened by me that ye'd lie to the woman ye love?"

"Quickly, Danty," Nora said. "Get us away from this scoundrel."

Danty climbed into the driver's seat and whipped the horse. Joseph followed after, trotting along beside the wagon.

"Shannon, do ye believe him?" Joseph asked frantically as the wagon gathered speed and he began to fall behind. "Do ye believe I left ye to die in a snowbank?"

Finally Shannon turned her head and looked over her shoulder at him. "Please, Joseph," she said, her eyes sad and confused. "Please just leave me and my family alone!"

"But Shannon, ye mustn't believe him. He's a liar!" he called after the departing wagon. But he didn't think she heard him.

And even if she had, he didn't think she would have believed him. After all, he was nothing but a common bog boy.

UNABLE to afford a room in the hotel, Joseph sought a camping spot down by the river with the other poorer settlers. Even here, it seemed, in the middle of the Oklahoma Territory, he was destined to take his place among the lower classes.

Tired and heartsick, he walked down to the stream, knelt and splashed his face with the cool, refreshing water, trying to wash away the humiliation of his encounter with the Christie family.

Nearby, a young man was dipping a bucket into the stream while his wife scrubbed dishes, and a baby and two other children splashed between them.

"Aren't you Joseph Donelly?" the man asked.

"I am," Joseph replied.

"I saw you box in Boston, many times. Children, look here! This is the man we're all so grateful to."

Even though Joseph was a grimy, tattered wreck, the family stared at him as though he were a celebrity.

"Yer grateful to me?"

"Oh, yes. By betting on you I made enough money to bring my family west. Come, share some supper with us. We have a bit left over and we'd be honored if you'd accept it."

The man's wife scooped some beans onto a plate and Joseph accepted it gratefully.

As he ate he glanced around the camp. "There's an awful crowd of people goin' after land," he said.

"It's a catching fever, all right. It's attracted all kinds of peculiar folk. Take a look over there. See that pious woman? I hear she was a prostitute once."

Joseph turned to look, and there, by a horse and buggy, a woman was kneeling and praying as she clutched a Bible to her chest. Joseph set his plate aside and walked over to her.

"My goodness," he said. "I thought it was ye, Molly Kay."

Molly reached beneath her Bible and pulled out a pistol. "If you're a remnant of my previous life, go away. I've reformed."

"It was I who gave ye that pistol, Molly," he said with a smile as he moved from the shadows into the light of her campfire.

Molly squinted up at him. Then she leaped to her

feet. "Joseph! I was punished with guilt when I turned you from my house, but now I've been atoned."

With Bible in one hand and gun in the other, she threw her arms around him. "Though your sins be as scarlet, they shall be as white as snow," she quoted. "So saith the prophet Isaiah."

"Ye've been Bible-ized to pieces, Molly, since I saw ye last," he said, taking the seat she offered him on a crate.

"I've been scrubbing my soul for all the men I fooked. There I go cursing again. It's hard work, resurrecting a woman like me."

Joseph laughed and patted her shoulder. "I, too, put me mind off love. Hammered spike after spike in a million miles of rail—but she's followed me here, and now that I've seen her I'm all agitated again."

"Then it's not just love. It's destiny. You're drawn to one another, moth to candle flame."

Joseph thought of Stephen and a sharp pain coursed through his belly. "But I gave her to another man, and a lyin' scoundrel, too. What should I do, Molly?"

Molly scratched her bonnet with a deep perplexity. "I'd advise you with ease if I was still a whore. But now that I'm all reborn, I can't make head nor tail of anything."

"Just answer me with yer heart."

Molly looked into his eyes, which were filled with pain and passion. "If you love her, Joseph, act on it. Go to her, find her, and make your peace with her. Until you've done that, you won't know where you stand."

In the noisy square vendors were selling everything from wagon wheels to bottled water. Competing lawyers sat on wooden crates, wranglers sold horses, women scrubbed clothes, gamblers played roulette, banjos and harmonicas wailed away, and carpenters hammered and sawed.

At one end of the square stood the hotel, the plain two-story wood building with a glamorous facade. Outside the hotel stood Stephen, negotiating with a wrangler.

"Come down five dollars and I'll buy the pair," he said.

"There's a hundred men I could sell these horses to," the old codger replied.

An upstairs window opened and Shannon leaned out. "Make sure they're not distracted, Stephen," she called to him. "I don't want a horse that's fighting me, or nervous or timid or shy."

"Stop worrying, Shannon. I'll look after you."

Stephen mounted the horse to test it while a frustrated, but obedient Shannon withdrew inside.

She turned from the window to her mother, who was running around the room, straightening and cleaning.

"That Stephen irritates me to death sometimes," she said. "He's so bossy."

"Don't pout, Shannon. Buying a horse is a man's job."

"But I'll be riding it tomorrow, Mother. I might even be called upon to gallop," she added sarcastically.

"That's liberty enough for a girl of your station."

Shannon sat down at a vanity and watched her mother in the mirror as Nora bustled around the room. "Mother, this is a hotel. You don't have to dust it."

"I'm merely creating order in this otherwise straggly place." She cast a critical look over her daughter's appearance. "Shannon, your hair, tie it up."

"It doesn't matter," Shannon said, studying her reflection without interest.

"Don't argue with me. Stephen will lose respect for you if you neglect your dignity."

Nora snatched a brush from the vanity and pulled Shannon's long wild hair up into a prim little bun. Shannon winced in the mirror like a young child having her ears washed.

"You treat me like a baby, Mother."

"Only when you act like one. Stand up. Turn around. Do up this button. There. Now smile. No, that's not a smile, that's an impudent grin."

"Mother!" Shannon stamped her foot in exasperation. "I have no liberty!"

"You had a try at liberty and nearly lost your life." She turned away from her daughter and walked over to the bed. "Come. I don't trust this mattress. Help me turn it over."

Shannon did as she said, but the other side was no cleaner. Gradually, she gained control of her temper. After all, her mother was only teaching her what she felt was important. Unfortunately, Shannon had experienced some hardships that had caused her to question things in life that her mother held in high esteem. She was no longer sure she held the same values.

"Mother . . . do you think that you and Father are compatible at all?"

"No, I don't."

"But you must have been once. Why else would you have married him?"

After spreading and tucking the sheet, Nora sat on the edge of the bed and patted the place beside her. Shannon sat down.

"When we were young," she said, "your father and I fell in love. It was passionate, romantic, even reckless now and then. But we were of the privileged class. Its rules were ours to uphold. Marriage is a compromise,

Shannon. A man and a woman surrender up a portion of themselves."

"But don't you miss it . . . the passion and the recklessness?"

Nora took Shannon's hand in hers. "It's better to have security, my modern little child. Security lasts. Passion doesn't."

Shannon tried to take her mother's words to heart, but it was difficult. She thought of the security she would have with Stephen . . . and the passion she had felt with Joseph.

Seeing him had resurrected those old needs and desires. As much as she wanted to believe her mother, it appeared that in some cases passion, too, could last for an insufferably long time.

MOLLY and Joseph strolled along the dark streets, toward the center of town, which blazed with torches. The bustle of daytime business had given way to nighttime rowdiness. Amid brawling and sporadic gunfire, men staggered, drunk and wild in the streets, as tension mounted in anticipation of the big race.

"It's Sodom and Gomorrah, Joseph," she said, "brimstoned into one."

Joseph grabbed her, pulling her out of the way of a fellow who was being ejected headfirst from one of the saloons. "How will I find her in all of this?" he asked, peering through the crowds. "And how will I get hold of her long enough to talk to her and make peace with her?"

"Ah, destiny will find a way," Molly replied confidently.

As they passed a tent brothel one of the girls—the same one who had propositioned him earlier—lifted her skirt, revealing a shapely ankle and a bit of calf. "I'm all yours mister," she said, repeating her pitch. "Fifty cents."

"Oh, 'tis you again," he replied wearily.

Molly pushed between them as though to shield Joseph from the temptations of the flesh. "Don't degrade yourself, dear," she said as she looked the girl up and down with a critical, practiced eye. "You're worth at least a dollar."

Approaching the town center, they could hear a hillbilly band tuning up. Settlers came running from everywhere and assumed square-dance positions at the crossroads. Tension, ready to be released in the form of rowdy fun, filled the air with expectation.

On the opposite side of the square, out of Joseph's sight and hearing, Nora Christie stepped out onto the porch of the hotel.

"Daniel Christie," she called. "Where are you, you wayward fool of a man?"

Behind her walked Stephen, his elbow extended, Shannon's white gloved hand resting primly upon it.

Daniel sauntered up to the porch with Danty Duff. Both wore enormous cowboy hats and their boots jingled with silver spurs.

"Howdy, Nora!" he said, tucking his thumbs into his belt. "Would you like to be my wife?"

Nora glared at him in disbelief, her eyes scanning his costume with open contempt. "I'm already your wife, you idiot."

He jumped up onto the porch and grabbed her hand. "Come dance with me, Nora."

"Not in a million years. Daaaniel!"

She squealed and kicked as he clumsily picked her up and carted her off to the dance. Danty ran after them while on the platform with the band a caller shouted to the crowd between jubilant riffs on the fiddle,

"Circle to the left,
Go round the land!"

Then allemande left
With your left hand . . . !"

A somewhat calamitous square dance fell together, punctuated by pistol shots and shrieks of delight.

Shannon and Stephen watched from the hotel porch. They made a nice couple, standing together, radiating dignity.

Shannon smiled a little sadly. "I hope they both enjoy their lives this far away from home. Ireland is a long way off, and they're old to be changing their ways."

Stephen looked down at her, concern on his face. "Something troubles you, Shannon."

"I'm fine."

"Let's not have secrets between us. There's discontent in your eyes. Speak openly to me."

She hesitated. "I'm afraid to. I think you'll be angry if I do."

"And if I'm angry? It will never outweigh the affection I feel for you. Tell me."

His comforting words gave her the courage to confess. "These people terrify me. The way they live and carry on; sometimes I fear I might be tempted again and fall back into ruin."

Stephen turned to face her, taking both her hands in his. "Shannon, you and I can outride any person here. Tomorrow, side by side, we'll claim enough fine land to protect us from the world. On it you will have your ranch and a mansion made of stone."

She reached out and clutched the front of his shirt. "Oh, Stephen, can you ever forgive me for running away from you?"

"Of course I can. You're forgiven now."

"I've never seen my father treat my mother so," she said with misgivings.

Stephen watched as Daniel twirled a reluctant Nora

through the steps. "Well, you needn't worry, my dear. I won't carry *you* off into all that savagery."

"But I might like to dance," she admitted reluctantly.

"You can't be serious."

Shannon released his arm and stared up at him. "Stephen, look at me. I know I've been reckless. My recklessness has taught me to appreciate my anchored life with you. But I'm a woman, Stephen. My appetite for life is huge."

He looked her squarely in the eye and said without emotion, "Control it."

Then he took her by the arm and led her off the porch. "Let's go for a walk away from all this madness."

DANTY stood at the side, watching the dancers, whooping and clapping enthusiastically. Suddenly he was grabbed by the arm and spun around—by Joseph.

"Where is she?" Joseph demanded.

"Saints preserve us, lad, haven't ye had enough abuse for one lifetime?" Danty asked. Then, seeing the determined look in Joseph's eyes, he sighed and nodded toward the hotel. "Last I saw her she was standing on the hotel porch . . . with her fiancé," he added pointedly.

Joseph scanned the crowd and the porch, which was now empty. Nervously he ran his fingers through his bedraggled hair. "How do I look, Molly?" he asked.

"You're a filthy mess. But never mind about those things. Just be your charming self and you'll sweep her off her feet."

Joseph took a deep breath and plunged into the crowd, leaving Molly alone with Danty.

Danty removed his giant hat. "Me name is Danty Duff," he said.

She smiled coquettishly. "And mine is Molly Kay."

Danty bowed; Molly curtsied.

"Yer a religious woman, I see." He pointed to the Bible, which she had clutched to her chest.

Molly looked around at the dancers and down at the Bible. Then she took one long, searching look at Danty, who had donned his most beguiling smile.

Flinging the Bible behind her, she hiked up her skirt and grabbed Danty by the arm. "Not so's you'd notice," she said as she pulled him into the circle.

The caller's voice rang out through the square.

> "Partner right,
> Do a right and left grand!
> Hand over hand
> Go round the ring . . . !"

High-stepping all the way, Daniel twirled Nora through the steps. As Stephen and Shannon walked by, circling around the dancers, Daniel reached out and grabbed Shannon, pulling her into his arms. "Be off with you, lad," he told Stephen. "My daughter is dancing with *me*."

"But—" Before Stephen could speak his mind, he was scooped away by Nora.

Stunned by this turn of events, Stephen followed in Daniel's path, spinning Nora through the paces.

Daniel whooped his happiness as he galloped Shannon around the circle.

She laughed. "I think the Wild West suits you, Father. You're happy as a boy."

"Thanks to you, you little rascal, cahooting us all this way. But are *you* happy? That's the question."

"I am, Father," she said with less enthusiasm than he had exhibited. "I am."

After a few turns around the square Shannon was twirled back to Stephen. At that moment Molly and Danty gamboled by.

"You're a limber little gentleman, Danty Duff," Molly said.

"You're limber yourself, Molly Kay."

They were directed to switch partners again and Danty found himself dancing with Nora, who nearly fainted to find herself in the arms of her servant.

Meanwhile, Shannon found herself thrown into the arms of . . . him!

"Joseph!"

She shrieked with alarm, and he appeared to be as rattled as she. Then he summoned the youthful arrogance that had always stood him in good stead. He puffed out his chest and said, "I'm of the opinion that ye and me are in love."

"You're wrong!"

"Then why does fate refuse to keep us apart?"

Two other pairs of dancers crashed into them from the front and the back, causing them to slam against each other. Both gasped at the contact.

"You're not my fate!" she cried. "And stop acting like a fool."

She turned to walk away from him, but he grabbed her and pulled her back into his arms.

' Meet your partner," the caller shouted.

> "And give her a swing!
> Then promenade right,
> Go round the ring . . . !"

With his arm tightly wrapped around her waist, Joseph propelled Shannon around and around. Nora, who was dancing with Stephen, saw them and shrieked, "There he is. It's the devil again! This never would have happened, Stephen, if you'd only shot him in that duel like you were supposed to."

She shoved Stephen toward Joseph and Shannon

just as the partners were switched and Shannon was spun back into Stephen's arms.

"Don't fall for his corruption, Shannon," he warned her. "Your future is with me."

The couples switched again, and Joseph grabbed her away from Stephen. "Ye'd have that ass for a husband?" he asked. "'Twas I you fled from Ireland with."

The dancers went through a series of trading partners and Shannon found herself dancing with her father, Danty, and then a man who was as filthy as a troll. Shannon shrieked as he licked his broken teeth and smiled at her lasciviously.

A second later she found herself back in Stephen's arms.

All this spinning back and forth was making her terribly dizzy. "I'm unraveling!" she screamed, halting in her tracks.

Her hysteria stopped the dance. The musicians ceased playing as everyone stared at her. Tears began to roll down her face as her emotions overwhelmed her.

Stephen put his arm around her shoulder and glared at Joseph. "Look what he's done to you, Shannon."

"Me? What I've done to her?" Joseph replied.

Stephen shoved Joseph hard on the chest. "You're a peasant. She doesn't love you. It's *me* she loves. I'm educated, schooled in the law, bred with manners, and trained in markmanship. Name one thing that *you've* accomplished in the world."

His chest and ego bruised, Joseph shoved Stephen back. "I made history in Boston for a time. Unbeaten I was in bare-knuckle brawls, admired by the highest of men."

Stephen snorted. "Boxing is a pagan sport."

"It's more honorable than jiggin' a pistol around!"

Their tempers got the better of them and they attacked each other, falling to the ground, where they wrestled in the dirt.

"Stop it!" Shannon yelled. "Both of you! I thought *I* was the object of your dispute!"

Lying in the dirt, they both turned their heads to look up at her, ear to ear.

"Well . . . you are, Shannon," Stephen said, somewhat sheepishly.

"You'd never know it. The two of you strutting and bragging, who's the better boxer, who's the better shooter, who's got the biggest you-know-what!"

"Shannon!" Nora cried.

"Men!" Shannon stomped her foot. "All bluster and no substance. Neither one of you is worthy of me. And as for that race for land, I'll be running it for myself alone."

Joseph and Stephen scrambled to their feet.

"But Shannon—" Stephen reached for her.

"Alone!" she cried, throwing off his hand. "And for company the rest of my days, I'll be satisfied with horses, thank you. Horses are better than men. They sleep standing up!"

Daniel threw back his head and roared. Nora sputtered and fumed. Shannon stormed off into the night.

"Stephen," Nora said when she had caught her breath, "don't just stand there with your mouth open—go after her and be stern with her. She needs to be put in her place."

"There's not a man on earth'll ever put *her* in her place," Joseph said.

Nora pushed Stephen and he followed Shannon into the darkness. But not Joseph. He had already endured quite enough and he was furious about the whole matter.

"What did I do wrong, Molly?" he asked, slapping his pants and sending the dust flying.

"You let your pride get in your way," Molly replied. "Pride always goeth before a fall."

"To hell with her then," he said. "Danty, ye heard me father on his deathbed. He told me to find some land. I've followed Shannon Christie far enough. If she can be selfish, then by God, so can I."

Joseph stomped away in the opposite direction from where Shannon and Stephen had headed.

Danty sighed. "'Tis a sad state of affairs when matters o' the heart go awry."

Molly smiled knowingly. "Ah . . . don't worry about those young people. He'll make it right with her yet, you just wait and see if he doesn't. He'll be chasing that skirt of hers again come morning."

Seventeen

BEHIND the hotel hung a maze of clotheslines. Laundry flapped in the breeze: sheets, trousers, shirts, blouses, stockings, long underwear, chemises, and bloomers. At the water trough behind the clotheslines, Nora Christie, highborn lady, knelt and gingerly dunked her husband's shirt into the water, holding it by her fingertips.

From the other side of the yard Shannon left her clothes in their basket and strode toward her mother, pushing the hanging clothes aside as she went.

"For heaven's sake, Mother," she said. "Those clothes will never come clean if you don't get your hands wet." She knelt beside her mother and grabbed the shirt. "Here, watch me. You have to plunge and scrub, plunge and scrub." She demonstrated while her mother watched in wonder.

Nora took the shirt from her and repeated the action. "Like so?"

Shannon smiled at her affectionately, as though a bond had just been established between them. "Yes, exactly like that. But you must say the words—plunge and scrub, plunge and scrub. It's very important when you're first learning . . . or so I've been told."

Galloping hoofbeats interrupted their conversation as a couple of riders came pounding up. Daniel Christie sat upon a handsome bay, the enormous cowboy hat still engulfing his head. He also wore a new western-style shirt and denim trousers.

Stephen Chase rode with him on a pinto.

"Nora," Daniel shouted as they pulled their horses to a halt and dismounted in a cloud of dust, "I've been shot!"

Nora gasped and dropped the shirt into the trough. "Shot! Oh, my God, Daniel!"

"Well, shot *at* anyway," he added when Stephen cast him a sideways look. "The cavalry fired at us. We crossed the starting line and broke the law."

"You won't be riding in that race tomorrow, you old fool," Nora said with authority.

"Don't be so sure." Daniel pushed his gigantic hat back on his forehead and tucked both thumbs into his belt, his chest expanding, a rebellious light in his eyes. "The Wild West suits me, Nora. There's no telling *what* I might do."

Meanwhile, Stephen had hurried over to Shannon, who, having assured herself that her father was healthy, had resumed her scrubbing.

"Shannon, I found it," he said, unable to contain his excitement. "Twenty miles straight west of here: the plot of land you've dreamed of."

Shannon didn't answer but squeezed the water from the shirt and laid it in the basket.

"Describe it to her, Stephen," Daniel said.

"You'll love it, Shannon. The earth is dry and dusty here, but where we'll live there's a winding stream, and the grass on the gentle hills around it grows high, and rich, and green."

Her dreamland. And Joseph's dreamland. For a

moment she allowed herself to remember all those times when they had lain in that dark room and spoken of their hopes. Even then she had seen that green land, the bubbling stream, the gentle sloping green hills that reminded her of her childhood.

Stephen was standing over her, his face eager and expectant. But all she felt toward him was anger, anger that he would infringe upon her dream.

"It's paradise itself," he continued. "And by waiting to marry, we can claim a quarter section each."

She said nothing, but grabbed another shirt from the basket and plunged it into the water.

"Is it not exactly what you've told me you wanted?" Stephen asked, sounding a little hurt and angry.

"It is."

He knelt beside her on one knee, but only after checking the ground carefully first to see that he wouldn't get his pants dirty. Shannon noted the mannerism and thought how typical it was of Stephen. Before, she would have thought such a gesture gentlemanly and sophisticated. Now she thought it prissy, and she wondered if Stephen had even once in his life gotten his hands dirty. What would he think of her if he knew that she had stood in freezing mud up to her knees and shoveled until she collapsed?

Joseph had thought her courageous and hardworking, and he had told her so. Somehow she thought that Stephen would have considered her coarse and common.

"Are you upset with me, Shannon?" he asked. Putting his hand beneath her chin, he forced her to look up at him.

She brushed his hand away and stood. "Of course I'm upset, Stephen." Picking up the basketful of wet laundry, she carried to the clothesline. "I told you last night after the dance, I want to choose my land myself."

He rose and followed after her. "Shannon, stop this childishness," he said in an authoritative, condescending tone that not even her own father had ever used with her. "Are we not here, your parents and I, in this godforsaken place, because *you* wanted this? I couldn't take you with me today. It was too dangerous."

"I don't *mind* a little danger now and then," she said, wearing a defiant expression that was very similar to the one her father wore when he set his mind about something.

Stephen reached out and grabbed her hands, holding them firmly. With a stern look on his handsome face he said, "Tomorrow we will ride as one, together, side by side. We *will* claim our land and then we'll marry and finally settle down. You do want to settle down, don't you, Shannon?"

"Yes," she said with a sigh. "I want to settle down."

Mollified, he leaned over and kissed her gently on the forehead. "There now," he said. "That's better. I hate to see you angry. It isn't your nature to be so. You're really such a sweet and gentle soul."

Sweet and gentle soul? The words grated on her nerves as she watched him walk away, following Nora and Daniel toward the hotel. She didn't want to be thought of as sweet and gentle. Joseph had never called her that. He had said that he admired her spirit, her tenacity, her courage. He had called her a fighter, and she much preferred that image of herself.

Sweet and gentle, my foot, she thought.

She began to hang the laundry with a vengeance, trying to keep her temper under control. How dare Stephen go out and choose her land for her. How dare he intrude upon her dream, which she had paid for so dearly . . . a dream that she had risked her life and nearly died for.

Finally, winded from her effort, she stopped to mop her brow.

"Hello, Shannon," said a familiar voice. Her heart leaped and she whirled around to see Joseph standing there, that mischievous grin on his face.

She stared at him for a moment, then turned her back on him and continued hanging the clothes.

"I'm surprised that you've sought me out again, considering all the opposition you've met in your pervious attempts," she said.

"But I haven't had a moment to speak to ye alone without yer family and that arse of a fiancé of yers hangin' about. Yer lookin' well, Shannon." His eyes raked over her as though he were memorizing every line of her face and form.

Uncomfortable with the heat that rose in her beneath his scrutiny, she pulled a sheet from the basket and hung it on the line, creating a wall between them.

"How did you get here?" she asked in a conversational tone, deciding to treat this as a casual meeting between two old friends. "My family and I came by train."

He peeked around the sheet, and she quickly hung up another.

"I came by train meself," he said.

She wondered how he could have afforded the train fare. The last time she had seen him he had been destitute. But then, she knew him well enough to know there was no holding him back when he wanted something. He was, after all, a scrapper.

"And I suppose you're looking forward to running in the race tomorrow," she said, knowing the answer.

"I always said I'd get me land." He pulled the sheet aside. She hung her mother's drawers in his face, knowing he wouldn't touch those.

"I've even bought meself a horse," he said proudly. "And a fine and elegant creature he is at that."

She smiled, a little sadly, awkwardly. "Time takes care of everything, doesn't it? It all seems such a long,

long time ago." In her mind's eye she could see their humble little room, the streets they had walked together, the evenings when he had sat in his chair and struggled to learn how to read.

"Aye . . . Boston . . . that was . . ." His eyes glazed over for a moment as though he, as well as she, were seeing those times and places. Then he shook his head slightly and snapped out of his reverie. "Yer family and yerself will be relieved to hear that I've given up on tryin' to bring the two of us together again. I believe things have worked out as they should. Do ye not agree?" he asked, his eyes searching her face.

Shannon nodded. But without conviction.

"I was just wantin' to make peace with ye," he added. "After all we've been through together, didn't seem right somehow that we should be enemies."

"Good luck tomorrow, Joseph," she said, offering her hand to him, putting her pain and anger over his desertion aside for a moment.

He took her hand in his and the vibrancy in the man set her afire. How could just the touch of his hand do so much, when a kiss from her own fiancé left her cold?

"And best of luck to you, Shannon," he said sadly. Then he turned to walk away. Hesitating, he turned back to her, an intense light burning in his green eyes. "Shannon Christie, ye never gave up. Ye knew what ye wanted in Ireland, and look at ye, here ye are in the Oklahoma Territory, ready to run yer race." He smiled and shook his head, his eyes full of admiration. "Yer a corker, Shannon. What a corker ye are!"

Then he turned and left, disappearing among the lines of flapping laundry.

Overcome with emotion, Shannon stood, looking at the empty spot where he had been, tears filling her eyes. What might have happened had he not left her that night in the snow? she wondered. Would they have run the race together? Claimed their dream together?

She shook her head and closed her eyes, trying to shut out the memories, the dreams and loving feelings. Joseph *had* deserted her, and Stephen had found her. And that was all that mattered now. That was all that would ever matter.

WITH a strange feeling of elation at having seen her, and despair for having to leave her, Joseph walked away from Shannon, throwing the sheets and blankets aside as he picked his path through the maze of soggy laundry. Pushing the last fluttering pillowcase out of his way, he found himself face-to-face with Stephen Chase.

His blood instantly raced to his face and he felt his cheeks growing hot with anger.

"What are you doing here after my explicit warning to you to stay away?" Chase demanded. "Answer me."

"I've nothin' to say to ye," Joseph returned. "At least nothin' ye'd like to hear."

He started to walk away, but Chase blocked his path. "You brought her to me in the cold that night and asked me to care for her. I've cared for her and more since then. Now stay away from her. Do you hear me? You've nothing to give a woman of her kind."

The insult stung deeply and Joseph's hands knotted into fists as his side. "And what've ye to give her?"

"Land. The land of her dreams. I've seen it and I'm claiming it tomorrow afternoon."

"Out of my way."

Stephen opened his coat and showed Joseph his holstered guns. "I'm warning you, boy, don't ever talk to her again. And don't come anywhere near me during that race. There's a bullet in here that has been thinking of you since the morning you ran from our duel."

Ran? His blood boiled, but Joseph fought to retain control over his temper. "I'll ride anywhere I please. Yer not in Ireland anymore," he said. "And I'll ride for meself. Not for Shannon, not for anyone but *meself.*"

Something in Joseph's eyes must have registered on Chase because he moved aside and allowed him to pass.

So, he's going to give Shannon the land of her dreams, Joseph thought as he walked away from Chase, feeling the man's eyes boring into his back. *A lot you know about Shannon Christie. Rather than be given anything by any man, she'd rather take it with her own hands.*

But the thought gave him little comfort and did little to lessen the sick feeling in his gut. Shannon was as beautiful as ever. And forever lost to him.

LATER that night Shannon sat on the edge of her bed in her hotel room, brushing her long hair. She wore an elegant white linen nightgown with lace at her throat and wrists. There was no point in dressing like a heathen, even in the Wild West, her mother had told her when they had packed for the trip.

"Knock, knock," said her father as he opened her door and stuck his head inside the room.

"Come in," she said, delighted as always to have his company.

"You're as pretty as a candle, daughter of mine," he said. "Can you spare me a good-night kiss?"

"Of course, Father."

He entered and sat down on the cot beside her. Pausing, he listened to the bustling crowd in the street outside. A broad smile split his round face. "What an adventure, eh? All thanks to you, you renegade." He stopped and studied her face for a moment. She wore a faraway expression that he had seen many times over the last year. "You aren't even listening to me, are you?" he said, gently reprimanding her.

"Yes, I am," she replied. She reached over and took his hand.

"Do you think he followed you here?" Daniel asked.

She appeared surprised that he would guess her thoughts, then she said, "No, he has no need for me. And I have none for him."

He said nothing, just gazed at her sadly.

"You don't believe me, do you?" she said.

"What I believe isn't important, my child," he said. "In matters of the heart it's what *you* believe that counts."

She sighed and leaned her head on her father's shoulder. He wrapped his arm around her, drawing her closer, attempting to impart some comfort.

"I believe," she said slowly, "that I must forget him . . . but there are certain things we did together, certain lovely, funny, touching things about him that my heart won't forget, no matter what I do."

Christie held his daughter tightly and placed a kiss on her cheek. "Once before I told you to follow your heart, and afterward I cursed myself because I feared I had sent you to your ruin. I don't know if I can give you that advice again, child, even if I thought it were right."

"I understand, Father. I'm not really asking for your advice this time. I know what I have to do."

"And what is that, child?"

"I have to follow my head for once, and not my heart. I only wish it didn't hurt so badly."

"I know, my dear. I know."

Daniel Christie wished that he could do something, say something to offer solace to his only child. But he knew that broken hearts, more than broken limbs, took time to mend.

But when would she be whole again? It had already been such a long time and he had seen so little healing.

God, he prayed, *let it be soon.*

JOSEPH downed his whiskey in one gulp, welcoming the liquid heat that burned all the way down his throat to his stomach. The drink—and all the ones before it—raced into his bloodstream, softening the edges of the scene before him. The gamblers, drinkers, and prostitutes all wore smiles of contentment as pleasant and warm as his own. Actually, they were all a bit fuzzy and he couldn't see if they were smiling or frowning, but he also didn't give a damn.

He set down his glass, threw back his head and began singing.

> "Her beautiful eyes . . .
> Were a terrible curse!
> Three days in his grave
> She ran off . . ."

He abandoned the song, his mood evaporating. "Impossible woman," he muttered drunkenly. "Came by train, she tells me. Train! All those months I tried to forget her, dynamitin' mountains and drivin' spikes—I was layin' down the very track that brought her here!"

Wobbly on his feet, he leaned against the wall. But, as the building was a tent, the wall was canvas and wouldn't support his weight. He promptly fell backward on his arse. The crowd roared as he staggered to his feet.

"To hell with everybody," he told them. "That's me thought for the night. He's got her land all picked out—the land of her dreams. Tomorrow I ride for me, for *meself*! And I'll ride anywhere I please . . . on me own fine horse."

Straightening his coat and assembling the tattered remains of his dignity, he stumbled out the door and into the street.

He crossed the square and headed for the hitching rail by the blacksmith forge where all the horses were tied. But when he arrived, he stopped abruptly, groaned, and crossed himself.

"Sweet Mary, Jaysus, and all the saints preserve us," he said.

An old blacksmith, wearing a leather apron, sauntered out of the forge. "That there was the oldest horse I ever saw in my life," he told Joseph. "Couldn't believe anyone paid good money for that pile of horseshit."

There on the ground lay Old Dependable. And one look told Joseph plainly . . . Old Dependable was very dead.

THE next morning the bustling tent city had become a ghost town. The teeming crowds were gone, and in their wake lay broken tents and mountains of litter. An eerie silence dominated the dusty path that had once been the main street of this strange town.

The clatter of hoofbeats—powerful hoofbeats— disturbed the silence as Shannon cantered into town upon a powerful roan. She reined the horse to a stop in the middle of the rubble.

"Father! Mother!" she cried, looking in all directions.

Then another horse galloped along the back of the tents, its rider waving two stakes with yellow flags that fluttered wildly.

"Stephen!" she shouted. "I can't find them anywhere."

—— 299 ——

"Neither can I," he replied as he pulled up his horse beside her. "But the race is soon to begin."

"Where would they be?"

"I don't know, but we can't concern ourselves with them now. I'm sure they're fine. Hurry, Shannon!"

After one more frantic glance around, she took the stake he was holding out to her and they galloped away.

Toward the starting line.

HORSES and wagons raced in crisscross trails, colliding with each other, their owners shouting and swearing as they stirred the hot dust into choking clouds that even further hampered the visibility of the riders and drivers. The biggest land run in the history of Oklahoma was about to begin.

Frantically, families performed last-minute repairs on rickety wagons, cowboys jostled for space, and Indians stood by, watching with lively curiosity as the tension mounted.

In the middle of this chaos a commotion caused even the most self-absorbed to turn and watch for a moment. A young man with dark hair sat upon a stallion that was bucking and kicking as though its backside were being pricked by the devil's pitchfork.

"Whoa!" Joseph shouted, trying to bring the green-broke stallion, which he had purchased only an hour before, under control. "Whoa there, ye black-hearted son of Cromwell!"

Joseph hung on for dear life as the creature tried to kick everything in its sight. People scrambled to escape those flying, lethal hooves. Wagons veered out of his way and other horses reared. Some of the spectators laughed at him, while others cursed him and made lewd suggestions about what he should do with the animal.

"Damnation," he muttered under his breath. "Help

me out here, Da. Or this beast will surely land me in Canada!''

"THIS is breaking the law, Nora," Daniel said to his wife as they huddled together in a gully that divided a fertile, verdant tract of land. Cheerfully he held up a flagged stake. "Isn't it exciting! Finally we're having an adventure of our own!"

They peeked up over the gully, but the only living creature for as far as the eye could see was their horse.

"I don't like you taking charge of the business side of our life," Nora said with a sniff.

He reached over and thumped her companionably on the shoulder as though she were an old drinking buddy. "Oh, you do so. Now listen up. This stake goes in the ground over there. That's your job. I'll tell you when. Meanwhile, I will run this horse in circles. It's got to look sweaty and tired . . . even dead would be good. Got it?"

"Yes, but—I'd feel better if we were living with the children," she said sadly.

"Shannon's not a child anymore."

Nora looked around at the prairie and shivered. "It's scary out here, Daniel," she said as though confessing some deep sin. "I keep thinking a redskin's going to pop up and scalp us."

"There are no Indians around here, Nora. Once there were. This land was theirs before the government pushed them off."

"Pushed them off their land?"

A sadness touched Daniel's eyes. "Aye. Someone's always getting pushed off their land somewhere in the world."

He leaned over and placed a quick kiss on her cheek, the first impetuous affectionate gesture he had made toward her in years. Her eyes widened with surprise.

"Bah," he said. "You needn't be afraid of anything, Nora. We'll do fine. Pretend we're starting out in life, instead of ending up."

Nora stared at her husband as though looking at a stranger. Then her face softened, and she appeared younger than she had in years. "I suppose we could try, Daniel," she said with a small grin as she shyly returned his peck on the cheek. "Yes, we could try."

STEPHEN and Shannon rode their horses closer and closer to the line, fighting their way through the thickening crowd. Fiercely tense and competitive, Stephen urged his horse ahead of Shannon, jostling anyone in his path aside.

"What's happening ahead?" he called back to Shannon.

She could see a cloud of dust and hear the cries of people who were gathered in a circle around some sort of confusion and violence.

When they neared the scene, Stephen saw what was going on and grinned. Shannon saw, too, and momentarily hated Stephen for his smug smile.

Joseph was still struggling with Greenbroke, hooves flying, Joseph clinging to the reins and the saddle horn.

"The race is that way, lad!" Stephen shouted, taunting him.

Stephen edged his horse closer to the stallion and deliberately waved his stake with its yellow flag at the horse. Startled, the horse reared and Joseph tumbled head over heels to the ground.

"Forget the horse and fall on your face on the first piece of land you can find!" Stephen yelled to him. Then he laughed and moved on.

Shannon nudged her horse closer to Joseph. "Take him by the bit, Joseph," she called as she rode by. "Grab him hard by the bit and show him who's boss."

Joseph looked up at her from where he lay on the ground and watched as she rode away toward the line. The line that he had to get to, or he didn't have a chance.

He jumped up and grabbed the stallion's reins and the end of the bit. The animal reared, lifting him off the ground, then continued to buck and writhe.

So much for that, he thought as he dangled in the air for a brief moment. *There's no doubt who's the boss here . . . 'tis the bloody horse.*

CAVALRYMEN, wearing their sharp blue uniforms with freshly polished brass buttons, stood at the line, bugles, watches, and guns in hand. Cannons stood at ready nearby. A thick line of horses, wagons, and expectant settlers stretched in either direction as far as the eye could see.

On line, Shannon took the kerchief from her neck and wrapped it around the lower part of her face, covering her nose and mouth. Any minute now they would all be eating dust.

Stephen inched his horse forward, aggressively pushing other riders aside.

Bugles sounded a warning alarm. The cavalrymen's stopwatches indicated only seconds to go. Tension was as thick in the air as the dust. An awesome silence stole over the ranks.

Suddenly a rider bolted ahead too early and one of the cavalrymen nearest him drew his pistol and shot him off his horse.

Other horses reared in panic. A few people shouted, then silence descended once more.

At precisely noon the cavalry cannons fired.

Shannon whipped her horse, riding as though demons were chasing her, swept along in a furious wave of excitement like nothing she had ever felt before. She knew, even as she rode, that she would remember and feel the exhilaration of this moment for the rest of her life. Never again would she have a chance like this, and she rode like a madwoman. Racing . . . racing for her dream.

All around her, horses, wagons, buggies, buckboards, bicycles, and people on foot thundered across the open land. The ground shook and the dust flew.

The Oklahoma Land Rush was on!

Eighteen

As the horses and wagons thundered by, leaving him in their cloud of dust, Joseph panicked. If he couldn't even get on this cursed horse, how was he ever to have the chance to pursue his dream?

Memories flashed through his mind as he tried again and again to mount the beast, only to have it shy out from under him. He thought of all the beatings he had taken to arrive at this time and place. He recalled the bitter winter when he and Shannon had nearly starved and frozen to death in the streets. He thought of all those days in the hot sun, pounding spikes on the railroad.

This bloody animal wasn't going to ruin it all for him now.

Hanging on to the stallion's bit, Joseph looked him squarely in the eye. "I have no wish to fight ye," he said with deadly deliberation.

A second later, his fist shot out and he punched Greenbroke hard, right in the nose. The blow dazed the animal just long enough for Joseph to swing up into the saddle. This time he *wasn't* going to be thrown. He swore a quick oath on his father's grave that he would ride this beast into hell itself, but he wasn't coming out of that saddle.

The stallion thrashed and tried to bolt in the wrong direction, but Joseph jerked savagely on the reins. Suddenly Joseph found himself headed in the right direction.

He was in the race!

And better than that . . . his horse was outrunning them all!

The creature flew as though its tail were on fire, passing settlers whose dreams lay broken in the dust. Wagons toppled, wheels broken off, horses panicking, bucking, ripping their harnesses apart. Buggies collided with wagons and everywhere could be heard screams of frustration and pain.

Joseph hung on, flying by on his whirlwind of a horse, his face so low that the stallion's mane slapped him across his cheeks and whipped into his eyes. But he didn't even notice. All he could see was the vision of his dream . . . his land . . . and it was just ahead . . . he could feel it!

In the distance he saw two familiar figures, a tall thin man in a black coat, and a woman with radiant copper hair that was blowing wildly in the wind. Stephen and Shannon. Just ahead. And he was gaining on them. He did what he could to steer the horse in that direction.

Meanwhile, Shannon had no idea he was following her. She, too, was focused, her eyes constantly scanning the horizon for that spot . . . that precious spot she knew she would recognize in her heart the moment she laid eyes upon it.

She reached up and ripped the kerchief off her mouth. Quickly she glanced over at Stephen and saw him whip and spur his horse.

"Faster, Shannon!" he yelled. "Hyah!"

He thrashed the horse, whipping its left flank, then its right. Pulling up beside another rider, he pressed forward, trying to pass him. Shannon watched the two ride neck and neck for almost a minute, then Stephen reached out and snatched the rider's stake out of his saddlebag and threw it to the ground. The other rider was forced to rein in his horse and circle back to get the stake.

Triumphantly, Stephen galloped ahead.

They, too, passed scenes of chaos and destruction. In the clamor and anarchy husbands dived off their horses and wives leaped from wagons, driving stakes into their land, then stood, weapons in hand to protect it. There were violent disputes: men fighting, stakes broken, guns fired, and people killed. The land was littered with failure and devastation.

But Shannon couldn't allow herself to even see it, let alone take it in. Somewhere, maybe just over the next rise, was her dream . . . and by God, she wasn't going to stop until she had claimed it!

NERVOUSLY, Nora Christie stood, stake grasped in both hands, while her husband circled around her, exhausting his sweating horse.

"That poor animal looks as though he's about to drop, Daniel," she said irritably. Her nerves were about to snap and she had to scold someone.

"Good, that's the way he's supposed to look. Can't have him fresh and rested, now, can we?" he said, still wearing that joyful grin that was driving her crazy.

Didn't he know that they were doing something terribly illegal? They could be shot for this, and he was enjoying every minute of it.

Briefly, she entertained the thought that this Daniel before her, the one wearing the impish smile with the fire of adventure shining in his eyes, was reminiscent of the young man she had fallen in love with so many years ago. She had been the same way—full of fire and vinegar—back then. But somewhere along the way she had grown dry and brittle. She had thought it was expected of her . . . now that she was a wife, a mother, and mistress of a household.

Maybe this *was* like starting life all over again, after all.

Then she felt it, a trembling of the earth beneath her feet, quickly followed by a rumble like thunder in the distance.

"Lord protect us, Daniel!" she cried as an avalanche of wagons and horses poured over the hill. "Here they come!"

"Stand by, partner," Daniel said with more calmness that she had ever thought possible. "Pretend you're out of breath."

"Pretend? My heart's up here in my nose!"

Christie rode off toward the wave of wagons, then turned and galloped back as fast as he could. As he jumped off his horse he shouted, "Now, Nora!"

Valiantly, she stabbed the stake into the ground.

With settlers clattering past them, Daniel Christie put his arm around his wife's shoulders and they posed, proudly, the yellow flag from their stake waving in the wind.

Just a couple of gosh-darn homesteaders.

WHAT had once been a tight line of contestants had now fanned out and spread across the Cherokee Strip. Yellow-flagged stakes dotted the land, while jubilant and somber settlers either celebrated the future or turned back to the past, their wagons and spirits broken.

Shannon and Stephen rode ahead of the pack, their high-priced steeds and excellent horsemanship serving them well.

They topped a small incline and Stephen shouted, "There it is!"

Her eye followed where he was pointing, and she saw a piece of land that was, indeed, straight out of her fantasies. Verdant and lush, with trees and a charming stream rippling through it, the property called to her heart, welcoming her home. A happiness, a sense of fulfillment and peace welled up inside her, a joy like none she had ever know. She was home.

But then she heard hoofbeats pounding behind her, and she could tell that some rider was gaining on her. Glancing over her shoulder, she was astonished to see that it was Joseph, racing toward her . . . worse yet, toward her land!

She and Stephen approached the stream and Stephen whipped his horse, urging him across. But Shannon saw the slippery rocks and hesitated.

"Come, Shannon, hurry!" Stephen yelled at her.

Impatiently, he halted on the other side. Distracted by his imperious command, she spurred her horse at the wrong moment and it faltered and fell. She tumbled into the water, hitting the hard rocks with a force that knocked her breath from her body.

"Stephen," she gasped, "help me." She held out her hand to him.

But instead of sympathy, Stephen gave her a reprimand. "What is wrong with you? Get up! Grab the reins! A child could have made that jump."

She struggled to her feet, weighted down by the wet dress. Then she saw Joseph come galloping up to her, splashing through the water. Yanking on his reins, he pulled his horse to a stop. The animal reared up on its hind feet, but he retained his seat.

"Whoa, are ye all right, Shannon?" he asked. He held out his hand to her. "Here, take me hand." But as she reached for him his stallion began to rear again. "This bloody horse has a mind of his own, he does."

Shannon reached for him again, and for a moment she looked deep into his green eyes. "No, Joseph," she said, making her decision. "Ride! Go! Go!"

Fired by her urging, Joseph spurred his horse and splashed across the stream. Stephen raised his riding crop to strike him, but Joseph pulled back his fist and punched him soundly on the right jaw. Chase fell off his horse into the water.

Joseph galloped off toward the marker; Stephen was frantic.

"Damn you, Shannon!" he shouted. "Do you want your land or don't you?"

Joseph rode hard, straight for the marker. He grabbed his stake from his saddlebag, and without stopping or even slowing, he leaped from the stallion and ripped the marker from the ground. He glanced up for a moment, long enough to see his horse thundering out of sight across the hills. Joseph had the sinking feeling that Greenbroke wouldn't slow down until he reached the Canadian border.

Holding his stake high, he paused, savoring the moment. Shannon and Stephen came galloping over the hill and Joseph shouted, "This land is mine . . . by destiny!"

But then he looked at Shannon, and he hesitated, holding the stake just above the ground where the marker had been.

"Go ahead, Joseph," she called to him. "Claim it."

"Claim it?" Stephen exclaimed. "Shannon, why are you doing this? He's nothing but—"

Stephen looked from Shannon to Joseph, then he exploded with rage. Whipping his horse, he charged straight at Joseph. Shannon screamed as Stephen's horse nearly plowed Joseph down, but in the last second Joseph grabbed hold of Stephen's horse and the horse stumbled and fell.

"Look out, Joseph!" Shannon screamed.

But her warning came down too late. The heavy animal rolled right over Joseph, knocking him to the ground with bone-breaking force.

His head smashed hard against a rock, and he lay there, not moving, blood oozing from the wound on his temple.

"Oh, my God," Shannon cried as she leaped off her horse and ran over to him. "Joseph!"

But Stephen jumped off his horse as well and caught her halfway, grabbing her by the arm. "Leave him, Shannon. Don't touch him. The land is ours now."

Shannon whirled around and pushed Stephen, causing him to stumble backward. "Leave me alone, Stephen!" she shouted at him, her face red with fury. "Haven't you done enough already. Just go!"

Turning her back on Stephen, she ran to Joseph, dropped to her knees beside him, and cradled his head in her arms.

Stephen watched her from a distance, a look of painful awakening on his face.

"Joseph, Joseph . . ." Shannon brushed the hair back out of his face and gingerly touched his wound. "Joseph, look at me."

Joseph gazed up at her with waning strength. "I feel meself dyin'," he said.

"No! Stay looking at my eyes."

He struggled to, but his lids fluttered closed. "Shannon . . . all the land in the world means nothing without ye. Yer father was me father's landlord, and I tried to prove meself to ye, but I've got nothin' to prove. I know nothin' of books or alphabets, or sun or moon or which goes round the other."

"It doesn't matter, Joseph." Weeping, she held his head against her bosom. "None of that matters to me."

"But this I do know," he continued. "Joseph loves Shannon. The rest is dark and cold. . . ."

He took a deep breath, and his head lolled to one side.

"No! No! Joseph, Joseph, no!"

She gently laid him on the ground, placed her hand on his chest, and felt no beat. She leaned her ear down to his face but could hear no breath.

"Oh, Joseph, my dear, sweet Joseph."

Stephen slowly dropped to one knee beside them. His pompous pride was gone and he spoke with bewildered innocence and humility. "Shannon, I've lied to you all these months. He didn't abandon you that night. He brought you home and placed you in my arms. I lied so you'd forget about him. Please understand I did it to protect you."

Shannon gathered all the pain inside her and struck out at Stephen, slapping him as hard as she could across the face with the back of her hand.

"Don't continue to lie to me, Stephen Chase. You did it to protect yourself. He loved me, and you hated him for it. Now get away from me, Stephen. I don't ever want to see your face again."

Stephen stood slowly, woodenly, as though the life had gone out of him. He glanced over the countryside and saw that even the distant sections of land had been claimed. Walking over to his horse, he threw his stake aside. Then he mounted and rode away, leaving Shannon alone.

She gathered Joseph's body into her arms and held him tightly.

"Oh, Joseph," she wailed. "I'm so furious with you now! This was our dream together! You selfish man! Were you blind?"

As though from far away Joseph could hear Shannon's voice, begging him to return. Opening his eyes, he was shocked to find himself floating . . . floating high and weightless like a cloud above the earth. He glanced down and saw his body there on the ground with Shannon bent over him, pleading for him to come back to her.

A force that he had never felt before was pulling him upward, higher and higher into the golden sunlight. He felt like a bird . . . even lighter than a bird as he soared, leaving the pain of his body and the heaviness of his heart behind. The light beckoned him, drawing him into its life-giving rays. His spirit rejoiced in its freedom . . . a liberation he had never known.

"Come back to me, you fool!"

Even as Joseph climbed higher into the light, reveling in its warmth, he could hear her calling him.

"Please, Joseph, I love you. I need you."

She loved him.

His spirit ceased to rise, caught and anchored by her words.

Shannon loved him . . . and, most of all, she needed him.

After one wistful glance at the warm, golden light, he looked downward. Shannon was shaking his body, his head rolling from side to side.

"Come back to me, Joseph. Please, please, come back."

Joseph felt a strange rush, a falling sensation, as though he had plummeted off a cliff. With a start he realized that he was back in his body. He could feel her hands on his shoulders, the wetness of her tears on his cheeks.

"I loved you from the moment that I stabbed you in the thigh!" he heard her saying. "I've always loved you!"

He opened one eye and looked up at her beautiful face. "I often wondered about that," he said with a mischievous grin.

Shannon shrieked with joy. "Joseph! You're alive! But you died!"

"Aye. But as sure as guns, I won't be dyin' twice."

Shannon began kissing him, his lips, his cheeks, his forehead, even his wound. Each kiss revived him more and he struggled to sit up.

Finally, on his hands and knees, he crawled with her across the grass to his stake, which was lying on the ground where he had dropped it.

He grabbed it and held it out to her. "Together?"

"Yes!"

As one, they held the stake with its yellow flag and plunged it into the ground, affirming their future together on their land. Two lives, two hearts . . . one dream.

Five Years Later

"Joseph, Jo-seeeph!" Shannon cried as she stepped down from the porch of the handsome farmhouse and looked around the fields that surrounded the house. The bountiful harvest of wheat lay ripening in the sun, blown in golden waves by the gentle breeze.

She walked out to the barn, a fine sturdy barn with a fresh coat of red paint, and saddled a pretty little white mare. Galloping out of the stable, she took off down the road, her long copper hair free in the wind, her skirts billowing around her knees.

"Joseph!" she called. "Joseph, where are you?"

At the edge of the field a tiny head popped up and the smiling face of her four-year-old son beamed at her.

"Hello, Joseph, you handsome little man," she said as she dismounted and swept the child into her arms. "And where's your da?"

"Where do you think I am, ye reckless redhead?" said a voice behind her. She turned to see her husband standing there, a scythe in one hand, a palm full of ripe grain in the other. "I'm puttin' in an honest day's work."

Hand in hand, Shannon and little Joseph walked over to him. Shannon looked down at the grain in his palm and smiled. "It's going to be a beautiful harvest, Joseph."

He grinned that mischievous smile that always went straight to her heart. "Do ye think so?" he asked.

Shannon looked down at her son and saw the same grin reflected on his small face. Leaning over, she gave her husband a long, leisurely kiss.

"I know so, my love," she said with an assurance that reached to the bottom of her heart. "I know so."